Stronger Than the River

HISTORICAL CHRISTIAN ROMANCE

VIVIAN BELLE

STERLING RIDGE PRESS LLC

Cover designed by Sterling Ridge Press LLC

Published by: Sterling Ridge Press, LLC www.sterlingridgepress.com

ISBN: 978-1-966093-43-5
Printed in the United States of America

First Edition: March 2026

For permissions, contact: support@vivianbelle.com or visit www.vivianbelle.com

Dedication

For every woman who became strong because she had no other choice— and for the moment she discovered that strength and softness could live in the same hands.

You were always more than what you carried.

Vivian Belle

"Be still, and know that I am God." — Psalm 46:10

Contents

Chapter 1

The Absaroka Mountain Range came into view through the stage window somewhere around the fifteenth mile, and Caleb Sterling leaned forward in his seat to watch them rise.

He'd spent three years in Denver, surrounded by the Colorado Rockies, and he'd thought he understood what mountains looked like. The Rockies were grand in the way that public buildings are grand, impressive, and well-proportioned, their peaks arranged along the horizon with something almost like order. The Absarokas were nothing like that. They climbed out of the valley floor without symmetry or apology, their ridgelines jagged where the Rockies were smooth, their snowfields sitting in the creases of the rock like old bandages on wounds that hadn't healed.

Caleb pressed his hand against the survey case on his lap, a battered leather case containing the transit, chain, and field instruments he'd carried to every job site since his first commission out of Chicago. The tools a civil engineer used to measure the land before he built on it. The Pacific Northwestern Development Consortium had hired him to survey a bridge site across the Yellowstone River in a town called Providence Ridge, a small settlement on the far side of the river. It depended on a cable ferry for its only crossing. If the site proved sound, he would oversee the construction of a timber truss bridge to replace the ferry. A project that would require weeks of work, a construction crew, and the steady hand of an engineer who trusted his judgment. He hadn't built a bridge in three years, not since the collapse in Wyoming. He'd kept to smaller work in Denver: road grading and culvert repair, and minor infrastructure. The kind of projects where nobody died if a calculation was wrong and the stakes were low. He'd told himself he was being cautious. The truth, which lived in the part of his mind that refused to stay quiet, was that he'd been hiding.

His copy of the Psalms sat in his coat pocket, a small leather-bound edition that had traveled with him from where he had grown up in Chicago to Wyoming to Denver and now into a valley he'd never seen. The book had meant different things at different times. Lately, it meant the most.

The stage hit a rut that nearly sent the case off his lap, jolting him out of the kind of thinking that had kept him poor company for most of this trip. Through the window, the valley was narrowing; the mountains pressing closer on both sides; the river growing louder as the road descended toward it. The trees began to thin as the road curved toward the water, and the air sharpened with the raw cold that rises off a river still carrying snowmelt.

Moments later the driver called back that the ferry was ahead, half a mile, and that if it was running on schedule, they'd make the crossing before the afternoon freight backed up the landing. Caleb leaned toward the window, pressing his shoulder against the frame to get a better angle on the water. The river was more visible now, not just audible, a wide, flat stretch of blue/green water moving with a speed that surprised him. Eastern rivers he'd bridged ran politely between their banks, contained by centuries of human reshaping, but the Yellowstone moved like something that hadn't been told it had boundaries, pushing against the banks with a force he could almost feel. The slight green color of it told him something: the spring runoff hadn't started in earnest yet. The river was still running on winter flow, which meant that what he was seeing now was the Yellowstone at its calmest, and its calmest was already more river than most of the crossings he'd engineered back east.

The ferry landing emerged from the tree line as the road leveled out: a timber platform built at the river's edge, wide enough and solid enough to hold a loaded freight wagon, its planking scarred by years of iron-rimmed wheels and livestock hooves and weather. A cable system stretched across the Yellowstone from bank to bank, two lines of braided hemp as thick as a man's forearm, anchored to timber posts sunk deep into the earth and humming with the tension of the current pulling against them. Moored at the platform was the ferry itself, a flat-bottomed scow broader than any he'd seen on eastern crossings, its planking weathered to the color of driftwood. The low side rails and loading ramp that angled down to the platform looked like a jaw waiting to be fed. The whole apparatus was more substantial than he'd expected, built not for convenience but for survival, every joint and cable and timber sized for the kind of loads that frontier communities depended on: freight wagons, livestock, and families with everything they owned lashed to a buckboard.

A woman was working the mooring lines at the near end of the platform. She had her back to the approaching stage, a dark braid lying over one shoulder, her hands running along the hemp cable. She wore a heavy coat against the April cold and work boots that had seen more mud than polish. She stood with her weight balanced evenly and her feet planted apart, the stance of someone accustomed to surfaces that moved beneath her. Even from the stage window, Caleb could see the economy in the way she held herself and moved, each gesture serving a purpose, nothing wasted, nothing decorative.

The driver pulled the team to a stop at the head of the landing and set the brake. The horses stamped and blew, unhappy with the river's sound. The woman at the mooring lines turned at the sound of the brake, and Caleb saw her face for the first time through the stage window.

Green eyes, direct as a surveyor's line. Her frame was compact beneath the heavy coat, and the discrepancy between her size and the authority with which she occupied the landing registered as a surprise. She was an attractive woman, much different from women in Denver who seemed purposely put together, arranged, and deliberate. She was something he didn't have a word for yet, standing on a timber platform at the edge of a river that could kill her, looking at him with an expression that suggested she was accustomed to strangers and unimpressed by most of them.

He opened the stagecoach door and stepped down into mud that took his boots to the ankle and approached the ferry.

"Callahan Ferry," she said, speaking past him to the driver. "Two bits for the stage. Four bits for the passenger with his trunks."

Caleb stepped forward with his survey case in one hand and his hat in the other. "Nice to meet you. I'm Caleb Sterling, the engineer contracted to build a bridge for Providence Ridge."

Her expression shifted at the word "bridge," a tightening around the jaw that was there and gone so quickly a less observant man would have missed it. But he had spent his professional life watching for the moment when a structure began to show stress, the hairline fracture that preceded the failure. What he saw in her face in that half-second wasn't hostility exactly, but something older than hostility, something that had its roots in a ground he couldn't see.

"Belle Callahan," she said. "I run this crossing."

"Pleased to meet you, Miss Callahan. If there's anything I can do to help with the loading, I'd be glad to lend a hand while the stage is being—"

"I have a system, Mr. Sterling. Your help isn't part of it."

She turned back to the mooring lines. Caleb stood on the landing with his survey case, his hat still in his hand, experiencing the distinct and unfamiliar sensation of having been assessed, measured to the inch, and filed in a category he suspected was located somewhere between unnecessary and unwelcome.

He expected a ferry operator to be loud, rough, and careless with details. Instead, he found a woman who looked as if the valley had made her with the same rules it used for rivers and rock—no waste and nothing false. She moved with a sure step and a quiet balance, and it wasn't softness that caught him. It was control, worn so naturally it masqueraded as grace.

He watched her work while the driver maneuvered the stage into position on the ramp. She directed the loading with hand signals the driver clearly understood, positioning the team and the coach on the scow with a precision that accounted for the weight of the horses, the distribution of the luggage, and the angle of the current against the hull. She checked the cable tension by running one hand along the hemp and tilting her head, reading vibration and resistance through her fingertips the way he read levels and plumb lines through his instruments. The correction she made to the guide rope, shifting it to a different notch on the overhead cable to adjust for the stage's weight, was so small he nearly missed it. Every movement of hers spoke of knowledge and experience. Every decision carried the weight of repetition, of seasons, of a thousand crossings in conditions he could only guess at.

Caleb paid his fare, placing the silver coins on the mooring post where she'd indicated with a nod, and boarded the scow beside the stage.

A rancher waited on the bank with a loaded packhorse. The horse balked at the ramp, its whole body communicating a profound objection to the concept of floating. The rancher pulled at the halter and spoke under his breath to the horse.

Belle walked to the horse without hurrying. She placed one hand on the animal's neck, just below its jaw, where the pulse ran close to the surface. "Easy now."

The horse dropped its head, its ears coming forward, and stepped onto the scow with the docility of an animal that remembered that it trusted the woman whose hand was on its neck more than it feared the water beneath the planking.

The correction took no more than three or four seconds. He'd never seen anyone read an animal's resistance that quickly or answer it with that little effort. She hadn't grabbed the halter or matched force with force. She'd identified the fear and addressed it. The packhorse's fear had dissolved under her hand the way ice dissolves in a current.

He was still thinking about that when she cast off and the river crossing began. The cable hummed overhead with a sound like a fiddle string bowed too slowly, a sustained vibration that Caleb felt in his teeth. The current pressed against the scow's flat bottom with a force he could track through the planking, a steady lateral push that wanted to carry them downstream. Belle Callahan stood at the guide rope, adjusting the scow's angle against the current with corrections so fluid they seemed less like decisions and more like breathing, as if it were a part of her. Her body responded to the river's pressure the way a musician's fingers respond to a melody, not by thinking but by knowing.

Caleb stood at the rail of the scow and let himself feel the crossing. Not measure it, not calculate the cable tension, not estimate the current speed, and not assess the load distribution. He let himself feel it all: the cold air off the water, the vibration of the cable through the deck, the particular vertigo of standing on a surface that was solid and moving across a body of water that could swallow everything in its path. The Yellowstone didn't care about ferry operators or engineers, or consortium contracts. It ran because gravity pulled it, snowmelt fed it, and the mountains channeled it, and everything else, every human structure built across its surface, existed at its tolerance.

He turned his head to watch Belle. She was adjusting the guide rope as they approached the midpoint, her braid swinging against her shoulder blade with the motion. The muscles in her forearm were visible where her coat sleeve had ridden up. Her hands on the rope were scarred, her knuckles crosshatched with small white lines, and her palms thickened with calluses that spoke of years of hard work.

The far bank was approaching, and beyond it, climbing up from the river's edge along a single muddy road, was the town of Providence Ridge. Wood-frame buildings, horses tied to hitching posts, and a freight wagon parked in front of what appeared to be the mercantile. It was smaller than the consortium's report had suggested. Smaller and more real, the kind of town that existed because people needed it to exist, not because anyone had planned it, and the mountains behind it were so large and so close that the buildings looked less like structures than like afterthoughts the valley had permitted.

A young man stood on the landing as the scow approached. He neither waved nor called out, just watched the scow approach with still, measuring attention. Even from the water, Caleb could see the family resemblance: the same dark hair, the same square-shouldered stance, and the same quality of contained readiness that he'd associated with the woman at the guide rope.

Belle brought the scow alongside the landing with a precision that left less than six inches between the hull and the platform timbers, and she did it while maintaining a conversation with the rancher about his pack horse's temperament.

The stagecoach driver guided his team off the ramp and up the bank toward town without incident. The rancher led his horse off with a tip of his hat. Caleb stepped onto the landing with his survey case and offered a nod to the young man, who returned it with the minimum warmth that courtesy required and not a degree more.

"Thank you for the crossing, Miss Callahan," Caleb said, turning back toward the ferry.

She was already loaded for the return trip; a woman in a calico dress waited on the scow with a basket and her horse. He watched the ferry pull away from the landing; the scow catching the current and the cable going taut, and Belle at the guide rope. He stood there watching for longer than a man with a survey to begin had any reason to stand and watch a ferry cross a river.

The bridge site was upstream from the landing, on a stretch of riverbank the consortium's geological survey had identified as suitable for footings: stable composition, adequate depth to bedrock, and a straight run of river with consistent current. Caleb walked the muddy path along the bank, his boots sucking at the spring mud with every step, and the river running beside him with its low, constant voice. The short walk gave him time to do what the crossing hadn't permitted, which was to sort through the information he'd collected in the last half hour and put it into categories that made sense. The cable ferry was well-engineered. The operator understood hydraulic principles. What was harder to categorize, what refused to sit quietly in the professional column where he was trying to file it, was the way she'd calmed a twelve-hundred-pound horse with a few words and a hand.

He reached the survey site and set down his case. The ground was good beneath his boots, firm under the spring mud, the kind of soil that accepted a stake cleanly when you drove it. He assembled the transit on its tripod, leveled the bubble, and began the measurements that would tell him whether a bridge could stand here: bank elevation, distance to the waterline, angle of descent, and the current's speed measured by timing a cottonwood branch from one survey flag to the next. He recorded each figure in the small gridded notebook he carried in his case, his pencil marking the page in the shorthand he'd developed over a decade of field-work.

Caleb worked through the morning and into the early after-noon, driving stakes, recording data, and pacing the bank to get the feel of the terrain in his legs. Twice he caught himself looking downstream toward the ferry landing, and twice he told himself he was studying the cable system because the anchor points and cable tension spoke to the riverbank's capacity to hold a load.

The river kept speaking to him as he worked. It had a different voice here than at the crossing, deeper and steadier where the chan-nel narrowed past the survey site, and the sound of moving water had never been a neutral thing for Caleb, not since Wyoming. There had been a river in that canyon too, smaller than the Yellow-stone but fast and cold, and after the bridge collapsed, it had carried the wreckage downstream for a quarter mile before the timber caught on the rocks. A freight driver named Thomas Halstead and Caleb's younger brother James had gone into the water with the bridge. They'd been hauling lumber across a span Caleb had certified as sound four months earlier, on the strength of a fore-man's assurance that the foundation work had been completed to specification.

Caleb moved to sit on a boulder at the river's edge and opened his notebook to review the day's measurements. The figures were clean, the geological composition matched the consortium's re-port, the bank was stable, and the current was navigable for con-struction staging. He should have been satisfied with that, should have closed the book, and walked to Providence Ridge to find the boardinghouse.

Instead, he turned to a fresh page and wrote something that had no business being in an engineering notebook.

Cable ferry, Yellowstone crossing at Providence Ridge.
Operator: Belle Callahan.
System well-maintained. Cable tension is consistent. Load distribution managed with notable precision. The operator demonstrates an unusual command of hydraulic principles. Horse management is exceptional. Voice carries a quality of authority that appears to be innate rather than performed. Hands scarred from cable work. Ran the crossing as if she'd built the river herself and was still deciding whether to let the rest of us use it.

Caleb closed the notebook and slid it into the case, fastening the leather straps, and began the walk toward town.

Chapter 2

Caleb walked the half-mile from the river into town, following the dirt road that served as the town's spine. By the time he reached the boardinghouse porch, the sun had dropped behind the mountains and left the valley in shadow. The boardinghouse was a two-story frame structure, the largest building on the street, with only the mercantile across the road approaching it in size. He noted the construction as he climbed the porch steps: good joinery at the corners, the sill plate level and true, and the porch planking replaced recently enough that the nails hadn't yet begun to weep rust. Someone had built this with care, and someone was maintaining it with the same care.

He pulled the front door open and stepped inside, the warmth of the building closing around him after the cold walk from the river. The dining room occupied most of the first floor: a long table flanked by benches and mismatched chairs. Beyond the table, a doorway led to what he assumed was the kitchen, given the heat and the smell of fresh bread intensifying from that direction.

Ahead, a narrow staircase rose to the second floor. Near the foot of the stairs, a small writing desk served as a check-in counter, a ledger open on its surface beside an inkwell. The whole interior carried the same quality he'd noted in the construction outside: maintained, orderly, and held to a clean standard.

A woman came through the kitchen doorway, wiping her hands on her apron. She was solid, no-nonsense, with her hair pinned tight and her apron showing the evidence of a day's work. Her gaze went to his face first, then to the survey case, then to his boots, and then back to his face.

"Mrs. Hanscombe, I assume," he said. "I'm Caleb Sterling. I believe the consortium wrote ahead about a room."

"You assume correctly. Your trunks arrived this morning, and I had them put in your room." She spoke the way a woman speaks who has checked in a hundred boarders and sees no reason to make a ceremony of the hundred-and-first. "Second door on the left, top of the stairs. Supper's at six. Try not to be late."

"Yes, ma'am. I appreciate it."

She studied him for another half-second, the way a woman studies a new piece of furniture to decide whether it belongs in the room or merely occupies space. Whatever conclusion she reached, she kept it to herself and turned back toward the kitchen.

Caleb climbed the narrow but solid stairs, the treads worn smooth in the center from years of boots ascending and descending.

His room was small and clean. A narrow bed occupied the far wall with a wool blanket folded square at its foot; the mattress firm when he pressed a hand against it. A pine dresser with three drawers stood against the near wall, its surface bare except for a white cloth runner. A desk sat beneath the window, and on it a kerosene lamp with a trimmed wick and a glass chimney wiped clear of soot. A washstand held a porcelain basin and a pitcher of water that was cool when he tested it with his fingertips.

His trunks sat at the foot of the bed. He knelt beside the larger one, unlatched the brass clasps, and lifted the lid. His rolled maps were on top, secured with leather ties, and beneath them the survey stakes nested in their wooden box alongside the gridded notebooks he'd purchased from a stationer in Denver by the dozen. He carried the maps to the desk and stood them upright against the wall where they wouldn't unroll. Then he stacked the notebooks beside the lamp.

The second trunk held his personal effects, what remained of a life packed into a space smaller than the desk. Shirts, trousers, and a shaving kit went into the dresser and onto the washstand shelf with the efficiency of a man who had unpacked in enough rented rooms to do it without thinking. At the bottom of the trunk, wrapped in a cloth, was his Bible, the leather binding soft and dark from years of handling. He carried it to the desk and set it beside his notebooks.

He poured water into the basin and washed his face and hands, removing the road dust and riverbank mud from beneath his nails. The water turned brown in the basin. He dried his hands on the towel, changed into a clean shirt, and ran a comb through his hair before checking the mirror above the washstand. The face that looked back was travel-worn but presentable. He was in need of a good haircut; he was beginning to look like a wild, untamed mountain man. He tucked his shirt in, straightened his collar, and left the room, pulling the door shut behind him.

The staircase creaked under his weight as he descended, and the sound of conversation and crockery rose to meet him before he reached the bottom step.

The long table he'd seen on arrival was now filled with diners. Two men who appeared to be mill workers sat at the near end, talking low about a problem with a saw carriage. A man, Caleb took for a traveling packer, sat near the middle, his coat folded beside him and a canvas satchel on the floor by his boots. He was eating with the steady, unhurried appetite of a man accustomed to meals taken wherever he found them.

At the far end of the table, a man sat with the ease of someone who had long since claimed his preferred seat, a spot where the entire room could be viewed. He was well-dressed in a wool suit that had been tailored rather than ordered from a catalog, his collar and cuffs pressed sharp, and boots that carried a shine. His face was smooth-featured and composed.

He looked up when Caleb approached the table and then rose from his chair. "Mr. Sterling, I presume. Horace Pritchard, Pacific Northwestern Development Consortium." He crossed the distance between them with three easy strides, extending his hand. "Mrs. Hanscombe mentioned you'd checked in this afternoon. I've been looking forward to your arrival."

The grip was firm and brief. "Mr. Pritchard," Caleb said. "The consortium mentioned in its letters that you'd be here ahead of me."

"Two weeks now." Horace gestured toward the table. "Long enough to develop a genuine appreciation for Mrs. Hanscombe's coffee, which is strong enough to stand a spoon in and worth every scalded inch of your throat. Please sit."

Caleb took the seat nearest Horace. Mrs. Hanscombe came from the kitchen carrying two bowls of stew, which she set before the mill workers without ceremony. She returned with bowls for Caleb and Horace, along with a plate of bread sliced thick and a crock of butter.

Caleb bowed his head and prayed before eating.

The stew was beef and root vegetables, well-seasoned and heavy enough to settle into a man after a day of travel and work. He ate while listening to everyone around him. The mill workers discussed a saw carriage problem with the specificity of men whose livelihoods depended on the equipment functioning correctly. The packer ate and offered the occasional observation about road conditions between here and Livingston, which were poor and getting worse with the snowmelt.

Horace spoke the way water finds a downhill channel: smoothly and naturally. He asked Caleb about the trip from Denver. He mentioned the bridge project in terms of development and opportunity. Furthermore, he used the word "we" in ways that Caleb noted without responding to, the collective pronoun of a man who preferred shared ownership of his ideas.

"And the ferry crossing," Horace said, leaning back in his chair with his coffee cup held loosely in one hand. "How did you find the ride over?"

"It's an efficient operation," he said. "The cable system is sound. Well-maintained."

Horace nodded. "Miss Callahan has managed the crossing for several years now. Capably, by all accounts. Of course, the bridge will provide something more permanent. More reliable."

One of the mill workers glanced up at the word bridge, then returned to his stew.

"You've had a chance to walk the proposed bridge site, I take it," Horace said as he buttered a piece of bread.

"Yes, sir. I ran preliminary measurements on the bank and the current."

"And your impressions?"

"The geological survey the consortium commissioned was competent. The bank composition is suitable for footings. The river's width and current speed are within a workable range. I'll need more time before I commit to specifics. A few days of measurement at minimum, and I'll need to observe the water at different times of day."

"Of course. Thoroughness is precisely what the consortium hired you for," Horace leaned forward. "The town committee has been anticipating your arrival. There's a meeting scheduled for tomorrow evening, right here in this room. You'll have a chance to present your initial assessment and hear what the townspeople have to say about the project."

"Who sits on the committee?"

"Amos Pemberton, who owns the mercantile across the road. Owen Gallagher, the lumber mill foreman. Mrs. Hanscombe. Marshal Tom Callahan, the local law. A few of the larger ranchers, when they can be persuaded to ride in. Some other locals. It's a small committee, but they take the bridge seriously. This crossing is the town's lifeline."

"And Miss Callahan?" Caleb asked. "Does the ferry operator have a seat?"

Horace's expression shifted, a flicker of amusement or calculation that passed too quickly to read with certainty. "Miss Callahan attends when she chooses, as do her siblings. She has opinions about the crossing, as you might imagine. The committee respects her knowledge of the river, though opinions differ on how far that respect ought to extend when it comes to bridge decisions."

Caleb let that settle without responding to it. He finished his coffee and set the cup down.

"The consortium has invested considerably in this project, Mr. Sterling," Horace continued, his voice dropping in volume as he leaned in. "A permanent crossing changes everything for Providence Ridge and the towns beyond here. Trade, access, property values. The men who build this bridge will be building the future of the valley, and that's not a small thing."

"No, it isn't."

Horace studied him for a moment, then smiled and pushed back from the table. "Well. I'll let you settle in. Tomorrow will be a full day, and the committee meeting will give you a sense of the lay of the land, so to speak." He stood, folded his napkin beside his plate, and offered Caleb a nod that managed to feel like a dismissal. "Good evening, Mr. Sterling. I'm glad you're here."

He watched Horace climb the stairs, each step measured and deliberate, and listened until a door opened and closed on the second floor.

The mill workers had already gone. The packer was pulling on his coat and settling his bill with Mrs. Hanscombe at the desk near the stairs. Caleb rose from the table and carried his dishes to the kitchen doorway, where Mrs. Hanscombe intercepted them with a look that suggested boarders were not expected to bus their own dishes.

"That was a fine supper, Mrs. Hanscombe. Thank you."

"Breakfast begins at six in the morning," she said. "The coffee will be on before that if you're an early riser."

"I am."

"Very well then Mr. Sterling. You have a pleasant evening." She said before walking into the kitchen.

Caleb walked to the front door and stepped out into the evening air.

The mercantile stood directly across the road from the boardinghouse, its false front rising a full story above the actual roofline in the way of frontier towns that wanted to look more established than they were. The porch was wide enough for townsfolk to gather on, and a bench sat against the front wall with the worn look of something that had held its share of conversations.

Caleb walked across the street and stepped onto the porch. He cupped his hands against the window glass to peer inside. The interior was too dark to make out much, but he could see the shapes of shelved goods lining both walls, the outline of a counter near the back, and what appeared to be a postal window beside the register. A handwritten card in the lower corner of the window glass read Pemberton's Mercantile & Supply in careful lettering. He stepped back and continued up the road.

A smaller building next to the mercantile served as a land office; its single window displaying a notice, he paused to read. However, the light had faded too far to make out more than the heading, which appeared to involve property filings. Beyond it, a narrow frame building with a painted sign he couldn't quite decipher sat dark and locked. He noted the gaps between structures, the alleys where firewood was stacked against side walls, and the way the buildings thinned as the road moved west toward the livery.

Higgins Livery & Feed Yard and Hart Blacksmith & Wheelwright occupied the far end of the street, one on each side of the road. The livery's corral held a handful of horses standing quietly in the chilly evening air. The blacksmith shop was still open; the forge glowed through the wide doors with a low orange heat that threw the shadow of the anvil across the back wall. A man worked at the forge with his back to the road, the ring of his hammer carrying in the still air with the clean, rhythmic sound of iron being shaped.

Also, on the opposite side of the road, a saloon occupied a building that looked older than most of its neighbors, its windows amber with lamplight and its door propped open despite the cold. The sound of voices drifted out, low and conversational, the unhurried talk of men at the end of a working day. Caleb passed it without stopping, but noted the name painted above the door.

Next was the town marshal's office; low lamplight glowed from within.

By the time he returned to the boarding house, the dining area had been cleaned and the kitchen door was closed. Caleb climbed the stairs to his room, lit the kerosene lamp, and sat at the desk.

He opened his notebook to a clean page and began writing: the bank elevations he'd measured that afternoon, the current speed he'd calculated, and the soil composition he'd assessed with a hand auger. He sketched the ferry crossing from memory. The cable system rendered in the clean lines of an engineering diagram, the anchor points and their relationship to the bank, and the angle of the cable's catenary under the load of a full crossing. He noted the cable material, the mooring post dimensions, and the approximate age of the hemp based on its color and stiffness.

Somewhere between the mooring post dimensions and the note about hemp age, he stopped writing. He couldn't see the river through the dark window, but he could hear it, that low murmur carrying up through the valley in the stillness. The sound carried the thought of Belle Callahan with it, standing at the guide rope, reading the river's push through her hands, and answering it with adjustments so quiet they looked like instinct rather than skill.

He sat with that image longer than he intended. Then he turned his attention back to the notebook, picked up his pencil, and wrote a clean heading for the committee meeting agenda. He organized his thoughts for the meeting that would take place tomorrow evening in the dining room downstairs. He reviewed the geological survey that the consortium had commissioned before his arrival. He made a list of questions for the committee regarding property easements and road access.

When there was nothing left to organize, he closed the notebook and picked up his Bible from the corner of the desk. He opened it to the Gospel of Matthew and read the Sermon on the Mount.

When he finished, he extinguished the lamp. The room went dark, and in the darkness the sounds of the building settled around him. Farther away but present, he heard the murmur of the Yellowstone running in the dark. He lay on the narrow bed and listened to it for a long time.

Chapter 3

The trail was rutted from a week of freeze-and-thaw. Belle's mare picked her way through the mud with the resigned patience of a horse who had made this ride a thousand times and expected to make it a thousand more. Her brother, Liam, rode beside her on his gelding. The trail followed the river along a low bluff where the cottonwoods grew thick, their bare branches interlocking overhead. Through the gaps Belle could see the Yellowstone running below, its surface catching the last pale light of the sky.

Her shoulders and hands ached. The hemp cable left its impression in her palms on heavy crossing days, a deep, burning soreness that traveled from the base of her fingers through the meat of her hand and up into the tendons of her forearm. There had been eleven crossings today, including a freight wagon loaded with milled lumber that had shifted its weight mid-river and required her to hold the guide rope at an angle that put the strain entirely on her left side. She'd managed it. She always managed it. But the cost of managing it settled into her body as she rode home.

The homestead came into view as the trail crested the last rise before the clearing. The cabin sat in the center of the clearing with a barn behind it, both built from timber her father had felled, notched, and raised with his own hands.

Beyond the cabin, her sister Winnie's garden occupied a fenced plot on the south-facing slope where the soil drained well. Belle could make out the seed trays next to the house Winnie had started weeks ago, wooden flats lined with river sand and covered with cheesecloth to hold the warmth. Winnie's faith in the growing season was like Winnie's faith in most things—practiced early and defended with a stubbornness that outweighed her slight frame.

Belle nudged the mare forward, and they covered the last stretch of trail into the yard. The barn door was open, and the smell of hay reached her as she swung down from the saddle. Her boots hit the packed earth of the yard, and her knees protested, stiff from the cold and from hours of standing on the scow's planking. She pulled the saddlebag from the mare's back, then turned to hand the reins to Liam. He dismounted and gathered both sets of reins in one hand with the unhurried competence of a young man who understood horses the way his sister understood the river. He led both animals into the barn without a word, his broad shoulders disappearing into the darkness of the doorway.

She walked toward the house and paused before stepping up onto the porch. She looked back toward the south, toward the river. The Yellowstone's voice carried from below the bluff, low and steady, the same sound she had fallen asleep to every night of her life in this cabin. A sound that ran beneath every memory she had, like the bass note in a hymn. It was louder in spring than in winter. Tonight it carried the particular resonance of a river that was gathering itself, accepting snowmelt from a hundred high-country drainages and adding it drop by drop to the volume that would, by June, turn the crossing from a manageable current into something that tested every cable and every nerve she had. She knew the river's calendar the way other women knew the calendar of holidays and planting seasons, by the sound it made and the color it ran and the way the cable hummed differently as the water rose.

Something about today sat differently than other days. She could feel it in the space behind her breastbone, a small, unnamed disturbance that had nothing to do with the ache in her shoulders or the weariness in her legs. She didn't examine it. She turned from the river's voice, climbed the porch steps, and went inside.

The cabin's front room served as parlor and dining room both, a single open space with a long pine table her father had built and a stone fireplace occupying the wall to the left. The fire was banked low, the coals glowed, and the warmth reached Belle as she hung her coat on the peg by the door. Beyond the front room, the kitchen was separated by a half-wall. Her sister Winnie was standing at the cookstove with a wooden spoon in her hand and a dishcloth over one shoulder, her fair hair pinned up in a loose knot that was already coming undone on one side.

"You're late," Winnie said, without turning from the pot she was stirring.

"The lumber freight from Livingston came through around four."

"That's the second lumber shipment this month." Winnie lifted the spoon, tested the broth, and returned it to the pot.

Belle crossed the front room to the narrow hallway that led to the two back bedrooms, hers and Winnie's, with Liam's loft above, reached by a ladder in the hallway. Her room was small and sparse. A bed with a pieced quilt their mother had sewn. A dresser next to a basin and pitcher, a shelf that held her Bible and comb, and a tin of the tallow balm Winnie rendered every autumn from the first butchered steer. She poured water from the pitcher into the basin and washed her hands and face, scrubbing the cable grease from beneath her fingernails and the grit of the river from her skin. The water was cold, and she didn't mind it.

She stripped off her shirt and split skirt and changed into a clean calico dress, the cotton soft against her arms after a day in wool and canvas. The dress was faded at the cuffs and mended twice at the hem, practical and plain. The kind of dress a woman wore at home when there was no one to dress for except family and no reason to care about appearances beyond cleanliness. She sat on the edge of the bed and worked the tallow balm into her hands, rubbing it into the cracks along her knuckles and the rough patches on her palms where the cable had worn the skin to leather. The balm smelled of sage and lanolin, a scent she associated so completely with evening and home.

When she returned to the kitchen, Winnie had moved the pot to the back of the stove and was pulling a tray of biscuits from the oven. The heat rose from the cast iron in a shimmer that fogged the window above the counter. Belle opened a cabinet and took down three plates, three cups, and three sets of flatware, and carried them to the table. She set each place without thinking about the arrangement: the plates centered on the edge, the forks on the left, the knives on the right, and the cups above. There were four chairs at the table. Three of them had seats worn smooth from use. The fourth, the one at the head nearest the fireplace, no one sat in it.

"The venison stew turned out better than I expected," Winnie said, carrying the pot to a trivet she'd placed at the center of the table. "I added dried rosemary from last summer. There wasn't much left."

"We'll get more this year; hopefully the patch by the creek will come back."

Winnie returned to the kitchen for the biscuits, setting them on a cloth-lined plate beside the pot.

The front door opened, and Liam came in, bringing with him the cold air from outdoors and the smell of hay. He hung his coat beside Belle's and crossed to the washstand in the kitchen, where he scrubbed his hands and forearms with the bar of lye soap Winnie kept on a dish beside the basin. He dried his hands on a towel, pushed his dark hair back from his forehead, and took his seat at the table—the chair to Belle's left, the same chair he had occupied since he was old enough to reach the table's surface without a stack of books beneath him.

Belle folded her hands in her lap. Liam and Winnie did the same, and the cabin went quiet save for the fire's low crackle.

"Lord, we thank You for this food and for the hands that prepared it," Belle said. "We thank You for the work of this day and for bringing Liam and me home safe. Bless this meal to our bodies and our lives for Your service. Amen."

"Amen," Winnie and Liam said together.

Winnie served the stew in generous portions; the broth was rich and dark, the venison tender from the hours it had spent over low heat. The biscuits were golden on top and soft in the center, the kind of biscuit that split cleanly when pulled apart and held butter without crumbling. Belle ate with the quiet, thorough appetite of a woman who had burned every calorie she'd consumed since lunch in the labor of running a cable ferry, and for several minutes no one spoke because the food was good, and the warmth of the cabin was settling into all three of them at once, loosening the day from their shoulders.

Winnie broke the silence. "How many crossings today?"

"Eleven." Belle buttered a biscuit and set the knife down. "Three freight, four passenger, two livestock, and two-stage runs."

"Sounds like it was a good day," Winnie said.

"Liam, did you check on the bay horse while you were in the barn?" Belle asked.

"Loose shoe on the left front. I filed down the clinch and reset it, but the hoof wall's starting to crack on that side. She needs a proper shoeing."

"Can it wait until next week?"

"It can wait. But not much longer than that."

"Take her in on Tuesday morning before you come to work," Belle said.

Liam nodded and returned to his stew. He ate steadily, without waste, his attention distributed between the meal and some interior landscape that Belle had long since stopped trying to map. At nineteen, her brother had grown into the dimensions of a man while retaining the reserve of a boy. He had their father's shoulders and their mother's dark eyes, and he carried both inheritances with a quiet gravity that made him seem older than his years.

"Did you hear?" Winnie said, reaching for a biscuit. "The bridge engineer arrived today."

Belle's hand paused on her cup. "Where did you hear that?"

"Mrs. Fairchild was at Pemberton's this afternoon when I went in for flour. She came in on the same stage. She said he's a civil engineer from Denver. The one the consortium hired."

"He arrived," Belle said. "He introduced himself."

Winnie waited for more. When nothing came, she tilted her head. "That's all?"

"That's all there is to say."

"Mrs. Fairchild said he was well-spoken. And that he carried some kind of instrument case and didn't complain about the mud, which she found noteworthy."

"Mrs. Fairchild notices a great deal about strangers."

"Mrs. Fairchild notices a great deal about everything, which is why she's useful." Winnie smiled. "What's he like?"

"He's an engineer; he's observant. He introduced himself and offered to help with the loading, and I told him I had a system."

Winnie's smile deepened. "You told him his help wasn't part of your system."

"That is what I said."

"Belle."

"I was polite."

"You were more than likely efficient in the way you said it. There's a difference." Winnie looked across the table with the particular expression she reserved for moments when she believed her older sister was being unnecessarily fortified against the world. It was an expression that managed to convey affection and exasperation in equal measure.

Liam said nothing. He ate his stew while his eyes moved between his sisters with the unhurried attention of a young man who had long ago learned that the conversations between Belle and Winnie contained information on multiple levels. The most useful information was rarely in the words themselves.

"The committee meets tomorrow evening at the boarding-house," Belle said, steering the conversation toward ground she could control. "Horace Pritchard arranged it. The engineer will introduce himself properly and present his preliminary findings."

"Will you go?" Winnie asked.

"I haven't decided."

"You'll go," Winnie said, with the calm certainty of a prophet delivering an outcome she considered already settled.

Belle didn't argue because Winnie was right, and they both knew it. The bridge survey concerned the ferry, and the ferry concerned Belle, and nothing that concerned the ferry would proceed without her attention. "We need coffee, salt, and lamp oil from the mercantile this week. And a new file for the cable splice kit, if he has one."

Winnie accepted the redirection of the conversation with the grace of a woman who had won the point and saw no need to press it. "I'll pick those items up the next time I'm in town."

After supper, Belle and Winnie cleared the table and washed the dishes in the basin near the kitchen window. Belle washed and Winnie dried. The warm water eased the stiffness from Belle's hands as she worked the cloth over each plate.

Liam had moved to the chair by the fireplace. He had a leather strap across his knees and was working a needle through the torn edge, mending it with small, even stitches. The firelight caught the side of his face and made him look for a moment so much like their father that Belle had to look away and concentrate on the plate in her hands.

"Liam," Winnie said from her station at the drying rack. "Did you see the new horse at the livery when you were in town last week?"

He looked up from the strap. "The chestnut?"

"Yes, Mrs. Fairchild mentioned it. Said it was a fine animal."

"It is." Liam's voice warmed in the particular way it warmed when the subject turned to animals. "Three-year-old mare, good conformation, clean legs. Paul Higgins bought her from a rancher up near Big Timber who was selling off stock. She'd make a solid saddle horse with proper handling."

"What would proper handling look like?" Winnie asked.

"Groundwork first. She's green, but she's willing, I could tell. You can see it in the way she stands—ears forward, weight even, watching everything but not spooking at it. A horse like that wants to trust you. You just have to give her a reason." He paused, his needle still in the leather. "On another note... I found out there's a parcel of land along the river outside of town, Mercy Bend, that would make good pastureland. The man selling it is getting on in age, and wants to move with his children to Oregon. There is a small home on the property. It's flat ground, good grass, and has a creek running through the property that drains into the Yellowstone River. If a man had the means to fence it—"

His needle resumed its work through the leather, but his sentence died as if it had walked to the edge of something and decided to step back. Belle heard the silence where the rest of the thought should have been. She heard what lived inside it—the shape of a want her brother carried quietly and never pressed, because pressing it would mean asking for something the homestead couldn't afford.

She should have said something. She should have turned from the dishes and asked him to finish the thought, to say what he meant about the pasture and the fencing and the life he was beginning to imagine for himself that didn't include the ferry. But her mind was crowded tonight with the image of a man standing on the landing that morning with his hat in his hand and his survey case at his side. He had looked at her with an expression that held no bluster and no condescension. Only the quiet attention of someone who was learning his surroundings.

She pushed the image away and rinsed the last plate.

"That chestnut sounds like a fine horse," she said, and even as the words left her mouth, she knew they were insufficient; a door closed gently when it should have been opened wide. But Liam nodded without looking up, and the moment passed.

Winnie hung the dishcloth over the edge of the basin and kissed Belle on the cheek. "I'm turning in. Don't stay up too late."

"Good night, Win."

Winnie disappeared down the hallway, and a few minutes later the soft sound of her door closing reached the front room. Liam finished the leather strap, held it up to the firelight to inspect his stitching, and rolled it into a coil that he set on the mantel. He rose from the chair, crossed the room, and paused at the foot of the ladder that led to his loft.

"Belle."

"Hmm?"

"The engineer. On the landing today." He stood with one hand on the ladder rung, his face half in shadow. "He watched you run the crossing. The whole way across, from the time you cast off until you docked on the far side. He didn't look at the river or the mountains, or the cable. He watched you."

Belle kept her expression level. "He's surveying the crossing. That's his job. I'm sure his attention was not on me."

Liam held her gaze for a beat longer than the words required. "Good night, Belle." He climbed the ladder, and the loft floor creaked as he settled into his bed.

She banked the coals and set the fire screen. Then she took her shawl from the peg and stepped out onto the porch.

The night was cold and clear. The kind of April evening when the frost came early, and the stars arrived all at once, not gradually but suddenly, as if someone had pulled a cloth from a lantern and revealed the whole of heaven in a single motion. The Absarokas rose black against the eastern sky, their ridgelines sharp. The air smelled of pine and frozen earth, clean and thin, the kind of air that made a person conscious of each breath as a separate, deliberate act.

Belle sat on the top step and drew the shawl around her shoulders. The porch boards were cold beneath her, the chill seeping through her skirt.

The river's voice reached her from the south, low and constant, filling the silence. She had been listening to this voice for as long as she could remember. As a child, she had believed the river was praying. The sound it made at night was the same sound her father made when he bowed his head at the table, a low murmur directed at something vast and unseen. She didn't believe that anymore in the literal way a child believes it, but she had never entirely stopped feeling it—the sense that the river's sound carried something sacred in its current, something that predated the valley and the mountains and every human structure built along its banks. On nights like this, with the stars overhead, the cold air sharp in her lungs, and the sound of the river, the world arranged itself around her in a way that felt like mercy. The weight she carried through the day—the ferry, the homestead, the ledger of expenses and repairs and responsibilities that never grew shorter—settled into a proportion she could bear.

She thought about the ferry's income. Eleven crossings at the rates she charged put the day's earnings at a figure she calculated without effort, the arithmetic as habitual as breathing. It was enough to cover the week's supplies with a margin left for the farrier's fee and the cost of the splice file. It was not enough to repair the south-bank mooring post, which needed new timber before the spring runoff tested it, or to replace the section of hemp cable that would need to be replaced soon. The ferry sustained them, but it sustained them the way a river sustains a valley—by running without stopping, by demanding that everything along its banks keep pace or be left behind.

She thought about the bridge contract. She had known it was coming. The consortium's interest in a permanent crossing had been discussed at committee meetings for the better part of a year, and Horace Pritchard's arrival two weeks ago had confirmed what the discussions had promised. A bridge across the Yellowstone would change everything for Providence Ridge—the access, the commerce, and the speed at which goods and people moved through the valley. She understood that. She wasn't so proud or so short-sighted that she couldn't see the benefit a bridge would bring to the town that depended on her ferry. But understanding it and accepting it were different acts, separated by a distance she hadn't yet crossed, because the ferry was not merely her livelihood. It was the structure her father had built, the system she had inherited, and the work that defined her place in the valley and gave her days their shape and purpose. Without it, she was a woman with a homestead, two siblings to support, and a set of skills that applied to a crossing that would no longer exist in the future.

She thought about the engineer. Caleb Sterling. She replayed the moment on the landing—his hand extended, his hat in the other, the survey case at his feet. He'd introduced himself with the directness of a man accustomed to being received well. She had responded with a directness of her own that was not rudeness but was near enough. I have a system, Mr. Sterling. Your help isn't part of it. She'd meant it. She had a system, and strangers who arrived with offers of assistance were, in her experience, strangers who intended to rearrange the system to suit themselves.

But his response hadn't matched the pattern she expected. She had expected bluster, or offense, or the particular condescension of a man who believed a woman operating heavy equipment was a novelty to be managed. Instead, he had nodded, stepped back, and observed her working. The expression on his face hadn't been admiration, though it lived in the same territory. It hadn't been an assessment, though an engineer's eye was clearly at work behind it. The closest word she could find was attentive. A deep, focused attention of a man who was watching not to judge or to correct, but to understand. As if the crossing and the woman running it were a text he wanted to read carefully before he formed an opinion.

She had been watched before. Strangers watched her every day because a woman running a cable ferry was unusual enough to draw the eye. But those looks carried a predictable quality—surprise, curiosity, sometimes disbelief—and she had learned to let them slide past her the way water slides past a hull, felt but not resisted. This had been different. His attention had carried weight, the kind of weight that settled against her awareness and stayed there, and the staying was the part she couldn't account for.

She pushed the thought away. She was tired, and tired minds wandered into territory that rested minds knew better than to enter. Belle drew her shawl tighter as she rose from the step, stiff and cold, and went inside.

She latched the cabin door and stood for a moment in the dark, listening to the steady breathing of her siblings in their beds, and she thought that this was enough—that the homestead and the ferry and the three of them were enough—and she was almost certain she believed it.

Chapter 4

The first crossing of the morning was a rancher's wagon loaded with fencing wire. The river was running quickly, the current strong enough to press the hull at an angle that required constant correction at the guide rope, and the fencing wire shifted every time the scow pitched against the cable's tension. Liam stood at the downstream rail with one hand on the cargo tie, keeping the load from sliding. Belle worked the rope through the overhead pulley and read the water's push against the hull.

Three more crossings followed before mid-morning. A pair of horsemen bound for Livingston. A freight wagon brought flour sacks from the mill in Tomblin. The driver, a man named Graham who crossed twice a week and handled his team without instruction. A rancher's wife and her daughter, the girl perhaps seven, who stood at the rail with her fingers wrapped around the cable stay, watching the water with the uncomplicated fascination of a child. Belle collected the fares and ran the crossings and felt the morning settle into the rhythm that her body knew better than any other rhythm in her life.

She was resetting the guide rope when Caleb Sterling appeared on the Providence Ridge side landing.

He'd come on foot from the direction of town, his survey case in one hand and his hat pushed back on his forehead. His boots had lost the polished shine they had had yesterday. He set his case down at the top of the ramp and stood waiting, his posture patient and unhurried.

Belle finished her adjustment to the rope and walked to the mooring post where the fare box sat. "Callahan Ferry," she said. "Two bits for a foot passenger."

He placed two coins on the mooring post and boarded without comment. The scow shifted slightly under his weight as he stepped onto the planking. He moved to the upstream rail and looked downriver toward the bridge site. He had positioned himself where he could watch the cable mechanism without blocking her path between the guide rope and the mooring cleats.

She cast off the mooring line, and the current caught the hull, and the crossing began.

Belle worked the guide rope in small corrections, adjusting the scow's angle against the cable to account for the current's push, which was stronger today. The rope hummed through the overhead pulley with a low, steady vibration that she could feel in her forearms. She corrected the angle by two notches and felt the hull settle, the scow tracking straighter against the push of the river.

She felt Caleb watching her the way she felt the current against the hull, a pressure that arrived from the side and required no correction but refused to go unnoticed. He was watching the rope, the pulley, and the angle of the cable where it met the overhead stay, and he was watching her hands where they gripped the hemp. The combination of the two produced an awareness in her that she didn't enjoy.

The far bank came up, and Belle docked the scow against the mooring post with a hard thump. A half-inch correction should have been made twenty yards back, and she hadn't because her attention had been distributed between the water and the man at the rail. She secured the mooring line and opened the rail gate.

"Much obliged, Miss Callahan."

He gathered his case and stepped off the scow. She heard his boots on the ramp, the crunch of gravel as he reached the bank, and then the sound of his stride growing fainter as he walked upstream along the bank toward the survey site. She stood at the mooring post and tracked his figure moving along the waterline until the cottonwoods obscured him, and by the time she turned back to the scow, she was angry at herself for watching him.

The river crossings continued. Belle ran two more before noon, the work pulling her back into the rhythm that left no room for anything except the rope, the water, the cargo, and the fare.

By the time the noon break came, the sun had climbed high enough to take the chill from the air. The light on the river had shifted from the flat gray of early morning to something brighter. Belle ate her noon meal on the south-bank landing, bread and dried venison from the cloth bundle Winnie had packed that morning, sitting with her legs hanging over the edge of the ramp and the river running below her. Liam sat beside her, eating his share with the steady, unspeaking appetite of a young man who treated meals as fuel and conversation as an optional expenditure.

From the landing, she could see the bridge site upstream. Caleb was visible at the waterline, crouched over something at the bank's edge. He had driven new stakes, a row of them running from the high-water mark down to the gravel bar where the bank's gradient steepened. He had his notebook open on his knee and was writing, his pencil moving in short, precise strokes. As she watched, he rose from a crouched position, paced fifteen steps upstream, drove another stake, then returned to the first position and sighted along the line of stakes with an instrument she couldn't identify at this distance. He repeated the process three times, each repetition covering the same ground but from a different angle, as though the bank's measurement changed depending on where a person stood to take it.

She knew what he was doing. He was checking the soil composition at multiple points, calculating whether the bank could bear the weight of bridge footings that would need to hold against a river whose spring floods had torn out cottonwood trees with root systems twice the depth of anything a man could drive into the ground.

She finished her bread, wrapped the cloth around the remaining venison, and handed it to Liam. "I'm going to walk up to the bridge site."

Liam took the cloth without comment. His eyes moved from Belle to the figure at the waterline and back to Belle.

"If the mail stage comes through, collect the fare and hold the crossing until I'm back," she said.

"I reckon I know how to hold a crossing," Liam said.

She walked upstream along the bank path, the cottonwoods thinning as the ground rose slightly toward the survey site.

He looked up from his notebook and straightened, tucking the pencil behind his ear when he heard her approaching. He was standing between two rows of stakes that ran perpendicular to the bank, marking a corridor perhaps thirty feet wide, and within that corridor he had driven shorter stakes at intervals she estimated at five feet, each one tagged with a strip of white cloth that fluttered in the wind coming off the water.

"Miss Callahan," he said.

"Mr. Sterling." She stopped at the edge of his stake line and looked at the corridor he'd laid out. "You've been busy."

"Yes...the consortium's geological survey was competent, but it measured the bank at a single point. A single point doesn't tell you what the bank does under stress. I need gradient readings at multiple intervals to calculate where the footings would bear weight and where they'd shift."

"They'd shift anywhere south of that third stake." Belle pointed to a marker twelve feet from the waterline. "The gravel bed drops off there. It looks solid until the water comes up quickly, and then it gives. The last time that happened was in seventy-nine."

Sterling looked at the stake she'd indicated. He looked at the bank below it, then at the waterline, then back at the stake. "How far did the water rise that year?"

"Four feet above the current line. Came up in two days during a warm spell in late April, when the snow in the mountains released all at once instead of over a week."

"And the seventy-eight flood? The geological survey references it as a hundred-year event."

"It wasn't a hundred-year event. It was a rain-on-snow event that the survey treated as a baseline because they didn't have anyone to tell them the difference." Belle crossed her arms over her chest. "A hundred-year flood comes from sustained snowmelt over weeks. Seventy-eight was four days of warm rain falling on a snowpack that was already saturated. The river didn't rise the way it rises in a normal spring. It came up overnight, six feet in under twenty hours, and it carried whole trees. The bank you're standing on lost eight feet of ground that spring. The ferry cable snapped, and my father had to re-anchor on the new bank line."

Sterling opened his notebook again. "Where was the bank line before seventy-eight?"

"Where your farthest stake is."

His pencil moved across the page in his notebook in shorthand, small, precise marks arranged in columns. When he looked up, his expression hadn't changed. He didn't adjust his stakes. He didn't step back to reconsider the corridor he'd measured. He simply closed the notebook and returned the pencil to its place behind his ear.

"What about ice dams?" he asked. "Does the channel dam upstream in winter?"

"Every year, at the narrows two miles above the crossing. The ice builds on the gravel bar where the channel splits around the island, and when it breaks in March or early April, it sends a wall of water and ice through here that scours the banks on both sides. The south bank takes the worst of it because the channel curves toward it below the narrows."

"How high does the ice-dam surge run?"

"Two to three feet above whatever the water's doing at the time. If the river's already up from early melt, the surge adds to it. In eighty-two the dam broke during a week of warm rain, and the surge put water on the ferry platform."

He started writing again. She watched him and felt the particular irritation of a woman who has offered expertise and cannot tell whether it has been received or merely recorded. He had asked questions that were specific and technical, questions that demonstrated he understood the difference between a seasonal flood and a rain-on-snow event, between a gradual rise and a surge. He'd listened with his full attention, the same attention she had felt on the ferry.

But he still didn't move his stakes.

"You're measuring the bank where the consortium's survey told you to measure it," Belle said.

"I'm measuring the bank at the site the consortium designated for the preliminary survey."

"The preliminary survey didn't account for the seventy-eight flood line or the ice-dam scour."

"Which is why I'm collecting additional data." He met her gaze. "Including yours."

"Including mine," she said. "Written down in that notebook between your angle readings and your gradient figures, filed alongside the numbers you'll use to build the bridge that replaces my ferry."

He was quiet for a moment. "I was hired by the consortium and approved by your the town committee to survey this site and build a bridge. That is the scope of my work here. I didn't come to Providence Ridge to disrupt your livelihood or to dismiss your work with the ferry. From what I've been told, the ferry is how you make your living, and I understand what that means."

"You understand it as a fact," Belle said. "You don't understand it as a morning that starts at dawn and doesn't end until every crossing is run and every mooring line is checked and every fare is counted, because that is the only thing standing between my family and the kind of failure that doesn't leave room for a second chance."

"No," he said. "I don't understand that. I haven't lived it." He held the notebook loosely at his side. "But I've been hired to do a job, Miss Callahan, and I intend to do it honestly. If the data tells me this site won't hold a bridge, I'll say so. If it tells me the site needs to be moved, I'll recommend it. The consortium's preferences don't change the soil composition or the flood history."

"And if the data tells you to build right here, on this bank, at this crossing, you'll build it. Regardless of what it costs, the person who's been running this crossing since she was seventeen years old."

"If the data supports it, that's my job. I won't pretend otherwise."

The honesty of it landed harder than condescension would have. A man who lied to her, who dressed the bridge project in reassurances about coexistence and partnership, she could have dismissed. She had dismissed men like that before, the ones who arrived in the valley with promises wrapped in language designed to make the listener feel included in a decision that had already been made. This man was not doing that. He was telling her plainly what he intended and what he couldn't change. The plainness of it left her with nothing to push against except the truth, which was not his fault and not something she could argue away.

"We don't need to be friends, Mr. Sterling."

"No, we don't," he said. "But I'd prefer it if we could be. I appreciate accurate data about this river from someone who knows it better than my instruments do. Everything you've told me this morning is information I can't get from a transit reading or a soil auger. I'd rather have it than not."

"The committee meets tonight," she said. "At the boarding house."

"So I've been told."

"Then you should know who you'll be talking to. Amos Pemberton owns the mercantile. He wants the bridge at the Main Street approach because it keeps commerce running through the center of town, which keeps his business alive. He's practical, and he can be shrewd, but he'll listen to your data if you present it without telling him what to think."

"And Gallagher?"

"Owen Gallagher is a rancher and the lumber mill foreman."

"Is Gallagher allied with Horace Pritchard?"

Belle looked at him. His question told her something she filed away without comment. He had been in Providence Ridge for a day, and he had already begun reading the committee's architecture, which meant he was either sharper than she'd given him credit for, or Horace had made his alliances obvious enough for even a newcomer to see.

"Horace has been here for two weeks," she said. "In that time he's bought several rounds of drinks at the saloon for anyone that will listen to him ramble. He's attended every public gathering, made himself agreeable to every woman at the mercantile counter, and offered Owen Gallagher terms on a lumber supply contract that will keep the mill running through winter. The purpose of that lumber no one seems to understand, but that is none of my concern. Horace is friendly and generous and patient, and every bit of his friendliness has a purpose."

"You don't trust him."

"I don't trust anyone who arrives in my town flaunting money, telling me how much better things are about to get with the improvements that are coming."

Caleb studied her. Not with the assessing look of a man calculating whether she was an obstacle or an asset, but with the steady attention of someone who was listening to what lived beneath the words and taking it as seriously as the words themselves.

"Mrs. Hanscombe sits on the committee," Belle continued. "She runs the boarding house, as you know. She holds no land interests and votes her conscience, which makes her difficult to predict and impossible to buy. My uncle, Marshal Tom Callahan, sits as well. He keeps order, and when he speaks, the room listens because he's earned the right to be heard. Several other townspeople, including my siblings, attend the meetings at times as well."

"And you?"

"I attend when I choose. I speak when it concerns the ferry crossing." She paused. "Some of those in attendance respect my knowledge of the river. Others tolerate it because they depend on the ferry and don't want to offend the woman who runs it."

He held her gaze for a beat that lasted longer than professional conversation required, and in that beat she saw recognition in his eyes, and she knew he had heard her. He had heard the thing underneath, the particular weariness of a woman whose expertise was welcomed when it was useful and set aside when it was inconvenient.

"Thank you for the information," he said. "About the committee and about the river. Both are useful."

She walked away from the bridge site along the bank path, rattled and frustrated.

She was halfway back to the landing when she understood what was bothering her, and the understanding arrived not as a thought but as an irritation she could finally locate, a splinter she had been pressing against without finding.

He had listened to everything she had said. He had written it down. He had asked questions that proved he understood what she was telling him. He hadn't condescended, hadn't interrupted, hadn't offered the patronizing reassurance that men offered women when they wanted the conversation to end. He had treated her river knowledge as data that carried the same weight as his own measurements, and he had said so without making a performance of it.

And she had enjoyed it.

Not him, and not his attention, specifically, and not the way he stood at his survey stakes with his pencil behind his ear and his notebook open, recording her words in the same hand that recorded his angle readings. What she had enjoyed was the experience of being listened to as though what she knew mattered, as though the years she had spent on the river translated into a currency that an educated man from Denver recognized as legitimate. She had spent five years since her father's death earning the town's respect through labor, and the respect she'd earned was real, but it was the respect given to a person who performs a necessary function, the way a town respects a well that produces water. Caleb's listening had been something else. It had been the attention of a man who wanted to understand not just what she knew but how she knew it, and the distinction between those two things was small enough to miss and large enough to unsettle her.

She would rather not be unsettled by Caleb Sterling. She didn't want to be unsettled by any man, for that matter, because "unsettled" was a word that led to other words, words like "interested," "distracted," and "vulnerable," and those words led to a place she had closed the door on years ago when she buried her father and took the ferry rope in her hands and learned that the only grip worth trusting was her own.

The landing came into view through the last stand of cottonwoods, the ferry platform sitting steady. Liam was coiling a mooring line. He looked up as she approached, and his gaze moved past her, upstream, toward the bridge site. Liam's eyes stayed there for a moment, measuring something, and then he returned his attention to the rope in his hands.

"Mail stage hasn't come through yet," he said.

"That's fine."

"You were up there a while."

"I told him about the flood history. The consortium's survey didn't account for the seventy-eight event or the ice-dam cycle."

Liam nodded. He finished the coil and set it on the mooring post.

The afternoon crossings came, and Belle ran them. A livestock buyer with two horses on lead ropes. An empty freight wagon returning to Livingston. Each crossing required the same series of adjustments, the same attention to the guide rope and the cable tension.

But between the crossings, in the minutes when the scow sat empty, her thoughts returned to the survey site, to the row of stakes with their white cloth tags, to the man standing between them with his notebook. She thought about what he'd said. *I appreciate accurate data about this river from someone who knows it better than my instruments do.* She turned the sentence over the way she turned a splice knot, examining it from each side, testing where it held and where it gave. It had been a compliment, or something shaped like one, buried inside a professional request, delivered without emphasis. A man who intended flattery would have said it differently, would have softened his voice or looked at her in a way that signaled the personal underneath the professional. Caleb had said it the way he stated his measurements, as a fact he had verified and saw no reason to qualify.

That was the part she couldn't put down. A man who flattered, she could dismiss. A man who stated facts, she couldn't, because facts required a different kind of refusal, and she didn't have one ready.

The last crossing of the day carried a pair of miners headed south toward the pass, their mules loaded with packs, their faces burned by wind and altitude. Belle docked the scow as the light began to lengthen across the valley, the sun dropping toward the western ridge, the river's surface turning from blue-green to something darker as the shadows of the cottonwoods reached across the water. She secured the mooring lines and checked the cable tension for the evening, running her hand along the hemp where it met the anchor post, feeling for the particular looseness that signaled wear. The cable was sound.

Liam brought the horses, and they mounted for the ride home. The air was cooler, and Belle pulled her coat tighter around her shoulders as the mare carried her up the bluff and onto the trail that followed the river toward the homestead.

They rode without speaking for a quarter mile before Liam said, "He's a thorough man, it seems."

"He's an engineer. Thoroughness is the job."

"He drove those stakes multiple times today. Pulled them, re-measured them, and drove them again. Most men would have set them once and called it done."

"Most men aren't trying to build a bridge across the Yellow-stone."

Liam was quiet for a moment. "He watched you walk back to the landing earlier today after you left the survey site. He stood there with his notebook, and he watched until you were past the cottonwoods."

Belle kept her eyes on the trail ahead. The mare picked her way through a rut where the freeze-and-thaw had softened the ground, and Belle let her choose her footing and said nothing, because there was nothing to say to a sentence like that.

"The committee meets tonight," she said. "I'm going."

"I know you are," Liam said.

Chapter 5

The boardinghouse dining room had been rearranged for the committee meeting. The long table was pushed against the far wall. The mismatched chairs had been pulled into a rough semicircle facing the end of the room where Caleb stood with his survey maps weighted at the corners by four of Mrs. Hanscombe's coffee cups. The cups were heavy stoneware, thick enough to anchor the paper against the draft that leaked through the gap beneath the front door.

The cookstove in the kitchen still held its evening coals, the residual warmth seeping into the dining area. Oil lamps burned at three points along the walls, their light catching the edges of his maps where the ink lines of the survey elevations stood crisp against the pale paper. He had spent the last hour going over these drawings in his room. He had labeled the elevations and marked the proposed landing site with a red circle.

Caleb heard boots on the porch, and the low murmur of greetings exchanged. The first through the door was a man he hadn't met, a solidly built figure in a good wool coat. He scanned the room with the quick, appraising look of a man accustomed to taking inventory. He catalogued Caleb's maps with a glance and took a seat. This would be Amos Pemberton. Belle had described him as practical and shrewd, and the apron he wore said he had come straight from the mercantile.

Horace arrived next, descending the boardinghouse stairs in a pressed wool suit. He crossed to Caleb's position at the maps and stood beside him for a moment, examining the drawings with proprietary satisfaction.

"These are excellent, Mr. Sterling. Very thorough." Horace's voice carried the warm assurance it always carried, pitched to be overheard without appearing to project. "The committee will appreciate the details."

"The detail is the minimum necessary," Caleb said. "A bridge proposal without elevation data is a guess, not a plan."

Horace smiled and then moved to a chair at the end of the semi-circle, a position where he could observe the entire room.

More men filed in. A rancher Caleb didn't recognize, broad across the chest with the permanent weathering of a man who spent his days in open country. Two others took seats beside the rancher, their coats still buttoned against the chill they had carried in from outside. A man Caleb identified as Owen Gallagher by the sawdust that clung to his wool shirt. Owen took a seat beside Horace, and the proximity registered in Caleb as confirmation of what Belle had told him that afternoon about their alignment.

Mrs. Hanscombe emerged from the kitchen carrying a tray of coffee cups and a coffee pot, which she placed on the table. And then she moved to stand near the kitchen doorway.

Marshal Tom Callahan arrived, filling the doorframe for a moment before stepping inside and removing his hat. He was taller than Caleb had expected, with the same dark coloring Belle carried in her hair. He wore his badge pinned to his coat. He nodded hello to Amos, then Owen, and finally let his gaze rest on Caleb for two measured seconds before he sat in a chair at the end of the semicircle nearest the door.

Caleb was reviewing the sequence of his presentation in his mind, the order in which the data would build the committee's understanding from the ground up, when the front door opened again and three more people entered.

The young man from the ferry came in first. Tall and broad through the shoulders. He found a position along the far wall and stood with his back to the plaster.

The second was a young woman Caleb hadn't seen before. She was soft in appearance, with fair hair worn in a neat arrangement beneath a bonnet, and an expression that carried warmth. She took a chair near the middle of the semicircle, smoothing her skirt as she sat with the composed, unhurried movement of a woman comfortable in social settings. She looked at Caleb once, briefly, with an assessment that was neither hostile nor welcoming but simply thorough.

Belle Callahan entered the room next.

Caleb had prepared for the meeting with the same rigor he brought to a bridge calculation. He had organized his data, sequenced his argument, anticipated the committee's likely objections, and rehearsed the figures until they moved through his mind with the smooth inevitability of a proof that arrives at its conclusion without detour. He hadn't prepared for the woman who walked through the boardinghouse door in a dress the color of a summer sky, fitted at the waist and buttoned high at the collar, her dark hair gathered and pinned in a way that showed the line of her neck and the angle of her jaw. She wasn't wearing her heavy coat and work boots; he had cataloged in his professional memory as the fixed elements of her appearance. She was the same woman who had stood at his survey stakes that afternoon, telling him the river didn't care about his measurements. The discrepancy between the two produced a sensation in his chest.

She took a chair beside the younger woman. Her posture was straight, her hands folded in her lap, and her expression composed in a way that conveyed readiness rather than ease.

Horace stood and addressed the room with the practiced warmth of a man who had given introductions before, in other towns, for other projects. He spoke briefly about the consortium's investment, the significance of a permanent crossing for commerce and growth not only for Providence Ridge but also for the settlements and communities beyond here. He introduced Caleb as the lead engineer, cited his credentials and experience, and yielded the floor with a gesture that managed to suggest both generosity and ownership.

Caleb stepped forward.

"The proposed bridge site is located at the Yellowstone River crossing, approximately two hundred yards upstream of the existing ferry landing," he began, placing his hand flat on the map to indicate the position. "The site was selected by the consortium's geological survey on the basis of bank stability, river width, and proximity to the existing road approach from town. My preliminary fieldwork has confirmed the bank composition as suitable for bridge footings, with qualifications I'll address."

He moved through the technical details with the unhurried precision of a man who respected both his data and his audience. He described the timber truss design, the load specifications, and the footing dimensions calculated to bear the weight of freight traffic and livestock. Furthermore, he described the materials—Douglas fir for the primary members, stone for the pier footings, and iron hardware for the joints and bracing. He described the timeline: twelve to fourteen weeks from groundbreaking to completion, dependent on weather and material delivery from Livingston.

Everyone in the room listened. Amos leaned forward in his chair, his attention fixed on the elevation drawings. Owen's attention moved between the maps and Horace, as if checking the drawings against some prior conversation the two of them had conducted. Marshal Tom sat still, his hat on his knee, his face carrying no expression that invited interpretation.

"The proposed bridge can connect to the main road through town easily once complete," Caleb said, tapping the red circle he had drawn. "This will keep commercial traffic routed through the center of town."

"What's the cost estimate?" Amos asked.

"Preliminary figures put the construction at approximately four thousand dollars, including materials, labor, and contingency for the footing work. That figure may adjust once I complete the soil analysis at depth."

"And the consortium's financing?" He asked as he turned to Horace.

Horace stood again and addressed the room. "The consortium has committed full funding for a bridge at the approved location. The committee's role is to approve the site, and Mr. Sterling's role is to build it. The financial structure is sound."

"Sound for whom?" Belle asked as she stood.

The room's attention shifted. Caleb watched the whole flow of the room's energy redirecting toward Belle with her hands at her sides and her chin level. He watched something else happen too, something smaller and harder to name: the quality of that attention changed as it settled on her.

"Sound for the consortium, certainly," Belle continued. "The consortium invested in this project. The consortium hired the engineer. The consortium will profit from the increased land values a bridge creates. That much is clear. What is not clear is what happens to the ferry crossing while this bridge is under construction. Twelve to fourteen weeks of construction that will occupy the riverbank adjacent to the ferry landing. Three months during which heavy materials will need to cross the river on the only crossing available, which is my ferry. Has anyone in this room calculated what that does to the commercial traffic the ferry currently handles? Has anyone asked whether the ferry can absorb construction freight on top of regular crossings without additional equipment, additional cable, or additional labor?"

She paused. The room was still.

"And when the bridge opens," she continued, "what happens to the ferry? A bridge and a ferry serving the same crossing cannot both survive. Every person in this room knows that. The bridge opens, and commercial traffic moves to the bridge because it's faster and it doesn't require a fare. The ferry becomes a convenience for the days the bridge is impassable, which is to say it becomes a charity."

The silence that followed had the quality of air before a shift in weather, weighted and watchful. Caleb stood at his maps with his hand still resting on the elevation drawing, and he looked at Belle Callahan standing in the middle of a room and felt the daggers being thrown his way from her eyes.

She wasn't less formidable away from the river. She was something more complete. The woman at the ferry had been competent and direct; her authority earned by the work her hands performed in the presence of anyone who cared to watch. The woman standing in this room, in the fitted sky-blue dress with the lamplight catching the line of her jaw and the green of her eyes visible from where he stood, carried that same authority through different ground.

"Miss Callahan raises a fair question," he said. "The ferry's operational continuity during construction is a legitimate engineering concern, and it should have been addressed in the preliminary proposal. It wasn't. That's a gap in planning. "

The room's attention shifted back to him, and in the shifting he caught Belle's reaction, which wasn't gratitude or surprise but something briefer and harder to read.

"During construction, the ferry would continue to operate on its current schedule," Caleb said, directing his answer to Belle. "Construction materials would be staged on the north bank and crossed separately, on a schedule coordinated with you to avoid interference with commercial traffic. The logistics are manageable, but they require cooperation between us all."

"And after?" Belle asked. "When the bridge is standing, and the ferry is no longer the town's only option?"

"That is a question for the committee, not for the engineer," Caleb said. "I can build the bridge. I cannot tell this town what to do with its ferry. But I can tell you that a ferry and a bridge serve different functions in different conditions, and a town with both has a redundancy that a town with only one does not. Whether that redundancy is worth maintaining is a decision that belongs to the people who live here."

"Miss Callahan's concerns are noted and will be taken under consideration," Horace said.

Belle turned to look at Horace. Caleb couldn't read her expression from this angle, but he read her posture, the particular stillness of a woman who had heard the phrase taken under consideration before and knew what that meant. She sat down, a movement that was controlled and deliberate.

The meeting continued. Owen asked about the current proposed bridge location and whether alternate sites had been considered. His question arrived with the casual specificity of a man who already knew the answer he wanted. Caleb addressed it with the data, describing the soil composition and gradient analysis at three points along the river. He watched Gallagher receive the information with the attentive blankness of a man listening for the number he needed rather than the number that was given. Horace offered supporting commentary that Caleb didn't need and hadn't requested, smoothing the committee's path toward the conclusion the consortium had already reached. Marshal Tom asked one question—whether the bridge design accounted for ice-dam surges—and when Caleb answered with the figures Belle had given him that afternoon, the marshal looked at his niece for a moment, then returned his attention to the maps and said nothing further.

The meeting dissolved the way such meetings do in small towns, not with a formal adjournment but with a gradual loosening, people rising from chairs and reaching for coats, and conversations splitting into smaller clusters that drifted toward the door. Amos crossed to the maps and studied them at close range, asking Caleb a series of specific questions about the road approach that told Caleb the mercantile owner was already calculating the bridge's effect on his freight deliveries. Mrs. Hanscombe began collecting the used coffee cups, moving through the thinning crowd with unhurried purpose.

Caleb looked for Belle and found the space where she had been sitting empty. He turned toward the door and saw her exiting.

Caleb took his coat from the peg near the stairs and stepped through the front door onto the boardinghouse porch.

Belle was at the foot of the porch steps, one boot on the bottom step and one on the packed earth of the road.

She turned when she heard his boots on the porch planking.

"Miss Callahan." He descended the steps and stopped at a distance that was close enough for conversation and far enough for propriety. "I'd like to discuss your objections, if you have a moment."

"My objections were stated clearly enough inside, Mr. Sterling. I don't see what a second hearing accomplishes."

"It accomplishes my understanding," he said. "If there are concerns about the bridge project that go beyond the operational questions you raised tonight, I'd rather hear them now than encounter them when the pilings are in the ground."

She studied him, and her expression carried the careful reserve of a woman deciding how much truth a conversation could bear.

"Engineers have tried to improve the crossing before," she said. "When I was fourteen, a survey party came through and drove stakes along the same stretch of bank you've been measuring. They had maps and instruments and a proposal that would replace the ferry with a timber bridge at what they called the optimal crossing point. My father told them the river would take anything they built at that location within three spring floods if the bridge was not built correctly. They told him his experience was anecdotal."

"What happened?"

"They built a footbridge further upstream. Timber pilings, plank decking, and twenty feet of clear span. The consortium that funded it ran out of money before it was completed. The first spring flood took the south footing. The second took the north. By the third year there was nothing left but two broken pilings at the waterline that the river used as current breaks until the ice finished them off."

"My calculations account for the flood history," Caleb said. "Including the data you gave me this afternoon about the seventy-eight event and the ice-dam cycle. The footing design I'm proposing is built for a hundred-year load, which includes the rain-on-snow events you described."

"The river does not read calculations, Mr. Sterling."

The sentence arrived with the flat certainty of a woman who had spent her life on water that did what it chose regardless of what men wrote in notebooks.

"No," he said. "It doesn't. Which is why I recorded your flood data. The river may not read calculations, but the woman who reads the river is worth more to this project than transit measurements. I said that to you this afternoon, and I meant it."

She was quiet as she studied his face. The cold air pressed against both of them, sharp and insistent, carrying the mineral smell of the river from below the bluff where the Yellowstone ran unseen in the dark. A horse stamped at the wagon. The jingle of its harness carried in the still air with the clear, metallic ring of cold metal on cold metal.

"You surprised me tonight," she said. "When I stood up in that room, I expected you to defend the proposal. Not to call the gap in it before anyone else could."

"The gap was real," he said. "Defending a proposal with a gap in it is how bridges fail."

Belle looked at him for a moment longer, then turned and walked away. As she moved, the air between them shifted. Caleb caught a scent that didn't belong to the river or the cold air. It was something lighter, something that carried the warmth of a woman's skin beneath the sharp April night, lavender or violet water, faint enough that a man standing six inches farther away would have missed it entirely.

His engineering mind, the part of him that processed the world through measurement and calculation and the orderly progression of cause to predictable effect, went silent. For one breath—one full, involuntary breath—there was nothing in his awareness except the scent of that faint perfume and the woman walking away from him toward a wagon where two people waited. The silence inside his own head was so complete that it frightened him, because Caleb Sterling hadn't stood in the presence of a woman and lost his capacity for structured thought since before the bridge collapse in Wyoming.

She reached the wagon. The man, whom he assumed was her brother, offered a hand to help her up. The woman, who must be her sister, was already seated on the bench with her hands folded in her lap. Belle settled beside her and didn't look back his way.

The wagon pulled away. The sound of the horses' hooves on the hard-packed road carried for a long time in the cold stillness, growing fainter gradually until it was indistinguishable.

Caleb went back inside. The dining room was empty now, except for Mrs. Hanscombe, who was restoring the table to its usual position. Caleb crossed to the table where his maps still lay and began rolling them, the paper crackling softly in the quiet room.

"Miss Callahan made her points well tonight," Mrs. Hanscombe said, without looking up from the chair she was repositioning.

"She did."

"She generally does." Mrs. Hanscombe set the chair in its place with a firm, final movement. "Whether the committee hears her points as well as she makes them is a separate question, and not one that reflects on her."

Caleb tucked the rolled maps under his arm. "No, ma'am. It isn't."

Mrs. Hanscombe looked at him then, one of her direct, assessing looks that Caleb had come to understand were not idle but investigative. The gathered data of a woman who formed her opinions from observed behavior and revised them only when the evidence required it. Whatever she found in his face, she kept it to herself and turned back toward the kitchen.

"Breakfast begins at six, Mr. Sterling."

"Yes, ma'am. Good evening."

Chapter 6

The wagon rattled over the last rut before the homestead clearing, and Belle felt the jolt travel through the bench seat into the base of her spine. The tension of the evening had settled and compacted into something that would keep her awake long past the hour she should have been asleep. Liam drove without speaking, his hands steady on the reins, his attention on the trail. Winnie sat between them on the bench, her shoulder pressed against Belle's.

The cabin windows were dark. The homestead looked smaller at night when the only light was starlight and the only sound was the river below the bluff and the horses blowing as Liam pulled them to a stop near the barn. Belle climbed down from the bench, her boots landing on the hard earth of the yard with a dull report that scattered the chickens roosting beneath the porch.

Winnie went inside and lit the kitchen lamp while Belle helped Liam unhitch the team. Liam unbuckled the traces while Belle backed the horses from the shafts. The barn was dark except for the lantern Liam lit and hung from the center post, its flame painting the stalls and the hay, and the tools along the wall in a warm, unsteady yellow. He pulled the harnesses and hung them on their pegs, his movements efficient, his face unreadable in the half-light.

"Go on in," he said. "I'll finish here."

Belle left him with the horses and crossed the yard to the porch. The cold had deepened while they were in town; the temperature dropping the way April temperatures dropped in the valley, without ceremony or transition, one hour passable and the next sharp enough to sting the skin. Her dress wasn't made for this kind of cold. It was a meeting dress, a town dress, chosen for its clean lines and its buttons that fastened properly, not for the ride home in an open wagon after dark. She climbed the porch steps and went inside.

Winnie had the fire rebuilt and was setting the kettle in place as Belle hung her coat.

Belle pulled a chair from the table and sat down. Her hands rested on the pine surface, palms down, the wood cool beneath her fingers.

Winnie set three cups on the table and poured tea; the chamomile's faint, grassy scent lifting with the steam. She settled into her chair across from Belle and wrapped both hands around her cup.

"Well?"

"Well, what?" Belle answered.

"You were magnificent."

"I said what needed saying. Whether it changes anything is another matter."

"Amos listened. I watched his face when you asked who decided the town needed a bridge without consulting the woman who runs the crossing. His jaw moved the way a man's jaw moves when he's heard something he should have thought of himself."

"He listens to whoever is talking. Tomorrow morning Horace's voice will be the last voice in his ear, and my concerns will be filed under the same heading they always get filed under."

"That's unkind to Amos."

"It isn't unkind. It's the history of how our committee in town works. The men carry more weight than the woman. That isn't cynicism, Winnie. It's a fact."

The front door opened, and Liam came in. He hung his coat beside Belle's and crossed to the washstand, where he scrubbed his hands, dried them, and took his place at the table. Winnie poured him tea without asking.

"Uncle Tom stayed quiet tonight," Liam said.

"Uncle Tom asked one question," Belle said. "About ice-dam surges. The engineer answered with the data I gave him this afternoon."

Liam held the cup between his hands, the steam curling past his face. "The engineer gave you credit for that data in front of the entire room. He said the flood history came from you. He didn't have to say that."

Belle looked at her tea. "It was accurate information. An engineer who ignores accurate information isn't much of an engineer."

"He also said the gap in the proposal was real," Liam said. "He stood in front of the entire committee and said the ferry should have been accounted for before the first stake went in. That was pointed at Horace as much as it was pointed at anyone."

Belle said nothing. She had replayed that moment on the wagon ride home, turning it over in her mind. Caleb Sterling had stood at his maps with the committee watching and called the failure. The move was either honest or strategic, and the fact that she couldn't tell which one it was bothered her.

"What concerns me the most," she said, "is what happens after the bridge is built. Not during. After."

Winnie tilted her head. "Go on?"

"Caleb Sterling laid out a plan for construction. Twelve to fourteen weeks with a coordinated ferry schedule. All of it sensible, all of it workable. But when I asked what happens to the ferry once the bridge opens, nobody in that room spoke up. Horace said my concerns would be taken under consideration. Taken under consideration is what men say when they intend to do nothing and want the woman who raised the question to sit down."

"Now, Belle—" Winnie said.

"The practical truth is that a free bridge kills a fare-based ferry. The ferry becomes what I do on the days the bridge is closed for inspections or the river takes out a footing. And I cannot feed three people on the income from a crossing that operates only when the bridge fails."

The room was quiet. The fire crackled. Winnie looked at her tea.

"There's another possibility," Winnie said. "One you haven't considered because you're looking at the ferry as the only thing that keeps us going."

"The ferry is the only thing that keeps us going."

"It's the thing that keeps us going for now. But a bridge brings people, Belle. More commerce, more freight, and more families settling because the crossing is reliable year-round instead of seasonal and dependent on one cable and one operator. More families means more trade at the mercantile, more demand for eggs and garden produce, more children needing teaching, and more households needing goods that someone in this valley could provide. It means we may someday have a proper school building and a church. It means expansion opportunities for the growing lumber mill. The bridge doesn't have to be the end of what we have. It could be the beginning of something we haven't imagined yet."

"I've imagined it," Belle said. "I've imagined what happens when the ferry fares stop and I have no way to replace them. That's what I've imagined."

"I'm not dismissing your fear. I'm asking you to hold it beside the other thing. Both can be true. The ferry will suffer, and the town will grow. You losing income and Providence Ridge gaining opportunity aren't contradictions. They're two sides of the same change."

Belle looked at her sister. Winnie's face was steady, her eyes clear. She wasn't arguing. She was doing what she always did, which was to place two truths on the table side by side and refuse to choose between them until she had studied each one fully. Belle couldn't do that. Belle's mind moved in straight lines, from problem to solution, from threat to defense. Winnie's mind moved in circles, taking in the whole of a situation before landing anywhere, and the difference between them was the difference between the ferry rope and the garden—one pulled against a fixed point, the other grew in every direction at once.

"I hear you," Belle said. "I do. But hearing it doesn't change the facts."

Winnie nodded and didn't push further. She sipped her tea, and the matter rested where she'd placed it, visible on the table between them, available for Belle to pick up when she was ready. If she were ever ready.

Liam set his cup down, his attention moving between his sisters with the patience of a young man. But something in the set of his shoulders had changed during Winnie's speech, a shift in posture that Belle read and braced herself for.

"The Mercy Bend parcel of land is forty acres. I mentioned before that the property runs along the Yellowstone. Flat ground, native grass, sheltered from the north wind by the treeline. Good water access from the creek that feeds into the Yellowstone. There is a small home there already. A man could fence the property for the cost of posts and wire. The posts could be harvested from the property itself," Liam said.

"Forty acres is a lot of fencing," Belle said.

"I can cut my own posts. The wire is what costs." He paused. "I spoke to Paul at the feed store last week. He told me Morrison Phelps up on the Shields Creek is selling off part of his herd soon. Young stock, good bloodlines, and healthy animals. Morrison's getting older, and he's reducing his operation. Paul said, Morrison intends to sell six head of yearling heifers for sixty dollars."

Winnie leaned forward. "Sixty dollars for six heifers? That seems low."

"Morrison's not trying to get rich. He's trying to place his animals where they'll be handled well. He's that kind of rancher. Paul said Morrison sold a bull to the Fergusons two years ago at a price that was practically a gift because he knew the Fergusons would treat the animal right."

"And you've been thinking about this since you talked to Paul?" Winnie asked.

"Before that. I've been thinking about it for some time now. What it would take to run a small herd through the winter. The hay costs, the shelter, and the calving in spring. I've talked to two ranchers about what a first-year operation needs, and I've written it down."

"Really?" Winnie asked.

Liam nodded.

"Liam, that's wonderful," Winnie said. "You've been planning this properly."

"It's just figures on paper."

"Figures on paper are how every ranch in this valley started. What would you need? Beyond the stock and the fencing."

Belle listened as her brother laid out the shape of his ambition in careful, practical strokes—the hay he'd need to put up the first summer, eight tons minimum for six head through a Montana winter. The shelter he could build from timber cut on the ridge, a three-sided run-in with a south-facing opening that would block the worst of the wind. The salt blocks. The veterinary costs if an animal fell sick. The mortgage terms at the bank in Livingston for small agricultural loans, which he'd asked about during a supply run three weeks ago.

Winnie asked questions that drew him further out. Where would he winter the herd? Whether the creek along the parcel froze solid or kept a running channel. How he would manage the fencing alone. Each question opened another room in the structure Liam had been building, and each answer revealed a young man who had thought about this with a thoroughness that surprised Belle.

"What would the loan come to?" Belle asked.

Liam looked at her. His expression shifted, the energy dimming slightly the way a lamp dims when the wick is turned down.

"A hundred and forty dollars would cover the stock, the fencing wire, the first season's hay supplement, and a margin for unexpected costs. The bank in Livingston offers agricultural loans at eight percent for three years. The repayment would be about fifty-four dollars a year."

"And if the first winter kills half the herd?"

The words came out harder than she intended. She heard them leave her mouth and felt the familiar, immediate regret of a woman who had spoken from fear rather than from the part of herself that wanted to say something better. She was proud of him and his ambitions, but she was frightened, because Liam wanting something of his own meant him moving toward a life that didn't need her any longer.

"If the first winter kills half the herd, I'd still have three heads and the land and the fencing, and I'd start again in the spring," Liam said. "That's what ranchers do. They lose stock and they start again. The ones who quit after the first loss were never ranchers to begin with."

Belle held his gaze. Something passed between them that was larger than the conversation, rooted in the years they had spent working on opposite sides of the same rope—Belle pulling, Liam holding, both of them doing the work because the work needed doing, not because either of them had chosen it. Liam had been forced into working the ferry the same way Belle had, through loss and necessity, and the difference between them was that Belle had made the necessity into an identity. Liam had kept it as a task, something performed with competence but without the possessiveness that Belle wrapped around it.

"That is a great deal of money," she said. "If the herd didn't make it, or the hay costs ran higher than your estimates, or something happened that you couldn't plan for—the debt would follow you. Banks don't forgive agricultural loans because the borrower had a bad year. They foreclose. I've seen it happen to families in this valley, Liam. Good families, hard-working families, who borrowed against a future that didn't come through."

"I know," he said. "I've thought about it."

"I'm asking you to consider this cautiously before doing anything."

Something shifted in his face. A small, careful opening, the kind of expression a person wears when they have been expecting a locked door and find it merely closed.

"The risk of this scares me, Liam," Belle continued. "I want you to know that before you take this any further."

Liam nodded. "That's fair," he said.

He finished his tea and pushed back from the table. "I'm turning in." He crossed the room to the hallway and paused at the foot of the ladder. "Belle."

"Yes."

"Thank you for listening; I appreciate it."

He climbed the ladder to his loft as Winnie rose and cleared the cups. She reached for her mending basket from the shelf and settled into a chair close to the fireplace, pulling a wool stocking over her left hand and examining the heel where the fabric had worn thin. She threaded her needle and began working the wool yarn in small, precise stitches, the firelight catching the needle's flash each time it rose from the fabric.

Belle took the almanac from the mantel and opened it on her lap after she sat in a chair across from Winnie. The pages were thin and closely printed, columns of planting dates and moon phases and weather forecasts that she had no intention of reading. The almanac was a prop. It was the thing she held when she didn't know what to do with her hands and didn't want Winnie to notice.

Several minutes passed. The fire settled lower. Winnie's needle moved in its steady rhythm, in and out, the thread pulling through the wool with a faint sound that was barely audible.

"Mr. Sterling watched you the whole time you were talking tonight," Winnie said, without looking up from her mending. "It was interesting to observe."

Belle's fingers tightened on the almanac.

"He wasn't watching the way men watch when a woman is causing trouble in a room," Winnie continued, her needle not pausing. "I've seen that kind of watching. It has a particular quality. Tight around the mouth. Waiting for the interruption to end so they can resume what they were doing. Mr. Sterling wasn't doing that. He was watching the way a man watches when he is seeing something that fancies them."

"He was watching his bridge get challenged. Any engineer would pay attention to that."

"I agree, Belle, but it was more than that...he was paying attention to you."

Belle turned a page of the almanac. The paper made a dry, sharp sound in the quiet room. "You're reading into it."

"I'm reading what was there. I have good eyes, Belle. I sat in the middle of that room, and I watched every face while you were speaking, because somebody in this family ought to be paying attention to what's happening around us."

Belle looked up. Winnie's face was bent over the stocking, the needle working its steady path.

"I think Mr. Sterling may be a bit interested in you," Winnie said.

"He is not interested in me. He is interested in building a bridge, and I am the obstacle that he will have to deal with daily. That is the sum of his attention."

"You don't believe that."

"I believe exactly that."

"Then why did your hands just tighten on that almanac when I said his name?"

Belle forced her fingers to relax, closed the book, and set it on the table beside her. "Mr. Sterling showed professionalism this evening. That differs from interest."

"Professionalism doesn't watch a woman walk to her wagon after a meeting and stand on the porch in the cold until the wagon is out of sight. I saw that too, Belle."

Belle's stomach did something unfamiliar, a quick, involuntary contraction that had nothing to do with the tea or the hour or the chill that still clung to the cabin's corners despite the rebuilt fire. The sensation arrived uninvited and departed quickly, leaving behind only the awareness that it had been there, like a word spoken too quickly to catch.

"You're making something from nothing," she said.

"I'm making an observation from evidence." Winnie set the darned stocking aside and reached for the next one from her basket. "You have never had a beau, Belle. Not once. I understand why. I understand what you've carried and what it cost you and why you closed that door. You had every reason to close it. But you are twenty-two, not eighty-two. The door doesn't have to remain closed forever."

"I didn't close a door. There was no door to close. There was a ferry to run and a family to keep, and no time for anything that didn't serve those two purposes."

"Caleb is a handsome, educated engineer who stood in a room full of men tonight and called out his own employer's mistake before anyone else could use it against you. He did that in front of the entire committee. In front of Horace. He didn't have to do that, Belle."

"That doesn't mean—"

"It means something, and you owe it to yourself to stop cataloguing him as a threat long enough to notice what else he might be."

Belle stared at the fire. "Even if I were inclined to pay attention to such things, which I am not, this is the worst possible moment. The bridge threatens the ferry. The ferry is our livelihood. Paying attention to the man who is building the thing that could ruin us is not romantic. It's foolish."

"Or," Winnie said, threading her needle, "it's God placing someone in your path at exactly the moment you think you need him least." She looked up, and her face held the expression Belle had seen a thousand times and never once grown immune to—the warm, unshakeable sureness of a younger sister who loved her fiercely and saw her clearly and refused, with every stubborn fiber of her gentle heart, to let Belle vanish into herself. "You have spent five years taking care of Liam and me. You have fed us, housed us, kept this homestead standing, kept that ferry running, and kept us safe. Nobody in this family or this town questions what you've given. But somewhere in all that giving, you stopped letting anything come back to you. And I think maybe it's time you stopped staring at the river long enough to notice what's standing on the bank."

Belle opened her mouth and closed it. Winnie returned her attention to the stocking in her hands. Her needle resumed its path through the wool with the unhurried confidence of a woman who had said what she intended to say and was content to let it sit where it landed.

"Good night, Win," Belle said as she stood.

"Good night, Belle." Winnie looked up one more time, and the curve at the corner of her mouth deepened. "Pay attention, Belle. The Lord doesn't send men like Caleb Sterling along every day."

Winnie went back to her mending as Belle walked down the hall to her room and closed the door behind her with a soft, definite click.

She sat on the edge of her bed, unpinned her hair, and let it fall. The weight of it against her shoulders felt like the release of something she'd been holding all evening without realizing she was holding it.

Her sister's words rolled around in her mind: *Pay attention, Belle.*

She lay down and pulled the quilt to her chin and listened to the river run, willing herself to sleep.

Chapter 7

Winnie walked ahead of Belle through the front door of the boardinghouse with a cloth-covered plate balanced in one hand and her Bible in the other. The boardinghouse dining room had been transformed again; the long table pushed against the wall as it had been for the committee meeting, but this time the chairs faced the far end of the room in straighter rows. Oil lamps burned low along the walls despite the morning light that came through the front windows.

Winnie delivered her plate to the sideboard near the kitchen, where two other covered dishes already waited for the social hour that would follow worship, and took her seat. The Callahans sat where they had sat for years: left side, second row, Belle in the chair nearest the aisle. She had been thirteen when she started sitting on the aisle beside her father, close enough to take his elbow if he listed or to press her knee against his when he began to slump during a hymn.

Belle smoothed the fabric of her skirt across her knees as her eyes wandered around the room. Caleb was seated on the right side of the room, directly across the narrow aisle from her. He sat with his back straight and his hands resting on his thighs. He wore a white shirt, buttoned at the collar and the cuffs, and his unruly dark hair had been combed to the side.

"Psalm forty-six," the traveling preacher, a man named Reverend Hale, said. "I ask you to listen, not follow along in your Bibles. Just listen as I speak and take comfort in God's word."

Reverend Hale, lean and angular, had the road-worn look of a preacher who spent more days on horseback than behind a pulpit. He had the complexion of a man whose face had been shaped equally by weather and by the expression he wore most often, which was a smile that brought a twinkle to his eyes. He stood at the small wooden stand at the front of the room and opened his Bible.

He read the psalm from beginning to end. Belle heard the opening about God as refuge and strength, about not fearing though the earth give way and the mountains fall into the sea. She heard the passage about the river whose streams make glad the city of God. She heard the verse the minister paused on and then repeated and held before the room the way a man holds a lantern above dark water.

Be still, and know that I am God.

Reverend Hale closed the Bible and spoke about those verses for twenty more minutes, and in that time he said nothing that Belle had not heard before and everything that Belle had not been willing to hear. He spoke of stillness as the hardest work a person could do. He spoke about the difference between trusting God with the outcome and trusting your own hands to produce it, and how the two looked identical from the outside and were as different as the river's surface and its current. He spoke about surrender not as weakness but as the recognition that a person's grip, however strong, was not the thing holding the world in place.

Belle sat with her hands folded and her back straight, and felt the minister's words land on her the way a thumb presses a bruise to test whether it has healed. It had not healed. She carried the bruise in the particular place where faith and self-reliance met, the juncture she had built her adult life around. The belief that if she worked hard enough and held tight enough and never depended on another person to do what she could do herself, then the river and the homestead and her siblings would remain under her protection. Nothing would be lost the way her father had been lost. The minister spoke about surrender, and Belle's hands tightened on each other in her lap, because "surrender" was the word for what happened when you let go. And letting go was the word for what her father had done, and she couldn't separate the two meanings no matter how many Sundays she sat in this room and tried.

She looked at the floor. The boards were worn smooth by years of accumulated traffic in a building that served as a dining room, meeting hall, and sanctuary in turn. She studied the grain of the wood because studying it meant she didn't have to look at anything else.

Mrs. Hanscombe rose from her chair near the front when Reverend Hale finished speaking. She was not a small woman, and she carried herself to the front of the room with the authority of a person who had been leading the singing in this makeshift congregation for years and intended to keep doing so until the town built a proper church or she was carried out of the boardinghouse in a pine box, whichever came first. She held a hymnal open in her left hand, though Belle suspected she needed the book about as much as the Yellowstone needed a map to find its way to the Missouri.

"Rock of Ages," Mrs. Hanscombe announced. "Those who have hymnals, page forty-three. Those who don't, follow along as best you can."

The first notes of the hymn came from Mrs. Hanscombe's voice alone, a soprano that had lost its highest register to age but gained in return a warmth that the highest register couldn't have carried. She sang the opening line, and the room joined on the second, voices layering over one another with imperfect, earnest harmony.

Belle knew this hymn. She had known it since before she could read the words in the hymnal, because her father had hummed it on the ferry platform on mornings when the river was calm and the work was steady. His face on those mornings had carried an expression she had spent years trying to forget and couldn't, because it was the face of a man who believed in something greater than himself at one time.

He had stopped humming the hymn shortly after her mother had passed. The humming went first, then his steadiness, then the mornings when he showed up sober, then the mornings when he showed up at all. The progression had been so gradual that Belle hadn't recognized it until she was standing on the ferry platform alone at sixteen, running the crossing by herself because her father was in his bedroom with the door closed and the curtain drawn.

Her knuckles went white as she gripped the empty chair in front of her. Winnie's hand came down onto Belle's left hand, where it gripped the chair and covered it, warm and firm.

The congregation continued to sing, and Belle heard the words about clinging to the cross. She tried to focus on something in the room to make the memories of her father retreat. And then she heard a distinct voice from across the aisle. A bass-baritone, low and unhurried, rich in the way that a voice is rich when it has been used for years in the service of songs the singer knows by heart. She glanced over to see Caleb singing without a hymnal. His voice didn't strain for the low notes or thin at the upper edges of the melody. It held the center of the tune and moved through it with patience.

The hymn ended, and Mrs. Hanscombe returned to her seat. Reverend Hale offered a closing prayer, brief and plain, and Sunday worship concluded without ceremony.

Chairs began to shift and conversations opened across the rows as people rose, the room's volume climbing from the hush of worship to the animated warmth of neighbors speaking with one another. Women moved to the sideboard and began uncovering the dishes that waited there, and moments later Mrs. Hanscombe brought a coffee pot from the kitchen.

Belle stood and smoothed her skirt and stepped into the general current of the social hour. She accepted a cup of coffee from a rancher's wife. The coffee was strong, stronger than what Mrs. Hanscombe usually served, and the taste of it told Belle that the beans had come from somewhere other than the mercantile's regular stock.

"That's a fine roast," Amos Pemberton's wife said from beside the sideboard, turning her cup in her hands. "Where did you come by it, Mrs. Hanscombe?"

"Mr. Pritchard. He brought me a pound of it from Livingston. A generous contribution to the Sunday table, if I do say so myself."

As if summoned by the mention of his own name, Horace materialized from the cluster of men near the front of the room and joined the women at the sideboard with smooth, unhurried ease. He wore a pressed wool suit and that particular smile that Belle had learned to read over the past few weeks as the expression of a man who wanted to be seen.

"I couldn't let Mrs. Hanscombe serve the Lord's Day gathering with plain beans from the mercantile," Horace said, addressing the small group that had formed near the coffee. "Livingston has a roaster who does a fine job with the South American imports, and I thought Providence Ridge deserved a taste of what a proper Sunday coffee should be."

"That's very kind, Mr. Pritchard," Pemberton's wife said.

"It's the least I could do. I rather enjoy the privilege of a good cup of coffee."

Mrs. Hanscombe picked up her cup and turned to Belle with the deliberate pivot of a woman choosing a new conversation.

"Belle, you look well this morning. Come sit with me a moment."

Belle followed her to a pair of chairs near a window that someone had pulled from the rows and angled toward each other. Mrs. Hanscombe settled into hers with the solid, grounded movement of a woman who had been on her feet since before dawn and intended to take her rest when it was offered. She gestured at the chair beside her, and Belle sat down.

"Your sister's molasses cakes are the best on that sideboard," Mrs. Hanscombe said. "Don't tell Margaret Pemberton I said so. She brought her version of them as well, and she's quite proud of them."

"Winnie would trade her the recipe for a good word about her garden," Belle said. "She put in the early peas this week, and now she's worried they'll freeze."

"They might. April is a liar in this valley. But peas are hardy." Mrs. Hanscombe sipped her coffee and regarded Belle over the rim. "How did you find the sermon?"

"Reverend Hale speaks plainly. I appreciated that."

"He does. No flourishes. The man says what he means and gets right to the heart of the matter, which is more than most traveling preachers manage." Mrs. Hanscombe lowered her cup to her knee. "Speaking of men who are plain in their manner, Mr. Sterling has been a quiet but courteous guest so far."

"He's been in Providence Ridge for a bit over a week now. I expect you've had time to form more of an impression than that," Belle said.

"I have. He's punctual to meals, he cleans up after himself, and he bows his head before he eats. Every meal. Not for show, either. I've observed plenty of men who bow their heads for show. Mr. Sterling closes his eyes and his lips move, and when he raises his head, he picks up his fork the way a man picks up a tool after he's asked a blessing on the work he's about to conquer."

Belle held her coffee cup in both hands and said nothing.

"I've taken to sitting with him some evenings," Mrs. Hanscombe continued. "After supper, when the dining room clears. He stays at the table with his Bible open, studying it the way he studies those survey maps of his: carefully and thoroughly. I came through one evening to bank the fireplace, and he looked up and asked me whether I'd read the book of Ruth. Imagine that. A young man asking an old boardinghouse keeper whether she's read Ruth." She shook her head with a fondness that was half amusement and half something deeper. "We've had some fine conversations. He has a thoughtful mind, that man. He listens when you talk, which is rarer than it should be."

"Has Mr. Pritchard joined your evening conversations?" Belle asked.

Mrs. Hanscombe's mouth did that thing again, the almost imperceptible flattening that communicated more than most people's full expressions. "Horace Pritchard retires to his room after supper or wanders down to the saloon. He is sociable in this dining room when the socializing serves a purpose and private when it doesn't. I have nothing ill to say about the man. He pays his bill on time and keeps his room in order." She paused. "But he doesn't sit at my table in the evening studying his Bible. There is a difference between a man who is pleasant on the surface and a man who has a central focus on God, and I have lived long enough to know which one I trust to return my good china."

Belle stared into her coffee cup as she listened.

"Mr. Sterling asked me about the town the other night," Mrs. Hanscombe continued. "About the families here, who's been here longest, and if the community comes together in times of need.

He wasn't asking to make conversation. He was asking because he wanted to know. There's a difference in that, too."

"He's thorough and inquisitive," Belle said. "An engineer's habit, I suspect."

"Perhaps. But I believe he's genuinely interested in our town. He asked whether the children had a full-time teacher, and when I told him they didn't, he said that was a shame, and I believe he meant it." Mrs. Hanscombe finished her coffee and set the cup on the windowsill beside her. "I've housed a great many men in this building, Belle. Drifters, teamsters, railroad men, and miners passing through on their way to somewhere else. Most of them are decent enough and forgettable. Some of them are decent and memorable. Once in a rare while, a man sits at my table who is not passing through, even if he thinks he is. Mr. Sterling is that kind, I believe."

Belle looked across the room. Caleb stood near the far wall with Amos and another man she recognized as one of the ranchers from the north end of the valley. He held his coffee cup and listened to whatever Amos was telling him with the unhurried attention she had first observed on the ferry. As she watched, Horace crossed toward the group and inserted himself into the conversation with the fluid ease of a man who considered every gathering of two or more people an opportunity. He clapped Amos on the shoulder and said something that made the rancher chuckle. Caleb nodded and offered a response that was too quiet for Belle to hear across the room. Horace's smile broadened.

"Mr. Pritchard is generous with his coffee and his company," Mrs. Hanscombe observed, following Belle's gaze. "He'd have the whole room believing he built this town with his own hands if you let him talk long enough. The coffee that he brought is good; I'll grant him that. But I dare say… we should keep an eye on him."

Belle turned back to Mrs. Hanscombe and found the older woman watching her. "I should check on Winnie; please excuse me."

"Of course, dear." Mrs. Hanscombe patted Belle's knee. "Tell your sister if the peas survive the frost, which I'm sure they will, I'll buy whatever she can spare."

Belle rose from the chair and carried her cup to the sideboard, where Winnie was wrapped in conversation with a young woman Belle recognized as the Gresham girl. They were talking about something that made both of them lean in with the particular absorption of women exchanging practical knowledge. Belle caught enough of the conversation to understand it involved rising bread and the temperature of a cookstove's firebox.

The room had reached the peak of its social hour's warmth; the voices layered and continuous. The coffee had made its second round, and the food on the sideboard had diminished. Liam stood near the door with Uncle Tom, the two of them engaged in a low conversation.

Belle turned to Winnie again and touched her elbow. "We should start for home soon."

Winnie nodded and excused herself from the Gresham girl. She collected her empty plate from the sideboard and followed Belle toward the door.

Belle was three steps from the doorway when Caleb appeared and opened the door for them.

She stopped and looked at him. His face was composed, and carried no expression she could read as an overture or an expectation.

And yet the act of it, the simple fact that he had opened a door for her, hit her deeply.

She gave him a nod, small and controlled. He returned the nod, and Belle stepped through the doorway and onto the boarding-house porch.

She crossed the porch, descended the steps, and walked toward the wagon where the horses stood tied to the rail. Liam rushed ahead of her and went to untie the lead horse. When Winnie reached her side and glanced her way, a knowing grin shone on her face.

"Don't," Belle said.

"I didn't say a word."

"You're about to."

Winnie leaned in close. "He crossed an entire room to hold a door for you, Belle. An entire room. Did you notice that? My heart swooned just watching it."

"He opened a door, Winnie. Men open and hold doors all the time. It is not a declaration."

"It is when a man crosses a room to do it."

Belle reached the wagon and took Liam's offered hand to climb up onto the bench. She settled into the seat and fixed her attention on the road ahead.

"Mrs. Hanscombe spoke highly of him," Belle said.

Winnie arranged herself beside her. "Did she now?"

Liam climbed up and took the reins, and the wagon lurched into motion. Belle fought the urge to turn and look back. She held that discipline for a full ten seconds.

Caleb Sterling still stood on the boardinghouse porch with his coffee cup in one hand and his other hand resting on the porch rail, watching them leave.

Belle turned her attention back to the road ahead and felt her cheeks flush.

Chapter 8

The Yellowstone was running a full hand higher than it had been the previous morning, the water dark with sediment from the overnight rain that had come down off the Absarokas in sheets and fed every drainage between the high ridges and the valley floor.

Belle and Liam had the scow loaded by mid-morning with a mining-supply wagon that had come down from Livingston. The teamster, a broad man named Ferris, drove a four-mule team hitched to a freight wagon stacked with iron pipe, coiled cable, crates of blasting caps packed in sawdust, and two barrels of kerosene lashed to the bed with chain. The wagon alone was heavy enough to settle the scow three inches deeper in the water than a standard freight load. The mules stood at the center of the platform where Liam had positioned them, their ears flat, their hooves stamping against the wet planking as the current pulled at the hull beneath them.

Belle ran the numbers before casting off. She calculated the load against the water speed, the cable tension against the angle, and the margin she had between the scow's draft at this weight and the river bottom at the channel's deepest point. The numbers were close.

"Current's strong," Liam said from the downstream rail where he was checking the cargo lashings on the freight wagon's near side.

"I know it."

Belle finished her inspection of the guide rope where it threaded through the overhead pulley and tugged it twice, testing the cable's response through the rigging. The cable hummed under tension, a sound she could interpret as precisely as a fiddler reads pitch. Both main cables were taut; the upstream line and the downstream line holding their catenary in the parallel arc that told her the anchor posts on both banks were solid and the tension was distributed.

"Let's cross," she said.

Liam nodded and moved to his position, one hand on the cargo tie that held the freight wagon's rear axle against the deck cleat. Ferris stood beside his horses with his hands on the lead animal's halter, talking low to the team. Two stagecoach passengers who had been waiting on the south bank landing sat on the upstream bench: a man in a dark coat and a woman with a carpetbag on her lap.

Belle cast off the mooring lines. The current took the hull immediately, and the scow swung downstream a quarter turn before the cables caught the drift and held. She leaned into the guide rope and corrected the angle, pulling the platform back into line with the crossing path, her shoulders absorbing the lateral force of the current through the rope and the pulley, and the overhead rigging. The hemp bit into her palms through her work gloves. The scow steadied, found its line, and began to track across the river on the cables.

The first third of the crossing went clean. The current pushed, the cables held, and Belle worked the guide rope in the small, continuous corrections that kept the platform's angle matched to the water's pressure. Liam held his position at the cargo tie. The horses shifted but held their ground. Below the platform, the Yellowstone moved with a force she could feel through the soles of her boots.

They reached the midstream channel where the current ran fastest, and Belle felt the change in the guide rope before she saw it. The tension shifted. Not in the rope itself, but in the geometry of the system above her, as though the cable supporting the pulley had elongated by a fraction of an inch on one side. She looked up at the main cables. The upstream cable was holding its arc. The downstream cable, the one closest to the heavy side of the load, was holding too, but something in the braid caught her eye, a place where the outer strands of the hemp appeared to be separating from one another in a pattern that had no business being there.

The first strand parted with a sound like a whip crack, sharp enough to carry over the voice of the river and the stamp of the mules. Belle's hands tightened on the guide rope. She looked at the cable and saw the second strand go, the braid unwinding at the point of failure.

The third strand snapped, and the geometry of the crossing changed.

The scow lurched downstream as the weakened cable lost its share of the load, and the upstream cable took the full force of the current. Belle hauled on the guide rope to correct the angle, but the correction only drove the scow harder against the one cable that remained at full tension, and the platform began to swing in a slow, sickening arc toward the downstream side. The freight wagon's lashing creaked against the deck cleat as the load shifted. One of the kerosene barrels slid six inches toward the downstream rail before the chain caught it. The horses lunged against the platform's tilt, their hooves scrabbling on the wet planking. Ferris threw his weight against the lead horses's halter to keep the team from pulling the wagon sideways.

"Liam!" Belle called across the platform.

He was already moving. He braced himself against the freight wagon's upstream wheel and pushed, his boots dug into the deck planking. But the scow was still swinging, the downstream cable still degrading, and Belle could hear more strands letting go in a rapid sequence of percussive snaps that punched through the noise of the river.

She needed an anchor point on the bank. She needed a second line to hold the platform's downstream side while she worked the scow into the shallows on the remaining cable. The south bank was closer, forty feet of fast water between the platform and the gravel bar where the landing's mooring posts stood driven into the earth.

Belle looked at the south bank and calculated the throw. The loose mooring line coiled at the stern of the platform was sixty feet of hemp, heavy enough to carry across forty feet of wind if she put her body behind the throw and aimed upstream of where she needed the line to land, letting the current carry the rope's arc downstream to the catcher. The problem was that there was no catcher on the bank. Liam was on the scow.

A figure came at a run from the upstream direction, moving along the bank at a full sprint with his coat flapping behind him.

Caleb reached the water's edge and stopped, his eyes on the scow, the failing cable, and the platform's downstream tilt. He waded into the shallows up to his knees, then his thighs, the current shoving against his legs, and he planted himself fifteen feet from the bank with his arms open and his weight braced against the river bottom.

Belle grabbed the mooring line from the stern coil. She set her feet wide on the tilting platform and threw the line toward the bank with everything her shoulders could give it. The rope arced out over the water, the coils unwinding in a flat spiral that the wind caught and dragged, and the end of the line landed in the fast water six feet upstream of where Caleb stood. He lunged for it. The current pushed the rope past him, and he caught it with both hands as it swept by, the hemp snapping taut between the platform and his grip, and the force of the connection jerked his body downstream a foot before he dug his heels into the riverbed and held.

The line pulled against him. Belle could see the strain of it in the angle of his body, leaning upstream against the current's drag on the rope. He was holding the mooring line taut enough to give the platform a second reference point, a downstream anchor that kept the scow from swinging further while Belle worked the guide rope to bring the platform's heading around toward the shallows.

She hauled on the guide rope with both hands, her shoulders burning under the strain as she forced the scow's angle against the current, using the upstream cable's remaining tension and Caleb's anchor line to vector the platform toward the south bank. Liam put his weight against the freight wagon at the center. Ferris held the horses. The scow moved through the water in a slow, dragging arc that felt like steering a barn through a flood, every foot of progress fought for.

The current drove Caleb back another foot. Then two. He stumbled, went down to one knee in the water, and came back up without releasing the rope. His face was contorted with the effort of holding position against a force that wanted to carry him downstream, and the image of it burned itself into Belle's vision.

The scow's hull scraped gravel. The shallows caught the platform's downstream edge and slowed the swing, and Belle felt the moment the river's grip on the scow loosened. She pulled the guide rope through two more notches, driving the platform harder into the shallows. Liam grabbed the stern mooring line and leaped from the platform into waist-deep water, wading to the nearest mooring post and looping the surrounding line. The scow ground against the bank and held.

Belle secured the guide rope and crossed the platform to the loading ramp. Ferris was already talking the team down the ramp and onto the bank with the steady, competent voice. Liam stood at the mooring post with the line in his hands, his trousers soaked to the waist, his chest heaving.

Belle stepped off the platform onto the bank.

Caleb was standing ten feet from the water's edge. The water had taken him to the chest at its deepest. His shirt was plastered to his frame, his hair was wet against his forehead, and his hands, where they gripped the rope, were white at the knuckles. He was shaking. The cold of the Yellowstone River in mid-April was not a mild cold. It was a cold that came down off glacial snowfields and carried the temperature of the mountains that fed it, and a man who had stood in it to his chest for the time it took to bring a loaded ferry to bank would feel that cold in his bones for hours.

She walked toward the river's edge. "Thank you," she called out. The words came out rough, stripped of everything but the thing they meant.

He let go of the rope. His hands opened slowly, the way hands open when they have been gripping something so hard the muscles have to be convinced to release. He shook his head once.

"You'd have saved it without me; it just might have taken longer," he said.

They both knew that was not true. They both knew that without his anchor point on the bank, the ferry would have swung downstream until the remaining cable either held or didn't. If it hadn't held, the ferry would have gone into the main channel of the Yellowstone River at high water.

Belle turned from him and walked to the storage trunk bolted to the platform rail at the scow's stern. The trunk was a pine box with a hinged lid and iron hardware that she'd built the second year after taking over the ferry, large enough to hold the splice kit, the fare ledger, a set of hand tools, and the folded wool blanket she kept for the crossings when the cold or the spray made the work unbearable. She lifted the lid, pushed aside the splice kit and the coiled marlinspike, and pulled the blanket free. It was gray wool, heavy, smelling of the trunk's pine boards and the faint mineral residue of river water that had soaked into it and dried and soaked again across seasons. She carried it back to where Caleb now stood on land.

She held the blanket out to him. He reached for it with both hands, and in the transfer, her fingers came down against his where they closed on the wool. His hands were cold. The cold startled her, as did the sensation of someone else's skin against hers. She let go of the blanket and stepped back.

He wrapped the blanket around his shoulders. His shaking didn't stop as he gathered the fabric at his chest and gripped it.

"Liam," Belle said. "Help me pull the cable in."

Liam was at her side in three strides. They walked to the bank-side anchor post where the downstream cable terminated, and Belle began pulling the slack line in hand over hand, coiling the wet hemp on the ground. When the damaged section reached the bank, she crouched beside it.

The damage was obvious at close range. On the underside of the cable, the side that faced the water when the line was strung between its anchor posts, strands had been cut. Not frayed. Not worn. Cut. A blade had been drawn across the hemp at intervals along a span of roughly eighteen inches, severing strand after strand on the bottom of the braid while leaving the top-facing strands intact. The cuts were clean, the edges of the fibers smooth where the blade had parted them, positioned on the one side of the cable that was invisible during a routine inspection from the platform or the bank.

Belle ran her fingers along the cuts. The edges of the severed fibers were smooth, not splintered. A blade had done this.

Liam crouched beside her. He looked at the cuts, and his face changed, color leaving it.

"That's not wear," he said.

"No, it is not."

She looked at the clean edges of the severed strands and felt something cold settle into the center of her chest that had nothing to do with the river or the wind.

She heard Caleb's boots on the gravel behind her. He stopped three paces from where she crouched beside the cable. She stood up and turned to face him, and the words that came out of her mouth arrived before the thinking part of her mind could intervene.

"Did you do this?"

He looked at her, then at the cable, then back at her.

"Did you cut my cable, Mr. Sterling? Did you come down here at night and take a knife to the line that holds every soul who crosses this river?"

He didn't step back, nor did he raise his hands in defense or protest. He stood with the blanket around his shoulders and the water still running from his clothes and listened to the accusation with an expression she couldn't read, because it was neither anger nor surprise nor the careful blankness of a man composing a denial.

"No," he said. "I didn't."

"You want the ferry to fail. You need the ferry to fail because a bridge is easier to justify when the alternative is a cable crossing that cannot hold a loaded wagon on high water. Every person in this valley knows that. This cable that holds my crossing has been deliberately cut in a way that makes it look as though my operation cannot bear the freight this town depends on."

"Miss Callahan." His voice was level. "I was in my room at the boardinghouse last night. Mrs. Hanscombe served supper at six yesterday evening, and I ate breakfast at half-past six this morning. You can confirm that with anyone who ate at that table in the boardinghouse. I was at the bridge site by eight this morning, and I've been there since."

"I don't know what I can confirm."

"May I look at the cable? I'd like to see the damage."

She held his gaze for a count of three. The fear that had produced the accusation was still in her, still pressing against the inside of her ribs. But the man standing in front of her was the same man who had waded into the Yellowstone ten minutes ago without removing his coat or his boots. The man whose hands were still red from the rope burn of holding her mooring line against a current that could have carried him to the bend downstream. The accusation she had made and the evidence of what he had done stood side by side in her mind, and they didn't fit in the same frame.

She stepped aside. Caleb moved past her and crouched beside the cable where it lay on the gravel. He picked up the damaged section with both hands and turned it, examining the braid the way she had examined it, but his attention moved differently than hers had.

He set the cable down and stood. When he turned to face her, his expression had changed.

"This was done with a knife," he said. "The cuts are too clean for anything else. Whoever did this knew what they were doing. The strands are severed on the underside at intervals, not at a single point, which distributes the weakness across a span instead of concentrating it. A single-point cut would have been visible in the cables hang. This method keeps the braid's shape intact under no load because the upper strands hold everything in position, and it fails progressively under heavy load, which is exactly what you saw on the water."

"I know what I saw on the water."

"I expect you do." He held her gaze. "The damage is deliberate. It was done by someone who understands cable construction well enough to sabotage it without leaving obvious evidence."

Belle looked at the cable on the ground between them. She looked at Liam, who stood three feet away with his hands at his sides and his jaw set. She looked at Caleb, standing in her wool blanket with the river still dripping from his trouser cuffs.

"The ferry is shut down," Belle said.

Liam nodded once.

"Nobody crosses on that cable until I've repaired it and inspected every foot of line on both sides." She turned to the stagecoach passengers waiting to cross the river. "The ferry is closed. If you need to cross, there's a shallow ford at Mercy Bend, two miles upstream. It'll take a wagon if the driver is experienced and uses caution. Liam will walk you to the trailhead and point you right."

Ferris spat onto the ground and adjusted his hat. "How long till you're running again?"

"Late tomorrow or possibly the next day."

"I'll need to cross again before then," Ferris said.

"And I've got a crossing that someone took a knife to. I have precious lives to protect, including yours. You'll have to reroute through Mercy Bend."

Ferris turned to his horses without further argument and began backing the wagon around toward the upstream trail.

"Liam. After you've shown them the trail, go into town. Find Mrs. Hanscombe and Amos. Tell them I'm calling an emergency committee meeting tonight at eight. Tell them what happened and to spread the word about the meeting tonight.

He nodded, then turned back to the trail and followed the travelers up the bank.

Belle turned to Caleb. She noticed that his lips had a bluish cast from the cold, and the shaking in his hands had not fully subsided.

"I need supplies from my barn," she said. "I'll be back within the hour. I don't expect you to stay here. Go to the boardinghouse and get warm. I've got this covered."

"I'll come with you," he said.

She should have told him that she didn't need the help. She didn't need a soaked, shivering engineer to accompany her on an errand she could complete alone. She looked at his hands, still red from the rope. She looked at the river where he had stood with the water at his chest.

"My mare is tied at the upper landing," she said. "Liam's gelding is there, too. Can you ride?"

"I can ride."

Belle turned toward the trail that led up the bank to the upper clearing where the horses waited. She heard his boots behind her, the wet squelch of waterlogged leather. They climbed the bank path in single file, and when they reached the clearing where her mare and Liam's gelding stood tied to the cottonwood rail, she untied both leads and handed him the gelding's reins.

He took the reins with rope-burned hands, mounted without complaint despite the wet weight of his clothes, and settled into the saddle with a competence that told her he had not lied about being able to ride. Belle swung up onto her mare and nudged her forward.

Chapter 9

Caleb rode two lengths behind Belle on Liam's gelding along the trail, the wool blanket pulled tight across his shoulders with one hand while the other held the reins, his wet trousers chafing against the saddle leather with every stride. The cold had settled past his skin and into the layer beneath, the deep muscular chill of a man who had stood in glacial runoff to his chest and whose body had not yet forgiven him for it. His boots squelched against the stirrups, waterlogged and heavy. The April air moving through the cottonwoods carried a bite that found every wet surface on his body.

Belle had not spoken since they mounted.

The trail narrowed where a deadfall cottonwood had dropped a limb across the path sometime during the winter, and Belle guided her mare around it without slowing. Caleb followed. The gelding was a steady animal, sure-footed on the rutted trail, and it carried him with the patient tolerance of a horse accustomed to a different rider's weight and habits.

The trail widened past the deadfall, and Belle's mare slowed enough that the gelding came alongside, the two horses falling into a matched walk with a gap of three feet between the riders.

Belle glanced at him. "The repair will take the rest of today and most of tomorrow," she said. "A long splice across the damaged section, reinforced with serving and sealed with pine tar."

"How long is a long splice?" Caleb asked.

"Depends on the diameter of the cable and the length of the damage. For my main line, I'll need to unlay six feet of rope on each side of the damaged section, taper the strands, and marry them back into the braid. The splice itself will probably take three hours if the hemp cooperates. The serving takes another two, and the tar needs to set overnight."

"You've done this before."

"Twice. Once after the ice breakup in the spring of eighty-one, took out a twelve-foot section at the midpoint anchor. And another time, after a freight wagon's brake chain caught the cable during loading and tore through four strands. A splice done right is stronger than the original cable at the join."

"The second cable looked sound from what I could see on the bank," Caleb said. "But I'd want to inspect it from underneath. The damage on the first cable was positioned where a topside inspection wouldn't find it."

"I know where it was positioned."

He let her comment stand without responding.

The cottonwoods thinned as the trail climbed toward a final rise, and the sky opened above them, a pale, washed blue of a Montana spring day. The mountains on both sides carried snow on their far upper ridges, the white broken by dark seams of exposed rock where the slopes were too steep to hold accumulation.

"How long have you been running the crossing with your brother?" he asked.

"Five years."

He did the arithmetic and assumed she couldn't have been more than a teenager.

"My father ran it before me," Belle said. "I took it over after he died."

Caleb nodded and said no more as the trail crested the rise and the land opened before them. At the center of the clearing sat a frame house, single-story with a loft peak visible above the roofline, its timber walls carrying the color of wood that had taken years of weather without paint. A porch ran across the front, rough-planked, wide enough for three chairs and a view down the valley to the Yellowstone.

The homestead was modest. There was no excess here. No second barn, no expanded home, no evidence of prosperity beyond the careful maintenance of what existed. The place was kept, and kept well, but it was kept at the margin.

Belle guided her mare into the yard and dismounted near the barn. Caleb pulled the gelding alongside and swung down from the saddle, his boots landing in packed earth with a heaviness that sent a jolt of cold up through his legs. He looped the reins around the fence rail beside Belle's mare and stood for a moment in the yard, taking in the homestead at close range.

The front door of the cabin opened, and a young woman came onto the porch. Caleb recognized her from the committee meeting and Sunday worship, the younger sister, the one who had sat beside

Belle and placed her hand over Belle's hand on the chair during the hymn singing. She was lighter in coloring than Belle, her hair fairer and pinned in a knot that was coming loose on one side, and she wore a housedress with a dishcloth over her shoulder. She came down the porch steps and across the yard toward them with a stride that accelerated as she got closer.

"What happened?" she asked. "Where's Liam?"

"The ferry cable was cut," Belle said. "Sabotaged. It failed during a loaded crossing this morning. Liam is fine. He's redirecting passengers and then going into town spreading the word for an emergency committee meeting for tonight."

Winnie looked at Caleb. "Mr. Sterling, you look as though you've been in the river."

"I have, Miss Callahan."

"He caught my mooring line from the shallows and held the platform while I brought the scow in," Belle said.

"You need to come inside," Winnie said to him. "Liam has spare clothes; they'll fit close enough, and there's a fire and coffee."

"I appreciate that, Miss Callahan. But your sister needs supplies from the barn, and I'd like to help carry them out before I take you up on the offer."

"The supplies will take ten minutes, if not longer," Belle said. "Winnie is right. You should go in."

"Ten minutes, then," Caleb said. "I'll last ten more minutes."

Winnie looked at Belle and then back at Caleb. "Ten minutes. Then you're coming inside, both of you, and I don't want an argument about it."

She turned and walked back toward the house.

Belle led him into the barn, and the interior was dim, the only light coming through the open door and through gaps in the plank walls where the boards had shrunk with age, throwing narrow bands of illumination across the hard-packed dirt floor. Caleb could see four small horse stalls, and the far end of the barn was storage with tools hung on pegs along the wall. A workbench ran beneath the tool wall, its surface scarred from years of use. Shelves to the side of the bench held supplies.

Belle moved through the barn with the certainty of a woman who knew where every item she needed was. She pulled a coil of heavy hemp from a peg on the far wall, testing the rope's flexibility with a quick bend. She unhooked a canvas tool roll from beside the workbench and laid it open on the surface, checking the contents: a marlinspike, a serving mallet, a fid, needles for whipping, and smaller cordage for the serving wrap. She reached to a high shelf and brought down a squat stoneware crock sealed with a waxed cloth lid, the pine tar she needed for sealing the finished splice.

"What else?" Caleb asked.

"A block and tackle from the back wall. I'll need it to tension the cable before I splice. And the serving cord on the shelf above your head, the spool of marline."

Caleb turned and reached for the spool. His hands were stiff from the cold; the fine motor control that an engineer depended on was reduced to a clumsy approximation, and when his fingers closed on the spool, they fumbled it. The marlin dropped, and he caught it before it hit the floor, a graceless recovery that sent a fresh wave of shivering through his shoulders.

Belle watched him from the workbench.

"You need to sit down," she said.

"I'm fine."

"You were standing in the Yellowstone for the better part of ten minutes and riding in wet clothes for another fifteen after that. Your hands are shaking badly enough that you nearly dropped a spool of cord. If I put you on the ferry platform right now, I wouldn't trust you to hold a rope."

"Then it's fortunate you're the one who will be doing the splicing."

She held his gaze for a second before she turned back to the workbench and began rolling the tools back into their canvas wrap.

"Hold this," she said, handing him one end of the hemp coil while she measured the length against her arm span. The coil was heavy, forty feet of cable-grade rope, and holding it required him to step closer to the workbench and brace the weight against his hip while she pulled the rope through in measured increments. The distance between them narrowed to the width of the rope running between his hands and hers. He could see the abrasions on her palms where the guide rope had burned through her work gloves during the crossing, the marks red and raised across the heel of each hand. Her hands moved with sureness, quick and precise on the hemp.

She finished measuring, tied off the coil, and took the rope from his hands. The transfer required her to close the distance by another six inches, reaching for the coil where he held it against his hip, and in the reach her forearm passed within an inch of his without touching.

She stepped back with the coil and turned to the workbench to gather the rest of the supplies. Caleb stood where he was and took a deep breath.

"Your sister seems like she manages this household with considerable authority," he said.

"Winnie runs the home the way I run the ferry. She'd object to the comparison, but it's accurate. She keeps the garden, the chickens, and the mending, and does most of the cooking. She sells eggs and produce to Pemberton's mercantile for whatever income it brings. She works part-time at the mercantile as well. Between the ferry fares and what Winnie earns, we manage."

"The three of you."

"The three of us."

"No other family?"

"Our uncle. Marshal Tom Callahan." Belle gathered the block and tackle from the back wall, the iron pulleys clinking as she lifted them from the hook. "He looks in on us, but he has his own life and his own concerns. We don't impose on him unless the situation requires it."

Caleb lifted the coil of hemp and the tool roll from the workbench, holding them against his chest. The weight of the rope pressed against the blanket still wrapped around his shoulders. "You were a teenager when you took over the ferry."

"I was. Seventeen, to be exact. We had what God provided us," she said. "And what we had was enough because it had to be."

She turned and started walking toward the barn door, and the conversation was over. He followed her, and they crossed the yard to the porch where the supplies could be staged for the ride back.

Winnie appeared in the doorway before they reached the steps. She held a folded stack of clothes in her arms, and she looked at Caleb with an expression that had moved beyond suggestion into instruction.

"Mr. Sterling. The coffee is on, and the fire is warm. You can change in the sitting room. I've set a screen."

Caleb took the clothes from her. His hands were still shaking; the tremor was visible in the fabric as he held it. "Much obliged, Miss Callahan."

He climbed the porch steps and crossed the threshold into the Callahan home.

The front room was small and clean; the walls bare except for a single framed piece of needlework near the door that read a passage he recognized from Proverbs. A fireplace anchored the far wall. The fire pushed warmth into the room in a steady wave he felt on his face and his hands the moment he stepped inside. A sitting area occupied the space in front of the hearth—two chairs and a mending basket on the floor beside one of them. A pine table with four chairs beyond that. Past a half-wall he could see the kitchen.

Winnie had arranged a folding screen in the corner of the sitting room, a three-panel frame covered in a fabric that created a space large enough for a man to change his clothes in privacy. Caleb stepped behind the screen and stripped the wet blanket from his shoulders, then peeled the soaked shirt from his back. The air against his bare skin was cold for a half-second before the fire's warmth found him. The relief of it was so immediate that he stood still for a moment with his eyes closed, letting the heat work into his clenched muscles.

He pulled Liam's wool shirt over his head. The shirt was close to his size, slightly broader in the shoulders than his own. He changed out of his wet trousers and into Liam's canvas pair, which were an inch short in the leg but otherwise serviceable. He hung his wet clothes over the top of the screen where the fire's heat would reach them.

When he came around the screen, Belle was in the kitchen and stood at the counter near the cookstove with her back to the sitting room. Winnie was beside her.

"Come sit, Mr. Sterling," Winnie said.

Caleb crossed the room and took a chair at the pine table. She set a cup of coffee in front of him; the steam rising in a thin column. He wrapped both hands around it. The heat from the cup penetrated his palms and reached the cold beneath his skin.

Belle took the chair opposite him. Winnie sat between them, completing the triangle.

"Tell me about the cable," Winnie said to Belle. "All of it."

Belle told her. She described the crossing, the failure, the progressive snapping of the strands, the platform's swing, the cargo shifting, and Caleb's intervention from the bank. She described pulling the cable in and finding the cuts. She described the pattern of the damage, the clean edges, and the placement on the underside where her inspection wouldn't catch it. She spoke with the clarity of a woman delivering a report, her voice level and precise, and Caleb watched Winnie receive each detail with the focused attention of a person building a picture from the inside out.

"Who would do this?" Winnie asked.

"I'm not sure," Belle said.

"But you have thoughts."

"I have thoughts I'm not ready to speak aloud yet."

Winnie turned to Caleb. "Mr. Sterling, Belle tells me you've been working at the bridge site since your arrival. You're there most days?"

"Most days, Miss Callahan. The site is just upstream from the ferry landing."

"And you saw nothing unusual? No one near the cables at odd hours?"

"I arrive at the site around eight in the morning on most days and leave before dusk." He paused. "This morning I heard the commotion while I was working and came at a run. That's the first time anything out of the ordinary at the landing drew my attention."

"You came at a run," Winnie repeated. She looked at Belle, then back at Caleb.

"Yes, ma'am."

"We're grateful, Mr. Sterling."

"Your sister already thanked me."

"I expect she did, and I expect she did it in as few words as possible. Belle thanks people the way she splices cable. Functional and strong, but not what you'd call decorative."

Belle looked at her sister. "Winnie."

"It's a compliment, Belle."

Caleb drank his coffee. The warmth spread from his hands through his arms, reaching the last of the cold in his chest, and the fire behind him pressed against his back through Liam's wool shirt. He set his cup down. "I should get back to the bridge site before the afternoon's gone. I've got measurements to finish, and you'll want the gelding back at the landing before your brother needs it."

"The measurements can wait," Belle said. She was looking at her coffee, not at him. "You stood in the river for me this morning. The least I can do is make sure you're warm, dry, and have food in your belly before you get back to your work."

Winnie refilled his coffee cup and set about preparing something at the cookstove in the kitchen.

Belle rose from her chair and crossed to the kitchen window, where a jar of tallow balm sat on the windowsill. She opened the jar and worked the balm into her hands, rubbing it into the rope burns on her palms. When she was finished, she set the jar back on the windowsill and stood looking out toward the valley beyond. As she stood there, Winnie said something to her from the stove about the state of the kindling box, and Belle answered her. Her voice when she answered her sister was different from every voice Caleb had heard her use. Not softer, exactly. Softer was not the right word for it. It was a voice with the guard taken down, a voice that lived in this home and nowhere else. The voice of a woman who was not running a ferry or addressing a committee or defending her livelihood to a room full of men who measured her by a standard she hadn't set. It was the unguarded voice of a woman in the comfort of her home.

Caleb held his coffee cup in both hands and looked at the fourth chair at the table. He looked back at the jar of tallow balm on the windowsill, the Bible on the shelf in the sitting room, and the mending basket beside the hearth. He looked at Belle again, standing at the kitchen window with her guard down, and she turned to face him.

"Mr. Sterling, I could use your help this afternoon. The cable repair is a two-person job, and I'm not sure how long Liam will be in town. If you're willing to set aside your survey work for the day, I'd be grateful for the extra hands."

"I'd be honored, Miss Callahan."

Chapter 10

The ferry landing looked different with no one waiting to cross the river. Belle had seen it empty a thousand times—first thing in the morning and after the last crossing of the day—but today the emptiness carried the residue of what had happened this morning, the way a room carries the shape of a conversation after the people in it have gone.

She dismounted and looped her mare's reins around the rail post nearest the bank. Caleb brought Liam's gelding alongside and swung down from the saddle. The dry clothes Winnie had given him fit well enough; Liam's shirt sitting close across his shoulders, the canvas trousers a bit short but serviceable. The color had returned to his face. He still moved with the careful economy of a man whose muscles remembered the river's cold, but his hands had stopped shaking.

Belle unstrapped the hemp coil from her saddle and carried it to the gravel bar beside the damaged cable. She set the coil down and went back for the tool roll, the pine tar crock, the block and tackle, and the spool of marline. She laid the canvas tool roll open on a flat section of the land and checked the contents again.

"I need to inspect the second cable before we start," she said. "If both lines are compromised, splicing one won't matter."

Caleb nodded. He stood beside the supplies she had staged and waited.

Belle walked to the upstream mooring post where the second cable was anchored and ran her hands along the hemp from the post to the waterline, feeling the braid through her palms. The cable was taut, the fibers dry above the waterline and damp where the hemp entered the river, and the braid held its twist without distortion. She stepped into the shallows where the gravel bar dropped into the current. The water was cold against her boots, climbing past her ankles to her shins as she waded to the point where the cable passed beneath the surface and angled down to the midstream anchor. She bent and worked her hands along the underside of the braid.

The hemp was sound. No separated strands, no clean edges, no irregularity in the twist. She checked the full accessible length, working the cable through her hands until the depth of the water made further inspection impossible without swimming, and every foot of it read the same: intact, undamaged, holding its rated tension.

She waded back to the bank and shook the water from her hands. "Second cable is clean."

"One cable was sabotaged," Caleb said. "Not both."

"One cable is enough to shut down the crossing. Whoever did this knew that cutting one line would cause a failure under load without destroying the entire system. If both cables had been cut, the scow would have gone into the channel the moment I cast off, and that's not a failure anyone could call wear or neglect. That's obvious sabotage. One cable, cut partway through at a point I can't see from the deck, fails under the strain of a heavy crossing and looks like the rope gave out because I didn't maintain it."

The splice would take the rest of the afternoon if the hemp cooperated, longer if it didn't. She knelt beside the damaged section and examined the break again.

She picked up the marlinspike and turned to Caleb. "I need you on the other side of the break, six feet from the cut. Hold the cable and keep tension on it while I unlay the strands on this side. When I tell you to feed slack, give me three inches at a time, no more. If you give me too much at once, the strands will twist back on themselves, and I'll have to start over."

"Three inches," he said. He moved to the position she had indicated, knelt on the gravel beside the cable, and took it in both hands.

Belle set the marlinspike into the braid at the edge of the damaged section and began to unlay the strands. The work was precise, the kind of labor that punished impatience and rewarded a steady hand. Each strand of the cable was a bundle of smaller fibers twisted into a rope within the rope, and unlaying them meant separating those bundles without damaging the fibers. Her father had taught her this. He had sat on this same gravel bar with a practice length of old rope and walked her through the long splice when she was fourteen, his hands guiding hers through the first unlay, his voice patient in a way it only was when he was teaching her the river or the tools. That had been one of his good days back then.

She worked the first strand free and laid it back along the cable's length, the fiber pale where the inner hemp had been protected from the weather, darker where it had been exposed. The second strand followed, then the third. Six strands in total, each one unlaid and tapered at the end so that when she married them back into the braid from the opposite side, the splice would carry the load without a lump or a weak point in the cable's diameter.

"Feed me slack," she said.

Caleb released three inches. The cable shifted in her hands, the tension adjusting, and she set the marlinspike back into the braid and continued the unlay on the far side of the damage. The work settled into a rhythm: the steel turning through the hemp; the strands separating under her fingers; the cable giving up its construction one twist at a time. Her forearms burned from the sustained grip. The gravel pressed into her knees through her split skirt.

Caleb held his position without shifting and without offering commentary. When she told him to feed slack, he fed slack. When she told him to hold, he held.

They had been at the splice for the better part of an hour when Belle finished the unlay on both sides of the damage and began tapering the strand ends. The taper was critical. Too blunt, and the splice would bulge, creating a stress point that would fail under load. Too thin, and the fibers wouldn't hold their purchase in the braid.

"How did you learn this?" Caleb asked.

"My father taught me the splice when I was fourteen. The rest I learned because I had to." She picked up the first tapered strand and began threading it into the opposing braid, working the marlinspike ahead of the strand to open a channel in the hemp. "When the ice took out twelve feet of cable in eighty-one, I couldn't afford to hire a rigger from Livingston. The ferry was shut down every day I didn't have a working cable, which meant no fares coming in at all. So I spliced it myself from memory and made many mistakes. It took me three full days of work."

"Three days?" Caleb said.

"I was eighteen and working from what my father had shown me on a practice rope four years earlier. The second time it happened, went faster."

She fed the strand through the braid and pulled it tight, checking the lay of the fibers against the cable's natural twist. The strand married into the braid cleanly; the taper disappearing into the construction as though it had always been part of it. She reached for the second strand.

"What is it like," Caleb said, "running this crossing as a young woman? The work itself—I can see what it demands. But the rest of it. The part that has nothing to do with cables and current."

Belle threaded the second strand before she answered. The marlinspike turned through the braid, the steel warm now from the friction of her grip, and the strand followed it into the cable with a resistance that told her the tension was right.

"The rest of it," she said. "You mean what it's like to stand on a platform and have a man twice my age tell me the load is fine when I can see by the waterline that it isn't. Or to quote a fare to a teamster and watch him look past me for whoever is actually in charge. Or to walk into the mercantile for rope and have the clerk try to sell me clothesline because he assumes I don't know the difference between quarter-inch and three-quarter."

"Yes, if you're willing to tell me."

"Then it's like doing the same job any man would do, except that every day starts with proving you belong and can handle the workload. The proving takes more out of you mentally than the physical work." She pulled the second strand tight and checked the lay. "I try not to let it get to me most days. I show up, I run the crossings, I maintain the equipment, and I collect the fares. But there are days when proving myself is a constant battle, and the work and my abilities are invisible."

Caleb was quiet for a moment, holding his tension on the cable. "In engineering, the invisible work is what holds the structure up. The footings, the cross-bracing, the calculations that happen before the first timber goes in. If those aren't sound, nothing above them matters. Most people only see what's above the ground."

Belle looked at him over the cable.

"Did you ever think about closing the ferry?" he asked. "When you were seventeen, and the burden fell on your shoulders. Did you consider walking away from it?"

"Where would I have walked? I had a sister who was fifteen, a brother who was thirteen, and a homestead with debts on it and a town that depended on the crossing. If I closed the ferry, the fares stopped. If the fares stopped, we lost the homestead. If we lost the homestead, Winnie and Liam had nothing."

"That's not the same as wanting to keep it."

The observation stopped her hands for a fraction of a second before she resumed the work. Nobody had said that to her before.

"No," she said. "It's not the same." She worked the strand through two more twists of the braid. "I kept it because the alternative was worse. And then I kept it because I got good at it. And then I kept it because it was mine, and being good at something that is yours is not a small thing when you are a woman in a place that doesn't expect you to be good at much beyond a kitchen and a garden."

"And now?"

"Now I keep it because I can't see who I am without it, and that frightens me." She didn't look at Caleb. She kept her attention on the hemp, the marlinspike, and the strand feeding into the braid. "Feed me some slack."

He fed her three inches. She continued the splice.

"What made you become an engineer?" she asked.

Caleb shifted his grip on the cable to resettle his weight on the gravel. He had been kneeling in the same position for some time without complaint, and the only evidence of discomfort was the way he moved his knees when she gave him a moment between instructions.

"I grew up in Chicago," he said. "In eighteen seventy-one, the city caught fire and nearly destroyed everything. I was seventeen when the city burned, and I spent the next few years watching men rebuild it. Not just the buildings—the idea of the city. The belief that something destroyed can be built again if the people who build it understand what went wrong the first time. I wanted to be one of those men. I wanted to understand how things hold, why they stand, and what makes the difference between a structure that lasts and one that doesn't."

"And bridges in particular...why?"

"Bridges are the purest form of the problem. A building sits on its foundation, and the ground holds it. A bridge spans empty space. It holds itself up by the logic of its design—the way the forces move through the timber, the way compression and tension balance each other across the truss. There's nothing underneath it except what you put there. If the engineering is wrong, the river takes it."

"The river takes it," Belle repeated.

"That's the part that drew me in. The honesty of it. A bridge over a river doesn't get to pretend. It either holds or it doesn't, and the river is the one that decides."

She understood what he was telling her more than he likely intended her to. A man who built bridges over rivers and a woman who ran a ferry on one had arrived at the same truth from different directions: the river didn't negotiate. It tested what you built, and what you built either survived the testing or it didn't, and no amount of reputation or argument or good intention changed the outcome. She threaded the fifth strand into the braid and pulled it snug.

They worked in quiet for a stretch after that; the splice nearing completion. Belle's hands moved through the final strands with the sureness of a pattern she could perform in her sleep. The quiet between them was occupied by the work itself—the sound of the steel in the rope, the creak of the hemp under tension, the river running its constant commentary fifteen feet from where they knelt.

When the last strand was married into the braid, Belle sat back on her heels and examined the splice along its full length, running her hands over the joined section and checking the diameter. The splice was clean and sound, and it would hold under any load the ferry carried.

"I need to let the braid settle overnight before I serve it," she said. "The strands will seat themselves into the cable's twist, and the serving will lie tighter for it. Tomorrow I'll wrap the marline over the splice and seal it with tar."

She stood and stretched her hands, opening and closing her fists to work the stiffness from her fingers. The rope burns from that morning's crossing had tightened across her palms during the hours of work, the skin pulling against the abrasions each time she gripped the marlinspike. She walked to the water's edge and knelt, dipping her hands into the river and letting the cold numb the sting.

Caleb stood from his position beside the cable. He stretched his legs and rolled his shoulders, the movements of a man whose body had been held in one position for longer than it preferred. Then he walked to the supplies she had staged on the gravel and gathered everything.

Belle dried her hands on her trousers and watched him from the water's edge. He rolled the canvas with the same precision he brought to his survey maps, the edges aligned, the ties pulled snug, and he set the finished roll beside the pine tar crock and the spool of marline. He had cleaned up her worksite with the competence of a man who understood that tools stored correctly lasted longer than tools thrown into a pile and ignored, and he had done it without asking whether she wanted help.

She walked back to the gravel bar and stood beside the block and tackle. "I want to talk about the cable."

"The cuts," Caleb said.

"Yes... the cuts." Belle crouched beside the damaged section, the portion she had cut free before beginning the repair. "Whoever did this understood cable construction. The cuts are placed between the outer strands, in the channels where the braid naturally compresses under load. A person cutting blind would slash across the surface and leave marks on the outer fibers that I'd catch in a morning inspection. These cuts go into the channels. They reach the inner strands without disturbing the outer braid."

"Which means the damage wouldn't show on a visual check from the deck," Caleb said.

"Not from the deck. Not from the bank. The only way to find these cuts is to work the cable by hand, bending each section and watching for the strands to separate under flex. I check my cables every morning, but I check tension and surface condition. I don't flex-test every foot of a two-hundred-foot line."

"Nobody would." Caleb crouched beside her and examined the cut ends, turning the cable in his hands. "The placement is deliberate in another way. The cuts are on the downstream line, not the upstream. Under a loaded crossing, the downstream cable carries the greater share of the lateral force because the current pushes the scow toward it. A cut on the upstream cable would weaken the system, but the downstream cable would compensate. A cut on the downstream cable puts the failure at the point of maximum stress."

"So whoever did this knows which cable carries more load in current."

"Or they watched the crossings long enough to see which cable goes taut under a heavy load and which one stays slack. You can see the difference from the bank if you know what to look for."

Belle turned the cable section over in her hands.

"This was done at night," she said. "There's no other time. I'm at the landing from first light until the last crossing, and the landing is visible from the bridge site and from the road. Anyone on the bank during daylight would be seen."

"I leave before dark and arrive after dawn. The interval between is unobserved."

"So someone came to the landing after dark, in the hours when no one was here, and cut the downstream cable with a knife sharp enough to part hemp without tearing it, at points precise enough to weaken the cable under load without destroying it outright." Belle set the cut section back on the gravel. "That's not vandalism. That's anger. That's someone who wanted the cable to fail in a way that looked like it failed on its own."

"If you hadn't pulled the cable in and taken the time to examine it," Caleb said, "what would the town have heard?"

Belle looked at him. "The town would have heard that my cable broke during a heavy crossing," she said. "More than likely word would have spread that I overloaded the platform, or that I failed to maintain the cable, or that the ferry is too old and too fragile for the loads the town needs to move across the river."

"The narrative would have been your failure. Not an attack."

"Yes."

"Which means the sabotage wasn't designed to destroy the ferry. It was designed to destroy confidence in it. And in you."

The precision of what he had said settled over her with the weight of something she had been circling.

"If the ferry looks unsafe," she said, "the argument for the bridge gets stronger. But we don't have enough information to point the blame toward any one person."

"No. But we have the method, and we have the motive, and those two things narrow the field considerably." Caleb stood from his crouch and looked downriver toward the town. "Someone is watching this crossing. Watching the ferry, watching the loads, watching the schedule. They knew when to cut and where to cut and how deep to go. That level of knowledge comes from sustained observation or from someone who told them what to look for."

"We both need to keep our eyes open," Belle said. "At the landing, at the bridge site, and in town. If something looks wrong or someone asks questions they shouldn't be asking, I want to know about it. And I'll do the same for you."

"Agreed."

Belle picked up the cut section of cable and carried it to the supply pile.

The afternoon had turned while they worked; the sun dropping to the west and the light shifting from the hard clarity of midday to the softer, angled quality that made the gravel bar glow pale against the dark water. She stood beside the supply pile and looked at the cable stretching from the mooring post across the river to the far bank, the downstream line still slack where the splice needed to cure. Tomorrow she would finish the serving and the tar, and by the following morning the ferry would cross again.

She looked at Caleb, who was standing beside the mooring post, his hand resting on the timber, his attention on the river. The light caught the angle of his jaw and the line of his shoulders in Liam's borrowed shirt. He stood with the particular stillness of a man whose body was tired and whose mind was still working, processing the afternoon's information.

He had worked beside her for several hours, following her instructions on a piece of work he had never done before. He had not, at any point during the afternoon, looked at her work and offered suggestions for improvement.

"Mr. Sterling."

He turned away from the river.

"Why did you help me this afternoon? You have survey work to do. You've been in the river once today and on horseback twice, and you're wearing another man's clothes. Why did you agree to help me when I asked?"

He was quiet for a moment. "Three years ago I designed and supervised a bridge build," he said. "When it was finished, the numbers told me something was wrong with the foundation work. A foreman told me it was sound. Our schedule was tight, bad weather season was closing in, and I wanted to believe him because believing him was easier than stopping the project and demanding we tear out what we'd built and start again." He looked at the river. "I let his assurance stand where my judgment should have. The bridge opened. Four months later it collapsed, and two men died on it." He paused. "This morning when I heard commotion, then heard a cable snap… I came at a run because that is what a man does when he hears something breaking and knows what silence costs. This afternoon you asked me to help you, and I did because it was the right thing to do. I have learned what happens when you sense that something is wrong and do not act on it. I have to know what happened here and who tried to put you in a bad light. The action that person took could have killed you as well as all your passengers. God was watching over you."

Belle stood on the gravel bar and felt the weight of what he had said arrive in a place she hadn't braced for. He had given her the reason he was the man standing in front of her—not the engineer, not the stranger who had waded into the Yellowstone that morning, but the man underneath both of those, the one who carried a failure that had cost lives and had rebuilt himself around the wound. For the first time since he had arrived in Providence Ridge, she could not place him against any man she had known. Men who came with promises and credentials didn't hand you their worst failure and then stand there without asking for anything back.

Belle turned to the road as she heard boots approaching. Liam walked toward them, his hat pushed back on his head and his face carrying the particular expression of a man who knew he had been gone too long and was calculating how much trouble the absence had earned him.

"Before you say anything," he called, "I have a reason for being gone so long."

"I wasn't going to say anything," Belle said. "I was going to let you explain yourself and then decide what to say."

"I went to the boardinghouse first to deliver your message about the emergency committee meeting. Mrs. Hanscombe had soup on the stove, and she wouldn't let me leave without eating, and you know how Mrs. Hanscombe is about feeding people who walk through her door."

"I do."

"So I sat down to eat, and I was halfway through a bowl of beef and barley when Uncle Tom walked in, and I told him what had happened this morning. He wanted the full account of the cable and the crossing, and the sabotage. You know how Uncle Tom is about getting the full account of anything."

"I do."

"That all took some time. And then he had questions. And then Mrs. Hanscombe refilled my bowl without asking, and Uncle Tom ordered coffee, and by the time I looked at the clock, it was past four." He glanced at Caleb, then back at Belle. "Tonight's meeting is confirmed. Eight o'clock, boardinghouse dining room. Everyone's been notified."

"Good. Go home. Change into dry clothes. I'll be there in a few moments."

"I can stay and help carry —"

"Liam. Go home."

He looked at Caleb, grinned, and nodded. "Much obliged for helping my sister, Mr. Sterling," Liam said.

"Glad to help."

Liam walked to his gelding, mounted, and turned up the trail toward the homestead. The sound of hooves on packed earth faded through the cottonwoods.

Belle gathered the remaining supplies into a stack she could carry in two trips to the mare. Caleb lifted the hemp coil and the block and tackle without being asked and carried them to the horse, securing the coil behind the saddle with the leather straps.

When the mare was loaded, Belle stood at the rail with the reins in her hand. Caleb stood three feet from her, his hands at his sides.

"The meeting is at eight," she said.

"I'll be there."

"The serving and the tar are tomorrow. I can manage them alone, but a second pair of hands speeds up the tensioning."

"I'll be here at first light."

She mounted the mare and gathered the reins. Belle rode the first twenty yards without looking back, but at the bend where the cottonwoods closed over the trail, she turned in the saddle, and Caleb was still standing at the rail, watching her go.

She smiled at him and then turned and continued toward home.

Chapter 11

Caleb stood near the head of the long table in the boarding-house dining room. There were no maps pinned at the corners, no elevation drawings, and no red circles marking proposed landing sites this evening.

Mrs. Hanscombe moved between the kitchen and the dining room, distributing coffee. When she finished, she set the pot on a folded cloth at the center of the table and took her position near the kitchen doorway, her hands folded at her waist, her attention already cataloguing every face in the room.

Amos sat at the table's midpoint, and Owen sat beside him. Two ranchers occupied chairs along the wall. Several men Caleb didn't recognize were spread around the table.

Horace descended the boardinghouse stairs at two minutes before the hour. He took his position at the far end of the table, where the entire room was visible to him. He nodded to Caleb as he sat.

Marshal Tom Callahan came through the front door. He removed his hat and hung it on the peg beside the door, then took the chair nearest the entrance.

The front door opened again, and Liam entered first, his face carrying the drawn quality of a day that had begun before dawn and would not end for hours yet. He moved to the wall and stood with his back against it, beside his uncle.

Winnie came next. She had changed from the house dress she'd been wearing at the homestead into something more presentable, her hair repined, a shawl across her shoulders against the April chill.

Belle entered last. She was still in her work clothes. The wool coat she'd worn to the landing that morning hung open over a shirt darkened with river spray and dried sweat, the fabric of her split skirt showing the hours she'd spent on her knees on the gravel bar. Her hands were at her sides, the rope burns visible on her palms even from where Caleb stood.

She sat beside Winnie, across from Amos.

Caleb felt the accumulated weight of the day in his body as he stood at the head of the table and looked around the room. "Thank you all for coming on short notice. I'll keep my portion brief because the person who knows the most about what happened today is in this room, and I intend to let her tell you." He paused, not for effect, but to let the room settle into the gravity of what he was about to say. "This morning, the downstream ferry cable failed during a loaded crossing. A very heavy load, I might add. The failure was not caused by wear, weather, or neglect. The cable was cut. Deliberately. The cuts were placed at points along the underside of the braid where they would not be visible during a surface inspection, and they were made with enough precision that the cable held under normal tension but failed under the strain of a heavy crossing. What happened today was sabotage."

The word landed in the room the way a stone lands in still water. Amo's hands, resting on the table, went motionless. Owen's restless attention fixed on Caleb and stayed. One of the ranchers along the wall shifted forward in his chair. Marshal Tom didn't move.

Horace, at the far end of the table, set his coffee cup down with the careful deliberation of a man absorbing information he found deeply troubling.

"The person who understands the ferry's cable system better than anyone in this room is Miss Belle Callahan," Caleb continued. "She discovered the damage, identified the method, and spent the afternoon repairing the cable. I'm asking her to address the committee with the full details."

He stepped back from the head of the table and took the empty chair beside the wall.

Belle rose from her chair and walked to the head of the table and looked at the room. "At approximately nine-thirty this morning, I was midway through a loaded crossing with a freight wagon, a team of horses, and a driver on the platform. The downstream cable began to fail at the midpoint of the crossing. The strands separated under tension in sequence over approximately thirty seconds, during which time I brought the scow into the shallows using the guide rope and the remaining cable. Mr. Sterling was at the bridge site upstream. He heard commotion and heard the cable give and came to the bank, entered the river, and held the mooring line from the shallows while I guided the platform to shore. The cargo, the team, and the driver received no injuries, thanks be to God."

She spoke with clarity. The room listened. Caleb watched the particular quality of attention that settled over everyone as Belle told them what had happened to her ferry, and he saw what he had expected to see: everyone listened differently than they had listened to her during the first meeting. In the first meeting, Belle had stood to challenge Horace, and the committee had received her with the measured patience of men deciding how much weight to give a voice they had already categorized. Tonight, the woman standing at the head of the table was the woman who had saved the crossing, and the categorization had been revised.

"After bringing the scow to shore, I pulled the damaged cable onto the gravel bar and examined it," Belle continued. "The cable had been cut in several places along a twelve-inch section of the downstream line. The cuts were made with a sharp blade, positioned in the channels between the outer strands where the braid compresses under load. The placement meant the damage would not show during a visual inspection from the deck or the bank. The only way to detect these cuts is to flex-test the cable by hand, foot by foot, and no operator performs that test on two hundred feet of line during a daily inspection because no operator has reason to expect that someone has taken a knife to her cable."

She paused and looked around the room

"The downstream cable was targeted specifically," she said. "Under a loaded crossing, the downstream line carries the greater share of force because the current pushes the scow toward it. Cutting the upstream cable would weaken the system but not produce a failure under load. Cutting the downstream cable puts the break at the point of maximum stress. Whoever did this understood which cable bears the heavier load, and they understood how to weaken it at a point and depth that would cause it to fail during a heavy crossing while appearing to have failed from neglect."

Amos spoke first. "How long until the ferry is operational?"

"I completed the long splice this afternoon with Mr. Sterling's assistance," Belle said. "The serving and tar seal go on tomorrow. The cable will be under full tension by early tomorrow evening. Crossings resume the following morning."

"And the second cable?"

"Inspected by hand from the bank to the waterline. It's sound."

"You're certain?" Owen asked.

"I am certain of what I can reach, Mr. Gallagher. The section between the waterline and the midstream anchor is below the surface and cannot be inspected without diving equipment, which I do not have. Within the limits of what is physically possible, the second cable is intact."

Owen leaned back in his chair. "If the ferry is this vulnerable to a man with a knife, the question has to be asked whether the crossing needs something more permanent. The bridge timeline, Mr. Sterling, is that something we ought to be discussing with more urgency given what's happened?"

"The bridge timeline depends on the survey work, the committee's approval, and the consortium's commitment to the approved location," Caleb said. "I won't accelerate a timeline at the expense of engineering. A rushed bridge is worse than no bridge."

"Nobody is suggesting we cut corners," Owen said. "I'm suggesting the town can't afford to depend on a crossing that can be shut down by a single act of vandalism."

"The town has depended on that crossing for years," Belle said. "It was shut down this morning not because the ferry is fragile but because someone committed a crime against it. If a man burned down the lumber mill, Mr. Gallagher, would the answer be that mills are too vulnerable, or would the answer be to find the man who struck the match?"

The analogy stopped Owen's line of argument dead in its tracks. Amos nodded once, a small movement, but visible.

"I've been briefed on the circumstances by Liam and by Mr. Sterling. I consider this a criminal act. I will be talking to anyone in this town who was near the ferry landing in the days before this happened. If anyone in this room has information, you can come to me directly," Marshall Tom said.

"Miss Callahan, I want to say how deeply troubled I am by what you've described tonight. The ferry is the lifeblood of this town, and an attack on it is an attack on every person who depends on the crossing." Horace said. "What can the committee do to ensure your safety and the security of the ferry going forward? I think we all want to hear what you need."

"What I need," Belle said, "is the same thing Marshal Callahan just asked for. If anyone has seen anything unusual at the ferry landing, on the road to the landing, or near the river at hours when the crossing isn't operating, I need them to come forward. I'm not asking the committee for protection, Mr. Pritchard."

Horace nodded, and the conversation turned to practical measures. Amos raised the question of security at the landing. Whether Liam could sleep at the ferry site. Belle answered that Liam was needed at the homestead and that she would not put her brother alone at the river in the dark when someone had already demonstrated a willingness to sabotage her equipment under cover of night.

"The spring rise is coming," Mrs. Hanscombe said from her station near the kitchen doorway. "Every year the river tests our town and the ferry, and every year something gives. This year we have a ferry that's been attacked and a bridge site that's barely staked. If we're going to protect both, we need to stop treating them as two separate problems."

"Mrs. Hanscombe is right," Amos said. "The sabotage endangered the ferry. But if someone is willing to cut a cable, the bridge site isn't safe either—survey stakes, equipment, and materials will start arriving. We need the committee and the entire town, for that matter, to see the full picture of the crossing, ferry, and bridge as one system."

"Which means the people responsible for each half need to be working in coordination," Marshal Tom said. "I can't investigate this properly if I'm getting information from two separate operations that don't talk to each other. I need a single picture of what's happening at that river."

Amos turned his attention back to Belle, then to Caleb. "I propose that the committee mandate formal coordination between the ferry operation and the bridge site moving forward. Mr. Sterling should conduct regular engineering inspections of the ferry cables and equipment, backing up Miss Callahan's inspections. Two sets of eyes on everything moving forward. Miss Callahan should be consulted on every phase of the bridge survey that touches river conditions and ferry operations. Both should walk the span of the river daily to note any changes or possible attempts to derail the forward progression of our bridge. Joint weekly reports should be provided to Marshall Tom; those same reports could then be provided to the committee during a meeting. That way all are informed, and we can all discuss any issues."

"I second the proposal," Marshal Tom said.

"I support it as well," Horace said.

The consensus of agreement moved through every person in the room.

The meeting continued for another twenty minutes, the conversation narrowing toward scheduling and the question of whether night watches at the landing were feasible. Belle answered the questions directed at her. Caleb answered questions about the bridge survey's progress and the vulnerability of his equipment.

Caleb watched Horace through the remainder of the meeting the way he watched a footing under load. Horace deferred to Amos on the question of supply chain concerns. He agreed with Marshal Tom on the need for coordinated information. He was the most cooperative man in the room, and in Caleb's experience, the most cooperative man in a room full of worried people was either the man with the least to hide or the man with the most.

As the meeting came to an end and people began to stand, Winnie crossed the room toward Caleb. She carried his folded clothes from earlier today and held them out to him. "Your clothes, Mr. Sterling. They dried well by the fire."

"Thank you, Miss Callahan. Much obliged."

Winnie smiled as Belle appeared beside her. "First light, Mr. Sterling."

"First light."

Belle turned and walked toward the door with Winnie beside her and Liam falling into step behind them.

Caleb stood in the dining room with the bundle of dried clothes in his hands and watched them go. He looked upward and closed his eyes. "Dear heavenly Father... watch over us all. Protect us from evil-doing."

Chapter 12

The marline bit into the braid as Belle wrapped the serving cord over the splice in tight, overlapping turns. Each pass pulled the thin cord flush against the hemp beneath it so that no gap showed between one wrap and the next. She had been at this for the better part of an hour, kneeling on the gravel bar with the cable stretched between the mooring post and the river. The cold air pressed against her shoulders through the wool of her coat with the particular sharpness of an April day that had decided to retreat back into winter.

Caleb knelt beside her, holding tension on the cable, his hands steady on the hemp and his weight braced against the cables pull. He had arrived at the landing this morning before she and Liam had.

Liam crouched near the small fire he had built, feeding a split of cottonwood beneath the pine tar crock. The crock sat on a flat stone ringed by smaller stones. He had the block and tackle laid out beside the supply pile, the canvas tool roll open, and the spool of marline within Belle's reach. He moved between tasks with the quiet competence of a young man who understood the rhythm of this work because he had grown up inside it.

Belle pulled the marline through another turn, snugging the cord against the splice with her thumb and forefinger, the fiber rough against the abraded skin of her palm. The serving was precise work, less physically demanding than the splice but less forgiving of distraction. Each wrap had to lie flat against its neighbor because a gap in the serving was a place where water would seep into the splice and rot the hemp from the inside over a season.

"How much more on the serving?" Caleb asked.

"Another eighteen inches. Then the tar." Belle pulled the cord through two more wraps, her thumb pressing each one flat. "Hold your tension. The cord seats better when the cable is taut."

He adjusted his grip without shifting his knees on the gravel. She felt the change through the cord as the cable stiffened a fraction under his hands, the serving pulling tighter against the splice beneath it.

Liam lifted the waxed cloth from the crock and checked the tar. "Getting soft," he said. "Another few minutes and it'll be ready."

"I don't want it pourable, Liam," Belle said. "I want it thick enough to spread with a stick. If it runs, it won't build layers."

"I know, Belle," Liam replaced the cloth and fed another piece of cottonwood beneath the crock. The wood caught, and the fire brightened, the flames licking up around the stone base with a sound like paper tearing.

Belle wrapped another turn of the marline. The repetitive motion had settled into her arms and her shoulders, the cord moving through her fingers in a rhythm she could sustain for hours if the work required it.

"Mr. Sterling," Liam said from his position at the fire.

Caleb turned his head, keeping his hands on the cable. "Yes?"

"When you go to a place like this, before there's a bridge, how do you decide where it goes? Is it the rock underneath, or the width of the river, or something else?"

"All three of those things," Caleb said. "The first thing I look at is the riverbed itself. I need to know what the footings will stand on. Sand shifts. Clay compresses under weight. Gravel drains well but doesn't bond to a footing. The best foundation is bedrock close to the surface, because the footing can be set directly onto stone and the load transfers straight down into the earth without anything between the structure and the ground that might move."

"Is there bedrock here?"

"At the survey site, yes. Fourteen feet down on the south bank, eighteen on the north. That's deep enough that I'll need coffer-dams to reach it, but shallow enough that the footing work is feasible."

Liam adjusted the crock's position on the stone, turning it so the fire reached the underside more evenly. "What's a cofferdam?"

"A temporary enclosure built in the water around the place where the footing goes. You drive pilings into the riverbed in a ring, seal the gaps between them, and pump the water out. That gives you a dry workspace at the bottom of the river where the masons can lay the footing stones. When the footing is finished, you pull the cofferdam out, and the river comes back in around the finished pier."

"You build a dry room at the bottom of the river," Liam said.

"That's right."

Belle pulled the serving cord through another wrap and pressed it flat. The conversation continued, Caleb's voice steady and unhurried, Liam's questions arriving with a directness that carried no self-consciousness. She had seen Liam ask questions before, at the mercantile, of Uncle Tom, of the teamsters who crossed the ferry with stories from Livingston and beyond. He asked the way he did everything, with an economy that wasted nothing. But the questions he was asking Caleb had a different quality. They were building toward something. Each answer produced the next question, not because the first answer was insufficient but because it opened a room Liam wanted to walk further into.

"The truss itself," Liam said. "The timbers that go across the top. How do those hold weight? A wagon crossing the bridge is pushing down on the middle, and the supports are at the ends. Why doesn't the whole thing sag?"

"Because the truss converts the downward force into two other forces that travel along the timbers to the abutments at each bank. The top chord of the truss is in compression. It's being squeezed. The bottom chord is in tension. It's being pulled. The diagonal members between them transfer the force from one to the other, and the geometry of the triangle is what keeps the structure rigid. A triangle can't deform without breaking one of its sides. A rectangle can. That's why every bridge truss you've ever seen is made of triangles, not squares."

Liam was quiet for a moment, his hand resting on the edge of the crock. "The ferry cables work like the bottom chord," he said. "They're in tension. The current pushes the scow sideways, and the cables hold against it, and the force goes out to the mooring posts at each bank."

Belle's hands paused on the serving cord.

"That's right," Caleb said. "That's exactly right. The mooring posts are functioning as abutments. The cable is a tension member. The geometry is different because the force is lateral instead of vertical, but the principle is the same. The cable transfers the force of the current to the fixed points on the bank."

Liam looked at the cable stretched between the mooring post and the far shore as though seeing the mathematics of it for the first time. The thing he had worked with for five years resolved itself into a language he hadn't known the cable spoke. Belle watched him from behind the marline in her hands. She saw the shift in his posture, the way his shoulders opened and his chin lifted half an inch. The particular stillness of a young man hearing his own experience described in terms that made it larger than what he had known it to be. His years of holding mooring lines and reading cable tension had been instinct and repetition. Caleb had just shown him it was engineering.

She returned to her wrapping. The cord moved through her fingers; the turns accumulating along the splice in the tight spiral that would protect the joined section from weather and wear. Twelve inches of serving remained. The tar would be ready by the time she finished.

"Will our bridge be different from other bridges you've built?" Liam asked.

"Every bridge is different because every river is different. The span here is wider than the last bridge I designed, and the current is stronger. The Yellowstone in spring carries more force per cubic foot than most rivers I've worked on because the gradient is steep and the snowmelt comes fast. I have to account for that in the truss dimensions and the footing depth, because the load on the piers during high water will be substantially greater than the load at low water."

"The spring rise is the test. If something is going to fail on the river, it fails in May or June."

"Correct. The bridge will face its heaviest lateral load during peak runoff, and that's the load I have to design for. If the bridge holds through its first spring rise, it'll hold through anything short of a flood that hasn't happened in living memory."

"What does an engineer do at a site before building starts? Before the first timber goes in."

Caleb shifted his grip on the cable and resettled his knees. "Walk the ground. Measure everything that can be measured. Bore test holes to find what's beneath the surface. Study the river at different times of day and in different weather. Talk to the people who know the river. Record their knowledge alongside the measurements, because the measurements tell you what the river is doing today, and the people who live on it tell you what it has done across a span of years that no survey captures."

He paused, and when he spoke again, his voice carried the quiet specificity of a man stating a professional fact. "The flood history for this section of the Yellowstone came from your sister. Her watermark readings and her knowledge of ice-dam surges are in my field notes alongside my own survey data. I wouldn't have that information without her, and the bridge design would be weaker for the absence of it."

Liam looked at Belle. She was aware of her brother's attention on her face, and she was aware of the particular care with which Caleb had said what he had said, and the credit given without performance.

She pulled the cord through the last series of wraps and tied the final hitch, drawing the marline tight against the cable and tucking the end beneath the last three turns. The serving was complete. She sat back on her heels and ran her hands along the full length of the served section, pressing her thumb against each wrap, feeling for gaps or soft spots where the cord might have loosened during the work.

"Tar," she said.

Liam lifted the crock from the fire with a folded cloth and carried it to the cable, setting it on the gravel beside Belle's knee. She removed the waxed lid, and the heated pitch rose in a wavering column, the smell thick and resinous, sharp enough to sting the inside of her nose. She took the flat spreading stick and dipped it into the crock, drawing out a thick ribbon of tar that stretched between the stick and the surface of the pitch before separating.

She laid the first stroke along the served section, pressing the tar into the wrapped cord with the flat of the stick, working it into the gaps between the marline turns so that the pitch penetrated the serving and sealed the splice beneath it. The tar went on black and glossy, the heat of it warming the hemp through the serving. She built the first layer in steady strokes from one end of the served section to the other, each pass overlapping the last. The work was slow. The tar cooled as she spread it, thickening on the stick, and she returned to the crock between passes to keep the pitch at the right consistency.

Liam held the crock steady when the gravel shifted beneath it. Caleb maintained his tension on the cable, the tar coating building up on either side of his grip, and when Belle reached the section nearest his hands, he shifted his hold three inches to give her access without being told.

"What about the forces during construction?" Liam asked, watching Belle work the tar. "When the bridge is half built, the truss isn't complete. What keeps it from falling?"

"Temporary bracing," Caleb said. "You build the truss in sections, starting from each bank and working toward the center. As each section goes up, you brace it with diagonal timbers that hold the incomplete structure until the next section connects to it. The temporary bracing absorbs the forces that the finished truss would handle on its own. When the last section closes the span and the truss is complete, the bracing comes out and the bridge carries its own weight."

"So the bridge holds itself up once it's whole, but during construction something has to hold it up from the outside."

"Yes."

"That sounds like the ferry," Liam said. "Belle holds the cable tension and reads the current, and keeps the entire system in balance from the outside, because the system can't balance itself. The scow doesn't know where to go. She tells it."

Belle applied another stroke of tar and didn't look at her brother. The comparison he had drawn wasn't wrong. It was, in fact, precise enough that it surprised her.

"That's a very good analogy," Caleb said.

"It's not an analogy. It's what she does."

"I know it is. Which is what makes it a good one."

Belle dipped the stick into the crock and drew another measure of tar. Her hands moved through the work while something shifted in her chest, a loosening that had no name and no clear origin, only a location somewhere behind her ribs where the breath came from. She spread the tar in long, even strokes over the served section, building another layer, and she listened to her brother talk to the man kneeling beside her about compression and tension and the geometry of triangles, and she didn't interrupt the conversation.

The morning moved through its hours. The cold retreated as the sun climbed above the cottonwoods on the far bank, the frost on the gravel bar burning off in patches that expanded and merged until the stones were dry and pale in the strengthening light. Belle applied another layer of tar, the last, working the pitch into the serving until the surface was uniform and sealed and the splice beneath it was entombed in cord and pitch.

Liam's questions hadn't stopped. They had moved from the truss to the footings, from the footings to the road approach, and from the approach to the question of how a bridge handles the expansion of timber in summer and the contraction in winter. Caleb answered each one with the patience of a man who wasn't simplifying. He used the words he would use with anyone asking the same questions, and he paused when a concept needed illustration, reaching for the gravel at his knees or the cable in his hands to show Liam what he meant. When Liam confused a term and Caleb corrected him, the correction came without condescension, offered the way a man hands another man a tool that fits the task better than the one he was using.

Belle saw her brother holding himself taller... prouder, though he was crouching by the fire. The change wasn't in his posture. It was in the angle of his attention, the way he leaned toward Caleb's answers, the intensity of a young man who craved learning and something more than what life had handed him. She had sensed for months that the ferry was holding Liam the way a corral holds a horse that has seen the open range, not with cruelty but with limits the horse has begun to notice. Seeing it happen in front of her while all three of them worked side by side, watching her brother come alive at another man's answers, his questions arriving faster, his attention locked on Caleb with an intensity she recognized because it matched her own intensity with the river, made something beneath her certainty go soft. The ferry couldn't contain him. She had known this in the part of her mind that dealt with problems she wasn't ready to solve, and now the knowing had moved out of that room and into the one where she stood.

If Liam left the ferry, she couldn't run it alone forever. The ferry wouldn't provide work for either of them forever either. The bridge would open. The traffic would shift. The crossing that had sustained three Callahans would sustain none.

She set the spreading stick across the mouth of the crock and wiped her hands on the rag from the tool roll. The tar was finished. The splice was sealed. She stood and stepped back from the cable and looked at the repair she had made.

The served section of the cable was sound. The pitch would cure overnight. Tomorrow morning she would run a test crossing with the scow empty.

She walked to the mooring post and looked at the scow. It sat in the shallows where it had been moored since the crossing failure.

The deck was empty. The cargo ties hung loosely. The guide rope coiled on the platform where she had left it.

Caleb walked to the water's edge and crouched to rinse the tar from his palms, the river running fast past his wrists. Liam banked the fire.

After they finished, the three of them stood on the gravel bar. The sun was well above the Absarokas, the light falling clean across the valley with the hard clarity of early spring. The warmth of it on Belle's face felt strange because it came at an hour when she would normally be midway through her fifth or sixth crossing of the day. She wouldn't have noticed the simple joy of warmth on her skin.

"You should come for supper, Mr. Sterling," Liam said. "Tonight. Winnie'll have food on the table at six, and I'd like to hear more about the cofferdam work."

Caleb looked at Belle.

"Winnie won't mind," she said.

"But will you?" he asked.

Belle could feel the warmth rush to her cheeks and knew she was blushing, something that rarely occurred. She dipped her head and looked at the ground. "Of course not. Liam invited you, and I extend his invitation."

"Caleb... just follow the road out of town toward the river when you come," Liam said. "Before you reach the river, there's a turnoff to the east. Stay on the main fork. The side tracks lead to other homesteads, but ours is the place on the rise."

"Six o'clock," Caleb said.

"Six o'clock," Liam confirmed.

They gathered the tools and the supplies. The horses were tied at the rail post where the bank met the trail, and Belle walked toward them to begin loading up her supplies. Behind her, she could hear Liam asking one more question, something about the cofferdams and the river's pressure. Caleb answered as they walked.

She reached the horses and strapped on her supplies. When she turned, Caleb was standing at the edge of the gravel bar where the trail began, his coat buttoned and his hat pulled low against the midday glare. Liam was walking toward her.

"I'm looking forward to supper this evening," Caleb said.

She held his gaze. "I am as well, Mr. Sterling."

She mounted and turned her mare toward the trail. Liam fell into step beside her, the two horses moving in their accustomed rhythm, and Belle didn't look back. She could feel his attention on her the way she felt the river's current through a rope, a steady pull she was only beginning to admit she had stopped bracing against.

Chapter 13

Paul Higgins's livery smelled of hay dust and liniment. Caleb counted out coins from his pocket and set them on the plank counter. Paul took the coins, wrote a line in his ledger, and walked into the stable without comment. He returned leading a bay gelding with a blaze face and a steady, unhurried gait, the kind of horse a livery keeps for hirers who want reliability over speed. Caleb checked the cinch, adjusted the left stirrup one notch shorter, and mounted.

He turned the gelding toward the main road and rode out of town. He had walked this route every day since arriving in Providence Ridge, the same ruts and the same bend where the road dropped toward the valley floor and the cottonwoods thickened along the creek drainage. He passed the last of the frame houses at the edge of town, and the land opened around him, the benchlands rising in gentle folds of brown grass on both sides; the Absarokas filling the eastern sky with their full vertical sweep from timber to rock to snow.

The turnoff appeared where he expected it, a wagon track branching from the main road before the final descent to the ferry landing. He turned the gelding onto it and followed the road as it climbed away from the valley floor.

He let the gelding choose its pace, which was an easy, ground-covering walk, and he let his mind do what it had not done in longer than he could remember, which was nothing.

No calculations. No load assessments. The work of the day was behind him. What lay ahead of him was a meal he had been invited to and the company of people he wanted to spend time with.

"Lord, thank You for this," he prayed as he looked toward heaven. "For the work this morning. For the simple company of good people, I'm looking forward to. For this road and this evening and whatever You are building that I cannot see yet. Thank you for placing peace in my heart today. I feel it, Lord; I truly do, and I welcome it. Bless us all this evening."

The road crested the last rise, and the homestead appeared on its gentle slope: the frame house, the barn, and the garden plot. The cabin's windows held lamplight. A thread of smoke rose from the chimney into the still air. The three Callahan horses stood in the paddock beside the barn.

Caleb rode into the yard and dismounted near the fence rail. He tied the hired gelding with a quick-release knot and loosened the cinch one notch so the horse could stand comfortably while he was inside.

He walked to the front door and knocked. The sound of his knuckles against the wood carried in the quiet yard, and he heard movement inside: the scrape of a chair and footsteps crossing the planked floor.

Belle opened the door.

She had changed out of her work clothes. The plum-colored calico she wore was fitted at the waist and buttoned to the collar; the fabric clean and pressed, and the effect of it against the lamplight behind her stopped his thoughts for the space of a full breath. He had seen her in a dress before, but the transformation still struck him with a force that had nothing to do with the dress and everything to do with the woman wearing it. Her dark hair was loosened from the braid she wore on the ferry, pinned instead in a soft arrangement that left a few strands curving along her neck. Her face, which he was accustomed to seeing set in focused concentration, was open and friendly, her green eyes steady on his, and her expression carrying the trace of something he wouldn't have called a smile but that occupied the same territory.

"Mr. Sterling," she said. "You're punctual. Come in."

The home was warm; the fireplace radiating a heat that met him two steps inside the door and pressed against his chest through his coat. Winnie stood at the cookstove with a long-handled spoon and a dishcloth over her shoulder. She turned when he entered with warmth in her expression.

"Mr. Sterling, I'm glad you've come," Winnie said. "Belle and Liam told me about your help this morning. We're grateful."

"I was happy to be of service."

"Take off your coat and hat and hang them on the peg by the door," Winnie said. "Supper's nearly ready."

"Is there anything I could do to help?" He asked.

"Yes sir, there most certainly is. I need a bucket of water from the barrel on the back porch."

She lifted a tin bucket from beside the cookstove and held it out to him. Caleb carried the bucket through the kitchen to the back door. The water barrel stood on the porch, lidded against the weather. He lifted the lid and dipped the bucket, the water cold against his knuckles as it rose past his hand. He carried it back inside and set it where Winnie indicated, beside the stove.

"Thank you," Winnie said.

The front door opened, and Liam came through carrying an armload of split firewood stacked from his forearms to his chin. He kicked the door shut behind him with his boot heel and crossed to the woodbox beside the fireplace, lowering the load into the box with a controlled drop that settled the splits in a neat stack without scattering bark on the floor.

"Mr. Sterling," Liam said, brushing wood dust from his sleeves.

"Liam."

"Glad you made it. Winnie's been cooking since this afternoon, which means she's serious about the meal."

"Correction. Belle and I cooked dinner together. And another thing, young man, I cook properly every evening," Winnie said from the stove. "Tonight is no different."

"Tonight you made a cobbler," Liam said. "You don't make cobbler unless it's someone's birthday or we have company."

Winnie pointed the spoon at him. "Wash your hands and set the table."

Liam went to the washstand and scrubbed up, then pulled plates and flatware from the cabinet and carried them to the table.

"Sit here, Mr. Sterling," Liam said, pulling the chair back.

"Please, you must call me Caleb. Let's do away with the formality," Caleb said as he took the offered seat.

Belle carried preserves to the table and set them beside the butter crock. Winnie brought a pot of venison stew, thick with root vegetables, the broth dark and fragrant. Biscuits followed on a cloth-lined plate. A pot of coffee completed the table.

Belle ladled the stew into Caleb's bowl first, then Liam's, then Winnie's, then her own.

"Liam," Belle said. "Will you say the blessing?"

They joined hands around the table. Belle's hand in his was small and scarred and roughened, the calluses on her palm pressing against his skin, and the contact moved through him with a warmth that had nothing to do with the stove.

Liam bowed his head. "Lord, we thank You for this meal and for the company at our table tonight. We thank You for the work of this day and for hands willing to help when help was needed. Bless this food to our nourishment and our lives to Your purpose. Amen."

"Amen," they said, and released hands, and the meal began.

The stew was good; the venison tender from long cooking, and the root vegetables soft. The biscuits were some of the best he had encountered west of Chicago; the tops golden and the centers yielding, the kind that could absorb broth without dissolving. He ate steadily and with the honest appetite of a man who hadn't eaten since breakfast, and across the table, Liam ate with the same directness, his spoon working through the stew in efficient strokes between sentences.

"Tell me about Chicago," Liam said, buttering a biscuit. "What was it like watching the city come back after the fire?"

"It was a lot. The city never quieted during the day," Caleb said. "Every street in every direction had scaffolding on it. You could hear hammers from the time you woke up until it was too dark to swing one. The commercial district was rebuilt in brick and stone, taller and more permanent than what had been there before. But the neighborhoods were rebuilt in wood, the same as before, because wood was cheaper and people needed to get back under a roof. My family's home survived the fire, but many of the homes near us did not. My father helped several of our neighbors rebuild."

"Your father," Liam said. "Is he a builder?"

"He is a skilled carpenter, but as a young boy he was trained as a home builder. His specialty is building furniture and cabinetry. He's particular about it in a way that drives his clients to frustration and his family to amusement. He would reject a plank of walnut for a defect no one else could see, and my mother would tell him he was building a sideboard, not a cathedral, and he would say the sideboard didn't know the difference, but he did."

Winnie laughed, a warm, quick sound that opened the room. "Your mother sounds like a woman with opinions."

"She has opinions about everything and expresses them freely and at great length. My sisters inherited the trait. Sunday dinner at the Sterling table is a competition for who can hold the floor longest, and my mother wins every week because she controls the coffee pot and refuses to refill anyone's cup until they let her finish her thought."

"How many sisters do you have?" Winnie asked.

"Three. Margaret, Ruth, and Anne. Margaret is the eldest of us. She's married to a fine man, has three children, and teaches piano. Ruth is engaged to be married this summer, and she has written me fourteen pages about the wedding so far, with more promised.

Anne is the youngest, eighteen, and she has more energy than the rest of us combined."

"Do they worry about you out here?"

"Margaret worries. She worries the way a firstborn worries, which is constantly and about things that haven't happened yet. Ruth trusts that I can take care of myself, which I appreciate. Anne writes me letters that are long and entirely about herself, which is precisely what I'd expect from a young woman. My mother doesn't allow her worry to show in the words she writes in her letters. She prays, which she considers more productive. She sends me beautiful letters about everything going on in Chicago and always includes a prayer for me to read and scripture."

"Well... I happen to agree with her and feel as if I would love your mother. Prayer is much more productive than worry," Winnie said.

"She would enjoy hearing you say so."

Belle had been listening. She sat with her spoon resting against the rim of her bowl, her attention moving between Caleb and her siblings with the quiet watchfulness of a woman who was more comfortable observing a conversation than directing it. Caleb had noticed this about her within the first five minutes of the meal: among her family, Belle occupied a different position than she held at the ferry or in the committee room. She was not leading. She was not managing. She was simply present, a woman at a table with people she loved, and the absence of the armor she wore in every other setting made her look younger and more at ease than he had ever seen her.

"Do you write to them often?" Belle asked.

"Every week. The letters take twelve to fourteen days each direction, so by the time my mother reads what I've written, the news is already old. But she says the letters matter more for the hand that wrote them than for the words they carry, and I suspect she's right about that too."

"She sounds wise," Belle said.

"She is. She raised five children in a bustling city. She is a woman who loves to learn; she's always reading a novel or studying the Bible. She enjoys singing in the church choir and volunteering everywhere she can to assist those in need. She loves the Lord and follows his word faithfully."

Belle's eyes held his for a moment. Her chin dipped a fraction, the smallest nod, as though the words had landed somewhere she kept private. She returned her attention to her bowl without comment.

"Liam," Caleb said, "you mentioned this morning that you'd been looking at property along the edge of town. Tell me more. What are your plans?"

Liam set down his biscuit and leaned back in his chair. "Cattle ranching. I've got the figures worked out. The forty acres I have my eye on has good grass and is sheltered from the north wind. A creek runs through it, so there's water year-round. A man could fence it for the cost of posts and wire, and the posts grow on the ridge. I've talked to several ranchers about first-year operations, and I've priced stock through a seller up on the Shields Creeks. Six yearling heifers for sixty dollars."

"That's a sound approach. Starting with heifers rather than a mixed herd keeps your first-year costs manageable and gives you calves in the spring."

"That's the plan. Build the herd slowly, keep the overhead low, and put up enough hay the first summer to carry through the winter." Liam paused. "I've been interested in animal husbandry since I was old enough to notice that a well-handled horse behaves differently from a poorly handled one. The ferry taught me about systems and maintenance. But livestock is what I want to put my hands on long term."

"You'd be good at it," Caleb said. "The way you think about the ferry cables and the crossing mechanics tells me you understand systems. Animals aren't so different from engineering in the fundamentals. They respond to consistent handling. They fail when you ignore the signs. The best stockmen I've met think the same way the best engineers do: they watch, they measure, and they adjust before the problem becomes a crisis."

Liam looked at him with the look of a young man hearing his ambition described as legitimate by someone whose opinion he had begun to value. Belle watched the exchange from across the table.

"I'm doing my best to think of the future. Not only for myself but also for that of my sisters. Belle has carried the weight of us all for far too long. I need to step up and do my part. I know the ferry will not provide for us in the future."

"I see. You are a young man who thinks deeply; I can tell. Perhaps you should talk to Amos Pemberton about fencing wire costs," Caleb said. "If he can't match the Livingston price, he might be willing to place a bulk order with you if you commit to the quantity early. Mercantile owners prefer guaranteed sales over competitive pricing."

"I hadn't thought of that."

"It's how things work in Chicago, at least. I expect Providence Ridge operates on similar principles, given that commerce is commerce regardless of the size of the town."

"Is Providence Ridge everything you expected it to be so far?" Winnie asked.

Caleb wrapped both hands around his coffee cup. "I expected a work site with a town attached to it. Most of the places I've been sent to build are like that. The town exists to service the project, and when the project is finished, the town either grows into something self-sustaining or it empties out within a year. Providence Ridge is smaller than I expected, yet it's different from any small town I've ever been to. The town existed long before a bridge was ever considered, and it'll exist after the bridge is built. The people here are unique; they are more caring and show more responsibility toward their town as a unit rather than sitting on the sidelines observing. That surprised me. I hadn't expected to find a place that felt settled. What this community has built is remarkable. There is a solid foundation here."

"Does it really feel settled to you?" Winnie asked.

"Yes... yes, it does. It feels like a place people love and intend to keep building upon. That's a rare thing in the territories."

Belle was cutting a biscuit in half, her knife moving through the center with a precision that split the bread cleanly along its natural seam. "Most people of your education and profession would leave a town this small when a project is finished," she said. "Is that what you intend to do?"

"I don't know yet," Caleb said. "I've never stayed anywhere longer than the work required. Every town I've been in, I've left when the project was finished and moved to the next contract.

That's been my life for years. I've been based out of Denver for the past three years, but was rarely home due to my work." He held her gaze. "But I've never been in a town such as this that made me wonder what staying would look like."

Winnie's hand paused on her coffee cup. Liam looked between Caleb and his sister. Belle held the halved biscuit in both hands and didn't look away from Caleb.

"Well," Winnie said, rising from her chair. "Who's ready for cobbler?"

She brought the cobbler to the table in a baking dish, the top browned and bubbled, the fruit beneath it a dark, rich stew of preserved berries that had been sweetened with sugar. She served it in generous portions.

Liam finished his cobbler quickly and pushed back from the table. "I need to see to the horses and close up the barn for the night." He stood and carried his dishes to the basin, and on his way past Caleb, he paused. "I'm glad you came, Mr. Sterling. I look forward to speaking with you again. I've got more questions about your work and experiences."

"I look forward to it," Caleb said.

Liam pulled his jacket from the peg beside the door and went out into the evening.

Winnie began clearing the table, stacking the bowls and gathering the flatware with quick, certain hands. Belle rose to help, but Winnie stopped her with a look.

"Take your coffee to the porch," Winnie said. "Both of you. The evening is mild enough, and I don't need help with the dishes."

"Winnie, I can—"

"Belle. Go sit on the porch."

Belle looked at her sister. Winnie looked back, and whatever passed between them in that exchange was legible only to the two women who had shared a household and a history long enough to conduct entire negotiations in silence. Belle picked up her coffee cup, crossed to the peg by the door, and pulled her shawl from its hook, wrapping it around her shoulders. She opened the front door and stepped onto the porch without looking back to see if Caleb was following.

Chapter 14

The porch ran the width of the house, rough-planked and wide enough for three chairs. The chairs were simple, straight-backed, and made from the same timber as the house. Belle sat in the one nearest the door with her cup cradled in both hands. Caleb sat beside her.

The Absarokas filled the eastern sky, their peaks dark against a band of pale blue that was the last of the day's light, the snow on their upper ridges holding the remnants of color while the timbered slopes below had already gone to shadow. The valley spread before the porch in a long, descending sweep of grassland. The air was cooling as the sun dropped; the temperature falling from the mild side of cold to the cold side of cold with the steady, predictable decline of a spring evening at elevation.

Belle drew the shawl closer around her shoulders. "Winnie is not subtle," she said.

"She is exactly as subtle as she intends to be."

Belle looked at him, and the corner of her mouth altered in the way he had seen once before, in the barn during his first visit, the suppression of something that wanted to become a smile but that Belle Callahan didn't release without deliberation. This time it made it further than it had before. The alteration reached her eyes, and what lived there was not amusement, exactly, but something warmer, something that acknowledged the absurdity of the two of them sitting on a porch in the cold because her sister had ordered them out of the kitchen with the authority of a field general.

"What does your evening look like on a typical day?" Caleb asked. "When the work is done, and the supper is cleared."

"This porch, most nights, if the weather allows it. Winnie and I sit out here with coffee or tea while Liam finishes the barn chores. On cold nights, we sit by the fire inside. I read occasionally. Winnie mends. Liam works on whatever piece of leather or equipment he's repairing." She looked out at the valley. "It's quiet. It's been the same for five years, with small variations."

"Does the sameness bother you?"

"No. The sameness is the thing I built. When everything fell apart, when there was no sameness, when every day was a different kind of trouble, and every week brought a new bill or a new crisis, I wanted nothing more than for things to be the same two days in a row. So I built that. I built a life where the morning looks like the morning before it and the evening looks like the evening before it, and for a long time that was enough." She paused. "Lately I've been wondering if 'enough' and 'good' are the same thing, or if I've been using one to avoid the other."

Caleb turned that over. It was the most she had said to him about the interior of her life, delivered as simply as she would deliver a fact about the ferry's cable condition or the river's strength.

"What do your evenings look like at the boardinghouse?" she asked.

"Some nights I enjoy Mrs. Hanscombe's company in the dining room after dinner. We study the Bible and engage in lively conversation. Other nights I work at the desk in my room. Review calculations, write letters, and update my field notes. I read. The Bible, mostly. Engineering journals at other times." He took a sip of his coffee. "It's a small room with a desk and a window."

"That sounds lonely."

"It has been. I didn't notice how much until I had something to compare it to."

Belle was quiet for a moment. She held her coffee between her palms, the cup close to her chest, the shawl pulled around her, and she looked at the mountains where the last light was retreating up the peaks.

"I don't know what God is doing in my life," Belle said. The words came quietly, aimed at the valley as much as at him. "I know He's doing something. I can feel it the way I feel the current shift before I see it in the water. Something is changing. In me, in the ferry, and in my family. In all of it. I believe there's a reason for what He's allowed and what He's provided. For the work He gave me to do, for my brother and sister, and for what we've held on to. I believe He hasn't brought us this far to leave us standing alone. But I don't know where He's leading, and not knowing is harder for me than any work I've ever done with my hands."

"I understand that," Caleb said. "Control is my native language too. The hardest prayer I've ever prayed is the one where I asked God to show me what I can't build myself. Show me what I cannot see with my own eyes."

She looked at him. In the diminishing light, her green eyes were darker, the color deepened by shadow, and the expression in them was unguarded. She was showing him something she didn't show at the ferry or in town, a part of herself that lived beneath the competence and the self-reliance, a woman who wanted more than sameness and was brave enough to admit it even when the admission frightened her.

"Belle," he said. "I want to tell you something, and I'd like you to hear it as plainly as I mean it."

She waited.

"Providence Ridge feels like somewhere I could belong rather than somewhere I was sent to and would be leaving. I feel something deep inside me... something telling me this is where I was meant to be. You and your brother and your sister have made me feel at home tonight, and that is something that has been missing from my life for longer than I care to think too deeply on. I appreciate it more than I have adequate words for."

Belle held his gaze. "I'm grateful you came," she said. "We all are."

"I'd like to call on you again, if you'd allow it."

Belle's hands stilled on her coffee cup. Her lips parted and closed again, and the breath she drew was slow and deliberate, the kind of breath a person takes when the ground has shifted beneath them and they are deciding where to place their feet. She looked at the mountains, then at the yard, then back at him, and Caleb watched her arrive at her decision.

"I would like that," she said.

"Would you allow me to come Sunday morning and accompany you to worship? Afterward, if you're willing, we could have lunch at the boardinghouse, and then perhaps a drive. I'd welcome the chance to see parts of this valley I haven't explored yet, and I can think of no better guide."

Belle's chin lifted half an inch, and the trace of a smile that had been working at the edges of her expression arrived fully, a real and undefended smile that changed her face, revealing something luminous beneath the composure.

"I would like that very much, Mr. Sterling."

"Caleb," he said.

"Caleb," she repeated, and the sound of his name in her voice was a thing he would carry with him back to town and into his small room at the boardinghouse, where it would occupy a space no field note or calculation had ever filled.

They sat on the porch and finished their coffee while the stars thickened overhead. The conversation moved to smaller things, the mild and unhurried talk of two people who had said what needed saying and could afford to be easy with what remained. Belle told him about the view from this porch in midsummer, when the wildflowers ran up the hillsides in sheets of purple and gold and the grass grew high enough to brush a horse's belly. Caleb told her about the lake in Lincoln Park where he used to walk on Sundays after church as a young man, and how the water there was nothing like the water here, flat and still and contained by stone walls, a tamed thing that had forgotten it was ever wild.

Belle listened with her face turned toward him, the shawl around her shoulders and the coffee cup resting on her knee. At one point during the evening, she did a thing that Caleb registered with a precision that surprised him. She set her cup on the porch floor and moved her hands to her lap and tucked them beneath the edges of the shawl, folding them out of sight. The gesture was small and private and entirely unconscious, the reflex of a woman whose hands carried the visible evidence of her labor, rope-burned and calloused and scarred from years of work that most men in the territory couldn't sustain for a season. She hid them. Not from shame, exactly, but from the awareness that hands like hers were not what a woman showed a man on an evening like this, and the awareness cost her something he could see in the slight tightening of her jaw.

He wanted to reach across the space between their chairs and take her hands out of hiding and hold them in his own, and the wanting was so specific and so immediate that it startled him. He didn't act on it. He sat in his chair and looked at the mountains and understood that the thing he felt for Belle Callahan had crossed a line he could not uncross, moving from admiration into something that had permanence in it, something that intended to stay.

The door opened, and Winnie leaned out. "Mr. Sterling, I wanted to say goodnight. It's been a pleasure having you at our table."

Caleb stood and turned to face her. "Miss Callahan, the meal was as fine as any I've had. I'm obliged to you and Belle both."

Winnie smiled at him. "You're welcome here anytime."

She withdrew, and the door closed.

Caleb looked at Belle, who had risen from her chair.

"I should go," Caleb said. "It's getting cold, and you should be inside."

"I'll walk you to your horse."

They crossed the yard in the dark, their boots quiet on the packed earth, and when they reached the fence rail where the hired gelding stood dozing, Caleb tightened the cinch and checked the stirrups. Belle stood three feet from him.

"Thank you for the evening," he said. "All of it."

"Thank you for coming. Liam enjoyed your company, and Winnie did as well."

He held her gaze in the darkness. "And you?"

The smile returned, smaller this time, quieter. "And I did as well. Very much."

"I'll see you at the ferry in the morning. And Sunday, I'll be here at half-past nine."

"I look forward to it."

He mounted and settled into the saddle. Caleb looked down at Belle standing near the rail in her plum-colored calico dress and her shawl, and he committed the image to a place in his memory that was not his field notebook and not his engineering calculations but something older and deeper, the place where a man keeps the things he cannot measure but refuses to lose.

"Goodnight, Belle."

"Goodnight, Caleb."

He turned the gelding toward the road and rode into the dark. The valley opened around him, the mountains black shapes against a sky so full of stars it seemed the darkness between them was the exception rather than the rule. The gelding's hooves struck the packed earth in a steady, unhurried rhythm, and the cold pressed against Caleb's face and filled his lungs.

The stars were so close he felt he could reach them, and the sky was so vast that a man could lose himself in it. His chest held a warmth that the cold could not reach, a fullness that occupied the space where the heaviness had lived for three years, not replacing it entirely but pressing against it in a way that changed the shape of what he carried.

He thought of Belle's hands hidden beneath her shawl, the gesture that cost her something she didn't know he'd seen. He thought of Liam's careful departure and Winnie's knowing smile. He thought of the fourth chair at the table, the one that had been empty for five years, and the way Liam had pulled it out for him, and the way sitting in it had felt like being handed something breakable and precious.

He lifted his face to the sky and spoke aloud, his voice small against the immensity of the valley and the mountains and the stars.

"Thank You, Lord."

Chapter 15

Belle pushed the biscuit apart with her fork and moved the halves to opposite sides of her plate. The preserves Winnie had set out were blackberry, the last jar from the previous summer's canning, opened for a Sunday breakfast that deserved better than Belle's appetite. She lifted a piece of the biscuit to her mouth, set it back down, and reached for her coffee instead.

She had been awake since before first light, lying in the dark with her quilt pulled to her chin while the house creaked around her and the Yellowstone murmured its low, ceaseless commentary through the walls.

Across the table, Liam ate with the steady, unhurried concentration of a young man. He had worked through two biscuits and a plate of eggs and was buttering a third biscuit. Winnie sat between them with her plate half-finished and her coffee cup held close to her chest, watching Belle.

"You haven't eaten a thing," Winnie said.

"I've eaten."

"You've rearranged."

Liam glanced up from his plate, looked at Belle, and returned to his biscuit without comment.

"I'm not hungry this morning," Belle said.

Winnie set down her coffee cup as Belle picked up the biscuit half and took a small bite.

"Belle."

"I'm fine."

"You're not fine. You're sitting at this table pulling a biscuit apart like it wronged you, and you've been up since before the rooster, which I know because I heard you tossing and turning. So either you're ill, in which case I need to know, or something is on your mind, in which case I also need to know."

Belle set down the biscuit and stared at her plate of food.

"Caleb Sterling is coming here this morning," she said. "He's taking me to church, then we're having lunch, and then going for a drive."

Liam picked up his coffee, took a long drink, and set it down. "Well, now... this sure explains a lot."

"Liam," Winnie said.

"I'm just saying. She's been staring at that plate like it owes her money." He pushed his chair back and looked at Belle with an expression that carried no surprise and no judgment. "I'll make sure the porch is swept and leave you two alone."

"Thank you."

He carried his plate to the basin and left his coffee cup on the table, a signal that he intended to return for it. On his way past the table, he stopped. "You need me to do anything else?"

"I need you to clear the table and take care of the dishes," Winnie said. She was already standing, her attention fixed on Belle with a focus that had reorganized the morning's priorities in the space of three seconds. "All of them. Wash, dry, and put away. I'll be with Belle."

"Yes, ma'am." Liam picked up Winnie's plate, and Belle's, and turned to the basin.

Winnie put her hand on Belle's shoulder. "Come with me."

Belle followed her sister down the short hallway to Winnie's bedroom. The room was small and neat; the bed made with tight corners, a wooden chair beside the window, and a trunk at the foot of the bed where Winnie kept her good clothes and a few things of their mother's: a tortoiseshell comb, a length of lace, and her hymnal with pressed wildflowers marking the pages their mother had loved. Winnie closed the door behind them.

"Sit," Winnie said, gesturing to the bed.

Winnie pulled the chair from beside the window and sat facing her. Close enough that their knees touched.

"Tell me," Winnie said.

"I don't know where to start."

"Start with what frightens you."

Belle looked at the closed door, then at the window, then at her hands resting on her knees. "Friday evening after dinner, you sent Caleb and me out onto the porch." She paused. "He asked if he could call on me. I said yes. Then he asked if he could come this morning and take me to church, and to lunch, and for a drive through the valley. I said yes to that as well."

"Good."

"It's not good. It's terrifying."

"Explain, please."

Belle looked at her sister. "Winnie, I don't know what I'm doing. I've never done this. I've never been called on by anyone. I've never sat beside a man in worship who wasn't Liam or Uncle Tom or our father. I have spent every day of the past five years being a ferry operator and a head of household, and those are things I know how to do. I know how to read a river. I know how to gauge the weight of a loaded wagon by how the platform sits in the water. I know how to keep the books close enough that we eat every night and keep a roof over our heads. Those are my competencies, and they are the only ones I possess. I don't know how to be a woman being courted by a man who reads engineering journals for pleasure and comes from a family that owns a house in Chicago."

"Belle—"

"I'm not finished." She held up her hands. "Look at these. These are not a woman's hands. These are the hands of a laborer. There is a scar on my left hand from a cable that cut to the bone. There are calluses on my palms thick enough to catch on cotton. I looked at my hands on the porch the other night, and I saw them as if I'd never seen them before, and what I saw was a woman who has no business sitting next to a man like Caleb Sterling."

She dropped her hands into her lap.

"Are you finished now?" Winnie asked.

"I think so."

"Good. Because I have a few things to say, and you're going to sit there and hear them." Winnie leaned forward. "First. Your hands. You are sitting here telling me that the hands that have kept this family alive, that have run a crossing most men in this valley couldn't manage for a week, that have pulled freight and livestock and passengers across the Yellowstone River every day for years—you are telling me those hands are a cause for shame."

"I didn't say shame."

"You held them up like evidence in a trial. I know what I saw," Winnie took Belle's hands in hers and held them. "These are the hands of the strongest woman I know. They fed me. They kept a roof over my head. They buried our father and kept us from the poorhouse when half the town expected us to fail. If Caleb Sterling cannot see the worth of the woman attached to these hands, then he is not the man I believe him to be, and he does not deserve to sit beside you anywhere."

Belle's jaw worked. She looked at the wall.

"Second," Winnie said. "You are not unworthy of his attention. You are a woman who has carried more weight than any person in Providence Ridge, and you have done it without complaint, without asking for recognition, without once letting Liam or me feel the cost of it. If you believe that a man's education or his family's circumstances make him too high for you, then you have confused station with character. You should not judge a man's worth by his schooling. Do not judge your own worth by the lack of it."

"It's not only the schooling. It's everything. He has seen cities. He has built grand things. He comes from a family that is whole. I come from a family that is now three siblings trying to hold the pieces of something that broke when Mama died."

"And what did you do with those pieces? You built a life. You held this household together. You continued the ferry operation that the entire town relies upon. That is not less than what he has built, Belle. It is simply something built with different materials."

Belle was quiet. Outside the window, one of the horses stamped in the paddock, the sound carrying in the still morning air. She could hear Liam in the kitchen, the thin clatter of dishes being washed and stacked.

"There is something I need to tell you," Winnie said. Her tone shifted, the firmness giving way to something more careful. "Something I have been waiting for the right time to say, and I've decided the appropriate time is now, because you need to hear it."

Belle looked at her.

"I have been keeping company with someone. A young man. His name is Luke Dixon."

Belle blinked. "Frank Dixon's son? From the Shields Creek ranch?"

"The same. He's been calling on me at the mercantile when I'm there working during the week. He comes in for supplies on Tuesdays and Thursdays, and he has been staying to talk. He's walked me partway home twice now, and last Tuesday he asked if he might come to our home sometime so that he could meet you and Liam properly." Winnie held Belle's gaze without wavering. "I wanted to tell you sooner. I nearly told you twice, but then the cable on the ferry was cut, and the committee meetings and the repairs. The timing was never right. But I'm telling you now."

"How long?"

"Three weeks. Nearly four."

"And you've been keeping this to yourself for a month."

"I have been waiting for the right time... and also I wanted to be sure of my feelings for Luke. I believe this may be the right time to tell you because now you know what it feels like to have a man notice you. I was a bit worried about telling you because you've never experienced having a beau or having a man pay attention to you in a positive way. I was afraid you would get upset. I was afraid that you would worry about my future and me wanting more out of life."

"Tell me about him," Belle said.

Winnie's composure eased by a fraction, the relief visible in the way her shoulders settled. "He's twenty-three. He works on his family's ranch with his father and his older brother. He's quiet but not shy—he speaks when he has something worth saying, and he listens when he doesn't. He brought me a bundle of early crocuses two weeks ago, wrapped in a piece of newsprint. They were half-wilted by the time he got them to the mercantile, but he'd ridden six miles to bring them."

"Does Amos know?"

"Amos knows everything. He hasn't said a word to anyone, as far as I can tell. Amos has watched over our conversations when Luke has come to the mercantile. He also speaks very highly of Luke's family."

Belle felt something break loose in her chest, a knot she hadn't known was there, and what replaced it wasn't sadness but a warmth that ached. Her sister, her quiet, steady, perceptive sister, had been holding this brightness inside her for weeks, waiting for Belle to have enough room in her own life to receive it.

"I'm happy for you, Winnie. I am. He sounds like a good man."

"I believe he is. I've been praying on it. Asking God to show me what is real and what is only pleasant." Winnie squeezed Belle's hands. "But do you see what I'm telling you? You are not alone in this. You are not the only Callahan woman sitting in a room wondering what on earth to do with a man's attention. The difference between us is that I've had weeks to get accustomed to the feeling, and you've had two days."

"Two days and no sleep."

Winnie laughed, a short, warm sound that opened the room. "Then we are more alike than you think, because the day Luke brought the crocuses to me at the mercantile, I lay in this bed that very night staring at the ceiling until midnight trying to decide if wildflowers from a rancher's son constituted an intention."

"Do they?"

"I believe they do. Half-wilted ones, especially. A man doesn't ride six miles with flowers unless he means something by it."

Belle looked at their joined hands. Winnie's were roughened from domestic work—laundry, gardening, the lye soap that dried the skin—but they were smoother than Belle's, the fingers longer, the nails more even. Belle turned her hands over in Winnie's grip and looked at the palms. The calluses were thick and amber-colored. The scar on her left hand was a raised white line that would never soften.

"He won't care about your hands, Belle."

"You don't know that."

"I know what I saw at supper on Friday night. I watched that man look at you, and what he saw was not your hands. What he saw was the woman who sat across from him and listened to him speak about his family as though every word mattered to her, because it did. I watched a man look at you as if you were the only person in the room. I watched a man mesmerized by a woman who doesn't realize how beautiful she is inside and out. It was like a love story happening before my very eyes. The only person at that table who couldn't see it was you."

Belle pulled her hands free and pressed them flat against her knees. The fabric of her nightgown was thin cotton, worn soft from years of washing, and through it she could feel the hard ridges of her calluses against her kneecaps.

"We need to get you dressed," Winnie said. She stood and crossed to the trunk at the foot of the bed. She lifted the lid, moved aside a few dresses, and drew out a dress that had not been worn in over a year.

The sage green calico was the best dress that either of them owned. Winnie had made it for her two Christmases ago from fabric she'd bought with egg money she'd saved for months, cutting the pattern from a dress of their mother's that had been too worn to mend. The bodice was fitted, the collar modest, and the sleeves full to the wrist. Small brass buttons ran from the collar to the waist. The color, when Belle had first tried it on, had done something to her eyes that Winnie had noticed, and Belle had dismissed. Belle had worn it at Christmas that year and to church three times after. Then put it away because the fabric was too fine for ordinary Sundays, and she wanted to preserve the dress for special occasions, which never seemed to come.

Winnie laid it across the bed and smoothed the skirt. "With Mama's comb in your hair and your good boots."

"Winnie, it's church at the boardinghouse, not a governor's ball."

"You will wear this dress, and you will wear it well, because you are a beautiful woman who has spent years putting yourself last." Winnie pulled the tortoiseshell comb from the trunk and set it on the bed beside the dress. "Today is a special occasion. Now wash your face, and let me do your hair."

Belle washed at the basin in Winnie's room, the water cold from the pitcher that had sat overnight. She dressed with Winnie's help; the sage calico fitting close through the bodice and falling in a clean line from the waist. Winnie buttoned the dress up; her fingers were quick and sure.

"Sit," Winnie said, guiding her to the chair that she had moved near the window.

Winnie stood behind her and began working on her hair. She loosened the braid Belle had slept in and drew her fingers through the length of it, separating the waves. Belle's hair was thick and dark and fell past her shoulders when it was down, which it seldom was.

Winnie worked in quiet concentration. She drew the front sections back from Belle's face and pinned them with the tortoiseshell comb, then let the rest fall in loose waves below the comb's edge.

"There," Winnie said.

Belle looked at the small mirror Winnie held in front of her, the one that had been their mother's, framed in pewter with a crack running through the lower right corner. The woman looking back at her wore sage green calico and her mother's comb, and her face was the same face Belle saw every morning at the washstand—the same strong jaw, the same green eyes, the same mouth that had been set against difficulty for so long it had forgotten there were other expressions available to it. But the dress changed the frame. The comb changed the line. Something about the way Winnie had arranged her hair softened what years of labor and weather had sharpened, not erasing it but allowing what existed beneath it to show through.

"I look like Mama," Belle said.

"You are just as beautiful as she was."

Belle set the mirror aside and looked down at the dress, the small brass buttons, and her hands resting on the skirt. The scars were still very visible on her hands. She was still the woman who ran the Callahan Ferry, who woke before dawn and hauled rope and read a river that could kill a careless man in under a minute. None of that had changed because she'd put on a dress. But she was also a woman sitting in her sister's bedroom on a Sunday morning, about to be called on by a man who had asked permission to call on her. The two truths existed in the same body without contradiction, and she was only beginning to understand that they could.

"Winnie," she said. "Will you pray with me?"

Winnie knelt on the floor beside her and took her hands. They bowed their heads.

"Lord," Belle said. "I come to You this morning asking for things I haven't asked for before. I have always come to You about the ferry or asking for guidance in raising my siblings. I have asked You to keep Liam and me safe on the water and to give me the strength to do the work You set in front of me, and You have been faithful, Lord. You have been so good to me every day."

"But this morning I am asking for something different. I am asking You to put peace in my heart, because there is none. I am asking for calmness because I haven't been calm since Friday evening, and I don't know when I was last this afraid of anything. I don't know what You are doing in my life. I can feel You moving through me, the way I feel the current shift before I see it in the water, and I trust You, Father. I trust that You haven't brought me to this place, to this morning, to hand me something that will break me."

"Show me the way. Show me who I am beyond the ferry and beyond the work and beyond the woman I have been for the sake of my brother and my sister. If this man is a part of Your plan for my life, give me the courage to stand in front of him without hiding. If he is not, give me the grace to bear it. But either way, Lord, I am asking You to show me who Belle Callahan is when she isn't holding a rope. Because I haven't met her yet, and I would like to. Amen."

"Amen," Winnie said.

They sat together in the quiet that followed the prayer, their hands still clasped. Through the window, the morning was advancing, as Belle heard the sound of hooves on packed earth, coming up the wagon track, steady and unhurried. She stood up to look out the window. A spring wagon crested the last rise, a single horse in the traces, a man on the bench seat holding the reins with relaxed competence, and a smile on his face.

"He's here," she said as she smoothed the skirt of her dress and took a deep breath.

Winnie opened the bedroom door, and they walked down the hallway.

The knock came. Three steady strikes of knuckle against wood, the same knock she had answered on Friday evening, except that on Friday she had been wearing her supper dress and expecting a guest for a meal. This morning she was wearing a sage green dress with her mother's comb in her hair, and she felt like a woman standing at the threshold of a life that was all new and unfamiliar.

Winnie touched Belle's arm. "Breathe, Belle. You can do this."

She put a smile on her face, crossed the room, and opened the door.

Chapter 16

Belle stood in the doorway, looking lovely and a bit nervous.

Caleb had spent the time during the ride from town telling himself that the morning was simple and that a man who called on a woman did so with composure and good manners and the steady confidence of intention. He had believed this up until Belle had opened her front door. The color of her dress did something to the green of her eyes that he had no engineering vocabulary for and no capacity to describe. The color of her eyes had deepened, or the dress had drawn the color of them forward, or both. Her eyes alone knocked his sense of calm into orbit. Her hair was down, arranged in loose waves that fell past her shoulders.

"Good morning, Caleb."

"Belle... good morning."

He offered his arm, and her fingers settled against the inside of his elbow through the fabric of his jacket. They crossed the porch and descended the steps into the yard. The spring wagon stood near the fence rail where he'd left it, the hired horse drowsing in the traces with one hind hoof cocked and its lower lip slack. Caleb guided Belle to the passenger side and offered his hand. She placed her palm against his, her fingers pressing into his skin as she stepped up onto the iron footrest and settled onto the bench seat.

Liam stood near the barn door with a bridle in one hand and a rag in the other. He had been polishing brass fittings, or had arranged himself to look as though he had been polishing brass fittings.

"Morning, Caleb."

"Liam. Fine day, isn't it?"

"It is. You'll want to keep left at the fork past the creek. The right side can be a bit rough."

"Much obliged."

"We'll be along shortly, Belle."

Caleb climbed onto the bench seat beside Belle. The wagon shifted under his weight, the springs compressing and settling, the hired horse lifting its head at the change in load. He released the brake and clicked the horse forward. The wagon lurched once and then found its rhythm on the packed earth of the yard.

Winnie stood in the doorway of the house. She raised one hand in a wave, and he nodded in her direction.

The homestead receded behind them, and the valley opened around them as they descended from the homestead's rise. The benchlands rolled away to the south in long folds of new grass, and the mountains filled the eastern horizon with their full sweep from timber to bare rock. The snow on the upper ridges was retreating, the line of white visibly higher than it had been a week ago. Below the snowline the timbered slopes held the particular green of conifers in spring, dark and dense and unbroken except where a clearing or a rock face interrupted the canopy. Overhead, the sky was the hard blue of high elevation and cloudless.

"I noticed something as I rode over this morning... the valley looks different from a wagon seat than it does on foot," Caleb said. "I've walked the main road to the bridge site every morning since I arrived, but I've only ever looked at the ground or right in front of myself. Then, once I'm at the bridge site, I pay little attention to the surrounding beauty. I've never stopped long enough to look up and just enjoy the view."

"That's because you were working and your focus was elsewhere," Belle said. "A person doesn't see a place the same when they're working in it as when they're passing through it for enjoyment."

"You see it, though. You've lived and worked in this valley every day for years, and I'd wager you still see it."

"I see the river. I see what the river is doing on a given day, what the current is telling me about the snowmelt in the mountains, and whether the water has risen or dropped since yesterday. The valley beyond the river..." She paused, and her attention moved across the landscape with the unhurried sweep of a woman reacquainting herself with something she'd set aside. "I used to see it more. When I was young, before the ferry was mine, I rode out here in every season and paid attention to what was growing and what was dying and where the elk were moving. I knew where every hawk nested on the benchlands. I could tell you what week the balsamroot would bloom on the south-facing slopes, and when the first lupine would come up in the meadow behind our barn."

"And now?"

"Now I see the ferry cable, and the water level, and the moor-ing posts, and the freight schedule. Those take up most of my attention." She turned to him. "But the valley is waking up, and I feel as if I am as well. I can see it in the cottonwoods along the creek—the buds are splitting, and by next week there will be leaves. The balsamroot is already showing on the south slopes. Another few weeks and the wildflowers will come up through the meadows in sheets of purple, yellow, and orange, and the grass will be high enough to brush a horse's belly before we know it. The whole valley will soon look like something a painter would give up trying to capture because no pigment would hold the colors right."

"I'd like to see that."

"You will. You won't be able to miss it."

The road curved past a stand of cottonwoods, and beyond them a fence line marked the edge of the property. Cattle stood in the near pasture, their coats rough and shaggy with the last of their winter hair, their heads down in the new grass.

"Whose place is this?" he asked.

"The Mercer family. They run cattle on acreage along the creek bottom. Bill Mercer and his wife came out from Ohio nine years ago with a small herd and a claim they filed sight unseen from a land office circular. Most people who file claims that way take one look at the winters and go back east. The Mercers stayed. They've built their herd up from what they brought, and they calve every spring without losing more than one or two."

"Good grass?"

"The best in the valley along this stretch. The creek keeps the bottomland watered through the dry months, and the benchland above it grows enough native grass for summer grazing. The Mercers cut their own hay from the meadow behind that tree line." She pointed toward a stand of cottonwoods where the creek bent south.

After the wagon crested a low rise and turned onto the main road, Caleb could see the town ahead. Even from this distance he could see movement near the front porch of the boardinghouse and figures arriving on foot and on horseback.

A hawk circled overhead, riding the updrafts with its wings locked and its tail feathers adjusting in minute corrections that kept it stationary against the wind.

"Red-tailed hawk," Belle said. "There's a nesting pair on the rimrock above Mercer's south pasture. They've been there as long as I can remember. The female is larger than the male, and she does most of the hunting. He guards the nest."

"You know that from watching?"

"From years of watching. From sitting on our porch in the evening and seeing them come in from their hunting with prey in their talons and drop to the rimrock where the nest is. From watching the female teach the young ones to fly in late summer, pushing them off the ledge and circling below in case they fell."

The hired horse had developed an opinion about pace. It wanted to walk faster as the town drew closer, the stable and its feed trough at the livery pulling it forward with the reliable magnetism of habit. Caleb held the reins steady and kept the pace where it was, not because the horse's eagerness was a problem but because the ride was nearly finished and he was not ready for it to be.

He had driven wagons to bridge and construction sites in several territories before. He had driven supply rigs to bridge camps on roads that barely earned the name. He had never driven a wagon on a Sunday morning with a woman beside him on the bench seat and the day opening ahead of them with no schedule. The entire morning so far carried the sense of being exactly where he was supposed to be doing exactly what he was supposed to be doing, and the unfamiliarity of that feeling was itself a kind of revelation, because Caleb Sterling had spent most of his adult life occupying positions that required him and had rarely, if ever, occupied one that simply fit.

They pulled up near the boardinghouse. Caleb set the brake, wrapped the reins around the handle, and came around to Belle's side of the wagon. He offered his hand, and her grip was firm and certain as she stepped down. For a moment they stood close beside the wagon, his hand still holding hers, and the warmth of her hand in his as unremarkable and as remarkable as anything he had experienced before. He released her hand and offered his arm, and they walked across the road to the boardinghouse.

The dining room was already configured for worship. The long table had been pushed against the far wall, and chairs were arranged in two sections facing the front of the room with a narrow aisle between them. Mrs. Hanscombe moved between the rows of chairs, adjusting them.

"Mr. Sterling, Miss Callahan," Mrs. Hanscombe said as they passed. "Good morning to you both." Her tone was even and warm; her observation contained in a single measured glance that moved from Caleb's arm to Belle's hand resting upon it and back to their faces without lingering.

"Morning, Mrs. Hanscombe," Belle said.

Caleb guided Belle toward the middle of the left section and settled into their chairs.

Reverend Hale stood near the front of the room, speaking with a man Caleb didn't recognize.

The front door opened, and Winnie and Liam entered. Winnie carried a covered plate that she delivered to the sideboard before making her way down the aisle. Both Liam and Winnie slid into the chairs beside Belle.

Reverend Hale moved to the front of the room and set his Bible on the pulpit. The conversations around the room subsided.

"I will read from Isaiah this morning," Reverend Hale said. "Chapter forty-three. Verses eighteen and nineteen."

Reverend Hale opened his Bible. The pages fell to the place he'd marked, and he read without hurrying.

"'Remember ye not the former things, neither consider the things of old. Behold, I will do a new thing; now it shall spring forth; shall ye not know it? I will even make a way in the wilderness, and rivers in the desert.'"

He closed the Bible and left his hand on the cover.

"Spring has come to this valley," he said. "You've seen it. You've walked through it. Some of you have been praying for it since January, when the snow was four feet deep on the valley floor and the road to Livingston was closed for two weeks running, and the only thing between your family and February was the firewood you'd stacked in October, the hay you'd put up in August, and the faith you'd carried since before any of it." He paused. "The snow is going. You can see the line retreating up the mountains. Every day it is a little higher than the day before, and below the line the ground is opening up, and the grass is coming through, and the creek is running with the water that was locked in those peaks all winter. The season is turning."

He moved from behind the pulpit table and stood in the aisle between the rows.

"Isaiah tells us that God says, 'Behold, I will do a new thing.' And then God asks a question. 'Shall ye not know it?' That is not a rhetorical question, friends. God is not making a speech. He is asking you directly whether you will recognize the new thing when it comes. Because the new thing does not arrive with trumpets. It does not come announced. It comes the way spring comes to this valley—slowly, beneath the snow, in the ground, in the roots, in the places you cannot see until the season turns and the evidence pushes through."

Caleb sat with his hands on his thighs and listened. Beside him, Belle sat still, her attention on the minister, her hands folded in her lap.

"Every one of you in this room is building something," Reverend Hale continued. "Some of you are building a herd. Some of you are building homes. Some of you are building a business or a family or a reputation, or simply a new life." His gaze moved across the congregation without settling on anyone. "And all of you have carried something through the winter that you are ready to set down. A loss. A debt. A failure that keeps you up at night. A fear that the thing you are building will not hold. I know this because I have ridden a circuit through these valleys for nine years, and I have sat at your tables and prayed at your bedsides and buried your people in the ground, and I have never met a soul in this country who was not carrying something heavy."

"The prophet tells us to let go of the former things. Not to forget them. Isaiah does not say forget. He says do not dwell there. Do not build your house on the ground of what was, because God is doing something in the ground of what will be, and if you are gripping the old thing with both hands, you will not have a hand free to receive the new one."

He returned to the pulpit table and placed both hands flat on its surface.

"Planting a seed in this valley requires faith. You all know this. The frost can come back in May, and I've seen it happen with my own eyes. I have seen it kill a garden in a single night, and I have seen the woman who planted that garden go back out the next morning and put new seeds in the same ground because she trusted the season more than she feared the frost. That is what faith looks like in this country. It does not look like certainty. It looks like a woman on her knees in cold dirt, putting seeds in the ground because she believes the summer is coming, even when the morning is still cold enough to see her breath."

Caleb felt the preacher's words settle deeply within himself. He had spent three years gripping the former things with both hands. Wyoming. The bridge that fell. The brother he could not bring back. He had built his life since on the foundation of what had been, measuring every decision against the catastrophe that preceded it, and the prophet's words landed on him with the weight of something that had been waiting for him to be still enough to hear it.

Beside him, Belle's hands had tightened against each other in her lap. In his peripheral vision he could see the compression of her fingers, the knuckles whitening, and he understood that the sermon had found her in the same place it had found him—the place where the old thing and the new thing occupied the same ground and a person had to choose which one to tend.

"I will make a way in the wilderness," Reverend Hale continued. "And rivers in the desert. That is not a promise of an easy country. That is a promise of hard country. The kind of country where roads wash out and the frost comes back, and the river rises higher than you can imagine. God does not promise to remove the wilderness. He promises to make a way through it. Your job is not to understand the way. Your job is to walk it. Plant the seed. Trust the season. And when the new thing springs forth, have the courage to say, I see it. I receive it. It is mine."

He bowed his head. "Let us pray."

Caleb bowed his head. In the stillness that followed the minister's words, before the prayer began, he moved his hand from his thigh and offered it to Belle.

Her fingers found his and closed around his palm.

"Lord," Reverend Hale said, "we come before You this morning as people who have survived another winter and are standing on the edge of another spring. We thank You for the ground that is thawing beneath our feet and the water that is running in the creeks and the light that is lasting longer each day. We thank You for the hands that planted last year's harvest and the hands that will plant this year's. We thank You for the roofs that held through the snow and the families that held through the cold and the faith that held through the doubt."

Belle's thumb moved against the side of his hand, a single, slow stroke. The pressure of it traveled through him, arriving everywhere at once.

"We ask You, Father, to give us eyes to see the new thing You are doing. Give us hands willing to release what we have been gripping and hearts brave enough to receive what You are offering. Where we have built on the ground of our failures, show us the ground You have prepared. Where we have trusted our own strength, teach us to trust Yours. Make a way for us, Lord, as You have promised. Through the wilderness of our doubt and the desert of our weariness, make a way, and give us the faith to walk it."

"We ask these things in the name of Your Son. Amen."

"Amen," the congregation said, and heads lifted.

The room shifted from sanctuary to social gathering as voices rose. Mrs. Hanscombe appeared from the kitchen with a coffeepot in each hand.

Caleb and Belle moved through the room in the easy current of the social hour. He brought her a cup of coffee from the sideboard and took one for himself, and they stood near the window where the light came through, and the room's conversations washed around them in overlapping waves.

At one point, a young man approached them. He was tall, clean-shaven, his dark hair combed with care, his Sunday clothes pressed, and his boots polished. He carried himself with a bearing that was respectful and slightly rigid, the posture of a young man managing his nerves by holding himself straighter than usual.

"Miss Callahan," the young man said. "Good morning."

"Good morning, Luke," Belle said. "It's good to see you."

The young man turned to Caleb and extended his hand. "Mr. Sterling, I'm Luke Dixon. My family ranches on Shields Creek."

Caleb shook his hand. The grip was firm and direct. "Mr. Dixon. A pleasure."

"The pleasure is mine, sir. I've heard a good deal about the bridge project. My family is looking forward to its opening."

"That's kind of you to say. Your family's ranch — how far from town is it?"

"Six miles from town. My father and my older brother, and I run cattle. We've been on that ground eight years now."

"A solid operation, then."

"We do our best." Luke shifted his weight slightly and turned back to Belle.

"Miss Callahan, I wanted to ask—if it would suit you, I would be honored to take Miss Winnie for a ride this afternoon. Liam would be welcome to accompany us. I understand from Winnie that you and Mr. Sterling have plans for the coming day, and I thought perhaps we might all meet back here around one o'clock for lunch. If that would be agreeable."

Belle looked at Caleb. "Would that suit you? Dining with the others at one o'clock?"

"I think that sounds fine," Caleb said. "It would be a pleasure. If you're agreeable, we could take our ride this morning, before lunch, rather than after. The morning is too good to spend indoors."

"I'd like that," Belle said.

"Thank you both," Luke said. "I'm grateful." He nodded to Caleb, then to Belle, and turned and crossed the room to where Winnie stood near the coffee pots with Liam beside her. Caleb watched the young man's approach—the way his stride lengthened and then shortened as he drew near, the way his posture shifted into something less armored when he reached Winnie. She looked up as Luke arrived, and her face opened with a brightness that came from below her usual composure and altered her entire expression.

Belle touched Caleb's arm. "I should tell you something about Winnie and Luke."

"I can see it from here."

"She told me this morning. Before you arrived. She's been keeping company with him for nearly a month. He comes to the mercantile on the days she works there, and he's walked her partway home twice. She was waiting for the right time to tell me. He rode six miles once to bring her crocuses."

"A man doesn't ride six miles unless he means something by it."

Belle's mouth curved. "That is almost exactly what Winnie said."

"Shall we go?" he said.

Belle set her coffee cup on the windowsill. "Let me tell Winnie."

She crossed the room to her sister and spoke briefly with her. He watched the sisters: Belle's hand on Winnie's arm, Winnie's quick nod, and the look that passed between them, carrying an entire conversation in two seconds. Belle returned to his side.

"She says to enjoy the morning."

They stepped onto the boardinghouse porch together. The spring air had warmed since their arrival. Caleb helped Belle up onto the bench seat, his hand steadying her.

He took his seat beside her, released the brake, and turned the horse away from the boardinghouse.

"Where would you like to go?" Caleb asked.

Belle was looking at the road ahead, and the expression on her face had shifted from the composed attention of the social hour to something less contained, something that lived closer to the surface. "There's a place I'd like to show you. I haven't been there in months, and I've been thinking about it this morning. It's not far."

"Tell me more."

"Take the left fork where the road ahead splits. The road follows the creek up into the foothills. I'll tell you where to turn."

Chapter 17

The road narrowed where it left the main fork; the wagon ruts sinking into softer ground where the drainage from the foothills kept the earth damp. Belle directed Caleb left at a stand of ponderosa pine that she had used as a landmark since she was old enough to ride this track alone.

The road climbed gently as it left the valley floor, rising through a series of low benches where the bunchgrass grew thick and pale.

"That drainage below us is where the creek meets the Yellowstone," she said, pointing toward a break in the bluffs where the water cut through cottonwoods and emerged onto a gravel flat before joining the river. "In May the creek runs bank-full with snowmelt, and the gravel flat disappears entirely. By August it's a trickle you could step across without wetting your ankles. Liam and I used to catch cutthroat trout in the pool below that junction in July. The fish stacked up there because the cold creek water met the warmer river, and they'd hold in the seam where the two temperatures mixed."

"How deep is the pool?"

"Four feet at midsummer. Deeper when the water's up. The bottom is gravel over clay, and the clay is what keeps the pool from draining between rains. My mother used to say that the pool was the most honest mirror in the valley because it showed you what the mountains were doing before the river told you. She grew up on this ground. Knew every seep and spring between the main road and the timber."

Caleb kept his attention forward, the reins loose in his hands. "Your mother's family was here before the town?"

"Before there was a town to speak of, yes. My grandparents came out from Pennsylvania with a wagon, holding everything they owned and filed a homestead claim on a piece of land they had never seen. My grandfather chose the ground for three reasons: the creek for water, the river flats for grazing, and the cottonwood stand for shelter from the north wind in winter. He was a practical man by all accounts. My grandmother planted apple trees the first spring they arrived."

"Apple trees this far north?"

"Everyone told her they wouldn't survive. The winters are too harsh, the growing season too short, and the altitude too high. She planted them anyway. She brought the rootstock from her family's farm in Pennsylvania, wrapped in burlap and straw. She said she wasn't going to build a home without an orchard, and the orchard would have apple trees because her mother's orchard had apple trees and her grandmother's before that. The trees survived every winter, and they were still standing as of the last time I was here."

The old logging road branched off to where the hills steepened; the track was barely visible now. Belle pointed it out as they passed.

"The loggers cut the lower slopes over twenty years ago, before my time. The timber grew back thicker than the original stand because the cutting opened the canopy and let the sun reach the ground."

"You know this land the way I know a set of plans."

"I know it because I've walked it many times. Because someone took the time to show it to me and name the things on it and explain why they mattered. My mother brought us out here every week when we were children. She knew the name of every plant that grew between the road and the timber, and she knew the use of each one. Which roots could be eaten, which bark could be boiled for tea, and where the wild onions grew in spring. She learned it from her mother, who learned it from the land itself, because when you homestead a place with nothing but what you carry, the land becomes your provision or your ruin, and you learn it accordingly."

The track dipped through a shallow ford where the creek crossed the road. The water was ankle-deep and clear, running fast over rounded stones that clicked and shifted under the wagon wheels. The horse splashed through without hesitation; the water darkening its fetlocks, and the wagon climbed the far bank with a lurch that pressed Belle against the bench seat's backrest.

Beyond the ford, Belle saw the cottonwoods.

They rose in a dense stand along the creek where it curved toward the river, their trunks pale against the darker timber of the hills behind them, their upper branches carrying the first visible swelling of spring buds that would become leaves within a week. The stand was old. The largest trees had trunks too broad for a man to reach around, and their root systems had lifted and cracked the earth along the creek bank in the slow, patient upheaval of decades.

"Turn here," Belle said.

The wagon track that branched from the road was barely more than two ruts through the grass, the space between them overgrown with bunchgrass and wild timothy that brushed the underside of the wagon as Caleb turned the horse onto it. A branch from an overhanging cottonwood scraped along the side of the wagon box with a long, rasping sound.

"This was my mother's family land," Belle said. "The Blecher homestead. My grandparents settled here when they first came to the valley."

The wagon moved through the cottonwoods. The light changed beneath the canopy, the open brightness of the benchlands giving way to the dappled, shifting quality of light filtered through bare branches that were just beginning to leaf. The sound of the river grew louder as they descended the gentle slope toward the clearing.

The clearing opened before them. It occupied a gentle shelf of ground above the river, bounded on three sides by cottonwoods and on the fourth by the slope that dropped through wild grass and scattered rock to the Yellowstone River below. The river was visible through the lower branches, its surface catching fragments of light, its current running strong and even in the main channel. The mountains filled the eastern sky above the treeline.

The cabin stood in the center of the clearing. It was small, a single room with a loft, built from logs that had weathered to the color of old silver. The roof sagged on one side where a support timber had shifted and given way. The porch was half-collapsed; the planking broken through in places where rot had eaten the boards from underneath, but the stone chimney rose straight and solid above the damaged roofline, its stones still fitted tight against one another.

Caleb set the brake, and the hired horse dropped its head and began pulling at the grass.

He came around to her side and offered his hand. Belle took it and stepped down. She stood beside the wagon and looked at the cabin and the clearing, and the apple trees, and a sense of peace washed over her.

"I come here," she said. "Not often. But when I need to."

Caleb stood beside her without speaking. His hands hung at his sides. He was watching the clearing with the attentive stillness she had come to recognize in him, the particular quality of attention he gave to things he intended to understand rather than merely observe.

"When the ferry or the household or the bills or the worry for Liam and Winnie becomes more than I can carry, I ride out here alone." She walked toward the cabin, and Caleb fell into step beside her. "I come here to think. To remember when things were simpler, when I was a child and the worst trouble I could imagine was getting caught in the rain." She stopped near the stone step that had served as the cabin's threshold, a flat slab of granite worn smooth by decades of boots crossing it. "I come here because my mama grew up on this ground, and standing on it is the closest I can get to being near her."

She sat on the stone steps. The granite was cool through the fabric of her dress, warmed only slightly where the sun reached it through a gap in the branches overhead. Caleb sat beside her, close enough that she could feel the warmth of his arm.

"Tell me about her," Caleb said.

Belle looked at the apple trees. There were four of them, planted in a row just east of the cabin, where they would catch the morning sun and be sheltered from the prevailing wind by the cabin it-self. They were gnarled, thick-trunked, and unpruned, their lower branches heavy enough to touch the ground, the bark furrowed deep with age. The buds on the branches were swollen and tight, weeks from opening, holding the blossoms inside the way a fist holds a secret it isn't ready to release.

"Her name was Mary. Mary Blecher before she married my fa-ther." Belle rested her hands on her knees. "She was the center of our family. Not in the way people say that about a woman because she kept the house, though she did keep it and kept it well. She was the center because everything moved through her. She decided when we ate, what we ate, who needed what, and when. She sang while she cooked, mostly hymns. She taught Winnie and me to sew, to garden, and to put up preserves in the fall. She had a garden at our homestead that produced more than any garden that size had a right to, and she gave the surplus to neighbors because it never occurred to her not to. She read to us at night. Scripture and stories both. She made our home feel like the safest place on earth just by being in it."

Belle hadn't spoken about her mother at this length to anyone outside her family in years, and the telling felt less like pulling something from a closed place and more like water finding a chan-nel it had traveled before.

"She used to talk about those apple trees," Belle continued. "How her mother watered them through the first summer with creek water carried in buckets, two trips a day, because the roots hadn't gone deep enough yet to find their own water. She said her mother talked to the trees the way some people talk to horses, with patience and expectation both, as though she believed they could hear her and would do their best if she asked them to. My grandmother died when I was ten, and my grandfather the year after, but the trees kept on as though nobody had told them they were allowed to stop. My mother was the same way. She kept on. She held our family in place the way these roots hold this ground, and I think she did it so quietly that none of us understood what she was doing until she wasn't there to do it anymore."

The river moved below the bluff, and a blue jay called from the cottonwoods upstream, two sharp notes that carried in the still air and faded.

"Mama died when I was twelve," Belle said. "A fever came through the valley that winter. It moved through the homesteads and the town, and it took many people. My mama was the youngest of them. I remember her last week on Earth. The doctor rode out from Livingston, and by the time he arrived, there was nothing he could do that hadn't already been tried. Winnie cried in the kitchen, and I held her. I didn't cry because someone had to be the one not crying, and I had already decided that person was me. Liam was eight, and he didn't understand why Mama wouldn't get up. He kept bringing things to her bedside. A bird feather he'd found near the barn. A piece of quartz from the creek. Offerings, the way a child offers the only currency he has."

She turned to look at the cabin door, hanging open on its one remaining hinge. The interior was dark beyond the threshold, the single room visible only in the shapes of what remained: the stone hearth, the loft ladder leaning against the far wall, and the outline of a window frame where the glass had long since broken and fallen away.

"My father sat beside her bed the night she passed away. He held her hand, and the stillness in him was something I had never seen before. I had seen my father angry, and I had seen him laughing, and I had seen him tired after a full day on the ferry, but I had never seen him that still before. He sat there as though he had already left this earth with her and was waiting for his body to follow." She paused. "He wept. I stood in the doorway and watched him weep, and it was the first time in my life I understood that a grown man could break. He never fully came back from her death. We not only lost our mama that day, we lost our father as well."

Caleb sat beside her on the stone step. He didn't speak. His hands rested on his knees, and the only movement in him was the slow, even draw of his breathing.

"Her death was the beginning of my father's ruin." Belle said the words without flinching. "Samuel Callahan was a good man before my mama died. He had built our home and barn with his own two hands. He had built the ferry. He taught us to read the river. He hummed hymns on the platform, and he could make Liam laugh harder than anyone. He loved my mama with everything in him, and when she died, that love turned into the thing that destroyed him, because he poured it into the only vessel that would hold something that big without asking anything back, and that vessel was a bottle."

"The drinking came gradually at first. A few weeks after her funeral, I found a bottle in the barn. Then another beneath the ferry landing in a place he thought no one would look. Then the mornings when he couldn't hold the guide rope steady, and I would stand beside him on the platform and correct the angle without saying anything, because saying something meant admitting what was happening, and admitting it made it real in a way I wasn't ready for."

She stood and walked to the well. The coping stones were warm where the sun struck them, and she rested her hand on the fitted surface and looked down into the dry shaft where the water table had dropped below the wells reach years ago.

"By the time I was fourteen, I was running crossings alone on the mornings he couldn't stand straight. I made excuses to the passengers. Told them he was ill, that he'd be back by afternoon. Sometimes the neighbors helped. Mrs. Phelps, the Gresham family, and Bill Mercer several times. They could see what was happening. Everyone in the valley could see what was happening. They came because the load was too much for a child to carry alone, and they stayed long enough to help me get through the day, and then they went home to their own families, and I went home to mine."

She turned from the well and walked to the apple trees. Caleb had risen from the stone step and followed her. She stopped beneath the largest tree and looked up into the branches where the buds waited.

"He died when I was seventeen," she said. "On the Yellowstone. During high water. He was drunk, and he was careless with his footing on the wet planking, and the river was running faster than it had any right to in early June, and he went in. I was on the platform. I saw it happen. I reached for him, but missed. The current took him."

She turned to face him. "I want you to know where I come from. I want you to know what shaped me. Why I hold everything the way I do, so tight that some mornings my hands ache before I've touched a rope. Why letting go feels like the most dangerous thing

I could do, because the last time I trusted someone to hold something, he couldn't hold himself." She walked back to the stone step and sat down. She watched as Caleb walked toward her. "The ferry became mine. The debts became mine. Winnie and Liam became mine. And I gripped all of it because gripping was the only thing I knew how to do, and if I loosened my hands for one day, one hour, I believed everything I loved would slip through."

She looked at him. "And now everything is shifting. The bridge will open, and the ferry will end. Liam is looking at land and cattle and a life that doesn't include me. Winnie has Luke Dixon bringing her crocuses on horseback. I can feel the ground moving beneath me faster than I can keep my footing. I know in my heart that God is asking me to let go, the way Reverend Hale spoke about this morning. I know it. I have wrestled with God about it, and every time I wrestle, I lose, because He is right and I am stubborn, and the two things cannot occupy the same ground forever."

A breeze moved through the cottonwoods, and the branches swayed above them. The shifting light played across the clearing in patterns that changed and returned and changed again.

Caleb was quiet as he processed everything she had just said.

"The night you had supper at our table," Belle said, "you told us about your family. Your parents, your three sisters. Margaret, Ruth, and Anne." She looked at him. "You said your mother raised five children. Three sisters and yourself make four."

The muscles along his forearm tightened. She watched his hands go still on his knees as if he were bracing for something.

"His name was James," Caleb said. "He was my younger brother. He was two years behind me, and he followed me west because he wanted to build a life in the territories as I did. He married a young woman from Cheyenne. They had been married less than a year."

Caleb's profile was sharp against the light that came through the cottonwood branches, his jaw clenched, the effort of the telling visible.

"Three years ago I oversaw a bridge in Wyoming Territory. The investors pressed the schedule. The materials supplier delivered timber that was not what had been ordered, pilings that were lighter than the plans called for. The foreman on the project assured me that the work was sound. I had doubts. I had written the discrepancy into my report, and the numbers I recorded told me something was wrong." He paused. "The foreman explained it away, and I wanted to believe the explanation because believing it meant the project stayed on schedule and the money held, and I didn't have to stand before the investors and tell them we needed to tear out what we'd built and start again. So I signed the report. I let the foreman's word stand where my own judgment should have stood."

Belle heard the care with which he stated each fact, the way he laid them down in sequence without softening a single one, and she recognized the discipline of it because it was the same discipline she had just used to tell him about her father. A person could tell the worst thing they carried in one of two ways: they could let it pour out of them uncontrolled, or they could set each piece down with their hands steady and their voice even and trust the listener to understand what the steadiness was costing. Caleb chose the second way.

"Four months after the bridge opened, it collapsed. Two men were on it. A freight driver named Thomas Halstead, hauling lumber across the span. And James. James was with him on the wagon. They went into the water with the bridge, and neither of them came out."

"The investigation cleared me. The foreman had falsified the foundation records, and the legal fault fell on him and on the supplier. But legal fault and the fault a man carries in his chest are different accounts, and I knew which one I owed." He looked at his hands, which rested on his knees. "I let someone else's assurance overrule what I knew to be true, and my brother died on a bridge I built."

"The three years you spent in Denver afterward," she said. "You told Liam about the road work and the smaller commissions... the work you did there."

"I took work where it was least likely that someone could die if I made a mistake. Culverts. Grading. Projects that mattered to the people who hired me but that carried little risk beyond a washed-out road or a delayed freight wagon. I told myself I was being careful. The truth is I was hiding, and I knew I was hiding, and I let the hiding continue because it was easier than standing on a riverbank again and trusting my own hands to hold the work they were given."

"What brought you here?" she asked. "To Providence Ridge. To a bridge over the Yellowstone River. To the one kind of work you were most afraid to do."

Caleb was quiet for several seconds. When he spoke, his voice carried a quality of measured precision, something that lived in the same place where her own faith lived: private and hard-won and not offered lightly.

"I believe God called me here," he said. "I don't say that the way a man says it when he wants to sound righteous or when he's trying to dress up a decision in better clothes than it deserves. I say it because it is the truest thing I know. I was in Denver, and I was working, and I was surviving, and the surviving had become a kind of death in itself because a man who is only surviving is not living, and God knows the difference even when the man pretends he doesn't." He looked at her. "The Providence Ridge contract came across my desk the way opportunities come to men in my line of work: through correspondence and reputation and the slow turning of professional circles. But when I read the description of this place, this valley, this river, this crossing that needed a bridge, something in me answered that had been silent for three years. I cannot explain it with any precision. It was not a voice, and it wasn't a feeling. It was more like a door opening in a room I had boarded shut, and the light that came through it was so clear and so certain that ignoring it simply wasn't an option."

He picked up a cottonwood twig from the ground beside the step and turned it in his fingers. "I prayed about it for two weeks. I read scripture. I asked God to show me whether this was His leading or my own restlessness dressed up as calling. And every morning for those two weeks, the answer was the same. Go. Build the bridge. Not because the bridge will redeem what happened in Wyoming, but because hiding from the work God made me to do is its own kind of faithlessness, and He didn't preserve me through that bridge collapse to spend the rest of my days building culverts in Denver."

"So you came."

"I did. With my survey case and my notebooks and three years of dread and a faith that was bruised but not broken. I stood on the bank of this river, and I felt in my bones that I was where I was meant to be. I didn't understand why. I didn't understand what God had prepared for me here beyond the bridge." He set the twig down on the step between them. "I am beginning to understand now."

Belle looked at the river in the distance. The current ran smooth and even in the main channel, the surface broken only where submerged stones created small riffles that caught the light and released it. She had lived beside this river her entire life. She had read its moods, fought its strength, lost her father to its current, and built her livelihood on a strip of water where a cable could hold a platform against its pull. The man beside her had lost his brother to a different river, in a different territory, under the span of a bridge he had built with his own calculations, and the two of them were sitting on ground that belonged to both their griefs and to neither.

"When you spoke at our table about your family," Belle said, "you told us about your three sisters. You didn't mention James. I knew there was someone you hadn't named. The way you spoke about your family had a shape to it, and there was a space in that shape where someone was missing. I didn't know what had happened, but I felt the absence."

"I haven't spoken his name aloud to anyone outside my family since the funeral," Caleb said.

Belle turned toward him. "Thank you for trusting me with him."

The words were plain and simple, but she meant them to be. A woman who had just told this man about her father's drowning, her mother's death, and the years she spent holding her family together was not going to dress her gratitude in lace. She was going to say what she meant and let it land.

"What happened in Wyoming was not your failing alone," she said. "The foreman lied. The supplier cheated. The investors pushed. You were one man in a line of men who each made a choice, and the choices compounded until they became a catastrophe. I know this because I have spent five years blaming myself for my father's death—for running the ferry so well that he had permission to stop trying, for not being able to reach him when he fell, for every crossing I made alone that told him he wasn't needed. And I have learned, slowly and against every part of my nature, that carrying blame for what I could not have prevented is not faithfulness. It is pride. It is the belief that if I had been better or stronger or faster, I could have changed what God allowed. And that belief is a wall between me and the Lord, and I have been dismantling it stone by stone for some time now."

Caleb's hand on his knee opened slightly, the fingers spreading and then settling again. She saw the movement and understood it the way she understood a shift in current: something had released in him, a fraction of the grip easing.

"I have a favorite verse from the Bible," Belle said, "and I carry it with me through every crossing I've made since my father died. The Twenty-third Psalm. 'Yea, though I walk through the valley of the shadow of death, I will fear no evil: for thou art with me; thy rod and thy staff they comfort me.' I used to think that verse was about the dying. About walking toward the end and not being afraid. But I have come to believe it is about the living. About walking through the valley that comes after the death, the shadow that falls over everything when the person you love is gone, and trusting that God is walking through it with you even when you cannot see Him and even when the shadow is so deep you forget there was ever light."

"I believe God led us both to this valley," Belle said. "You from Denver and I from my own hiding, which looked like staying but was just as much a retreat as yours. I believe He put us on the same ground beside the same river for a reason that has nothing to do with bridges or ferries and everything to do with what He is building in us that we cannot build in ourselves."

"I believe that too," Caleb said. "With everything in me."

They sat beside each other on the granite step, and the morning moved around them in the small, unhurried progressions of spring: a bird landing in the cottonwoods and launching again, the shadow of a cloud crossing the clearing and passing, and the hired horse pulling at the grass near the wagon with the steady, rhythmic sound of teeth tearing stems.

After a time, Belle stood up from the step. "Come. I want to show you something."

She led him past the cabin to where the clearing sloped down toward the river, and from there the full sweep of the Yellowstone was visible below the bluffs, running south through the valley in a long silver curve that bent toward the mountains.

"My grandmother loved this spot because of the view," Belle said. "My mama told me that. She said her mother would stand right here in the evenings and look at the mountains and the river and say that a woman who could see this far had no business living small."

"She was right."

"She was." Belle looked at the mountains and then at the man standing beside her, and the distance between the two things—the vast, impersonal beauty of the range and the specific, present warmth of Caleb Sterling standing three feet from her on her family's ground—was a distance she no longer needed to maintain.

They walked back through the clearing. Caleb stopped near the chimney and ran his hand along the stones where they rose from the cabin's foundation, his fingers tracing the mortar joints.

"These stones are fitted without a gap," he said. "The mortar has held for decades. Whoever built this chimney understood that stonework is the last thing standing when everything else gives way."

"My grandfather built it the first summer. My mama said he spent more time on the chimney than on the rest of the cabin combined, because a house was only as sound as the thing that kept it warm."

"He was right about that, too."

The morning had moved toward midday. The sun was high above the cottonwoods; the shadows pulling back toward the bases of the trees; the air carrying the warmth of a spring day that had committed fully to the season. Belle looked at the clearing one more time, the cabin with its sagging roof and its straight chimney, the apple trees with their tight buds and their patient, gnarled branches, the well with its perfect coping stones, and the river running below it all.

"We should head back," she said.

They walked to the wagon. Caleb moved to Belle's side and offered his hand to help her up.

She looked at his hand. She looked at her own. Her fingers bore the marks of the life she had lived for years—the calluses, the scars, the rope burns that healed and returned and healed again in the cycle that was as much a part of her as her name. She had hidden these hands beneath her shawl on the porch because they were not the hands a woman showed a man in the soft part of an evening. She had held them up in front of Winnie like evidence of a life that left no room for tenderness. She had folded them in her lap and asked God, in the silence of prayer, to show her who she was when she was not holding a rope.

She placed her hand in his and stepped up onto the footrest and settled onto the bench seat.

Caleb walked around to his side and climbed up beside her. He released the brake and gathered the reins, and the hired horse lifted its head from the grass and turned toward the track through the cottonwoods.

Belle reached across the space between them and opened her hand, palm up, on the bench seat.

Caleb looked at her hand. He set the reins in his left hand, and with his right he traced a single, slow line along her palm with the tip of his finger, following the ridge of a callus from the base of her fingers to the heel of her hand. The touch was deliberate and light, like a man reading something written in a language he was learning. Then his hand closed around hers, and the fit of it was warm and certain and unhurried, and he held her hand as the wagon moved through the cottonwoods and out onto the road where the valley opened ahead of them and the town waited beyond the next rise.

Chapter 18

Amos Pemberton was telling a story about a freight wagon that had lost a wheel on the road from Livingston, and the whole table was listening because Amos told stories the way he kept his shelves stocked, with an inventory of details arranged for maximum effect and a punchline he'd been saving since the second sentence. Caleb sat beside Belle at the center of the long table with a plate of roast beef and boiled potatoes in front of him and the warm, overlapping hum of a Providence Ridge Sunday dinner filling the surrounding room. The table was full. Mrs. Hanscombe had set it for the crowd that came when Reverend Hale's circuit brought him through town, and the crowd had come: the Pembertons, the Hales, each of the current boarders, several ranchers Caleb recognized from committee attendance, and Winnie, Luke, and Liam across from them.

Belle sat close enough by his side that he could feel the warmth of her arm through the fabric of his jacket. She was passing a bread plate to Liam and laughing at something Amos said about the freight driver's mule.

The laugh was what caught him. He had heard Belle speak with authority at the committee table, with tenderness on the porch of her homestead, and with the stripped honesty of a woman laying down every defense she owned on a stone step beside a ruined cabin. He had not heard her laugh. The sound of it was lower than he would have expected, unguarded, brief, and it changed the architecture of her face in a way that made the woman beside him look like someone he was meeting for the first time. As she laughed, Liam grinned at her from across the table, and the exchange between the siblings carried the ease of people who had earned their joy through years of shared difficulty.

Across the table, Luke Dixon sat beside Winnie with Liam on Winnie's other side. Reverend Hale had drawn Luke into a conversation about the Dixon ranch, and Luke was answering with the steady ease of a man speaking about work he knew from the ground up.

"We lost one calf in the late cold snap three weeks ago," Luke said. "The dam was a first-timer, and she calved in the open before we could get her into the shed. The rest came through strongly. My father says it's the best spring crop we've had in three years."

"Your father has a good eye for stock," Reverend Hale said.

"He selects for hardiness over everything else. Says a pretty cow that can't survive February isn't a cow worth owning."

Liam leaned forward. "That's the approach I'd take. Start with hardy stock and build from there."

"It's the only approach that works in this country," Luke said. He glanced at Winnie as he spoke, a brief look that carried no particular content except the desire to include her in what he was saying, and Winnie met it with a warmth that made the young man's ears color slightly above his collar.

The ranching talk folded into a wider conversation about spring conditions, Reverend Hale asking after other families along his circuit, Margaret contributing a remark about the Livingston road that prompted Amos to shake his head and mutter about freight delays. The table's threads crossed and separated the way they did at any communal meal, voices rising and falling in the easy rhythm of people who shared a valley and a Sunday and saw no reason to rush either one.

Liam leaned back in his chair with the loose-limbed ease of a young man. "How long before the bridge foundations go in?" he asked Caleb.

"Materials start arriving from Livingston tomorrow," Caleb said. "Owen's crew begins cutting the timber in the morning. Once the footings are set, the truss work moves fast."

"And once the footings are set, how long to completion?"

"It should be about twelve weeks from the first footing to the last plank. Longer if the river runs higher than predicted during construction."

Liam nodded.

Mrs. Hanscombe came through the kitchen doorway with a fresh pot of coffee. She moved along the table, filling cups with the efficient economy of a woman who had fed this town for years and saw the refilling of coffee as a civic duty rather than a courtesy. She set the pot on the table when she was finished and returned to the kitchen without comment.

The meal's conversation shifted and branched the way conversations shift at a full table, threads picked up and set down as different voices carried them. Margaret Pemberton told Winnie about Mrs. Dixon's planting schedule, and Winnie leaned forward with the particular attention she gave to anything involving soil and growing seasons. Reverend Hale spoke with a rancher about the road conditions further beyond town. Prudence, the girl who had helped serve the meal, sat nearby picking at her plate with the distracted appetite of someone whose attention kept drifting toward the conversation rather than the food.

At the table's far end, Horace occupied his accustomed seat. He held his coffee cup and wore the expression Caleb had catalogued across days of shared meals: pleasant, contained, a man whose attention moved across a room in the smooth sweep of someone who preferred to observe before he spoke. His gaze passed over Belle and Caleb, but the passage lingered a fraction longer than it needed to. He caught Caleb's eye and offered a nod. Caleb returned it.

Amos set his fork down and leaned back in his chair. "I've been hearing things. Mining interests in land just north of here. Silver prospects, possibly more. I don't have specifics, but enough men have passed through the mercantile with bits of gossip that I know someone with capital is paying attention to what's under this ground in our town."

"The timber company is growing," Amos continued. "Three new families have taken up homesteads recently. I've heard land is being bought up left and right. The bridge, once it opens, changes everything. Providence Ridge is on the edge of becoming something more than what it's been." He tapped the table once with his forefinger. "Which is why I'm expanding the mercantile. Not next year. This year. A second room, double the floor space, wider stock. Hardware, household goods, and a proper fabric section."

"It's about time," Margaret said.

"It is Margaret, I believe that with everything in me. An expansion like that means I need help," Amos said. "Not a clerk who can count change. I need someone who understands inventory, knows the people in this valley, can manage suppliers, and keeps accounts." He looked at Belle. The look was direct, the look of a businessman who had weighed his options and arrived at a conclusion. "I can think of no one in Providence Ridge more capable than you, Belle. You're a hard worker, and you do what needs to be done to get the job done. You've handled freight, negotiated with teamsters, and managed accounts. Those are the skills I need."

Belle set her cup down. Through Caleb's peripheral vision, he watched composure settle into her posture, the particular stillness of a woman receiving something significant and giving it the weight it deserved before she responded.

"That's a generous offer, Amos," Belle said. "I'll think on it."

"Take whatever time you need."

The meal continued in its natural course: the food eaten, the coffee cooling, and the afternoon pressing against the windows. Caleb spoke with Luke about the depth of bridge footings and with Reverend Hale about the passages in the Bible that he spoke on this morning. He listened to Liam and Luke compare hay yields with the practical intensity of two young men who approached the same subject from different ground but with the same appetite for the work. He ate, and he talked, and he enjoyed the company and warmth of those present around him.

Belle turned to Winnie and said something about the balsam-root blooming on the south slopes, and Winnie responded with a remark that made Belle's mouth curve into a half-smile, and the half-smile became the beginning of another laugh, quieter than the first, and Caleb sat beside her and let the sound settle into him.

The meal wound down eventually, plates emptied, and conversations found their natural endings. Pritchard rose from his chair and walked the length of the table to where Caleb sat, his stride unhurried, his hands at his sides.

"Mr. Sterling, might I have a word when you're free?" Pritchard said. "Bridge and consortium business. A few items I'd prefer to settle before the workweek."

"Certainly. I'll need to take Belle home first, and then I'm at your disposal."

Belle turned from her conversation with Winnie. "That's not necessary, Caleb. I'll ride home with Liam and Winnie. You tend to your business."

He looked at her, and she met his gaze with the steady, practical expression of a woman making certain that no one rearranged their obligations on her account.

"If you're certain," he said.

"I'm certain."

Pritchard nodded. "I'll wait. No rush." He turned and walked back toward his end of the table.

Chairs scraped back. Mrs. Hanscombe began clearing plates with Prudence at her elbow. The Sunday table dissolved into the ordinary motions of an afternoon reasserting itself, jackets and shawls retrieved from pegs, farewells exchanged, the particular loosening of a community that had gathered for fellowship and lunch and was now returning to its separate lives.

Caleb and Belle stepped onto the boardinghouse porch. Liam brought the Callahan wagon around from the side of the building. Winnie and Luke stood at the far end of the porch, conducting their farewell. Luke held Winnie's hand for a moment. Winnie smiled at him, and Luke's composure faltered in a way that made Caleb like the young man more than he already did.

Belle stood beside him at the porch rail.

"The apple trees at your grandmother's cabin," Caleb said. "You said the buds were weeks from opening."

Belle looked at him.

"I'd like to ride back out and see their blooms when that happens," he said.

"I'd like that," Belle said.

She stepped off the porch and crossed to the wagon. Liam offered his hand to help her up, and she climbed onto the bench seat. Winnie arrived from the far end of the porch, and Liam helped her up beside Belle.

The wagon pulled forward. Belle turned on the seat and looked back at Caleb standing on the porch. Her face carried a smile that was unguarded and full, the second one he had seen from her today, and he understood that both of them had been gifts she had chosen to give rather than expressions she had failed to contain.

He watched the wagon for a moment, then he turned from the rail and walked back through the boardinghouse door.

Pritchard stood just inside the entrance, near the window that looked out onto the porch. He held his coffee cup in one hand.

"Miss Callahan looked lovely today," Pritchard said. "The Callahans are a fine family. Providence Ridge is fortunate to have them."

Chapter 19

Mrs. Hanscombe wiped down the long table in the dining room with a cloth, her movements unhurried. Prudence, her part-time worker, followed behind with a second cloth, wiping each chair back and seat.

Horace watched Mrs. Hanscombe's progress along the table with an expression of mild, general pleasantness. When Mrs. Hanscombe moved into the kitchen and Prudence trailed after her carrying a stack of plates, Horace turned to Caleb.

"It occurs to me that a dining room with its walls still holding the conversations of a blessed Sunday is perhaps not the ideal setting for the matters I'd like to discuss," Horace said. "Would you care to take a walk? The afternoon is splendid, and I find that certain conversations benefit from open air."

"I could use the walk," Caleb replied.

They stepped onto the boardinghouse porch. The afternoon had settled over Providence Ridge with the quiet that belonged to

Sundays in small towns. A dog lay in the road near the mercantile porch, its chin on its paws.

Horace crossed the street, stepped up onto the boardwalk, and turned toward the livery end of town, Caleb beside him.

"I appreciate you making the time to speak with me today," Horace said. "I know you've had a full day."

"Sundays I typically keep for the Lord's day and refrain from work, but I sensed your desire to speak business on a day of rest was important to you."

"Yes... yes, and I thank you for taking the time to speak with me," Horace smiled. "Now then. I've been wanting to discuss the bridge timeline and generally make sure I'm up-to-date on where everything stands."

"The first shipment of materials arrives from Livingston tomorrow," Caleb said. "Iron hardware, bolts, bearing plates, and the anchor chain for the cofferdam work. Owen's crew begins milling the bridge timber in the morning. The Douglas fir we need for the primary truss members has been selected and marked, and Owen tells me the logs are already yarded and ready for the saw."

"Good. And the footing work?"

"The footings are the critical part. Before any timber goes up, I need dry working space at the bottom of the riverbed to lay the pier stones. That means building cofferdams, which means driving pilings into the river channel in a ring around each pier location, sealing the gaps between them, and pumping the water out by hand. On the south bank, bedrock sits fourteen feet below the surface. On the north bank, eighteen. The south pier goes in first because the shallower bedrock makes the cofferdam work faster and gives the crew experience before they tackle the deeper north side."

"How long for the cofferdams?"

"Three to four weeks for both, depending on how quickly the crew I have coming in from Livingston can drive the pilings and whether the river cooperates. The Yellowstone is still rising with snowmelt, and every foot of additional water makes the cofferdam work harder. Once the cofferdams are pumped dry, the masons lay the footing stone directly onto bedrock. After the footings cure, the timber truss work begins, and that moves considerably faster. If the weather holds and the materials arrive on schedule, it will take twelve weeks from the first piling to the last plank."

They reached the end of the boardwalk, where the planking gave way to packed earth near the land office. The land office was dark; its single window reflected the afternoon light. Beyond it, the road continued toward the livery and the blacksmith shop at the edge of town. The livery corral held a half-dozen horses standing in the shade of the hay shed, their tails switching at flies.

Horace walked with his hands clasped behind his back, his stride measured and comfortable. "The consortium is pleased with the pace of things. I want you to know that. The reports I've sent to the board have reflected well on your work, and the committee's confidence in the project has been growing steadily. Amos in particular has been vocal about the bridge's potential to transform commerce in the valley."

"Amos understands what a permanent crossing means for this town and his store."

"He does." Horace paused at the edge of the livery yard, turning to look back along the road toward the center of town. "There is another matter I've been considering. Not urgently, but with enough thought that I believe it warrants your professional opinion."

Caleb waited.

"Have you had occasion to examine the river north of the current survey site? Upstream, where the Yellowstone narrows before the bend?"

"I walked the banks two miles in each direction during my initial survey. The narrows upstream were noted in my field book, but the consortium's geological report designated the current site, and my measurements confirmed it as sound."

"I don't dispute that. Your work has been thorough, and the current site is viable. What I'm raising is whether it's the only viable site, or whether there might be a location that offers certain advantages the current position does not."

They began walking back toward the center of town. The road was empty in both directions. A pair of swallows cut across the space in fast, looping arcs, their shadows flickering across the packed earth.

"What advantages are you referring to?" Caleb asked.

"The narrows upstream offer a shorter span. I've ridden up there myself several times in recent weeks, studying the terrain, and what I've observed is a crossing point where the river is perhaps several feet narrower than at the current site. A shorter span means less timber, fewer structural demands on the truss, and potentially shallower bedrock, though I'd defer to your instruments on that. There's also the matter of the road approach. A bridge at the northern site would connect to open land on the far side of town, land that's flat and suitable for a freight road. That road would serve the ranches and homesteads on the north side without routing heavy traffic directly through the center of Providence Ridge."

Caleb listened with the particular attention he gave to any conversation that involved engineering. He registered the technical claims, setting each one alongside what he knew from his own survey data, and he registered the structure of what Horace had said, which was careful and sequential, each point building toward a conclusion he had not yet stated.

"You're suggesting the town might benefit from keeping heavy freight traffic off the main road," Caleb said.

"I'm recommending it's worth considering. Providence Ridge is growing. Amos announced his expansion today. The timber company is adding crews. New families are moving in. A bridge at the current site routes every wagon, every freight team, and every head of livestock through the center of a town that wasn't built for that volume. In two years, perhaps three, the road through town will need constant maintenance. The ruts will deepen. The boardwalks will take damage from the traffic. The mercantile porch will be covered in dust from the freight wagons. A northern crossing avoids that problem entirely by directing traffic around town rather than through it."

They passed the saloon, its door closed, its windows dark. The afternoon quiet pressed against the buildings on both sides of the road, and their boot heels on the boardwalk carried in the stillness with a regularity that sounded almost like a cadence being kept.

"The land north of town," Caleb said. "You mentioned it would be suitable for a freight road. What is up there now?"

"Open range, mostly. A few homesteads scattered around. Some of it is being looked at by parties with an interest in the mineral potential of the area. Amos mentioned it at dinner: the talk about mining prospects north of here. Where there's mineral interest, there's freight, and where there's freight, there's a need for reliable road access. A bridge that opens the north side of the valley positions Providence Ridge as the hub for that development rather than a bottleneck standing in its way."

Caleb recalled Amos's words at the table. Mining interests in land just north of here. Someone with capital paying attention to what was under the ground.

"There's another consideration," Horace said. "Owen Gallagher."

"What about Owen?"

"His ranch sits right on the narrows I'm describing. The Gallagher property runs along the river. I rode out there last week to get a closer look at the terrain, and I couldn't help but notice the condition of the place." Horace's voice shifted. "Owen is struggling, Caleb. I don't know if you're aware of the extent of it."

"I am not aware. I hardly know Owen at all."

"His livestock is gone. He lost most of it in the hard winter two years ago, and what survived he sold off to cover debts. His ranch hasn't run a productive herd in over a year. That's the reason he took the foreman position at the mill. Not because he wanted to leave ranching, but because the ranch couldn't sustain him any longer. He has seven young children and a wife to care for. He's carrying debt on the property, and the income from the mill is barely enough to provide for his family." Horace shook his head once. "A good man in a hard position. I've seen it before in other territories. A rancher puts everything he has into his land, and then the weather or the market takes it from him, and he's left holding ground he can't afford to keep and can't afford to sell because the value has dropped with the operation."

"A bridge at the northern site would increase the value of the surrounding land considerably," Horace continued. "Owen's property included. A permanent crossing with a freight road connecting to it turns that ranch from a liability into an asset. The land alone would be worth more than Owen's current debt." He paused. "I mention it because I believe we have an obligation to consider the broader impact of where we place this bridge. It's not merely an engineering decision. It's a decision that affects families."

"You've given this considerable thought," Caleb said.

"I have. I believe in being thorough, same as you."

"I appreciate the information about Owen," Caleb said. "I wasn't aware of his situation, and it gives me a clearer picture of the committee dynamics."

"I thought it might."

"As for the northern site, I'd need to think on this. Possibly send word to the board at the consortium office and see what they recommend, considering the information you just supplied. A shorter span is an advantage on paper, but it means nothing if the bedrock is deeper, or the bank composition won't hold a footing, or the flood profile at the narrows is worse than at the current location. Narrows concentrate current velocity. A bridge at a narrow point takes more lateral force per square foot on its piers during high water than a bridge at a wider crossing."

"Of course. I wouldn't expect you to evaluate the site without proper data, but you have my word; the consortium office is well aware of what is going on here."

"I see... I'd also need flood history for that specific stretch. The data Belle Callahan provided covers the current crossing point, but the narrows you're suggesting may have their own flood characteristics. Ice dams behave differently where the channel constricts."

"All reasonable requirements."

"There's something else to consider," Caleb said. "A location change isn't a simple matter of surveying a new site. The consortium approved the current location based on the geological report and my field confirmation. Moving the bridge requires a formal request to the committee, a written justification supported by survey data showing that the alternate site is superior to the approved one, and a revised cost estimate. The approval process alone would delay the timeline by four to six weeks, longer if the town committee requires additional review. That's four to six weeks of lost construction time during the best building season this valley offers."

"We do not need to consider this town committee at the moment. The consortium will do what is best for the town; it has the final word. The town's committee is just local representation... in the grander scheme of things... we both know that you and I and the consortium itself make the final decisions."

They were passing the mercantile again, retracing their path along the boardwalk. The dog that had been lying in the road was gone.

"Caleb, I want to be direct with you. The consortium values engineers who demonstrate flexibility. A man who can evaluate multiple options and recommend the strongest one, even if it differs from the initial proposal—that man demonstrates the kind of judgment the board rewards. They also value men who think forward, who see the larger picture. A consulting fee for the survey itself at this northern site is already guaranteed above what you are being paid for the contract you've signed. The consortium has provisions for this kind of arrangement."

"What kind of provision?" he asked.

"The details would be settled between you and the board. I don't set the figures. But the additional labor of surveying a second site and presenting the findings accurately goes beyond your current contract, and the consortium recognizes that. I'd see to it that the arrangement would be more payment than standard."

Horace's words were polished. The structure of them clean, every phrase load-bearing, every word positioned to support the conclusion without ever stating it plainly. A consulting fee for additional survey work. The consortium values flexibility. The meaning beneath the language stood as clear to Caleb as a stress fracture in a footing stone, visible only if you knew what to look for, invisible to anyone examining the surface.

He had heard language like this before. Not these specific words, not this specific offer, but the architecture of it, the way a proposition could be framed so that every individual sentence was reasonable while the sum of them asked a man to do something that reason alone would not justify.

"I'll think further on this," Caleb said. "If the consortium can provide the geological reports for that stretch of the river, I'll compare them against my existing data for the current location. If the reports aren't available, I'll need to conduct the survey work myself, which will take a minimum of two weeks with proper instrumentation."

"I believe reports exist. I'll make inquiries."

They had reached the far end of town again, the livery and blacksmith at the western edge where the road came in from Paradise Valley. The corral horses had shifted positions since they'd passed the first time, rearranging themselves in the shade. Caleb stopped walking. Horace stopped beside him.

"I should be clear about a few things," Caleb said. "I won't recommend a complete site change unless the engineering supports it. If the northern location proves inferior to the current one in bedrock depth, bank stability, flood profile, or road grade, the bridge stays where I put it. No consulting fee changes that. Furthermore, I will not delay the work on the current bridge site; the construction will continue on schedule. I see no reason to delay it simply because of a suggestion for a site change. If anything, a second bridge could actually be recommended."

"I understand." Horace's expression carried no trace of anything apart from agreement. "But I do insist that you think on this matter with seriousness."

They turned and walked back toward the boardinghouse.

"You know," Horace continued, "the committee in this town trusts and respects you. Miss Callahan and her family have clearly taken to you, and that is no small thing in a place where outsiders are measured carefully before they're welcomed."

Caleb said nothing.

"It speaks to your character. A man's reputation is built on the work he does, but it's also built on the trust people place in him, and you've earned a great deal of trust in a short time. The consortium recognizes that. I recognize it. But... I understand you've had a difficult professional chapter in your past," Horace said.

The words landed in Caleb's body before they reached his mind. His hands went still in his pockets. His breathing stopped for the space of one beat, the air held in his lungs as though his chest had forgotten the mechanism of release.

"I'm aware of the situation in Wyoming," Horace continued. "I mention it not to dwell on the past, but because I believe it's relevant to the present. A successful project here in Providence Ridge, at whichever site proves most sound, would go a long way toward putting that chapter behind you. The board sees this project as an opportunity for you, Caleb. An opportunity to demonstrate what you're capable of when the circumstances are right and the support is there. To reassure yourself, if nothing else, that you have done your job and done it well."

Horace stopped and offered Caleb a smile. "I'll leave you to your evening. Thank you for the walk. It's been productive, I think."

He crossed the porch and entered the boardinghouse. Caleb was standing alone on the boardwalk with the late afternoon pressing against his face and the town of Providence Ridge quiet around him in every direction.

Wyoming.

Horace had dug into his past. That was the fact of it, stripped of every courtesy and every layer of professional language the man had wrapped around it. Horace had gone looking for information about Caleb that had nothing to do with bridge specifications or survey data, or construction timelines. He had found it. He had held it through the walk, through the conversation about materials and cofferdams and Owen Gallagher's failing ranch, through the mention of consulting fees and the consortium's appreciation for flexibility, and he had played it at the end the way a man lays down his final card after the hand has already been won or lost.

The question was why. The question was what purpose the knowledge served in a conversation about an alternate bridge site. Horace's proposal carried a surface logic that Caleb could not dismiss outright: a shorter span, a freight road that bypassed the town center, and possibly lower material costs. Each element, taken alone, was the kind of consideration a reasonable man might raise about a significant infrastructure project. Taken together, they formed a structure whose foundation Caleb couldn't yet see completely.

And threaded through all of it, Wyoming. Threaded through it as encouragement, as reassurance, as the gentle reminder that the consortium knew what he carried and had the power to make the carrying easier or harder, depending on the choices he made in the weeks ahead.

Caleb turned from the boardinghouse and looked down the road toward the river. He ran the conversation through his mind from its first sentence to its last, testing each claim the way he tested a beam, applying pressure at the joints to see where the structure held and where it gave. The alternate site might be sound. The shorter span might offer advantages. Owen's situation might genuinely benefit from a bridge at his doorstep. None of those possibilities required Horace to know about Wyoming, and none of them explained why a consortium representative had taken it upon himself to ride out to the narrows on his own multiple times, study the terrain, assess Owen's financial condition, and build an argument for relocating a bridge that had already been approved on the strength of data Horace himself had praised as thorough.

Something was not right. The pieces fit together too neatly in some places and not at all in others. Caleb could feel it in the tension across his shoulders, in the pressure of his fingers against the wool lining of his pockets, and in the shallowness of his breathing that had not fully returned to its normal depth since Horace spoke the word Wyoming.

Caleb walked toward the river. He needed the open air and the movement of his legs before he could trust himself to sit still with what information he had been given and the questions that were swimming around in his mind as he tried to make sense of what exactly Horace was getting at.

Chapter 20

The heavy freight wagon carried supplies bound for a homesteader, and Belle felt every pound of it in the guide rope. The Yellowstone had entered its May temperament overnight, the current pressing against the scow's upstream rail with a broadside insistence that turned each correction into a negotiation between her arms and the river's opinion of where the platform ought to go. She leaned into the rope and hauled the angle back two degrees, her boot braced against the deck cleat, the hemp biting through her gloves where the weave had thinned across the palms.

Liam held the downstream rail, one hand on the freight lashing, his weight shifted to counterbalance the load as the platform tracked through the midstream channel. The wagon driver sat on his bench with both hands locked on the brake lever, his horses stamping against the deck planking every time the scow tilted a half-degree beyond their tolerance.

The rope hummed in Belle's grip. Not the steady, manageable vibration of an April crossing but a faster frequency, a sound that told her the cable above was absorbing force it hadn't absorbed just days ago. She adjusted her stance and pulled, and the scow answered, tracking the last forty feet to the north bank landing.

Liam caught the mooring line and made it fast. The driver released his brake, spoke to his horses, and the wagon rolled off the ramp with a clatter of iron rims on timber that echoed off the cutbank. Belle secured the guide rope and stretched her hands, pressing the knuckles of her right hand into her left palm to work loose the cramp that had settled between the tendons during the crossing.

She turned on the platform and looked upstream.

The bridge site had changed. Just last week it had been cleared ground and survey stakes and the organized stillness of a project waiting to begin. Today it was men and supplies and the ring of mauls driving pilings into the riverbank. A crew of eight worked under the direction of a man she could identify at two hundred yards by the way he stood. Caleb moved among the crew with authority. A small pile of stacked lumber lined the bank above the high-water mark. Iron hardware and assorted supplies lay arranged on a canvas tarp.

The footing excavation had begun. She could see the raw earth where the topsoil had been stripped back to expose the gravel and clay beneath, the first step in the descent toward bedrock fourteen feet below. Two men worked in the shallow pit with shovels while a third hauled buckets of loose soil up a ramp of planks laid over the excavation's lip. The cofferdam pilings that would eventually ring the pier location stood in a stack nearby, their ends sharpened to points.

The thing she had feared for months was becoming real. Timber and iron and the labor of men turning a proposal into a structure that would stand on the bank of her river long after the last ferry crossing had been run and forgotten. She had carried the knowledge of this since the first committee meeting, had argued against it, and then accepted it. Acceptance had come in stages, each one costing less than the one before, and what she felt now as she looked upstream at the excavation and the crew and the stacked materials was not sharp, panicked resistance. It was something quieter. A tenderness toward her own displacement, the way a woman might feel watching a child take its first steps—pride in the forward motion married to the private grief of knowing the child would never again need to be carried.

She walked to the edge of the platform and sat on the deck with her boots hanging over the water. Liam was coiling the mooring line into a neat figure eight on the deck beside the ramp, his movements automatic.

"Crossing traffic's been light this morning," he said, tucking the coil's tail through the final loop.

"It'll pick up. Thursday traffic runs heavier in the afternoon. The freight from Livingston reaches the north-bank road by midday, and the teamsters cross right before supper."

"I know. I was just making conversation."

Belle looked at her brother. He stood beside her with his forearms resting on the rail, his sleeves rolled to the elbows, the muscles in his arms visible in a way that reminded her, with a small jolt of recognition, that he was no longer the slight boy who had taken up the mooring line because there was no one else to take it. He was nineteen and broad across the shoulders and capable, and the realization landed not as a surprise but as a confirmation of something she had been watching happen without marking the day it became true.

"I'm sorry. I'm poor company this morning."

"You're fine company. You're just quiet." Liam tilted his head toward the bridge site. "You've been quiet since he visited this morning before he began working."

"I know."

Caleb had come to the ferry landing at eight, as he had come every morning this week. He had stood at the edge of the gravel bar while she finished her cable inspection, and they had talked for ten minutes about the supply delivery that had arrived from Livingston on Monday and the cofferdam schedule and various other things.

She had never been courted before, and now, four days into the quiet rhythm Caleb had established between them—the morning visits, the brief conversation, and the way he lingered a few seconds longer each morning before walking upstream to the bridge site—she understood something about courtship that no one had told her and that she could not have learned from watching other women receive it. The pleasure of it was not in the grand gestures. It was in the accumulation. It was in the knowledge that a man had restructured the first part of his working day around the simple act of seeing her, and that the restructuring was deliberate, chosen, and repeated. She found herself watching for him to arrive each morning.

Liam pushed off the rail and crossed the deck to check the upstream cable where it ran through the pulley housing. Belle stayed where she was, her boots above the water, the current running beneath her with the steady, unhurried power of a river that had somewhere to go and all the time it needed to get there. She looked upstream at Caleb again, a small permission she granted herself more freely now than she had a week ago. He was crouched beside the excavation, pointing at something in the pit wall, one of the crew leaning in to see what he indicated.

She was still watching when she heard the sound of a wagon and turned to see Winnie approaching.

She pulled the mare to a halt, set the brake, and climbed down from the bench seat. Belle watched her cross the gravel bar to the scow's ramp with a stride that carried purpose.

"Liam," Belle called as she stood up.

He came back from the pulley housing and stood beside her. Winnie stepped onto the platform, and her expression held the particular quality of a woman who was turning something over in her mind.

"I left the mercantile early; it's been a slow day, and Amos told me to go on home," Winnie said.

"So, what brings you here?" Belle asked.

"Owen Gallagher came into the store today to pick up hardware for the mill—bolts and chain, and other items Amos had ordered from Livingston. They were at the counter settling the bill, and I was two aisles over working the dry goods. They didn't know I could hear them, or if they did, they didn't consider that I'd think much of what they were saying."

"Owen told Amos that the consortium is considering a change to the bridge location," Winnie continued. "His words when he spoke were careful... as if he'd rehearsed them, and he seemed nervous. He talked about a narrower crossing north of this bridge site. He said there was talk of a freight road that could be built from this other bridge location that would open the upper valley to development, and that the consortium saw advantages in the alternate location."

"Owen Gallagher said this? Are you certain it was him?" Belle asked.

"Yes, I'm certain. I peeked around the corner of the aisle because I couldn't believe what I was hearing."

"What did Amos say?" Liam asked.

"Amos stopped writing. He set the pen down on the ledger and looked at Owen, and his look alone would have told you everything you needed to know about what Amos thought of what he'd just heard. He told Owen that the bridge was already under construction. He said the town committee has received no formal proposal for any location change, and that bridge locations do not move without just cause. He told Owen that he was speaking rubbish and asked where he'd heard this. Owen said he'd heard it from someone at the mill, but he didn't name who."

"Well, this sounds like someone just invented a story to stir up trouble and start gossip," Belle said.

"I agree. Amos told Owen that if the consortium had plans to change the bridge site, the committee would hear about it through proper channels, not through secondhand talk at a hardware counter. He was upset, Belle. Not shouting, but his voice carried an edge of anger to it. Owen didn't say another word... he just took his purchases and left."

Liam leaned against the deck railing and crossed his arms. "Owen works at the mill. He answers to Horace and Caleb for the lumber contract for the bridge. If Horace told him to plant this idea with Amos to stir up trouble, Owen would do it because Owen can't afford to refuse."

"Owen didn't sound like a man sharing his own opinion. He sounded like a man delivering a message he'd memorized," Winnie said.

Belle looked past her sister toward the bridge site upstream. The crew was still working. Caleb was walking the line of cofferdam pilings with one of the men, gesturing toward the river. The maul strikes carried across the distance, a dull, rhythmic percussion that marked the pace of the work.

"Owen's ranch is up where the river narrows," Belle said.

"I don't know what's going on or why Owen felt the need to say what he did. I thought you should know. Both of you," Winnie said.

"You were right to come tell us," Liam said.

Winnie nodded. "I should get home and tend to things that need doing now that I have a couple of extra hours in my day."

Belle walked with her sister off the scow and across the gravel bar to the wagon. Winnie climbed onto the bench seat and gathered the reins. The mare lifted her head from the grass she'd been cropping and stood ready.

"Winnie."

Her sister looked down at her.

"Thank you and don't fret about what you heard. I'm sure it was simply gossip, and I'm betting Owen just wanted to ruffle a few feathers for reasons we simply don't know."

Winnie gave her a small, firm nod and released the brake. The wagon lurched forward, and the mare turned onto the road heading back toward home.

Belle stood on the gravel bar with the May sun on her shoulders and the Yellowstone running high beside her, and she made a decision that took no more than the time required to turn her head and look at Liam on the platform.

"I need to speak with Caleb," she said. "Can you hold the landing?"

"Go."

The path between the ferry landing and the bridge site was worn now, a track beaten into the grass by the boots of the construction crew traveling between the road and the work area. She followed it past the cottonwood stand where the older trees leaned out over the water, past the point where the bank rose three feet above the river and the exposed roots of the cottonwoods hung like fingers reaching for the current below.

The bridge site opened before her as she came through the last of the trees. The excavation was deeper than it had appeared from the ferry platform. Two men stood waist-deep in the pit, their shovels working the clay layer.

Caleb was standing at the edge of the pit with his drawings unrolled across a plank table set on sawhorses. He looked up when she approached, and the expression on his face when he saw her was that of simple joy.

"Belle," he said.

"I need to talk to you... do you have a minute?"

He said something to the nearest crewman—words she didn't catch—and walked to meet her at the edge of the site where the worked ground gave way to the undisturbed grass of the bank.

"Winnie was just at the ferry," Belle said. "She was working at the mercantile this morning. While she was there, Owen came in for hardware, and she overheard him tell Amos that the consortium is considering moving the bridge to a site north of here. A narrower crossing. Something about a possible freight road."

Caleb's jaw tightened. The muscles along the hinge of his jaw drew inward as if absorbing the weight of what she'd said, and his hand, which had been resting at his side, closed into a loose fist and opened again.

"Amos didn't take it well," she continued. "He told Owen the committee has heard nothing about a location change, and that bridge sites don't move without cause."

"Amos is right," Caleb said. "They don't."

"Owen didn't sound like himself. Winnie said his words were careful, as if rehearsed."

Caleb looked past her toward the river. His hand opened and closed once more at his side, and then he was still.

"You're not surprised," Belle said.

He brought his attention back to her. The gladness that had been in his face when she arrived was gone.

"No," he said. "I'm not surprised."

"So there is some truth to what Owen speaks. Should I be concerned? How long have you known?"

"There's no reason for you to be concerned right now. The bridge at this location will continue; the contract is signed, and obviously construction has begun. I've known of what you are asking about for long enough to stew on it for a few days, and still I have not come to a conclusion as to why a bridge location change is being suggested." He held her gaze. "I've kept silent because I wanted to know more about what I was possibly dealing with."

Belle studied him. She could see that he was carrying something heavy and struggling with it.

"Belle," he said. "I'd like to come to your home this evening, if you and Liam and Winnie would allow it. There are a few things I need to tell you, the three of you, and I would rather not have this conversation at the bridge site or at the ferry landing where anyone might hear. I should have come to you sooner. I can see on your face that you know something isn't right, and you deserve to know what I know."

"Come for supper," she said. "We eat at six."

"I'll be there."

Chapter 21

Belle watched Caleb turn his coffee cup a quarter rotation on the dinner table, then turn it back. He had been doing this since Winnie had poured the second round of coffee, a small, repetitive motion that his hands performed while the rest of him participated in the conversation. He laughed at Liam's account of a mule that had refused to board the ferry that afternoon and had to be blindfolded and taunted with a handful of grain before it would step onto the ramp. He complimented the chicken and dumplings Winnie had made with sincerity. He asked Winnie about the garden, whether the late frost two nights ago had touched the pea shoots. But the cup kept turning, and Belle kept watching it.

"I've been thinking about riding to Livingston," Liam said, pushing his bowl to the side and leaning back in his chair. "Not next week, but soon. I want to sit down and speak with someone about a loan."

"For the Mercy Bend parcel?" Winnie asked.

"For all of it. The land, the stock, and the fencing. Morrison Phelps won't have those heifers forever; I'm sure someone will step in and buy them. If I'm going to make an offer, I need the financing settled. I'd rather walk into that conversation with terms on paper than with my hat in my hand, hoping for the best."

Belle looked at her brother. Days ago, this announcement would have tightened every muscle in her shoulders. She would have countered with the risks, the repayment figures, or anything else that was negative. She still carried the caution that years of feeding a family on ferry fares had woven into her thinking. But the woman sitting at this table tonight was learning to set her feelings and thoughts aside and to allow her siblings room to grow and reach for the things they desired, whether it included her.

"The road was passable in early April, but the washouts up near Mill Creek were bad," Caleb said. "By now the worst of the mud should have dried. If you go on horseback instead of by wagon, you can make the trip in a day if you ride hard."

"That was my plan. Leave before dawn, ride hard, stay the night at a hotel in Livingston, and be at the bank as soon as they open. Then ride back as soon as possible."

"Amos will give you a letter of recommendation," Winnie said. "A word from a known merchant may carry some weight with a bank officer who's never met you."

"I hadn't thought of that."

"Winnie thinks of everything," Belle said.

"Somebody in this family has to," Winnie said, and everyone around the table laughed.

After the laughter subsided, Belle let the moment pass, and then she redirected the conversation. "Caleb. You mentioned at the bridge site today that you had things you wanted to tell us. Whatever it is, we'd like to hear it."

Caleb's fingers stilled on his coffee cup. He looked at Belle, then at Liam, then at Winnie, and the expression he wore was one of confusion and concern.

"Sunday afternoon, after lunch at the boardinghouse, Horace asked me to take a walk with him," Caleb said. "He suggested we leave the dining room. He said certain conversations benefited from open air, and he wanted to discuss the bridge."

"On a Sunday?" Liam said.

"I noted that as well. We walked the length of town and back twice. The bridge timeline was the opening of the conversation, but it wasn't the purpose."

Belle rested her hands on the table's edge. Winnie sat with her coffee held close, her attention fixed on Caleb.

"Horace proposed an alternative bridge site," Caleb said. "Upstream, north of the current survey location, where the Yellowstone narrows before the bend. He'd ridden out to the narrows himself several times to study the terrain. He noted that the crossing there is shorter, which means less timber and fewer structural demands. He mentioned a possible freight road that would route heavy traffic around Providence Ridge instead of through it, to spare the town from the wear of constant wagon traffic as the valley grows."

"That's considerate of him," Liam said, and the dryness in his voice was unmistakable.

"He also brought up Owen," Caleb said. "He told me Owen's ranch sits on the narrows. That Owen lost much of his livestock due to a bad winter and sold off what survived to cover debts, and took the mill foreman position because the ranch couldn't sustain him. Horace said a bridge at that location would increase the surrounding land value enough to save Owen from losing everything."

"Since when does a consortium man concern himself with one rancher's debts?" Belle asked.

"That question has been keeping me up at night." Caleb looked at his hands where they lay flat on the pine. "There's more. Horace offered me a consulting fee. He said the consortium had provisions for this kind of arrangement. He implied I'd be paid generously."

Winnie set her coffee cup down. "He offered you money to consider moving the bridge."

"He framed it as compensation for additional survey work. Every sentence he spoke was reasonable on its own. The sum of them was something else entirely."

"What did you tell him?" Liam asked.

"Basically, I told him I'd review the geological data for the northern site if it existed. I also told him I wouldn't delay construction at the current site. I gave him nothing he could hold me to and nothing he could accuse me of refusing."

"There's one more thing," Caleb continued. His hands pressed harder against the table, his fingertips whitening at the nails. "At the end of the conversation, after I'd listened to his speech and responded as little as possible, Horace mentioned what happened in Wyoming. He referred to it as a difficult professional chapter in my past. He said the consortium was aware of it and that a successful project here would go a long way toward putting it behind me. He framed it as encouragement. As concern for my career." Caleb's jaw worked once, a single involuntary contraction. "It was not concern. He had investigated my history, found the worst thing in it, held it through the entire conversation, and placed it at the end to let me know he had it."

Liam's arms were crossed against his chest, his forearms tight. Winnie's hand rested on the table near her cup, her fingers curled inward. Belle sat with the stillness that came over her when the current beneath a conversation shifted and the surface no longer told the truth about what moved below.

"He's using what happened to your brother as leverage of some type," Belle said.

"Yes."

"To pressure you into supporting a bridge location that hasn't been formally proposed, hasn't been approved by the committee, and hasn't been requested by the consortium's own board."

"That is what I believe, though I cannot prove his intent. Every word he spoke could be defended as professional courtesy with subtle undercurrents. He built the conversation so that nothing he said could be held against him if repeated."

"That's what makes it dangerous," Winnie said. "A man who speaks plainly can be answered plainly. A man who wraps his meaning in courtesy so thick you can't hold it up to the light—that man is harder to confront."

"Winnie's right," Liam said. "What he did was offer you money and told you he was worried about your reputation."

"Which is why I haven't spoken of it until tonight," Caleb said. "I wanted to understand what I was dealing with before I put it in front of anyone. Yet, I still don't fully understand it. What I know is this: Horace rode out to the narrows on his own multiple times. He assessed Owen's financial situation in detail. He built an argument for relocating a bridge that his own consortium had approved at the current site. He offered me money outside of my contract. He researched my past. None of those actions are required by his role as a consortium representative, and none of them serve the bridge project as it stands."

Belle turned it over in her mind. The pieces Caleb had laid on the table sat there like survey stakes driven into unfamiliar ground—each one marking a point, none of them yet connected into a shape she could name.

"What does moving the bridge do for Horace?" she said. "That's the question I keep circling. A different location doesn't change the consortium's investment. The consortium funded a bridge over the Yellowstone at Providence Ridge. Whether it sits at the current site or two miles north, the consortium still builds a bridge, and the valley still gets a permanent crossing. The cost might change. The timeline would certainly change. But the outcome is the same for the men writing the checks."

"Unless the outcome isn't about the bridge," Liam said.

"The land," Belle said. "The land around the northern site. If a bridge goes in at the narrows, every acre within riding distance of that crossing becomes more valuable overnight. Owen's ranch. Our family land. The open range beyond it. The mineral prospects Amos mentioned during lunch last Sunday—someone looking into silver deposits north of here. Maybe Horace has his hands in that."

"Possibly. But Horace doesn't own land here. Why would he? He's not from around here," Winnie said. "Owen does. How does Horace profit from increasing someone else's land value?"

"I don't know," Caleb said. "That is the piece I cannot see. The pieces I have point toward something, but the foundation is hidden, and I won't guess at it because guessing leads to accusations I can't support."

Belle looked at him across the table, and the weariness in him was plain—not the physical tiredness of a man who had worked a construction site all day but the deeper fatigue of a man who had been carrying a weight alone and had just set it down.

"What do you intend to do?" she asked.

"Nothing different from what I've been doing. I'll build the bridge at the approved site. I'll fulfill my contract. There is no professional justification for a change right now, as far as I can tell, and I won't manufacture one because a man with polished manners and money suggested it. I'll continue working the way I am until official word is delivered to me by someone on the consortium board."

The firmness in his voice settled around the room.

"Then that's what we know," Belle said. "And what we don't know isn't something we can solve tonight at this table. We have questions without answers, and worrying about them past the point of usefulness helps no one." She looked at Caleb. "I think we should set this aside for the evening. Not forget it. Just set it down until there's a reason to pick it back up."

Caleb held her gaze. "Let's go for a walk?" Belle continued. "The evening is mild, and I think the air would do us both some good."

"I'd like that."

Winnie was already on her feet, clearing the table. Liam pushed back his chair and stood.

"I'll see to the barn," Liam said. He paused beside Caleb's chair and put his hand on Caleb's shoulder, a brief, firm pressure that carried more than any sentence could have managed. Then he was through the door and into the yard, his boots on the porch boards fading into the sounds of the evening.

Belle took her shawl from the peg by the door. Caleb held the door for her, and they stepped onto the porch together.

They walked past the garden fence and the chicken coop where the hens had settled for the night, their soft, drowsy clucking audible through the wooden walls. The path they followed led from the homestead toward the bluff where the land dropped gently toward the river.

They walked side by side without speaking. Belle could feel the tension in Caleb beginning to ease, a gradual loosening that showed first in the length of his stride. It slowed from the purposeful pace of a man leaving a difficult conversation to the unhurried gait of a man walking beside someone whose company was enough.

"The garden looked good," Caleb said. "Winnie has a talent for it."

"She has a talent for most things she puts her hands to. She'd object to hearing me say that, but it's the truth." Belle pulled the shawl closer around her shoulders. "She got the gift from our mother. Mama could grow anything in this valley. She had a garden that half the women in Providence Ridge came to for cuttings and seeds. Winnie inherited the gift for gardening—she knows when to plant and when to wait and when to let a thing alone, which is the hardest part of growing anything."

"It's the hardest part of building anything, too."

They reached the top of the bluff, where the ground leveled before its gentle descent toward the river below.

"Caleb."

He turned to her.

"What Horace did—using Wyoming against you—that speaks to who he is, not to who you are. Whatever Horace found in your past, he found a story with an ending he doesn't understand, because the ending isn't a man hiding from what happened. The ending is a man standing on a riverbank building the thing God called him here to build." She paused. "Don't let him take that from you."

Caleb reached for her hand. His fingers found hers in the space between them, and the contact was warm and deliberate, his hand closing around hers with a gentleness that held no hesitation. Belle felt the roughness of his palm against her own, and the sensation of two hands meeting that understood labor and carried the evidence of it was a tenderness she had not prepared for.

"I am grateful for you, Belle," he said. "For your steadiness. For the way you hear what I tell you and stand beside me rather than away from me. This evening would have been heavier than I could bear if I'd carried my burden much longer, and I didn't have to because you opened your door to me and you listened. I don't have words sufficient for what that means to me."

"You don't need sufficient words," she said. "You need to know that you're not alone in this world. And you're not."

His hand tightened around hers, a single, brief pressure. They stood together on the bluff above the river with their hands joined between them, and the valley held them in the particular privacy of a landscape so large that two people standing in it were invisible to everything except the stars beginning to show above the peaks and the God who had led them both to this ground.

Chapter 22

Caleb followed the road out of Providence Ridge toward the ferry landing with his field notebook in his coat pocket and his hat settled low against the brightness of the morning.

He had slept last night after returning home from visiting Belle and her family. Not the shallow, interrupted rest of a man whose mind would not release the weight it carried into the dark hours, but actual sleep, deep and unbroken. He had lain in his narrow bed at the boardinghouse with the window cracked to the night air, and the thoughts that had circled his mind for days had been quiet.

The road descended toward the river, and he could see Belle. She stood near the upstream mooring post with one hand resting on the cable where it rose from the post toward its catenary arc across the river. Liam was at the scow, coiling a mooring line on the platform's planking with the unhurried competence of a young man. The ferry was rigged for the day's crossings, the guide rope threaded through the overhead pulley, and the loading ramp set at the bank's edge.

Belle's hand left the cable. She turned toward the road, toward him, and her hands went still at her sides. She straightened from the slight forward lean of a woman who had been testing cable tension by feel, and she watched him come down the path.

"Good morning," she said as he neared the landing.

"Morning, Belle."

"The cables are sound. I checked the tension on both lines, and Liam inspected the mooring posts before I arrived. Everything reads the same as it did yesterday evening."

"Good. I slept well last night. First time in days."

"I'm glad," she said.

He turned his attention upstream toward the bridge site, and immediately something registered as being off. The small lumber stack was where it should be, a long pale line against the darker bank. But the area around the excavation had changed.

"Something's wrong," he said. "I can see it from here."

Belle and Caleb hurried upstream along the bank path with Liam not far behind.

Caleb first noticed that the survey stakes had been pulled from the ground. Every single one of them. The colored flags that had marked each stake scattered across the ground like scraps of cloth after a windstorm. The stakes themselves lay in a scattered line along the riverbank, some broken, some intact.

The footing excavation had been partially filled. River gravel and loose stone had been dumped into the pit, burying the clay surface the crew had spent two days exposing.

The cofferdam pilings that had been stacked on the bank were scattered down the slope toward the water. Several had rolled to the river's edge, their sharpened ends driven into the soft ground at the waterline by their own weight. Others lay at angles across the gravel where they had been thrown or kicked from the stack. Caleb walked to the nearest piling and crouched beside it. The sharpened point had been hacked at with a blade or the flat of a maul; the fresh wood splintered where the point should have tapered clean. He checked a second piling and found the same damage: the point blunted and split. The pilings that had already been driven partway into the bank stood untouched, their tops rising from the earth at the angles the crew had set them, too firmly seated to be moved by hand.

The iron hardware was off the canvas tarp. Bolts lay scattered across the grass and gravel. The bearing plates, heavier and harder to move, had been dragged to the edge of the tarp and left in a disordered pile. The anchor chain, which had been coiled on the tarp in a neat spiral, had been pulled off and left in a snarl of links ten feet from where it belonged. Some of the smaller bolts were missing entirely, lost in the grass or thrown into the river where the current had carried them.

Caleb's plank table lay on its side. The sawhorses had been knocked apart; the crosspieces separated from the legs and left where they fell. His drawings, which he had left rolled up in a trunk for protection, lay on the ground beside the overturned planks. He picked up the nearest one and unrolled it. The paper was damp from the night's dew, but the ink had held. The elevation drawings were intact. The site plan was legible.

He stood in the middle of the site and turned a slow circle, cataloging what he saw. He felt his anger as it rose into his throat and pressed against the back of his teeth.

Belle stood at the edge of the site, her gaze moving across the scattered pilings, the emptied stake holes, and the iron hardware glinting in the grass. "The morning my cable was cut. I stood on the bank and believed for a moment that everything I had built could be taken from me. That the work of my hands could be undone in a single night by someone who didn't care what it cost me." She paused. "I was wrong. The cable was repaired. The ferry crossed again. This will be the same. The work is yours, Caleb. Nobody can take that from you by scattering hardware and filling a hole with gravel." She looked at him. "But who would do this and why?"

The question stopped him for a moment as he considered. "Someone wanting to delay progress... or possibly someone wanting to make a statement."

He looked upstream, then downstream, then at the bank on the far side of the river. Someone had come to this site in the dark and had spent what must have taken a couple of hours pulling stakes, shoveling gravel, scattering hardware, and hacking at pilings. Hours of deliberate labor performed in the service of destruction.

The sound of voices reached him from downstream. The crew was arriving.

The first man to reach the site was Emmett Lassiter, the foreman Caleb had hired from the labor pool in Livingston. He was a broad-shouldered man in his forties who had spent twenty years building railroad trestles and road bridges across the territory. Emmett stopped at the edge of the cleared area and stared. The shock of what he saw before him was evident on his face.

A younger hand named Virgil stopped mid-stride and shook his head in disbelief. Another man, Paul, set down his tool satchel and stood with his arms loose, looking from the excavation to the scattered hardware with the bewildered frustration of a man whose labor had been erased overnight. The rest of the crew gathered in a loose cluster at the site's edge, their morning ease replaced by the tight-shouldered silence of men confronting damage they hadn't expected.

"Gather around," Caleb said.

The crew assembled. Eight men in work clothes, their faces carrying the range of reactions the scene produced: anger in some, confusion in others, and a careful watchfulness in Lassiter that Caleb recognized as the attention of a man who had seen construction sites targeted before and was already calculating next steps.

"Sometime between yesterday evening and this morning, someone came to this site and did what you see around you," Caleb said. "The survey stakes have been pulled. The excavation has been filled with river gravel. The cofferdam pilings have been scattered, and several of the points damaged. The iron hardware has been thrown off the tarp, and some bolts are missing. The damage is real, and it will cost us time."

"Here is what it will not cost us. It will not cost us the bridge. The engineering is sound. My measurements are in my notebooks. The design hasn't changed. The materials can be gathered, the excavation can be cleared, the pilings can be re-pointed, and the stakes can be re-driven. Every piece of this site can be rebuilt, because the work that matters—the calculations, the design, and the foundation geology—lives in places that a man with a maul cannot reach."

Emmett nodded.

"Paul, take Virgil and start clearing the gravel out of the excavation. Use the buckets and the plank ramp. Work from the south wall, where the clay is still clean, and move north. I want the original surface exposed by the end of the day if possible." He turned to the rest of the crew. "Emmett, I need you and two men to collect the scattered hardware. Check the river's edge for anything thrown into the shallows. Anything that went into deep water is gone, and we'll order replacements from Livingston. The rest of you, start bringing the pilings back up the bank. Stack them on level ground. Sort them by condition. The ones with damaged points go in a separate stack for reshaping."

Men moved toward their assignments with the energy of workers whose frustration had been given a direction. Caleb's mind raced with thoughts as he watched the cleanup efforts around him. Horace had first suggested an alternative bridge site on Sunday. Caleb had given him nothing. Owen had relayed information concerning a possible bridge location change at the mercantile on Thursday afternoon. Thursday night, Caleb had told Belle and her family everything. And now, destruction at this bridge site.

The progression pointed toward Horace. When persuasion failed, disruption followed. The logic was clean, almost too clean, the kind of sequential argument that invited the conclusion it was designed to produce. That was the part that troubled Caleb. Horace had built his Sunday walk with a precision that left no sentence exposed to accusation. A man who constructed conversations that carefully would not commission sabotage this traceable in its timing. The cable attack on the ferry weeks ago had been surgical; the cuts placed where they would escape visual inspection and fail only under maximum load. This damage was blunt, broad, and aimed at quantity rather than precision. The two acts shared the quality of intent but differed in craft, the way two letters written by different hands might argue the same point in different vocabularies.

Caleb didn't have answers. "I'd like to walk to town and speak with your uncle," Caleb said as he turned toward Belle. "Marshal Tom should know about this before the day goes further."

"I agree," Belle said. "I'll go with you."

She turned to where Liam was standing, watching the recovery work. "Liam. Can you manage the ferry while I'm gone? Caleb and I need to speak with Uncle Tom."

"I can manage it."

"If any heavy freight comes to the landing, tell them to wait until I'm back. I don't want you running a heavy load alone. It takes both of us for that."

"Understood."

Caleb spoke briefly with Emmett, who had returned from the hardware search with a handful of recovered bolts in his coat pocket. "Keep the recovery moving. I'll be back within the hour. If you find anything unusual, anything beyond the damage we've already identified, leave it where it is and wait for me."

"You'll have a full accounting when you return," Emmett said.

They walked toward the road that led from the river to Providence Ridge. Caleb matched his pace to Belle's, which was steady and unhurried despite the errand that drove them toward town.

"Belle."

She looked at him.

"Would it be too forward of me to hold your hand while we walk into town?"

The question came out plainly, without preamble or apology, because what he felt for the woman beside him had moved past the territory where preamble served a purpose.

Belle's stride didn't break. She looked at him with an expression that carried no surprise. "I rather like holding your hand."

Chapter 23

The marshal's office was a single room with a pine desk, two straight-backed chairs for visitors, and a gun rack mounted on the wall behind the desk holding a Winchester. A potbelly stove sat in the corner with a pipe running up through the ceiling. A front window that looked out onto Main Street. The single iron-barred cell occupied the back wall. The cell held a cot, a bucket, and nothing else, and in Belle's memory it had rarely been occupied, usually only by a mill hand or a ranch hand who had taken too much whiskey at the saloon and needed a night to come back to himself.

Belle's Uncle Tom was at his desk when they came through the door. He had a ledger open in front of him, a pencil in hand, and a cup of coffee sat nearby. He looked up when the door opened, and Belle saw his attention move from her face to Caleb's face and back to hers with the measured assessment of a man who had spent years reading people.

"Winnie and Liam," he said. "Are they safe?"

"They're fine," Belle said. "Winnie's at home. Liam's running the ferry."

Tom's shoulders settled a fraction. "Sit, both of you. There's coffee on the stove if you want it, though I can't say it's as good as what you find at the boardinghouse."

Belle took the chair nearest the window. Caleb took the other one. Tom leaned back in his own chair, his badge catching a line of light from the window where it was pinned to his vest.

"You both look like something is on your mind; tell me," Tom said.

Caleb leaned forward with his forearms on his knees. "Sometime during the night, someone came to the bridge site and did a considerable amount of damage."

He went on to describe it all in great detail, and Tom listened without interrupting. Belle watched her uncle receive the information. His face gave nothing back while the words were arriving. His eyes stayed on Caleb.

"When did you last see the site intact?" Tom asked.

"Yesterday evening. Before I walked to the Callahan homestead for supper."

"What tools would a man need to do this?"

"A shovel for the gravel. A blade or a maul for the piling points. Hands to pull the stakes. The hardware could be scattered by hand or boot. A man working alone could have done it, but not quickly."

Tom turned to Belle. "You saw the site yourself this morning?"

"I did. The damage is as Caleb described it."

Tom absorbed this. He reached for his coffee cup, looked into it, and set it back down without drinking.

"There's more," Caleb said. "And what I'm about to tell you involves Horace Pritchard."

Tom's gaze sharpened. He didn't speak.

"Last Sunday afternoon, Horace asked to speak with me after lunch," Caleb said. "He proposed an alternative bridge site at the northern narrows, upstream of the current location. He stated that the crossing would be shorter, the timber requirements reduced, and that a freight road through the upper valley would open land for settlement and commerce. He mentioned Owen Gallagher's land that is right there at the bridge site that he wants considered. Horace informed me of Owen's financial troubles. He described Owen's debts, the hard winter, and his livestock losses."

"Go on."

"He suggested I could receive an additional consulting fee, beyond the contract I have. Every sentence he spoke that afternoon could be defended as professional courtesy if repeated. I didn't agree to do anything, and I didn't refuse outright. I told him that I needed time to consider. He accepted that, or appeared to."

"Was there anything else?"

Caleb was quiet for a beat. "At the end of the conversation, after everything else had been laid out, Horace mentioned an incident that occurred in Wyoming that involved me. He referenced what he called a difficult professional chapter in my past. He framed it as encouragement. He told me that Providence Ridge could be a fresh start, that a man's past didn't have to define his future." Caleb paused. "The words were kind. The placement of them was not."

"Explain what happened in Wyoming," Tom said. "In your own words."

"Three years ago I supervised a bridge project in a canyon in Wyoming Territory. My measurements identified a discrepancy in the foundation work. A foreman assured me that the discrepancy had been addressed and the work was sound. I signed off on his assurance rather than halting the project and demanding the work be redone. The bridge opened. Four months later it collapsed under a freight load." He held Tom's gaze. "Two men died. One was the freight driver, Thomas Hale. The other was my younger brother, James."

Belle sat in the chair beside the window with her hands folded in her lap and felt the ache of what she was witnessing travel through her chest. She had heard this story already, but here, in her uncle's office, Caleb told it as a man submitting himself to the scrutiny of authority, laying the record bare.

"The investigation cleared me of legal fault," Caleb said.

"Did Horace put any of this in writing?" Tom asked. "The consulting fee. The alternate site. The mention of Wyoming."

"No. Every word was spoken."

Tom nodded slowly, the nod of a man fitting a piece into a structure he was building in his mind.

"The timing concerns me," Tom said. "Walk me through the sequence."

"Horace proposed the alternate site on Sunday. I gave him no commitment. Yesterday afternoon, Owen Gallagher mentioned the same bridge location change at Pemberton's mercantile. Yesterday evening, I told Belle and her family everything I've just told you, at their kitchen table. This morning I walked to the river and found the site destroyed."

Tom pressed his thumb against the edge of the desk. "The pattern argues for Horace. Pressure was applied on Sunday, reinforced yesterday through Owen, and destruction last night when persuasion hadn't produced results."

"It does argue for him," Caleb said. "That's what troubles me."

Tom looked at him. "Explain."

"The man who built that Sunday conversation built it the way I build a bridge footing. Every sentence was placed where it could bear the load of scrutiny. Nothing he said to me on that walk could be quoted back to him as a threat or an inducement. The consulting fee was framed as a professional courtesy. The mention of Wyoming was framed as kindness. A man who constructs a conversation with that kind of precision does not commission destruction that points directly back to himself within the same week."

"He knows you'll make the connection," Tom said.

"He has to know it. The timing is too clean."

Tom rose from his chair and crossed to the stove. He picked up the coffeepot, looked into it, and set it back on the iron plate.

"The cable sabotage on the ferry," Tom said, turning back. "Those cuts were placed on the underside of the braid where a surface inspection wouldn't find them. The damage was designed to look like wear, to fail under load, and to cast doubt on Belle's maintenance rather than announce itself as an attack. That was careful, patient work. Someone who understood cables did that."

"The bridge damage is nothing like that," Belle said. "Gravel shoveled into a pit. Stakes pulled by hand. Hardware scattered across the grass. It's broad. It's crude. It's just mean and was done to delay the bridge building... either that or send a message."

"Well… either the same person did both and is becoming less careful, or a different hand did the bridge site," he said as he returned to his desk and sat. His gaze moved between Belle and Caleb.

"Here is what I keep returning to," Tom said. "Horace was sent here by the consortium to oversee a bridge at the approved location. Moving the bridge to the narrows does not serve the consortium. It does not serve Horace's official role. The only people served by a bridge at the narrows are whoever controls the land there, the lumber mill, and whatever other business opportunities that could be out that way that none of us may be aware of."

"Owen owns the land right there at the suggested bridge site," Caleb said.

"Yes, he does." Tom folded his hands on the desk. "But that raises questions I cannot answer sitting in this room. Why would Owen commission destruction at the bridge site or the ferry? If Owen wants the bridge moved to his land, destroying progress at the current site does nothing. A smart man would raise the issue at a town meeting or contact the consortium himself and propose a bridge and back up his reasoning. If Horace is directing Owen, why would Horace sabotage the project he was sent to oversee? The logic breaks down, and when logic breaks down in an investigation, it means I'm missing something."

Tom stood and reached for his hat from the peg beside the gun rack and settled it on his head.

"I'm going to find Owen," he said.

"And Horace?" Belle asked.

"I'll speak with Horace as well. Something just isn't right, and I'll get to the bottom of it."

Tom moved toward the door, then stopped and turned back to face them both. "Keep doing what you're doing. Caleb, you build the bridge. Belle, you run the ferry. Do not confront Horace. Do not confront Owen. Watch your surroundings. Keep your attention sharp. If anything else happens at either site, you come to me immediately."

"We will," Belle said.

Tom opened the door, and they followed him out onto the boardwalk. Tom's horse stood at the rail outside his office, a tall sorrel gelding with a blaze face, saddled and bridled. He untied the reins with a single smooth pull, gathered them in his left hand, and mounted. The saddle leather creaked beneath his weight as he settled in. He looked down at Belle from the saddle, and his expression softened.

"I'll find you when I know something. Love you, Belle; now get back to work, the days wastin' away," he said.

He turned the sorrel north and rode up the main road at a trot

Belle and Caleb stepped off the boardwalk and turned toward the river.

"Your uncle listens closely, just like you do. I respect that; he thinks before he jumps into action," Caleb said.

"He's been the marshal here since before my father died. The town trusts him because he earns that trust every day. He doesn't bluster, he doesn't threaten, and he doesn't speak until he's thought through what his words will set in motion."

They walked in silence for a stretch; the road descending gradually as it left town.

"Caleb."

He looked at her.

"I need to say something to you that I should have said before now, and I don't want to wait any longer because waiting hasn't made it easier." She kept walking, her eyes fixed on the road ahead. "When I accused you of cutting my cable on the ferry—"

"Belle—"

"Let me finish." She breathed. "I have carried the shame of that accusation since the day it happened. You had given me no just cause. You had given me every cause to believe otherwise, and I looked at you, and I chose suspicion because suspicion was the only tool I had. I didn't know how to trust a man I had just met. I had been carrying my family and my ferry for so long that when something threatened either one, the only response I knew was to find someone to blame and attack." She paused. "I am sorry, Caleb. Deeply sorry. It was wrong of me to accuse you."

Caleb reached for her hand. She gave it to him, and his fingers closed around hers, warm and certain.

"I forgave you for that a long time ago," he said.

"I know you did. That's part of what makes this so difficult to say. You forgave me before I had the courage to ask for it."

"You were angry, and you were protecting your family. The accusation came from fear."

Belle looked at their joined hands. "I have not trusted any man the way I trust you since my father took to the bottle," she said. "Saying that frightens me. Because in my life, trust and loss have lived in the same house. I trusted my father, and the river took him. I trusted the ferry to sustain my family, and a knife in the dark nearly took that from us. Every time I have placed my trust in something, the world has tested whether the trust could survive what came next."

Caleb's thumb moved against the back of her hand, a single slow stroke that carried more tenderness than any word he could have offered.

"I'm not going anywhere, Belle," he said. "And I'm not something the river can take."

"You speak as if you're certain, Caleb, yet the river can take you in a moment's notice."

Belle stopped walking, and Caleb stopped beside her.

"We should guard the sites at night," she said. "Both the ferry landing and the bridge. Whoever is doing this works in the dark. We cannot prevent everything, but we can make it harder."

Caleb considered this. "For how long? We can't sustain a night watch from now until the bridge is complete. That's weeks of sleeping on the ground."

"Not weeks. A few nights. My uncle is speaking to Owen and Horace today. If that conversation stirs something loose, if whoever is doing this feels the ground shifting beneath them, they may strike again before they lose the opportunity. The next few nights are the ones that matter."

"You're thinking like a strategist."

"I'm thinking like a woman who has already had her cable cut once and would prefer not to rebuild it a second time." She looked at the ferry landing, then at the bridge site, measuring the distance between them. "Liam will need to be with us. Three sets of eyes cover more ground than two."

"Agreed."

"We have extra bedding. Blankets and canvas enough to sleep on the ground in shifts. Liam and I will bring those tonight. We can meet at the landing around eight o'clock."

Caleb looked at the river, at the bridge site where his crew was pulling the morning back from the damage the night had done, and at the ferry where Liam was bringing the scow alongside the south bank landing with the same competence as his sister.

"Eight o'clock," he said.

Chapter 24

The canvas ground cloth they had spread near the bridge site smelled of the linseed oil Belle had used to waterproof it, a sharp, clean scent that seemed out of place here in the dark. Caleb lay on one edge of the cloth with a wool blanket pulled to his chest, his coat folded beneath his head as a pillow. Belle occupied the far edge with her own blanket drawn around her shoulders.

The moon was full and high enough to wash the valley in a blue-silver light that rendered the ferry landing and the bridge site in clear silhouette. Caleb could see the scow moored against the south bank, its hull a dark, flat shape against the paler sheen of the water. Nearby, the survey stakes he and his crew had re-driven that afternoon stood along the excavation, the pale wood and the flags visible against the dark bank.

Liam sat thirty feet away, his back braced against a driftwood log. He had been there since half-past eight, and for the first hour his attention had been constant, his head turning at every sound the night produced.

By the second hour, his attention had slowed down. Caleb watched the intervals between Liam's movements lengthen from seconds to minutes, watched his shoulders settle lower, and watched the gradual, losing negotiation between a nineteen-year-old boy who had worked the ferry from first light to last crossing and the will that insisted he stay awake. Liam shifted his weight twice in quick succession, the correction of a man who had caught himself drifting, then shifted once more, then was still. His chin dropped forward by a degree, held there, and dropped further. His breathing changed; the rhythm deepening into the slow, even measure of sleep.

"He's asleep," Belle said. Her voice came low and quiet from the far side of the ground cloth.

"He earned it," Caleb said.

"I should wake him. We both ought to try to rest while we can."

"Let him be. I'm awake, and I don't feel as if sleep will come for me tonight. If I tire, I'll wake him later."

A pause settled between them, filled by the sound of the river and the high, thin calling of a nighthawk somewhere above the benchlands to the south. Belle sat up on the ground cloth, her blanket gathered around her, her hair loose against her shoulders.

Caleb rose and walked to the edge of the bank where the ground sloped toward the river. The Yellowstone ran smooth under the full moon; the surface carrying a faint, shifting luminance that moved with the current. He could see the far bank clearly: the dark line of cottonwoods, and the road climbing away from the north landing site of the ferry into the valley beyond. Nothing moved on either bank. No sound carried except the river and the small, persistent life of the night.

Belle came and stood beside him. She had brought her blanket with her, wrapped around her shoulders over her coat, and she lowered herself to the ground at the edge of the bank with her legs stretched before her. Caleb sat beside her. The ground beneath him was cold through the canvas of his trousers, and the air carried the particular chill of a May night in Montana, the kind of cold that came down off the mountains after sunset and settled into the low ground of the valley.

"Your uncle rode out to speak with me before I finished working for the day," Caleb said. "He spoke with me while the crew was still clearing the last of the gravel from the excavation."

"He came to the ferry as well. Just before we brought in the last crossing."

"What did he tell you?"

"That Owen had heard talk at the mill about a different bridge location. That was the extent of what Owen claimed to know. He said the talk was general, nothing specific, but he'd grown interested because the land being discussed sits on his own property. Uncle Tom said he believed Owen was telling what he knew, but not all of it. There was more sitting behind the words that Owen wasn't offering."

"That matches what Tom told me," Caleb said. "He said Owen's answers were honest but incomplete, the kind of answers a man gives when he wants to cooperate without revealing the full picture."

"And Horace?"

"Tom said Horace didn't deny a thing. He didn't confirm much either. He told Tom he'd suggested the northern site to me as a professional observation, that routing heavy freight traffic through the center of town was poor planning, and that the narrows offered a shorter span with less material cost. Every word he spoke was pointed toward nothing meaningful."

"Uncle Tom wasn't satisfied."

"No. He said the pieces he has don't fit the shape he's looking at. He promised to keep pressing."

Belle drew her knees up slightly and rested her arms across them, and watched the river. "Let's talk of something other than destruction and speculation; it serves no purpose. We can sit here and stew all night long or talk of things more pleasant."

"Tell me more about your parents," Caleb said. "Tell me what your home was like when they were alive. What your mother was like in her garden. What your father was like on the ferry before everything changed."

Belle was quiet for a moment, and the quiet was not reluctance. It was the quiet of a woman reaching back through the years to find the images that lived in her heart.

"Mama was one of a kind," Belle said. "She came to the valley with her parents when she was a little girl, and she never wanted to be anywhere else. She kept a garden three times the size of what Winnie keeps now. She could walk through those rows in the morning and tell you which plants had been visited by beetles in the night, just from the way the edges of the leaves had been chewed. She had a way with growing things that I've never seen in another person."

"Winnie has some of that," Caleb said.

"Winnie has more of it than she knows. The garden survives because Winnie tends it the way Mama did, not by reading a book about planting, but by watching the soil and the weather and the way the light falls on the rows at different times of day. Mama taught her that. She taught all of us, really, but Winnie was the one who listened more closely."

"What did she teach you?"

"To cook. To sew. To put up preserves that would carry us through the winter. Mama could take a bushel of green beans from the garden, a salt crock, and a copper kettle, and by the end of the afternoon the cellar would have twelve new sealed jars of garden goodness. She taught me to read when I was four. She sat me at the kitchen table every morning after breakfast with a Bible and a slate, and she wouldn't let me leave until I'd read a verse aloud and copied it out. I was furious about it at times and tried to rebel. Now I understand what she was doing. She was making certain that whatever came for us in this life, her children would be able to read the Word of God for themselves."

"She sounds like my mother in that way," Caleb said. "Different methods, but the same conviction."

"Your mother had a city to raise her children in. Schools, churches with steeples, and lending libraries. My mother had a kitchen table, a Bible, and her own stubbornness, and she made those three things equal to all of it."

A coyote called from the benchlands above the valley, a single rising note that hung in the cold air for the space of two breaths before a second voice answered it from further off. The sound traveled across the open ground and faded into the distance, leaving the night wider in its wake.

"She sang beautifully," Belle said. "Hymns, mostly. She had a voice that could fill the cabin without effort, the kind of voice that made you stop whatever you were doing and listen. She sang while she cooked. She sang while she sewed. She sang us to sleep every night, all three of us in a row on the big bed while Mama sat in the chair beside the window and sang until we couldn't hold our eyes open any longer. Winnie inherited her voice. Have you heard Winnie sing?"

"I have not."

"You will someday. When she's comfortable enough. Her singing voice is Mama's. The first time I heard her sing after Mama died, I had to leave the room, crying my eyes out. My heart still hurt so at the time."

"My father taught us the river," Belle continued. "Not just the ferry. The river itself. He took each of us down to the bank when we were old enough to walk the trail, and he taught us to read the current, to understand where the deep channels ran, and to know by the color of the water how much sediment it carried and what that meant about the runoff upstream. He taught Liam and me to fish before we could write our names; poor little Winnie had no interest in fishing. He taught each of us to hunt and to dress the game and bring it home, and Mama taught us to preserve the meat, to salt it and smoke it and put it up in jars so that nothing we took from the land was wasted."

"A household that provided for itself."

"Completely. Between the garden and the hunting and the ferry fares and what the land gave us, we needed very little from town. Mama and Papa built that life on purpose. They wanted us to know how to sustain ourselves, to be dependent on nothing but God and our own hands." Belle paused. "Every night after supper, when the dishes were done and the lamp was lit, Papa would sit at the head of the table and read from the Bible. I remember sitting beside him while he read, and I followed along in my own Bible with my finger on the words. After Mama died, the Bible stayed on the shelf."

Her words carried no bitterness. They were a fact, delivered with the same precision Belle brought to every measurement and every observation, a recording of what had been and what had followed.

"Sunday afternoons," Belle continued, "we used to ride over to my mama's parents' homestead. The old Blecher place. The one I took you to. We would go there after church, and Mama's parents would have dinner waiting. Liam, Winnie, and I spent those afternoons running through the grass, climbing trees, and playing in the creek. Those were the simplest days of my life, Caleb. No ferry. No freight schedule. No worry about cables or fares or the river rising. Just three children in a yard with their grandparents and parents watching from the porch."

"What happened to your grandparents?"

"Grandmother passed when I was ten; my grandfather found her in the house. She had collapsed while he had been outside. Mama always suspected her heart had been bad; she had been complaining of chest pains for weeks before she went home to the Lord. Grandfather followed her the next spring. Mama said he died from missing her, and I've never found a better explanation for it. He was lost without her. The homestead sat empty after that."

An owl called from the cottonwoods downstream, a low, resonant note that repeated three times and then ceased. Caleb looked toward the trees and saw nothing except the dark shapes of the branches against the luminous sky.

"Tell me about growing up in a city. I cannot imagine it. A child without space to run."

Caleb leaned back on his hands. "Chicago is nothing like this valley. The streets ran in every direction, and every one of them was full, morning to night. After the fire, when the rebuilding began, the noise was constant. Hammers, saws, wagon wheels on cobblestones, men shouting orders from scaffolding. I fell asleep to that sound for years, the way you fell asleep to the river. It was the voice of the place, and it didn't stop."

"Did you have a yard to play in?"

"A small one behind the house. Enough for a clothesline and my mother's small garden bed. My father built a bench against the back fence, and Margaret and I used to sit on that bench after supper and watch the chimney smoke from the neighbor's rooftops while the city settled. I didn't understand what open land felt like until my parents took us to my grandparents' farm in Ohio."

"Ohio," Belle said.

"Outside of Columbus. My mother's parents bought forty acres of bottomland along a creek, with a barn and a hay meadow, and a woodlot that seemed to go on forever. The first morning James and I woke up on that farm, we walked out the back door and stood in the yard, and neither of us spoke for what felt like an hour. We had never seen that much wide-open land or sky. We had never heard that kind of silence, the silence that has birds in it and wind in it and nothing else. James took off running toward the tree line, and I ran after him, and we didn't stop until we reached the creek at the far end of the property, both of us winded, our shoes soaked, laughing at nothing whatsoever."

"How old were you?"

"Nine. James was seven. We visited every summer and spent a week there until I was fifteen, and every time we returned home to

Chicago, the city felt smaller. The buildings felt closer. The streets felt louder. Something had shifted in me during those summers, a knowledge that there was a world beyond the city that breathed differently, that moved at a pace set by the seasons rather than the clock on the wall. James felt it too. We talked about it often, lying awake in our shared room at home with the sound of the trains running through the freight yards two blocks away. He would say, 'Caleb, one day I'm going west and I'm not coming back,' and I would agree, and neither of us was pretending."

"You both kept that promise."

"We did. We left Chicago after my schooling and traveled west. Our mother stood on the platform at the Chicago station and watched both her sons leave at once, and the look on her face that morning is something I will carry with me for the rest of my life. She didn't cry. She stood perfectly straight and held our father's arm, and she smiled, because she is a woman who would not send her sons into the world with the image of her weeping. But her chin was trembling, and my father's hand covered hers on his arm, and I knew what it cost them both."

Belle was watching him. The moonlight fell across her face, the line of her jaw, and the dark fall of her hair, and her eyes held the particular quality of attention that he had first noticed on the ferry the day he arrived, the listening that happened behind her eyes rather than in front of them.

"Tell me about James," she said. "Tell me who he was. What made him laugh? What did he dream of?"

Caleb looked at the river. The water moved past them with its slow, persistent sound, carrying the reflected light of the moon downstream toward the bend where the channel curved north.

"James laughed at everything," Caleb said. "He was the kind of man who found something amusing in every situation, no matter how ordinary. He could make a stranger smile inside of five minutes. He could walk into a room full of people he'd never met and leave with three invitations to supper. He had a way of looking at the world as if everything in it was a curiosity worth investigating. A new tool, a bird he hadn't seen before, or a card trick a man showed him. He wanted to understand how everything worked, and the wanting was so genuine that people opened up to him without thinking about it."

"He sounds like he was good company."

"The best company. There was nothing he was afraid to try. When we were boys and visited Ohio, our grandfather had a barn with a hayloft, and James spent an entire afternoon trying to fashion a pair of wings from canvas and barn wood because he wanted to know what it felt like to fly. He jumped from the loft into a pile of hay and broke his wrist, and while our grandmother was wrapping the wrist with a splint, he was already talking about what he would do differently on the second attempt."

Belle's mouth curved. "He sounds like Liam at that age."

"There is a resemblance. The same appetite for the thing just beyond reach." Caleb paused. "James wanted a homestead. He talked about it constantly in those last years: the spread he was going to build, the cattle he was going to run, and the house he was going to put up with his own hands. He wanted a large family. I remember him saying he wanted to build a table long enough that he couldn't reach both ends of it if he stood in the middle, and then he wanted to fill each chair around it with his children and wife."

"Tell me about his wife."

"A woman named Clara. He met her in Cheyenne at a church social. Clara was his match. She was steady where he was restless; she was patient where he was impulsive, and she loved him in a way that made the restlessness mean something. They were married within weeks of meeting one another."

"Where is she now?"

"California. After James died, she couldn't stay in the territory. Every road they had ridden, every building they had visited, and every piece of the life they had built carried him in it. She told me that the memories of him were not a comfort. They were a wound that reopened every morning when she woke and reached for the side of the bed where he had slept. She went west to start again."

"That is so sad. I feel sorry for her," Belle said. "And for him. For the life they should have had."

"I feel the same. They were a match made in heaven."

They sat without speaking for a time, and the silence between them was not an absence. It was the presence of everything they had given each other across the span of the evening, memories of days gone by.

The cold deepened. Caleb could feel it settling against his skin through his shirt, the temperature dropping as the hour passed midnight, the chill of the high country pressing down from the mountains and pooling in the low ground along the water. He looked at Belle and saw her draw her blanket tighter, her shoulders pulling inward against the cold, a shiver running through her that she tried to suppress by pressing her arms closer to her body.

He got up and retrieved his coat and sat back down beside her. He settled the coat around her shoulders and over her blanket, his hands adjusting where the collar sat against the back of her neck, drawing the front panels forward so the wool covered her.

"Thank you," she said.

They watched the river. The moon had crossed the midpoint of the sky, its light shifting as it moved, the shadows of the cottonwoods lengthening across the gravel bar. Caleb listened to the water and to the night, to the small sounds that rose and fell in the darkness, the rustle of a field mouse in the grass behind them, the distant call of the owl repeating its low refrain from a new position further downstream.

Belle yawned. She tried to close her mouth against it, turning her face away, but the yawn won, and when she turned back her eyes were heavy with the weight of a day that had begun before dawn.

"Come here," Caleb said, and he lifted his left shoulder slightly. "Rest. Even for a few minutes."

She leaned into him. Her head came to rest against his shoulder, and the warmth of her pressed against his side was the warmest thing in the valley.

"Caleb," she said, her voice low, already drifting.

"Hmm."

"What do you dream of for your future? When you think ahead, what do you see?"

He considered the question. Three months ago, in Denver, the answer would have been a contract and a rail ticket and another meaningless, low-risk build in another territory, the endless forward motion of a man with no desire or want for anything in his life.

"I haven't thought much about the future in a long while," he said. "I've been living one day to the next, taking the work that came and moving to wherever the work was. A man can live that way for years and convince himself it's a life."

"And now?"

"Now I hope for something I didn't know I was allowed to hope for. A home of my own. A place I stay, not a place I pass through. A family, if God grants it. A table long enough that I can't reach both ends of it."

He felt her smile against his shoulder, the small movement of her mouth through the fabric of his shirt.

"James's table," she said.

"His dream. But I reserve the right to claim it for my own future."

Her breathing was slowing. The intervals between her inhales were lengthening, the depth of each breath increasing, the gradual descent of a body surrendering to exhaustion. He waited, listening, and within minutes her breathing found the steady, even rhythm of sleep.

Caleb wrapped his left arm around her, drawing her gently closer against his side. He held her carefully, the way a man holds something he has been entrusted with, something whose worth he understands with the full measure of his attention.

A coyote called from the rimrock to the south, a rising, wavering note that climbed into the night sky and broke into a chorus as the others answered from their scattered positions across the benchlands. The sound was wild, undomesticated, belonging to the same country that produced the river and the mountains and the stars overhead, and it carried no threat. It was the valley speaking in its own voice, the voice it used when the human world went quiet.

Caleb listened. He listened to the coyotes and the river and the owl and the wind that had begun to gently stir through the cottonwoods in a low, continuous murmur. He listened to Belle breathing against his shoulder. He listened to Liam's deeper breathing from the log where the young man slept with his chin on his chest and his hands loose in his lap.

He thought about her question. What do you dream of for your future? He had given her the beginning of the answer before sleep had taken her, the home and the family and the table, and each of those things was true. But the full answer was larger than the words he had spoken, and it had been forming in him for days, one layer at a time.

He loved her. The knowledge lived in him without surprise, without the alarm that a man might expect to feel when a truth this large declared itself. It had not arrived as a single moment of recognition. It had arrived the way morning arrives in this valley, gradually; the light increasing by such fine degrees that a man couldn't say when the darkness ended and the dawn began, only that at some point he looked up and the world was illuminated and he couldn't remember what it had looked like before the light came. He loved the way she held a rope. He loved the way she read a river. He loved the way she carried her family and her responsibilities with quiet strength. He loved her honesty and her faith.

He knew what God had done within himself. The certainty of it sat in him with the solidity of bedrock. God hadn't sent him to Providence Ridge to build a bridge. God had sent him to Providence Ridge to find the woman sleeping against his shoulder, the woman who ran a ferry and raised her siblings and carried the memory of her parents. God had placed her in his path with the same deliberate hand that placed rivers in their courses, not by accident but by design, not as a reward for suffering endured but as the next thing, the thing that springs forth, the way through the wilderness that the prophet had promised and that Caleb had heard spoken over him in the boardinghouse on a Sunday morning that now seemed like the first morning of his life.

He would ask her to marry him. Not tonight. Not tomorrow. When the time was right, when the bridge was further along and the ground beneath them was stable enough to bear the weight of a future spoken aloud. He believed with everything in him that she would accept. The belief was not a presumption. It was the reading of evidence, the accumulated weight of every conversation, every look that lasted a breath longer than it needed to, every silence that said more than the words surrounding it, and every moment her hand had found his and held on.

He thought about his parents. His father standing in the small yard behind their Chicago home, his sleeves rolled to the elbows, his hands moving over a wood joint with the patience that was his signature, fitting two pieces together so precisely that the seam disappeared. His mother standing in the kitchen doorway watching his father work, her arms folded, her face carrying the expression of a woman who had chosen well and knew it, an expression that held neither triumph nor complacency but something deeper, a quiet, daily gratitude for the man she had married and the life they had built from the materials God had given them. Their marriage had been built like his father's furniture, with care and precision, with attention to the joints where the stress collected, with the understanding that the beauty of the thing was not in its surface but in the soundness of its construction. He wanted what they had.

Caleb smiled as he lifted his face toward the sky.

Lord, I am sitting here on the bank of a river You made, holding a woman You brought to me, in a valley You led me to, and I have no words large enough for what I feel. Thank You. Thank You for bringing me to this place. Thank You for every hard mile, every sleepless night, and every morning I woke carrying a weight I thought would crush me. You saw me through all of it. You saw me through Wyoming, through the grief that ate the center out of my life, and through the years I spent hiding. You did not leave me in that canyon of grief. You brought me here. You gave me a bridge to build and a woman to love and a town that feels like home, and I do not deserve any of it, but I receive it, Lord. I receive it with my whole heart. I love her. You know I love her, because You are the one who placed this love in me, and I ask You to guide me in what comes next. Give me the wisdom to be the man she deserves. Give me the patience to wait for Your timing. Give me the courage to speak when the time comes. And hold us both, Father. Hold us both in Your hand, the way You hold the river in its banks and the mountains on their foundations. I trust You. I trust what You are building. Amen.

The prayer finished in the silence of his mind, and the silence was full, and the fullness was peace. The moon touched the ridgeline. The stars burned on. The river spoke its low, unhurried word beneath the bank, and Caleb sat with Belle sleeping against his shoulder and his arm around her, and the whole of the valley stretched before him in moonlight, and he kept watch.

Chapter 25

Belle had been awake since half-past three. When she had opened her eyes on the riverbank, Caleb's coat was still around her shoulders over her blanket, and she was still against his shoulder, the warmth of his side a steady presence through the layers of wool and cotton. The valley had been locked in moonlight; the river running silver below the bank; the cottonwoods standing motionless against a sky heavy with stars. Liam had been awake, sitting on the ground cloth with his blanket pulled around him. Caleb had stirred when Belle shifted against him, his arm tightening around her for a moment before he lifted his head and looked at the sky as if reading the hour from the position of the moon.

She had urged them both to rest. The ground cloth was spread, the blankets were there, and neither of them had slept more than a few hours. She had promised to wake one of them in a couple of hours to take over. Caleb had resisted at first, but eventually fatigue won. He had eased himself away from her, crossed to the ground cloth, and stretched out on the near edge. Liam had already settled on the opposite side of the canvas, and within minutes both of them were breathing with the slow, even rhythm of men who had given their bodies permission to stop.

Belle had taken her position at the edge of the bank where the ground sloped toward the water, and she had found the stillness of the remaining hours before dawn calm and peaceful. She had let them both sleep. The promise to wake one of them in two hours had passed unclaimed, because the night was quiet, her eyes were open, and the peace of it felt like something she had been given and did not want to hand away.

Nothing had come during the watch. No footsteps on the trail. No figure moved through the cottonwoods toward the ferry landing or the bridge site. The night had held its silence, broken only by the river, the coyotes, and the owl that had called from the cottonwoods at intervals through the small hours. Belle had kept her watch without incident until the sky began to change above the mountains.

She was tired. The fatigue lived in her shoulders and behind her eyes, the particular heaviness of a body that had slept only a few hours. But beneath the tiredness, something else occupied her attention, something that had been sitting in her chest since the moment she woke and felt the weight of his coat across her body. She had leaned into him. She had asked him what he dreamed of, and he had answered her with words that carried the shape of a future, and she had listened to those words against the warmth of his side while sleep pulled her under.

Behind her, she heard movement on the ground cloth. The sound of canvas shifting under someone's weight, the rustle of a wool blanket being pushed aside, and then the low, involuntary groan of a young man protesting the transition from sleep.

Moments later, Liam lowered himself beside her, his movements stiff from the cold ground and the short sleep, and he sat with his arms resting across his knees in a posture that mirrored her own.

"Quiet night," he said.

"Nothing stirred. Not on the trail, not at the landing, and not at the bridge site."

"Caleb's still asleep."

"Let him sleep."

Liam nodded. He picked up a small stone from the gravel beside him and turned it in his fingers. "How long do we keep doing this? Tonight again? Tomorrow night? We can't keep this up forever."

"I know we can't. I wanted to watch last night because Uncle Tom spoke with Horace and Owen yesterday, and I didn't know what that conversation might stir. If a man feels the ground shifting beneath him, his first instinct is to act before the ground shifts further. I wanted eyes on the landing in case that instinct brought someone down here."

"It didn't."

"It didn't. Which either means there's nothing to stir, or it means whoever is behind this is patient enough to wait. Or it could mean something entirely different that none of us know."

"Or it means Uncle Tom's conversation didn't reach the right ears yet."

Belle looked at her brother. He was turning the stone between his thumb and forefinger with the absent concentration of a young man thinking past the surface of the question he'd asked.

"We should ask Uncle Tom for help if we decide to watch again," Liam said. "He could send someone, or come himself. But I think he needs to know what we're doing."

"I agree. I'll speak with him today."

"What's the plan this morning?"

"I need to ride home. Change clothes, wash my face, and have Winnie pack food for us. I'll be back within the hour. When I return, you can ride home and change clothes. We should probably wake Caleb up so he can walk to the boardinghouse and change and eat before his crew arrives."

"That leaves you alone at the landing when I go."

"For a short while, I'll be fine."

Liam tossed the stone toward the river. It struck the gravel at the water's edge with a flat click that carried in the still morning air. "I don't like leaving you here alone."

"I've been here alone before. This is no different."

"It feels different."

"I'll be fine... I doubt anyone will come and stir up trouble in the daylight."

The sound of canvas shifting reached her again from the direction of the ground cloth, followed by a deeper voice clearing its throat. Caleb appeared at the edge of her vision eventually, walking toward the bank. His hair was disordered from sleep, pressed flat on one side, and his face carried the softness of a man not yet fully returned to the day. He stopped a few feet from where she and Liam sat and looked at the river, then at the sky, then at Belle.

"Good morning," he said.

"Good morning."

He sat on the bank beside her and ran his fingers through his hair, pressing it into some semblance of order.

"Anything during the night?" he asked.

"Nothing. All was quiet."

"I slept harder than I intended. I meant to wake for a second turn."

"You needed the sleep."

He didn't argue. He looked at the river. "The river's up," he said.

"About two inches since yesterday morning. The warm days are pulling snowmelt faster than the ground can absorb it. We'll see over three feet of a rise before the month is out if the weather holds."

Liam stood and brushed the gravel dust from his trousers. "I'll start rolling the ground cloth."

He walked back toward the canvas, and Belle turned toward Caleb. "You should go to the boardinghouse and take advantage of Mrs. Hanscombe's good breakfast."

"What about you?"

"I'm going to ride home in a few minutes, change, and I'm sure Winnie will have biscuits ready."

Caleb reached across the distance between them and took her hand where it rested on her knee. His fingers closed around hers, firm and warm against the morning cold. "I'll walk to town. I should be back at the site before the crew arrives at eight."

"Be safe on the road."

"And you on the trail."

He held her gaze for a moment longer, then got up and walked toward the road.

"Liam," she said. "I'll be back within the hour. Keep your eyes open."

"Always do."

She stood and walked toward where her mare stood tied to the rail near the ferry. The horse had been there since the previous evening, hobbled with enough lead to reach the grass along the tree line, and it lifted its head at Belle's approach with the alert. Belle ran a hand along the mare's neck. Her coat was cool and slightly damp from the night air; the muscle beneath it solid and warm. She checked the horse's hooves, checked her legs, and found nothing amiss. She untied the lead from the rail and bridled the horse with the bridle she had hung from a branch the night before, the leather stiff from the cold until her hands worked it supple enough to slip the bit between the mare's teeth.

She swung up into the saddle, and the mare shifted beneath her, eager, already turning its head toward the trail that led home.

She turned the mare onto the trail and gave the horse its head. The mare moved into an easy trot, the ground-covering gait of a horse that knew this trail as well as Belle knew the ferry cable, and the rhythm of it settled into Belle's body.

The air was chilly, the temperature of a May morning that would warm quickly once the sun had risen further in the sky. Belle's coat kept the chill from reaching her skin.

The trail curved away from the river bluff and entered a denser stand of cottonwoods where the trees grew thick along both sides and the canopy closed overhead.

She looked up as a blue jay flew between branches, just as the mare's front legs caught something.

The horse's stumble was violent and instantaneous, its chest dropping as both forelegs buckled forward beneath the animal's weight. Belle felt the lurch in her spine, the sudden pitch of the saddle as the mare's head plunged downward, and her hands tightened on the reins by reflex. The mare scrambled for footing, its hooves scraping against the packed earth, in a panicked attempt to recover its stride. The mare lurched sideways, its balance gone, its weight pitching to the left.

Belle left the saddle. The world tilted, the cottonwood canopy spinning above her, the packed earth and the morning light trading places in a single, wrenching instant, and then the ground came up to meet her with a force that drove every thought from her mind.

Her left hand struck the trail first. The impact traveled through her wrist into the small bones of her forearm with a pain so sharp and complete that it registered before the rest of her body reached the ground. Her ribs struck something hard, a root or a buried stone that caught her below the arm and compressed the breath from her lungs in a single, involuntary gasp. Her head hit the earth. She took a deep breath, thought of Caleb, and then the darkness came.

Chapter 26

Caleb finished his coffee and pushed back from the table. He carried his plate and cup to the kitchen doorway, where Mrs. Hanscombe intercepted them.

"Thank you, Mrs. Hanscombe. Breakfast was fine as always."

"You look like you haven't slept a wink, Mr. Sterling. But you've eaten well, so I'll hold my questions. Have a blessed day."

"You have a blessed day as well," he said.

Caleb left the kitchen doorway and crossed the dining room toward the front door. Behind him, he heard the scrape of a chair at the far end of the dining table and the sound of boots approaching.

Horace met him at the door. The timing was precise enough that Caleb understood it had been calculated. Horace had been watching him closely the entire time it had taken him to eat his breakfast.

"Mr. Sterling. I have a few matters on which I'd value your perspective."

Caleb opened the door and stepped onto the boardwalk. Horace stepped out beside him and fell into stride as naturally as if they had arranged the walk in advance.

"I had a visit from Marshal Callahan yesterday," Horace said. "An unexpected visit, I might add. The marshal is a fine man, as I'm sure you'd agree, and I've had nothing but the highest respect for his office since I arrived. But I had the impression someone had raised concerns about my conduct with the marshal. I can't imagine who would have done that, or why."

Caleb kept his eyes on the road ahead. A meadowlark was singing from a fence post at the edge of town, its call a liquid, tumbling phrase that carried across the still air.

"The marshal visits whom he sees fit to visit," Caleb said. "I expect that's the nature of his business and none of my concern."

"Of course." Horace adjusted his coat lapels with a gesture that managed to convey both ease and precision. "I only mention it because I hope professional disagreements between us won't be allowed to become personal. We're both working toward the same end, Mr. Sterling. A bridge for Providence Ridge. A crossing that will serve this community for generations. I would hate for the kind of misunderstanding that sends a marshal to a man's door to cloud what has been, I think, a productive professional relationship."

"I don't consider anything we've discussed in the past personal, Mr. Horace."

"I'm glad to hear it. Truly." Horace walked in silence for several steps, and the silence had the quality of a man allowing one subject to settle before introducing the next. "I've been giving considerable thought to the bridge, as you might imagine. To the site, to the design, to the future this crossing will create. And I've been in contact with investors who have an interest in the development of land north of Providence Ridge."

"These investors have commissioned geological assessments that indicate considerable extraction potential," Horace continued. "Mineral deposits, Mr. Sterling, of the kind that could sustain an operation for years. The assessments reference specific mineral formations that are consistent with commercially viable deposits. I'm not a geologist, of course. But the men who conducted these assessments are, and their findings are substantial."

Extraction potential. Commercially viable deposits. Mining. Someone intended to pull minerals from the mountains north of town, and the geological assessments Horace referenced were not the speculative musings of a prospector with a pan and a prayer. They were commissioned surveys, which meant capital, which meant organization, which meant someone with enough money to pay geologists before the first shovel broke ground.

"The relevance to the bridge you are constructing," Horace said, "is a question of freight capacity, Mr. Sterling. An operation of the nature I'm foreseeing in the future would require heavy material transport on a scale that the current bridge approach, routed through the center of town, cannot efficiently sustain. The grade into Providence Ridge from the Main Street approach is adequate for commercial traffic and livestock. It is not adequate for wagons running at tonnage. A crossing north of the current site, at the narrows, would connect directly to the benchland roads without routing through town. The engineering advantages are considerable."

"The committee approved the current site, and so did the consortium," Caleb said.

"They did. And the current site is sound, as your survey confirmed. I'm not questioning your work. I'm raising the possibility of a second bridge location, north where I asked you to survey before."

A pair of riders appeared on the road ahead, coming from the direction of the river. Ranch hands, by the look of them—wide hats, working coats, horses carrying the dust of a morning's ride. They passed with nods, and Caleb returned the greeting. Horace raised a hand.

When the riders had moved beyond earshot, Caleb stopped walking.

"Mr. Pritchard. Why is this other bridge location so important to you personally? You represent the consortium. The consortium approved the current site. Why does a consortium representative push for an alternate location that his own board hasn't formally requested?"

The question hung between them in the morning air. A magpie called from the cottonwoods along the road, its harsh chatter cutting through the quiet. Caleb watched Horace's face.

His response came a half-beat faster than his usual cadence, as though the mechanism that governed his composure had needed to work slightly harder than it was accustomed to working. The smile he produced was correct in every particular—the right degree of warmth, the right measure of understanding—except that it arrived an instant after the words rather than with them, a fractional delay that a man who was not watching for it would never have noticed.

"I see the bigger picture, Mr. Sterling. The consortium hired me to represent its interests, and those interests extend beyond a single crossing. When I see an opportunity that could benefit everyone, I consider it my responsibility to bring it forward. Professional thoroughness."

"That's a broad answer to a specific question."

"It's the only answer I have." Horace adjusted his coat, and the gesture carried less of the ease it had held at the beginning of their walk. "I'm a practical man. I see what's coming, and I want Providence Ridge to be ready for it."

A man who could not answer a direct question plainly was a man whose answer would not survive daylight. Caleb filed the deflection alongside the unnamed investors, along with the language about extraction potential and heavy material transport. He resumed walking, and Horace fell into step beside him.

Horace let the silence between them extend for the space of twenty paces before he spoke again. "I believe in this strongly enough to put my own capital behind it. I will fund the northern site survey from my own pocket, in cash, and pay you double what the consortium would pay."

Caleb measured the offer the way he measured a span under load—testing where the weight fell, where the structure held, and where it gave. A consortium representative offering his own money to fund a survey his board had not requested. No man paid out of pocket for professional courtesy.

"The investors I mentioned would look favorably on an engineer who demonstrated the foresight to evaluate multiple options," Horace continued. "Very favorably, Mr. Sterling. These are men who reward sound judgment, and the kind of professional who takes a longer view of his career prospects is precisely the kind they prefer to work with."

"I'd appreciate it if you kept this between us," Horace continued. "I trust you will. These are sensitive matters, and the investors prefer discretion until the assessments are fully documented."

"I understand discretion," Caleb said.

Horace nodded. "What I haven't told you, and what I think you deserve to hear, is that the development coming to this valley will require engineering expertise for years. Not months, Mr. Sterling. Years. Roads into the benchlands. Infrastructure for operations that this community has not yet imagined. Structural work on a scale that would keep a capable engineer fully employed in meaningful, substantial projects for as long as he cared to stay."

The words landed in Caleb's chest with a precision that startled him. Years of engineering work. In a valley he had come to love. In a place where the woman he had come to care for lived.

"A man who positions himself on the right side of that growth now," Horace continued, "who demonstrates he understands where the opportunity is heading, would find himself in considerable demand. I would see to it personally that the right engineer was not overlooked."

Caleb felt the pull of it. The sensation was physical, a tightness in his sternum that he recognized not as greed but as longing. The temptation was real, and the recognition of it ran through him with the cold clarity of river water. He knew what Horace was doing. He knew the condition attached to the promise, though Horace would never state it plainly—give me another approved bridge location. Work closely with me in the shadows. Serve the investors whose names I will not speak and whose purposes I will not name, and in return I will give you the career of your dreams.

"The bridge at the current site is my priority," Caleb said. "The committee approved it, the survey supports it, and the community is depending on it. That's the work in front of me, and I intend to see it through. I cannot divert my focus on anything else at the moment."

"Of course," Horace said. "And I wouldn't ask you to do otherwise. The current site deserves your full attention. But I'm sure you could take a day off here or there... no one would need to know. I merely want you to know that the landscape is larger than a single bridge, and that the men who see that landscape clearly tend to find themselves well positioned when it develops." He paused. "I'll be in touch. I trust we understand each other."

Horace turned back toward town. His stride was measured. His posture was composed. He walked the way he always walked—a man whose outward carriage betrayed nothing that his words had not already offered. But he had offered his own money. He had referred to unnamed investors. He had dropped language that pointed at mining without naming it. He had promised Caleb a future of meaningful engineering work in exchange for a bridge approval that would serve interests Horace refused to identify, and he had asked Caleb to keep it between them. The accumulated weight of these things occupied Caleb's mind as he continued walking on the road toward the river, sorting each claim against what he knew, noting where the structure held and where it gave.

Chapter 27

"Where's Belle?" Caleb asked as he approached the ferry landing.

Liam turned from the river. "She hasn't come back yet. She left for home shortly after you left. I expected her back by now."

"Can you think of any reason that would keep her away this long?"

Liam's jaw tightened. "No. Belle never lingers when the ferry needs running. She is the most punctual person I know."

Caleb looked toward the trail. The distance from the landing to the homestead was approximately one mile, a ride Belle's mare could cover in minutes at a trot. She should have reached the homestead, changed, eaten, and returned long before Caleb had finished Mrs. Hanscombe's breakfast.

Something was wrong.

"I'll go and see if I can find out what's holding her up," Caleb said.

Liam hesitated for the space of a single breath, the instinct to go himself visible in the set of his shoulders. "Take my horse."

Caleb walked to the rail where Liam's gelding stood with its head low, cropping at the grass. He untied the lead with hands that moved faster than his thoughts, bridled the horse, checked the cinch, and swung into the saddle. The gelding responded to his heels and turned toward the south-bank trail.

He pushed the horse into a canter. The trail curved away from the river bluff, and the sound of water receded behind him. The trail straightened through a stretch where the cottonwoods thinned, then curved again into a denser stand where the trees grew thick on both sides and the canopy pressed low.

He saw the mare first. Belle's horse stood on the trail ahead, head down. The animal was calm; the settled posture of a horse that had been standing in one place long enough to lose its urgency. One hind leg was tangled in a length of rope that ran to a cottonwood trunk at the trail's edge.

Near the horse, on the ground, Belle lay on her side.

Caleb was off the gelding before the horse had fully stopped. He crossed the distance to Belle at a run, his boots striking the packed earth, the sound of his own breathing loud in the still corridor of trees. He dropped to his knees beside her.

Her face was turned against the ground, her dark hair fallen loose from its pins and spread across the earth. Her left arm was bent beneath her at an angle. He could see the rise and fall of her ribs—shallow but steady. Breathing.

He pressed two fingers to the side of her neck. Her pulse beat against his fingertips, present and regular.

"Belle."

He touched her shoulder, the fabric of her coat warm beneath his hand from the morning sun that had reached her through the canopy.

"Belle."

She didn't respond. He kept his hand on her shoulder and looked at the surrounding scene.

The rope on the mare's hind leg ran to a cottonwood trunk six feet from the trail's edge, tied at knee height. He followed the line of it with his eyes and found a second rope between two cottonwood trunks on opposite sides of the trail, stretched across the path. The spacing between the ropes was deliberate—one to catch the front legs, the second to entangle the hind legs as the horse stumbled. The placement was precise. The ropes were positioned in the densest section of the canopy, where the shade was deepest and the light most broken.

Two ropes, strung low, designed to trip a horse. Set on a trail only the Callahans used. Set during the night, while Caleb, Belle, and Liam had watched the river.

The recognition passed through him with a force that compressed the air in his lungs. He looked at Belle on the ground, at the angle of her arm, at the stillness of her body, and the weight and meaning behind Horace's earlier words vanished from his mind as completely as if they had never been spoken. What replaced it was singular and absolute and occupied every part of him at once. The woman on the ground was the woman he loved, and she was hurt, and everything else in the world was noise.

"Belle." He said her name a third time, his voice steady despite the current running beneath it. He kept his hand on her shoulder.

She stirred. A sound came from her—low, involuntary, the sound of consciousness returning to a body. Her right hand moved against the earth, fingers pressing into the packed trail. Her eyes opened, unfocused, looking at the ground inches from her face. She blinked. She tried to push herself up with her left hand, and the sound that came from her was sharp enough to stop his breath—a gasp that carried the full register of pain arriving unexpectedly.

"Don't move that arm," Caleb said. He shifted his position and placed his right arm behind her back, supporting her weight as she eased herself upright. His left hand found her uninjured arm above the elbow, steadying her. She sat up against his support, her face drawn tight with pain, her breathing shallow and controlled in the way of a person managing each breath as a separate negotiation with her own body.

"What happened?" she asked.

"Your horse was tripped. You were thrown."

She looked at the canopy above her. "I remember the mare stumbling. I remember the sky moving. Nothing after."

She looked at her left wrist. It was swelling; the joint already thickened, the skin taking on the dusky flush of blood pooling beneath the surface. She tried to rotate the joint and drew a sharp breath through her teeth. The movement produced pain that Caleb could read in the whitening of her knuckles, where her right hand gripped her knee.

"I don't think it's broken. But my ribs—" She pressed her right hand against her left side, below her arm, and the contact made her close her eyes. "Something caught me when I fell. A root or a stone."

She opened her eyes and looked past Caleb toward the trail. She saw the rope on her mare's hind leg. She followed the line of it to the cottonwood trunk. She saw the second rope stretched between the two trunks across the trail. Her face changed. The confusion that had softened her features since waking hardened.

"Someone did this intentionally," she said.

Caleb looked toward the ferry landing, drew in a deep breath, and called out, "Liam!"

His voice carried through the cottonwoods, rolling between the trunks and out over the open ground toward the river. He waited. Called again, louder this time.

An answering shout came back, distant but clear. Then the sound of boots, moving fast.

Liam came around the curve in the trail and stopped when he saw Belle on the ground.

"I'm all right," Belle said. "I think my wrist is sprained... my ribs bruised. I can see straight, and I can think. I'm pretty sure nothing is broken."

Liam knelt beside her on the opposite side from Caleb. He looked at her wrist, at the way she held her left arm against her body, and at the careful rigidity of her posture.

"Help me get her standing," Caleb said.

Caleb positioned himself on her injured side, Liam on the right, his grip firm on her forearm. Belle pushed with her legs and rose with a sharp intake of breath that she cut off before it could become anything louder. She stood between them, her weight distributed on both legs, her balance steady.

"I can ride if someone leads the horse," Belle said.

Caleb kept his hand on her arm. "We'll use Liam's gelding. Your mare needs that rope cut from her leg before she goes anywhere."

Liam crossed to the mare and crouched down. He worked the rope free with careful hands, unwinding it from the fetlock, and examined the mare's leg. The horse stood patiently, shifting its weight but showing no lameness.

Caleb brought Liam's gelding alongside Belle. "Left foot in the stirrup. I'll lift from the right."

She took the saddle horn with her right hand. Caleb placed his hands at her waist and lifted as she swung her right leg over the horse's back. She settled into the saddle with the careful rigidity of a person managing pain through posture, her spine straight, her shoulders held level.

He placed his hand on her knee to steady her, and he kept it there as they began walking. Liam untied the second rope from the cottonwood trunks and coiled it with the first, then took the mare's reins and fell into step behind them on the trail.

They moved slowly. The cottonwoods thinned as the ground rose toward the homestead, the canopy opening to admit the full warmth of the morning sun. Belle held herself upright in the saddle with a discipline that cost her something with each step the horse took; the slight jar of hooves on packed earth translated through the saddle and into her ribs. She didn't complain. Her jaw was set, her eyes forward, and her right hand steady on the saddle horn.

Caleb walked beside her with his hand on her knee. His thumb rested against the worn fabric of her trousers, and the warmth of her leg beneath the cloth was a presence he was aware of with every step, a small, steady confirmation that she was here, that she was upright, and everything was going to be fine.

Chapter 28

Winnie reached them in the yard before Belle could speak, her skirt gathered in one hand and her face carrying the expression Belle had seen from the saddle as they approached—the flash of panic already hardening into something more contained. Winnie's attention moved from Belle's posture in the saddle to the wrist she held against her body, to the rigid way she carried her left side, cataloguing each detail.

"What happened?"

"My horse tripped, and I was thrown," Belle said.

Winnie looked at Caleb, his hand still resting on Belle's knee. She looked at Liam, who led Belle's mare by the reins, coiled ropes slung over his shoulder.

"Get her inside," Winnie said.

Winnie turned and walked back toward the porch, her stride quick and purposeful. Caleb took the gelding's reins and led the horse forward. Liam followed with the mare.

When they reached the fence rail near the porch steps, Caleb moved to Belle's side. She shifted her weight to dismount, and the movement sent a flare through her ribs that locked the breath in her chest. Before she could try again, Caleb reached up and placed his hands on her waist.

"Let me," he said.

She didn't argue. She released the saddle horn and let him lift her down, his hands steady beneath her ribs, bearing her weight with care. He set her feet on the ground, and she stood for a moment against him, her right hand gripping the front of his shirt, the pain settling from sharp to bearable. Then he bent and gathered her up, one arm beneath her knees and the other behind her back.

Caleb carried her up the porch steps. Winnie held the door open, and he turned sideways through the frame.

Caleb lowered her onto a chair by the table. She settled with her back straight and her left arm held close against her side, her right hand flat on the pine surface of the table.

"Caleb, would you fill the basin with water from the barrel on---"

He was out the door before Winnie finished the sentence.

Winnie walked into the kitchen and gathered supplies.

"Winnie, I'm banged up, not dying," Belle said.

"I'll be the judge of that." Winnie said as she knelt beside the chair and took Belle's left hand. She turned her wrist slowly, rotating the joint through its range while watching Belle's face. The rotation produced a flare of pain that Belle contained behind closed teeth, but the joint moved. It moved through its full arc with resistance and protest but without the grinding halt that a fracture would produce.

"Can you make a fist?" Winnie asked.

Belle tried. Her fingers curled partway and stopped.

Winnie nodded and moved to her ribs. Her fingers pressed along Belle's left side below her arm, moving from front to back in a sequence that was methodical and unhurried, each point of contact a question asked through touch. Belle flinched when Winnie's fingers found the place where the pain was deepest. The flinch was involuntary and sharp enough to pull a sound from her that she would rather not have made.

"Deeply bruised," Winnie said. "There may be a crack underneath, but the treatment is the same, regardless. Binding and rest."

"I don't have time for rest."

"You have time for what your body requires, Belle, and not a minute less." Winnie stood. "Look at me. Follow my finger."

Winnie held one finger in front of Belle's face and moved it slowly from left to right, then up and down, watching Belle's eyes track the movement. She leaned close and studied Belle's pupils; her face inches away, her attention focused with the concentration of a woman performing a task that mattered more than any task she had performed that morning.

"Your pupils are even, and they're tracking," Winnie said. "You have a lump on your temple the size of a walnut. Does the light bother you?"

"No more than your fussing does."

Winnie smiled as Caleb set the basin of water on the table. "You, Mr. Sterling, must step outside for a moment. I'll let you know when you can come back in."

She then soaked a length of cotton sheeting in the cold water and wrung it until it dripped without streaming. She wrapped the cold cloth around her swollen wrist in a figure-eight pattern that held the joint immobile without cutting the circulation, tucking the ends beneath the wrap so they would hold. The cold bit into Belle's skin and traveled inward through the swelling, and the relief of it was immediate enough that she closed her eyes.

"Arms up," Winnie said. "As high as you can manage, and hold up your shirt so I can wrap your ribs."

Belle did as she was told, and Winnie took a wide strip of dry cotton sheeting and wrapped it around Belle's torso, binding the bruised ribs with a pressure that was firm without being cruel. She tied the binding off beneath Belle's right arm.

"Shirt sleeve up," Winnie said.

Belle rolled her sleeve to the elbow, revealing the scrapes along her forearm where the ground had taken skin during the fall. Winnie opened the salve jar and worked the balm into the abrasions with her fingertips, her touch light over the raw patches, thorough over the surrounding skin. When she finished, she set the jar on the table and placed both hands on Belle's face, one palm on each cheek, and held her there for a long moment. The contact said everything Winnie's composure had not permitted her to speak aloud.

"God was watching over you." Winnie said as she released her and stepped back. She washed her hands in the basin and dried them on the dishcloth.

"Caleb, you can come back in," she said loudly enough that he could hear her from outside. "Liam, I need you in here."

Liam and Caleb both came through the front door. Caleb took the chair across from Belle, and Liam stood near the table, his arms folded across his chest.

"Who in the world would do something like this?" Belle said. "Ropes strung between trees on a trail that only we ride. What purpose does that serve? What does someone gain by putting me, or Liam for that matter, on the ground?"

"I cannot even wrap my head around the why right now. But I'd venture to say they were set during the night," Caleb said. "While the three of us were watching the river."

Belle turned what she knew over in her mind, testing its edges. Whoever had strung those ropes had known the trail was unguarded. Had known that they were at the ferry landing and the bridge site through the night, their attention fixed on the river.

"Someone wanted to hurt you, Belle," Liam said. "Not the ferry. Not the bridge. You."

"But why?" Belle pressed her right hand flat against the table. "We've done nothing to anyone. The ferry operates the same as it has for years; I've not forbidden or refused a ride to anyone that could cause anger. The bridge is being built at the site that the committee and the consortium approved. Why would someone want to hurt any of us?"

"Is it a warning?" Winnie asked. "Something meant to frighten rather than injure?"

"A rope strung at a height to trip a horse is not a warning," Liam said. "It's built to put the rider on the ground. If Belle had been riding faster, if the mare had gone down harder—" He stopped.

"Is this tied to the ferry cable?" Belle asked. "To the bridge site?"

"That's what I've been sorting through," Caleb said. He leaned forward in his chair and rested his forearms on the table, his hands clasped. "I had a conversation with Horace this morning. Before I came to the landing."

"What did he say?" Belle asked.

"He mentioned your uncle's visit. He said Marshal Callahan had paid him an unexpected call, and he implied that someone had been putting ideas into the marshal's head about his conduct. He wanted me to know he was aware of it." Caleb paused. "Then he moved on to what he actually wanted to discuss. He pushed harder for the northern bridge site. He used language about extraction potential and heavy material transport north of town. He referenced geological assessments commissioned by investors who have an interest in the development of the land."

"He said investors had commissioned geological assessments that show commercially viable deposits," Caleb continued. "He said the current bridge approach through Main Street cannot sustain wagons running at tonnage, and that a crossing north of the current site, at the narrows, would connect to the benchland roads without routing through town."

"Did he say what kind of deposits?" Belle asked.

"No, he did not. He talked about operations that would require heavy material transport on a scale this town hasn't seen, and development that would need years of engineering work. Not months. Years. Roads into the benchlands. Infrastructure for operations this community hasn't imagined."

"He's talking about mining," Belle said. "Nothing else requires heavy material transport and years of engineering in a valley. Timber doesn't require that kind of infrastructure. Ranching doesn't require new roads built to carry tonnage."

Winnie sat down in the chair beside Belle. "Amos mentioned something about this...at the Sunday lunch we all had together. He said he'd heard talk about mining interests in this area, about land being bought up north of Providence Ridge. He didn't know who was behind it."

"The land office in town might have records of those purchases," Belle said.

"Horace offered more than information," Caleb said. "He offered his own money to fund a northern site survey. Not consortium funds. His personal money." He held Belle's gaze across the table. "And he subtly offered me a future. Years of engineering work in this valley. Roads, infrastructure, and structural projects on a scale that would keep me employed for as long as I cared to stay. He said he would see to it personally that the right engineer was not overlooked."

"In exchange for what?" Belle asked.

"He never stated the condition. He didn't have to. He wants a second bridge location approved at the Narrows, and he wants an engineer who will provide the documentation to support it. He asked me to keep the conversation between us."

Belle considered the pieces of the puzzle laid out before her, each one distinct, each one connected to the next by a logic that was becoming difficult to dismiss. The ferry cable—cut to discredit the crossing and create urgency for a permanent bridge. The bridge-site destruction—designed to cause delays and rattle those working on the site. The ropes on the trail—designed to sideline herself or Liam from the ferry and further destabilize the only crossing this valley had.

"Every act of sabotage pushes in the same direction," Caleb said. "And every conversation Horace has had with me serves the same purpose. Someone... more than likely Horace himself... wants a bridge built at the narrows, to serve freight road access for an operation Horace will not name. These acts of sabotage aren't random. They're designed to create pressure and force delays. But the thing I cannot account for is why the trail. Why the ropes? Why target you or Liam specifically?"

Belle had been listening with the part of her mind that sorted facts. The facts arranged themselves in a sequence, and when the last piece settled into place, the picture it formed sent a cold thread through her chest.

"Our land," Belle said. "Our grandparents' property sits north of Owen Gallagher's property," she continued. "If someone with mining interests is buying land north of Providence Ridge, and if the geological assessments Horace mentioned are real, then whoever is behind this may not only want a bridge to move their freight. They may want to buy up all the land in that area. Our land sits unattended; anyone could have been out there assessing what is below the ground, and we would not know any different."

"Belle," Liam said.

"Think it through," she said. "If the ropes were meant to frighten us, then the question is what the fear is supposed to accomplish. If someone wanted to persuade us to sell our land, the first thing they would need is for us to feel unsafe or shaken up, and the next would be for us to be needy. The ferry sabotage cost us income. The ropes cost me my ability to work for a few days. If these incidents continue, if the pressure builds, a family stretched thin enough and frightened enough might be willing to sell. It's a stretch, but it's all I can figure."

"You think someone is trying to drive us to sell that land," Winnie said.

"I think it's possible. I'm thinking broadly, and I could be wrong about the land. But the pattern holds regardless. Every act of sabotage weakens our position, could instill fear, and cause a loss of funds. Every conversation Horace has had with Caleb points toward mining interests that need access through the northern part of the valley. And the ropes on the trail were not set to damage the ferry or delay the bridge. They were set as a warning or a wake-up call intended to hurt a Callahan."

Caleb sat back in his chair. His expression carried the focused stillness of a man recalculating a load after a variable has changed. "If you're right, then Horace's offer to me this morning takes on a different shape. He wasn't only trying to secure an engineer for a second bridge. He was trying to secure cooperation from the man who works beside you daily."

Belle felt the truth of that statement settle into the bruised places beneath her ribs. She looked at Caleb across the table, and she saw in his face something that was neither anger nor fear but resolve.

"Liam," Belle said. "I need you to ride into town and find Uncle Tom. Bring him here."

"I'll leave now."

"Do not speak a word of what happened this morning. Not one word. Just tell him he must come now."

"What about the ferry?" Liam said.

"The ferry can wait. Now go, Liam. Caleb," she said. "I'd be grateful if you stayed here with Winnie and me. I'd feel safer with you here."

"I'm not going anywhere," he said.

Chapter 29

The front door opened, and Marshal Tom came through it with his hat in his hand and Liam a step behind him. Tom's gaze swept the room: the kitchen table, the basin of water, and the salve jar. His attention settled on Belle. Caleb watched the marshal's eyes move from the cotton wrap binding her wrist to the way she held her left arm pressed against her ribs to the swollen lump at her temple.

Tom crossed the room in three strides, crouched beside Belle's chair, and looked up into her face. "Are you all right?"

"I'm banged up pretty well. Nothing is broken."

Tom held her gaze for a long moment, and Caleb could see the effort it cost him to keep his expression level. The marshal straightened and looked around the room — at Winnie, who stood near the cookstove, at Liam in the doorway, and then him sitting beside Belle with her hand in his. Tom's jaw shifted, a small lateral movement that tightened the muscles along the side of his face before he controlled it.

He pulled a chair from the table and sat down. He set his hat on the pine surface beside the basin. "Tell me everything."

Caleb looked at Belle, and she gave him a small nod. "The three of us spent last night on the riverbank near the bridge site," Caleb said. "After the damage to the bridge site, Belle and I discussed the need for someone to keep watch overnight. Liam, Belle, and I camped on the bank within sight of the bridge and the ferry landing. The night passed without incident. No one approached either site."

"Who knew about the watch?" Tom asked.

"No one but Belle, Liam, Winnie and myself."

Tom sat with that. His hands rested flat on the table, his fingers spread. "Go on."

"At first light, Belle left the camp to ride back here," Caleb said. "She intended to change clothes and bring food back for Liam, who was staying at the river. Belle hadn't ridden far on the trail when her horse tripped. I was in town at the boardinghouse. I changed into clean clothes and ate breakfast."

"My horse caught a rope strung between two trees," Belle said. She shifted in her chair, and the movement pulled a tightness across her face that she smoothed before it fully formed. "The rope was set at a height that would catch the horse across its legs. She went down, and I went over her neck. There was a second rope strung between two trees as well. Someone set two separate ropes, spaced apart, on a trail that only Liam and I ride."

Tom leaned forward. "Two ropes."

"Two," Belle said. "The first brought the horse down. The second would have caught any rider who managed to stay mounted through the first."

"So whoever set those ropes on the trail knew — or guessed — that the three of you were at the river," Tom said. "And the obvious attempt was to cause injury... either to the horse or the rider."

"That is what we believe," Caleb said.

Tom looked at Liam. "The rope."

Liam stepped forward and laid the ropes on the table beside the marshal's hat. The hemp was pale, the fibers clean and tight in a braid that had not been exposed to weather or work. Tom picked up the coil and turned it in his hands, running his thumb along the cut end where the fibers had been severed.

"New hemp," Tom said. "The cut ends are clean — a sharp knife, not a saw." He looked at Liam. "Tell me about the placement. How high off the ground, how far apart, which trees, how the knots were tied."

"The first rope was strung between two cottonwoods, about twelve inches off the trail," Liam said. "Knotted around the trunk on each side with a timber hitch — the kind you'd use to secure a drag line. Tight enough to hold but designed to release cleanly if you pulled the free end. The second rope was a little higher, closer to eighteen inches, strung between cottonwoods a few feet away. Same knot."

"A timber hitch," Tom said.

"Both of them."

Tom set the rope on the table. "What else?"

Caleb felt Belle's hand tighten against his. "I had a conversation with Horace Pritchard after breakfast," Caleb said. "The conversation was presented as casual, but it was not."

"What did he say?"

"He began by implying that someone had been talking to you about his conduct. He said you had paid him an unexpected visit, and he wanted me to know he was aware of it. He didn't accuse me directly, but his manner suggested he believed it was me."

Tom's expression gave nothing away. "Go on."

"He moved from that to the bridge," Caleb said. "He pushed again for the northern site at the narrows. He referenced geological assessments commissioned by investors — his word — that indicate considerable extraction potential north of town. He said the current bridge approach through Main Street cannot sustain wagons running at tonnage, and that a crossing north of the current site would connect to freight roads without routing through town."

"He referenced heavy material transport on a scale this town hasn't seen," Caleb continued. "He spoke of development that would require years of engineering work. Roads into the benchlands. Infrastructure for operations that this community has not imagined. He said he would personally see to it that the right engineer was not overlooked." Caleb paused. "That was a promise of long-term employment. It was aimed at me specifically, and it was conditional on cooperation he didn't name but didn't need to."

"He's talking about mining," Tom said.

"That is what I believe," Caleb said. "Nothing else fits the language."

"Did he name the investors?"

"He did not. He offered his personal money to fund a northern bridge site survey."

Tom sat with that for several seconds. Caleb watched the marshal process the information.

"I want to be direct about something," Caleb said. "I've worked job sites across the western territories many times before coming here. Horace Pritchard is not the first man to approach me with an offer dressed as a conversation. I've been offered side work, asked to perform tasks under the table, and pressured to adjust figures. I know what it feels like when a man is buying your cooperation without saying the word purchase." He held Tom's gaze. "I felt that pressure this morning. Horace was careful and polished, but what he was doing was offering me a future in this valley in exchange for my professional support of a bridge location that served his interests. When I pressed him on the specifics of why he wanted this second bridge, his composure cracked. Not badly. But enough."

"Enough for what?" Tom asked.

"Enough for me to know that what lies beneath this is larger than just another bridge for a simple operation. Something is moving in the valley north of town. Something profitable, something organized, and Horace is either directing it or standing close enough to the men who are that the distinction doesn't matter."

Winnie came to the table and sat in the chair beside Belle. She set the poultice she had been preparing on the table. "Amos mentioned something about this at Sunday lunch. He said he'd heard talk about mining interests in this area, about land being bought up."

"If someone has been buying land north of town," Winnie continued, "the records would be at Ned Farley's land office. Every deed transfer in this area passes through his hands."

Tom nodded. "That's where I'm going when I leave this table."
The kitchen was quiet for a moment.

"Let me tell you all where I stand," Tom said. He placed both hands flat on the table. "We have three acts of sabotage. A cable cut to look like wear — precise, done by someone who understands rope. A bridge site torn apart — broad damage aimed at delay. Ropes on a trail aimed at putting a rider on the ground. The first two targeted properties. The last targeted my niece or my nephew."

"I have Owen Gallagher admitting that Horace offered to buy his ranch contingent on a bridge being built on the river where his land sits," Tom continued. "Late yesterday evening, Owen came to me and named Simon Doyle as a man Horace meets privately at the mill. Daily meetings at the end of the day, Owen says, between Horace and sometimes several men Owen does not know. Owen came to me nervous as a field mouse, and I believe his guilt has been eating at him. He knows more than he has told me, and I intend to give him the opportunity to tell the rest."

"Caleb, you telling me Horace is using mining language and offering personal money and long-term work is another piece," Tom said. "I questioned Amos yesterday about what gossip had come to him at the mercantile, and he told me he's heard chatter about mining and that land is being bought up north of town. He's noticed several men whom he does not know shopping in his store recently. They say little, but they are the observant type. The pieces are connecting."

"What will you do?" Belle asked.

"Two things, both this afternoon," Tom said. "First, the land office. I'll have Ned pull every property transaction north of Providence Ridge in the past year. I want to see who has been buying, how much ground they've acquired, and whether any of those names connect to Horace Pritchard or the consortium he represents."

"And second?" Caleb asked.

"Simon Doyle." Tom picked up the rope from the table and turned it once more in his hands, then set it down. "I'll ride out to the lumber mill and speak with him. I don't have enough to arrest anyone, and I cannot yet see the full shape of what is happening. But I know how to read a man carrying a burden. A man doing devious acts for someone else's benefit is a man who is not sleeping well. When you offer him a listening ear and the chance to set his burden down, most of them take it." He paused. "I know Simon Doyle personally. I've known him for years. I cannot see him as a man involved in something underhanded, and that is precisely why I need to look him in the eye and ask."

Tom looked at each of them in turn — Liam still standing near the door, Winnie at the table, Belle in her chair with her wrapped wrist and her bruised ribs, and Caleb beside her. "In the meantime, you all keep doing what you're doing. Caleb builds the bridge. Liam runs the ferry. Belle rests."

"I don't need—" Belle began.

"Belle. Rest. That is an order. Let your body mend. The ferry will be there tomorrow and the day after."

She didn't argue. Caleb felt her hand soften against his, the resistance draining from her grip the way tension leaves a rope when the load is shared.

"Keep your eyes on each other," Tom said. "Watch your surroundings. Liam, take one of your daddy's shotguns with you and keep it with you while you run the ferry. No one in this room confronts Horace, Simon, or Owen. No one speaks to them about what we've discussed here. Let me do my work."

Tom placed both hands on the edge of the table as if to rise, then stopped. His attention moved to Caleb. "Mr. Sterling. What are your intentions here in Providence Ridge besides the building of a bridge?"

The question arrived without preamble and without softening, direct in the way of a man who had spent decades sorting truth from talk and had no patience remaining for the distance between the two. The room fell still. Caleb could feel Winnie's attention from across the table, could feel Liam shift his weight near the door, and could feel Belle's fingers press once against his palm.

He met Tom's gaze and held it.

"My intentions as of this moment are to protect Belle and Winnie from harm," Caleb said. "As for the future, beyond the bridge build—I believe God has led me here for a purpose, and I intend to follow His lead faithfully. My intentions are pure, sir... I promise you."

Tom nodded—a single, measured movement—and stood.

"I'll come with news when I've spoken with everyone," Tom said as he picked up his hat from the table and set it on his head. "You all go on with your day. Be mindful. Be aware of your surroundings."

Tom walked to the front door. He paused with his hand on the latch and looked back at Belle. Something passed across his face that Caleb could not name but recognized, the particular expression of a man who has carried responsibility for people he loves and has just seen evidence that the carrying might, in time, be shared. Tom opened the door and stepped through it, and his boots sounded on the porch boards once, twice, three times, and then all was quiet.

Caleb sat at the kitchen table with Belle's hand in his and the afternoon light falling across the pine surface where the rope coil still lay beside the empty basin. Winnie rose from her chair and picked up the poultice she had been preparing.

"Let me see your ribs," Winnie said to Belle. "This needs to go on while it's still warm."

Belle looked at Caleb. "Go see to the horses with Liam," she said.

Caleb stepped out through the front door after Liam. The sun was high above the valley. He stood on the porch for a moment and looked at the mountains, and in the quiet he spoke a prayer that had no words, only the offering of a man who had been asked about his intentions and had answered with the truest thing he knew.

Chapter 30

The door closed behind Caleb, and Belle lifted her shirt so Winnie could apply the poultice. She unwound the cotton binding enough to lay the warm cloth against the deepest bruise below Belle's ribs, her fingers careful around the edges of the discoloration that had darkened. The poultice was warm and smelled of comfrey and something sharper beneath it, an astringent bite that cut through the sweetness.

"Hold that in place," Winnie said.

Belle pressed the cloth against her side with her right hand while Winnie rewound the binding over it, her movements sure and unhurried. When the binding was secure, Belle lowered her shirt and sat back in the chair. The warmth from the poultice spread through the bruised tissue beneath her ribs, not erasing the pain but blunting its edges, turning the sharp flare into something closer to a deep ache she could carry without wincing.

Winnie rinsed her hands in the basin and dried them. She poured two cups of coffee from the pot she had kept warm on the stove, set one in front of Belle, and sat down across from her. "How much pain are you in?"

"Enough that breathing requires planning," Belle said with a small grin. "My wrist is worse than the ribs. The ribs I can work around. The wrist means I can't grip the guide rope, which means I can't run the ferry, which means Liam runs it alone for a few days or it doesn't run at all."

"Liam can manage the ferry. You are staying here with me, and that's that." She took a sip of her coffee and watched Belle. "When Caleb carried you through that door this morning, I was standing right here. I saw his face."

Belle looked at the table.

"You were against his chest and your eyes were closed. But I watched him carry you, and I am telling you what I saw." Winnie continued. "He was terrified. Not the kind of fear a man shows when something startles him. The kind that lives in his heart. His hands were steady. His arms were steady. But his face — Belle, his face held the look of a man who understood exactly what he would lose if the damage had been worse."

Belle's throat tightened. She lifted her coffee and took a long drink.

"You didn't argue with him or fuss when he picked you up," she continued. "You closed your eyes and held onto his shirt, and you let him bring you inside."

"I was in too much pain to argue."

"You have argued through worse pain than this, and we both know it."

Belle set the cup down. The truth of what Winnie had said pressed against the place inside her chest where she kept the things she did not speak aloud. She had not argued. She had not told him that she could walk. She had gripped the front of his shirt and let him bear her weight.

"When the horse went down," Belle said, and then she stopped. She looked at the window above the washstand, where the morning light fell through the glass and pooled on the sill. "When the mare tripped and I went over her neck, I hit the ground and the pain came, and I lay there in the dirt trying to breathe for maybe a few seconds before I lost consciousness, and I had a thought."

"A thought about what?"

"Caleb. I lay on the ground with my ribs on fire and my wrist screaming, and what I thought was — I need him. Before I thought of anything practical, before I thought of anything that made sense, my first thought was of him."

Winnie said nothing. She sat with her hands around her cup and waited, and the waiting was the kindest thing she could have done, because it left space for Belle to continue or stop, and the choice was Belle's.

"That terrifies me, Winnie." Belle looked at her sister. "Not the ropes. Not whoever is doing this. The fact that I have given a man a place inside my heart where he can do the kind of damage Father did. The fact that I have let someone matter this much."

"Caleb Sterling is not Papa."

"I know he isn't."

"Do you? Because knowing it in your mind is one thing. Knowing it in the place where you make your decisions is another."

Belle felt the words land against the old wound, the one she had carried since she was seventeen and watched her father's body pulled from the river, the wound that said, *Love someone and they will fail you, depend on someone and they will drown.* She had lived inside that wound for five years. She had built the ferry operation around it, built her refusal to accept help around it, and built every wall she owned from the rubble of a father who had promised to get sober and never kept the promise.

"I know it in every part of me," Belle said. "That is what frightens me. Because if I know it — if I truly believe that Caleb is not the kind of man who breaks what he holds — then I have no more reason to keep him at a distance. The wall comes down, and there is nothing between me and the full weight of what I feel for him. Nothing to catch me if I'm wrong."

"What do you feel for him?"

Belle looked at her hands on the table — her right hand scarred and calloused from the ropes, her left hand wrapped in white cotton and held still against her body. These hands had run the ferry. These hands had spliced cables. These hands had held the family together through every season since her father died.

"I love him," Belle said. "I love him, and I don't fully understand it, because I have never felt this way about a man. I didn't know this was something I was capable of feeling. I thought whatever part of me could love a man like this had been closed off when Papa died, and I was wrong about that the way I have been wrong about most things that involve trusting another person."

Winnie's eyes were bright with unshed tears..

"I cannot imagine my life without him in it," Belle said. "I have tried. After he found me, and I came back to consciousness, the thing I could not bear wasn't the pain. It was the thought that if the damage had been worse, if the fall had taken more than it took,

I might never have seen him again. That thought was worse than anything the ground did to my body."

Winnie reached across the table and laid her hand over Belle's. "I have known since the first night he came for supper that he is the man God made for you, and you are the woman God made for him. The two of you have been circling each other like planets caught in the same gravity since."

Belle laughed. It came out rough and unsteady and surprised her, because laughter was not the response she had expected from herself in this conversation, but the image Winnie had drawn was so precise and so absurd and so true that the laughter was the only container large enough to hold all of it.

"Uncle Tom asked him about his intentions," Belle said.

"I know."

"And Caleb said he believes God led him here for a purpose."

"He did."

Belle traced the grain of the pine with her fingertip. "He didn't say the purpose was me. He didn't name it. He said he intended to follow God's lead faithfully."

"Belle," Winnie said. "The man carried you through the front door of this house and sat beside you, holding your hand while our uncle not so subtly interrogated him. He answered with his faith and his commitment to follow where God leads. You are where God led him. He knows it. Uncle Tom knows it. I know it. Liam knows it. The entire town of Providence Ridge has known it since he waded into the Yellowstone River to catch a rope for you. The only person still pretending this requires further evidence is you."

Belle looked at her sister. "I'm finished pretending."

Winnie smiled as the front door opened, and Caleb and Liam came in from the yard. Caleb had taken off his coat, and his shirtsleeves were rolled to the elbow, his forearms beneath them showing the lean, corded build of a man who had spent his professional life working outdoors. Liam followed him, his hat in his hand, his face carrying the focused expression of a young man who had a day's work ahead of him and was already calculating how to accomplish it alone.

"The horses are watered and fed," Caleb said. "We checked the barn and the chicken coop. Everything looks as it should."

"I need to get to the ferry," Liam said. He looked at Belle. "I'll turn away all heavy loads."

"You're not going without protection," Belle said.

"I know." Liam crossed to the corner of the room where the rifle stood against the wall. It was their father's Winchester, the stock worn smooth from years of handling. Liam picked it up and checked the chamber, then leaned the rifle against the table and looked back at Caleb.

"What should I tell your crew?" Liam asked.

"Tell Emmitt Lassiter I'm staying here today," Caleb said. "The plans and my notes are in the trunk at the site. Emmitt is the lead foreman, and he has my full authority to proceed with the work as laid out. If the crew needs anything or runs into a question that the plans don't answer, they can come to me here."

Liam nodded. "I'll tell Emmitt and the crew to keep a watchful eye throughout the day. Everyone on that site needs to be looking out for each other, not just working with their heads down. If anyone sees something wrong, anything at all, they come to me at the landing or they come to you here."

"Agreed," Caleb said.

Liam turned to Belle. "I don't want Caleb staying at the river alone tonight, and I don't want to be out there alone either. A man on watch by himself is asking for trouble from people who have already shown they're willing to cause it."

"What are you suggesting?" Belle asked.

"I'm suggesting Caleb stay here tonight." Liam looked at Caleb. "You and I sleep on the front porch. We can hear anyone coming. If someone decides this homestead deserves the same attention the trail and the bridge site have gotten, there will be two of us instead of one."

Belle looked at Caleb across the room. He stood near the door with the late afternoon light behind him, his sleeves rolled, his hair pushed back from his forehead, his expression carrying the quiet consideration of a man weighing a decision against its consequences and finding the consequences acceptable. She knew what Liam was saying, and she knew what it meant: Caleb at their table for supper and breakfast, and Caleb on their porch through the night. The proximity of it would have frightened her a month ago. It didn't frighten her now.

"That makes sense," Caleb said. "Staying here keeps me close to the homestead if anything happens during the night. It also makes it harder for Horace to seek me out for another conversation."

"Then it's settled," Liam said. He picked up the Winchester and slung it over his shoulder by the leather strap. He looked at Belle, and something in his face softened for a fraction of a second — the expression of a younger brother who had watched his older sister give everything she had to keep them safe and was grateful for the chance to carry some of the weight himself. "I'll be back before dark. Don't let her do anything that requires two hands, Winnie."

"I promise," Winnie said.

Liam put on his hat and walked out the door.

Caleb took the chair across from Belle. He sat with his forearms resting on the table, his hands open and still, the posture of a man who was not going anywhere and didn't need to be told what his presence in this room meant. He looked at Belle, and the look carried steadiness—no urgency, no demand, only the quiet certainty of a man who had chosen his ground and intended to hold it.

"How are your ribs?" he asked.

"Winnie's poultice is helping."

"And the wrist?"

"The wrist will keep me off the ferry for at least a week more than likely."

Winnie moved between the kitchen and the table, clearing the basin, setting a fresh pot of water on the stove, and beginning the quiet preparations that would become lunch. The sounds of her work filled the kitchen — the scrape of the kettle on the iron, the soft thud of a cutting board set on the counter, the rustle of dried herbs pulled from the jar on the shelf. The sounds were ordinary and specific, the sounds of a home being tended by a woman who understood that the most important thing she could do in this moment was make the house feel like what it was — a place where people were safe, where the world outside the door could carry its threats and its schemes and its ropes strung between trees, and inside these walls the bread would still be baked and the coffee

would still be poured and the people gathered here would still be
held.

Belle looked at the man sitting in the chair her uncle had occupied an hour before, the man who had answered Tom's question
with the plainest words faith could produce. She felt the full shape
of what her life was becoming settle around her with a weight that
was not a burden but a promise.

"Thank you for staying," she said.

"There is no place I would rather be," he said.

Chapter 31

Caleb wrote the list in a hand small enough to fit three columns on a single page. Liam ate biscuits and salt pork and read the instructions as Caleb wrote them. Winnie stood at the cookstove, turning eggs in the cast-iron skillet. Belle sat to Caleb's left, her plate cleared except for a biscuit she was pulling apart with her fingers in small, deliberate pieces.

"Emmett knows the footing plan as well as I do," Caleb said, writing as he spoke. "But I want you to tell him the northeast piling needs to be checked for plumb before they set any more stone. Second item. Another timber delivery is expected sometime today. Douglas fir for the main truss members. Emmett should inspect every piece. If any of it shows checking, waning, or rot at the heartwood, it goes back on the wagon. No exceptions."

"No exceptions," Liam repeated.

"Third. I've drawn a detail of the bracing angles for the south abutment. It's on the second page of the plan folio, inside the trunk at the bridge site. Emmett will need it when the crew gets to the knee braces this afternoon. And one last thing, if Horace comes to the site for any reason, Emmett should be polite and tell him nothing. No progress reports, no material counts, and no schedule information. If Horace asks where I am, Emmett should tell him I'm attending to personal business and leave it there."

"I expect Emmett will enjoy that particular instruction," Liam said.

Caleb signed the bottom of the page with his initials and set the pencil down. He folded the paper in thirds. Liam took the paper and tucked it inside his coat, then reached for his last biscuit, broke it in half, and used one piece to soak up the egg yolk on his plate.

The knock came at the front door while Winnie was pouring a second round of coffee.

Liam rose from his chair and crossed the room. He opened the door, and Marshal Tom stood on the porch with his hat in his hand and the collar of his coat turned up against the chill. His face carried the particular drawn quality of a man who had slept little and worked late, the lines around his eyes deepened by a night spent in motion rather than rest.

"Morning, Uncle Tom," Liam said. "Come in."

"I apologize for interrupting breakfast. I would have come last night, but I worked until well past midnight."

"Come sit," Belle said.

Tom pulled out the chair at the end of the table, and Winnie set a cup of coffee in front of him.

"I went to the land office yesterday and spoke with Ned Farley," Tom said. "He was evasive at first. I asked for general records. Homestead filings, property transfers, anything filed in the past twelve months. He pulled what he had and laid it on the counter:

small transfers, routine filings, the kind of paperwork that moves through a land office in any valley this size. Told me that was everything."

Tom paused and took his first drink of the coffee.

"But it wasn't everything. His right hand was flat on the ledger drawer. Pressed against it. The man was guarding that drawer the way a card player guards his hand when he's been dealt something he doesn't want the table to see."

"You pressed him," Caleb said.

Tom nodded. "I told him I was investigating sabotage and attempted bodily harm against my niece. I told him that obstruction by a territorial clerk in a criminal investigation carried consequences and that I intended to see the full record."

"He broke," Tom continued. "Opened the drawer. Pulled out a second set of records he'd kept separate from the public filings." Tom set his cup down. "Twenty-three property transfers were filed over the past eight months. All north of town. Totaling over three hundred acres of land."

"Who purchased the land?" Belle asked.

"Two men working on behalf of the Pacific Northwestern Development Consortium and Horace Pritchard himself. Farley processed every filing." Tom looked at Caleb. "The two buyers deferred to Horace on every question, and Horace was present for every transaction, whether the deed carried his name or theirs."

"Three hundred acres. That's a large amount of property," Caleb said.

Tom nodded. "Farley confirmed what we've suspected. The consortium's interest in Providence Ridge is not limited to the original bridge. The land purchases are positioning for mining operations. Silver, possibly gold. The geological survey the consortium commissioned before you arrived wasn't just measuring the riverbank for bridge footings. It mapped the mineral deposits in the mountains north of the valley. I imagine you were only provided the information you needed; the rest is probably in Horace's possession."

Caleb thought of the survey report he had reviewed in his first week, the pages he had assumed were thorough because thoroughness was what the consortium claimed to value.

"There's more," Tom said. "Farley admitted that six additional parcels are being targeted. Properties held by community members. The consortium hasn't made offers yet, but Farley was told the approaches would come soon." Tom held Belle's gaze. "One of those is your grandparents' property. They'll come for it."

"They can come," Belle said. "The answer will be no."

Tom turned his cup in a slow circle on the table, the ceramic scraping softly against the pine. "After the land office, I rode to the lumber mill. I found Simon finishing his shift. I asked him to walk with me, and we spoke privately."

"Simon confessed," Tom continued. "He admitted to being hired by Horace to commit acts of destruction against the ferry and against the bridge site. Horace paid him in cash. Now, I'm not sure if you all are aware, but Simon is facing foreclosure on his homestead. His wife has been sickly for months, and they can barely keep food on the table. Horace offered Simon a good sum of money, and Simon took it. There is one critical detail: Simon did not set the ropes on the trail."

Belle looked up.

"He swears to it," Tom said. "He confessed to the cable and the bridge site without hesitation, but he denied the trail ropes, and I believe him. When I told him about your fall, about the injuries, his face went white and his hands shook. I have sat across from men who were performing regret, and I have sat across from men who were sincere. I believe Simon was sincere; he was sick at the thought that you'd been hurt, Belle."

"Then who set the ropes?" Liam asked.

"Either Horace hired a second person," Tom said, "or Horace did it himself. I don't yet know which but I intend to find out."

"Did Simon say anything else about the arrangement?" Caleb asked.

"Horace approached him privately at the mill," Tom said. "The instruction was to cause incidents that would make the ferry look unsafe and delay the bridge construction. According to Simon, Horace wanted to shake up Belle and her family and the community. The purpose was pressure and fear. Pressure on you, Caleb, at first to abandon the Main Street bridge site. Then, from what you've said, it sounds like he started pushing for the second bridge besides what you were already working on. Fear among the townspeople that the ferry crossing was unreliable, and also fear was to be used as a distraction from activity going on north of town. Simon was told to cut the ferry cable to fail under load in a way that looked like wear. The bridge site damage was meant to look like vandalism by drifters."

"Fail under load," Belle repeated. "A loaded ferry with passengers and freight and livestock... we could all have been killed."

Tom said nothing. He let her words stand.

"Simon is in jail," Tom said. "He's not under arrest; I'm only holding him for now. He's willing to give a sworn statement."

"And Farley?" Caleb asked.

"I found a purchase in the records that didn't belong to the consortium. Fifty acres of property, bought with Farley's entire personal savings four months ago. He saw the direction the money was moving and placed his own bet. He kept quiet about the consortium's purchases because exposing them would have exposed his own. He's not a conspirator. He's a small man who saw an opportunity in someone else's scheme and took it, and his silence protected Horace as effectively as any threat."

Tom pushed his cup toward the center of the table. Winnie turned from the counter and refilled it without being asked, then stood beside Belle's chair with the pot held at her side.

"I need to ask you something, Belle," Tom said. "What do you want me to do about Simon?"

Caleb watched Belle as she traced the grain of the pine table with her fingertip, her hand moving over the surface as though reading something written in the wood that no one else could see.

"I've heard talk in town about the Doyle family," Belle said. "His wife has been very ill since their last child was born. All of their children are young. They've been struggling to hold on to what they have, and most people in Providence Ridge know it because in a town this size you can't hide that kind of hardship." She lifted her head. "Horace Pritchard found a man in desperate circumstances and used that desperation to turn him into a weapon. Punishing the hand while the man who guided it walks free serves no one."

Tom listened without interruption.

"If you charge Simon," Belle continued, "his family loses the man who brings income through the door. His wife is already poker-thin from sickness. His children are already going without, I'm sure. The homestead they're fighting to keep becomes the homestead they lose, not because of anything Simon's wife and children did, but because Horace saw a man drowning and offered him money."

"I'm not saying Simon bears no responsibility," Belle continued. "He does. He made a choice, and that choice put lives at risk, including mine. But he came to you willingly. He confessed. He's sitting in that cell because his conscience brought him there, and a man whose conscience brings him to confession is not the same as a man who has to be dragged."

Tom nodded once. The nod was slow, and it carried the full measure of a marshal's consideration. He looked at Caleb.

"And you?" Tom asked.

Caleb thought of the mooring line in his hands, the weight of the current pulling at his body while the scow swung toward the bank with Belle fighting the guide rope on the platform above. He thought of the cold that had lived in his bones for hours afterward. He thought of Doyle's family: a woman too sick to work and children too young to understand why their father might not come home.

"Belle has spoken," Caleb said. "I stand with her."

Tom took a long drink of his coffee and set the cup down. "Then Simon stays where he is for now. I'll use his sworn statement, and I'll keep him out of Horace's reach until this is finished. I'll have a good long talk with him before I release him."

"What are your next steps?" Caleb asked.

"I need more information before I can bring charges. Simon's word against Horace's isn't enough on its own. A clerk who hid records and a desperate man who took money don't build a case that holds. I need corroboration." He looked at Caleb. "I need you to write a formal account of every private conversation Horace has had with you since you arrived. Every offer he made and every time he pressured you. I need it in your hand, signed and witnessed."

"I'll write it today," Caleb said.

"When will you confront Horace, Uncle Tom?" Belle asked.

"Not today. I need a day to assemble everything properly. I want the documents organized and the statements sworn before I sit across from Horace, because when I do, I intend to leave him no room to maneuver." Tom reached for his hat. "I'm calling a committee meeting. Tomorrow night, at seven o'clock, at the boardinghouse. I need every member present, and I need the town to hear what's been happening to their valley."

Liam stood up from his chair. "I'll help spread the word about the meeting tomorrow."

"I'd appreciate that," Tom said. "You all have a good day, and I'll see you tomorrow evening."

He put his hat on and walked to the door. Liam followed him out onto the porch.

Chapter 32

Winnie had carried the seed basket onto the porch after the breakfast dishes were cleared. The basket was shallow and wide, woven from willow strips their grandmother had cut from the creek bank years before the ferry existed. Inside it, Winnie had arranged her collection of saved seeds in small cloth pouches and folded paper envelopes, each one labeled in her careful handwriting with the variety and the year of harvest.

"The pole beans did well in the south rows last year," Winnie said, holding an envelope to the light and shaking the seeds inside it. "I saved enough for three full rows this season. We'll have enough to can through August and still sell some to Amos."

"The south row gets shade from the barn in the afternoon," Belle said. She sat in the chair nearest the porch rail with her bandaged wrist resting in her lap, her right hand wrapped around a cup of coffee that had gone lukewarm. Her ribs ached beneath the poultice binding when she shifted position, a deep pull that reminded her to sit still.

"It gets shade after three o'clock," Winnie said. "Before that it's in full sun, and the beans only need the morning hours to set their flowers."

"You know best. The garden is your domain," Belle said.

Caleb sat in the chair beside Belle with his legs stretched in front of him, his boots crossed at the ankles. The folded pages of the account he had written for Marshal Tom were tucked into his shirt pocket. He had finished the document an hour ago, four pages of careful script detailing every private conversation Horace Pritchard had conducted with him since his arrival in Providence Ridge.

When Winnie held up a pouch of carrot seeds and frowned at the quantity, he leaned forward to look.

"Is that enough for the space you have?" he asked.

"It's thin," Winnie said. "Carrots need to be seeded heavily because not every seed takes, and you thin them after the first true leaves come in. This might cover one row. Last year I had enough for two."

"Could Amos order seed from Livingston?"

"He could, but the freight cost doubles the price, and by the time the order arrives, the planting window will have closed. Carrots need to go in early. They can take frost, but they need the cool soil to germinate." Winnie set the pouch aside and reached for the next envelope. "I'll make do with one row."

The sound of hooves reached the porch from the direction of the trail, and Belle turned her head. A rider was coming up the rise at a canter, the horse's legs dark with trail mud, the figure in the saddle sitting forward with the urgency of a man on an errand. Belle stood from her chair, and the movement pulled at her ribs hard enough that she pressed her right hand against her side. Winnie rose beside her.

The horse was Liam's gelding. The rider was not Liam.

Belle's stomach dropped. She gripped the porch rail with her good hand and watched the gelding come up the last stretch of the rise, its sides heaving. Emmett Lassiter pulled back on the reins as he approached the yard.

Caleb was already standing. "Emmett."

"Nothing's wrong," Emmett said, raising one hand as he led the gelding toward the rail. "Everyone's fine. Liam's fine. He loaned me his horse to ride out here because I told him this was a matter that probably shouldn't wait."

Belle released the rail. The blood that had left her face came back in a slow flush that she could feel in her cheeks and her ears.

Emmett reached into his coat and pulled out an envelope, cream-colored and sealed with wax. He climbed the porch steps and held the envelope out to Caleb. "A man rode into the bridge site not twenty minutes ago looking for you. He asked for you by name. I told him you weren't at the site today but that I knew where to find you, and I offered to deliver the message. He handed me this letter and rode off without another word."

Caleb took the envelope. "Thank you, Emmett. I appreciate you riding out."

"The crew is working hard. Liam delivered your instructions this morning, and we've got the northeast piling checked and the stone course underway. The timber delivery hasn't arrived yet." Emmett touched the brim of his hat and turned back to the gelding. "Good day, ladies. I need to get back to work."

He mounted, turned the gelding, and rode back down the rise.

Belle watched Caleb turn the envelope in his hands. He broke the wax seal and unfolded the letter inside.

She watched his face as he read. His expression became still. His eyes moved across the lines of text once, then returned to the top and read them again, and on the second reading his jaw clenched.

He folded the letter and slid it into the breast pocket of his shirt.

"Bad news?" Belle asked.

He looked at her. "The Pacific Northwestern Development Consortium has terminated my contract. Effective immediately. I am no longer the bridge engineer. The letter cites failure to maintain the project timeline and deviation from consortium directives regarding site assessment."

"That is Horace's doing," Belle said.

"The letter bears the consortium's seal and an officer's signature, of whom I imagine is somewhere within the valley as we speak, moving forward with whatever they are planning. But the grounds it cites are fabricated, and the timing is not a coincidence. Horace knows that Tom has been investigating. He probably knows Simon confessed. This is his response. If I have no contract, I have no authority at the bridge site, no income, and no professional standing in this town. He is cutting me loose before the committee meeting tomorrow."

Belle stood on the porch with the valley behind her and the mountains filling the sky to the east. She looked at the man standing three feet from her with a letter in his pocket that had just taken from him every material thing he had come to Providence Ridge to build. His contract. His wages. His professional reputation in the territory. The bridge that was supposed to be his redemption from

Wyoming, the structure he had poured his skill and his conscience and his faith into for weeks, was no longer his to build.

"What will you do?" she asked.

Caleb looked at her, and his face held nothing she was looking for. No retreat. No calculation. No flicker of a man weighing his options against his losses. What his face held was the expression of a man who had already made his decision and was at peace.

"I'm not leaving if that's what you're thinking," he said. "Not because of the bridge, though I intend to finish it. God led me to this valley, and the Pacific Northwestern Development Consortium does not have the authority to override that call. I will finish the bridge because this town needs it, and I will do it without the consortium's name or money behind me. But the bridge is not why I am staying, Belle. You are."

She crossed the porch to him. Two steps on the rough planks, her boots quiet against the wood, her bandaged wrist held against her body, and her right hand lifting to his face. She placed her palm against his jaw, the calluses of her rope-scarred fingers rough against the line of his cheekbone, and she lifted her left hand despite her bruised rib's protest. She held him between her hands, and she looked into his brown eyes from a distance of inches and saw in them the thing she had told Winnie she felt, reflected back to her with a steadiness that didn't waver.

She leaned in and kissed him.

The kiss was brief, tender, and it remade her world. His lips were warm against hers, and his hands came to her waist with a gentleness that held her without pulling. She leaned into him and felt his arms close around her. And for a span of seconds that belonged to no clock and no calendar, Belle Callahan stood in the arms of the man she loved and let the full measure of it exist without condition or defense.

She drew back.

"You are not building that bridge alone," Belle said.

"No," he said. "I am not. I'll have you by my side."

Winnie's voice came from behind Caleb, steady and practical and carrying the faintest tremor of emotion she was working to contain. "I will help. Whatever needs doing at the bridge site. If the crew needs food brought out, I will cook it. If they need tools handed up, I will hand them. If someone needs bolts driven, I will learn how to drive bolts. I want to be a part of this, Caleb."

Belle grinned. "I'm not of much use with one hand for now, but whatever I can do to help, I will."

Caleb looked at both of them with gratitude. "I accept the help and I appreciate it. I need to ride into town and show Tom the termination letter and give him the written account I finished this morning. The committee meeting is tomorrow evening, and Tom will want every piece of evidence assembled before he faces Horace."

"Go," Belle said. "We'll be fine here."

"I don't believe Horace will cause any more trouble today. He's made his move with the letter, but I worry about leaving you without protection."

"Papa's other Winchester is in the house," Winnie said. "Not that I expect we'll need it. I'm more dangerous with a cast-iron skillet, and any man with sense wouldn't come near us."

The laughter that escaped Belle was small and unexpected.

Caleb smiled. "And I hope I never have to witness the damage I'm sure you could do with that skillet."

Chapter 33

Horace Pritchard was descending the boardinghouse stairs when Caleb looked up.

The dining room held more people than it had held for any meeting since the bridge project began. The long table had been pushed against the far wall, the mismatched chairs arranged in rows facing the end of the room where Marshal Tom stood with a leather satchel on the chair at his right hand. Every seat was taken. Amos Pemberton sat in the front row beside his wife Margaret, his expression carrying the particular gravity of a man who understood that something consequential was about to happen in his town and intended to witness every moment of it. Mrs. Hanscombe stood at her post near the kitchen doorway with her hands folded at her waist. Owen Gallagher sat three rows back with his wife beside him, his hat in his hands. Several ranchers filled the chairs along the walls. Townspeople stood where there were no chairs left, their conversations lowered to the murmur of people who had come because word had reached them that this meeting was important.

Emmett Lassiter stood along the far wall near the front door, and beside him stood the other seven other members of the bridge crew.

Liam held his position along the wall nearest the kitchen. Winnie sat beside Belle in the front row, her shawl across her shoulders, her hands quiet in her lap. Belle sat with her bandaged wrist resting against her leg and her posture straight despite her ribs that still ached. When Caleb looked at her, she looked back at him with a steadiness that carried no anxiety, only the calm attention of a woman who had strong faith in God for whatever was about to take place in this room.

Horace reached the bottom of the stairs. He wore his pressed wool suit, the collar and cuffs sharp, and his boots polished. He surveyed the room with the quick, proprietary assessment of a man cataloging who was present. His expression registered the size of the gathering without alarm. He crossed to the side of the room where a narrow space remained between the last row of chairs and the wall, and he stood with his hands clasped in front of him, his posture composed, his face carrying the pleasant neutrality it always carried.

Marshal Tom stepped forward. "I want to thank everyone for coming tonight. I know this is short notice, and I know some of you rode a distance to be here. I called this meeting because there are matters before this committee and this community that have gone unaddressed long enough, and the evidence I've gathered over the past several days requires a public hearing."

Tom opened his leather satchel and removed a folded document. "I'm going to begin with a sworn confession given to me by Simon Doyle."

A murmur moved through the room. Caleb watched it travel across the faces nearest him, recognition on some, confusion on others.

Tom unfolded the document and read aloud. His voice was measured and unhurried, and the words he read were Simon Doyle's words of confession and signed at the bottom with his name. The confession detailed the sabotage of the ferry cable; the cuts were placed between the outer strands where the damage would not show during a routine inspection, aimed to fail under the weight of a heavily loaded crossing. It detailed the destruction at the bridge construction site. It named the man who had commissioned and paid for each act.

Horace Pritchard.

The name landed in the room, and the murmur that followed it was not surprise on every face but confirmation on some and shock on others. A rancher near the back wall shifted on his feet. Margaret Pemberton turned to look at Horace, and the look she gave him carried the particular disappointment of a woman who had extended hospitality to a man and now understood what that hospitality had sheltered. Amos sat facing forward with his jaw set.

Horace stood with his hands clasped and his expression carrying the mild attentiveness of a man listening to information that concerned him professionally but did not disturb him personally.

Tom folded the confession, set it aside and reached into the satchel again, withdrawing a second set of documents.

"I have obtained records from the land office." Tom held the papers where the room could see them. "These records show a pattern of property purchases north of town. The purchases were made over a period of months by two men employed by the Pacific Northwestern Development Consortium and by Horace Pritchard, also an employee."

"What kind of land is it?" a rancher near the wall asked.

"A variety from flat land to the mountains," Tom said. "The parcels are consistent with preparation for mining operations. The property to the north of town shows geological indicators that have attracted interest from minerals found there." He set the land office documents beside the confession. "The second bridge location that Mr. Pritchard has been advocating for since his arrival would place the crossing at a point that serves these northern parcels directly, routing heavy wagon traffic from the mining operations around the town and onto the territorial road without passing through Providence Ridge at all."

"He told me that the second location was about diverting freight tonnage away from the heart of this town," Amos said. "He said it was an engineering consideration."

"It was a financial one as well," Tom said as he withdrew the next document from the satchel. "This is a formal written account prepared by Caleb Sterling, the bridge engineer, detailing every private conversation Horace Pritchard conducted with him since his arrival in Providence Ridge." Tom looked at Caleb briefly, then addressed the room. "Mr. Sterling's account documents repeated attempts by Mr. Pritchard to pressure him into supporting a northern bridge location. These attempts included references to mining operations that the consortium had not disclosed to the committee, a private offer of personal compensation beyond his contracted salary, a veiled promise of future employment with the consortium contingent on his cooperation, and direct pressure from Mr. Pritchard."

Caleb felt the weight of every eye in the room pass over him and settle.

"Mr. Sterling refused every approach," Tom said. "He documented each conversation in writing and delivered the account to me voluntarily."

Tom set the document down and turned toward where Owen Gallagher sat. "Owen."

Owen sat for a moment with his hat in his hands, turning it by the brim, and then he stood. "Mr. Pritchard approached me last autumn. He knew my ranch was in trouble. He knew about the debt. He offered to buy my property at a price that would have cleared what I owed, but the offer was contingent on a bridge being built on the river where my property sits. I admit at first I was willing to do whatever Mr. Pritchard asked of me so that I could get out of debt which included spreading gossip, starting lies and following Caleb Sterling around town and reporting his doings back to Horace. I'm not proud of any of that. My apologies for what I have done."

He sat down and his wife reached for his arm

"There is one more piece of evidence," Tom said. He reached into the satchel and held up the cream-colored envelope Caleb had received the previous day. "Yesterday morning, the Pacific Northwestern Development Consortium terminated Mr. Sterling's contract as bridge engineer. Effective immediately. The letter cites failure to maintain the project timeline and deviation from consortium directives."

A woman Caleb didn't recognize spoke from the third row. "If they've terminated the engineer who is building our bridge?"

"That is a question this meeting will answer," Tom said.

"They fired him for no good reason," Emmett said from his position along the wall. "Every man on this crew knows Mr. Sterling built to specification, and we were ahead of schedule until the bridge site was attacked."

Several of the crew members along the wall nodded.

Tom set the termination letter on the chair with the other documents and turned to face Horace Pritchard.

"Mr. Pritchard. You've heard the evidence presented. You are welcome to address this committee."

Horace unclasped his hands and took a step forward. "I appreciate the opportunity, Marshal. I came to Providence Ridge as a representative of the Pacific Northwestern Development Consortium, and every investment I have made in this valley has been made with the full knowledge and support of legitimate business interests. The land purchases north of town are lawful transactions recorded in the territorial land office. There is nothing improper about a man investing in property he believes will appreciate in value. That is how the West is built. The second bridge location I proposed was based on my assessment that heavy wagon traffic from future commerce would be better served by a crossing that diverted that traffic around the town center rather than through it. That is a reasonable position, and I stand by it."

He paused and let his gaze move across the room. "As for Simon Doyle's confession, I would like to remind everyone that Mr.

Doyle is a man facing serious criminal charges who has every reason to shift blame. A desperate man will say whatever he believes will lessen his consequences. His accusations against me are exactly that. Accusations."

Mrs. Hanscombe spoke from her station near the kitchen doorway. "Mr. Pritchard, I have served you breakfast, lunch, and supper at my table for weeks. I have watched you eat my food and sleep under my roof and walk through my town as though you owned it. I have heard enough tonight to know that the man I fed was not the man he presented himself to be, and in my establishment that is a debt that cannot be settled with charm."

"There is a question that I need answered tonight." Tom looked directly at Horace. "Simon Doyle confessed to the ferry cable sabotage and the destruction at the bridge site. Those acts are accounted for. But there is a third incident that remains unresolved. Ropes were tied between trees across the trail between the ferry landing and the Callahan homestead. That trail is used by the Callahan family and almost no one else. My niece rode into those ropes on horseback. She was thrown from her horse and sustained injuries to her wrist and ribs."

The room erupted. Voices broke from three directions at once: the sharp exclamation of people who had not known, the lower sound of people who had heard rumors and now understood them to be true. A rancher's wife turned to look at Belle, and the look carried the fierce protectiveness of a community that regarded the Callahan family as its own.

Belle sat still. Caleb felt the tension in her posture beside him, the controlled stillness of a woman who didn't want to be the subject of the room's sympathy but would endure it because the truth required it.

Tom waited for the room to settle. When it did, he looked at Horace again.

"Simon Doyle did not tie those ropes. He confessed to every act he committed, and the ropes on the trail were not among them. That trail leads to one place, Mr. Pritchard. It leads to the home of the woman whose ferry you paid to have sabotaged." Tom paused. "I believe you are responsible for those ropes."

The room held its breath.

Horace said nothing.

The silence lasted five seconds, then ten. Horace stood against the wall with his jaw set and his eyes fixed on a point above Marshal Tom's head.

Amos Pemberton rose from his chair.

He stood with the deliberate motion of a man whose patience had reached its boundary, and when he turned to face the room, his voice carried the authority of the town's most established businessman addressing his neighbors in the place where their community gathered.

"I have heard enough," he said. "I will not stand by while outsiders come into this town and undermine the people who built it. I will not tolerate sabotage against the ferry that has served this valley for years. I will not tolerate the manipulation of this committee by a man whose every word has been designed to serve his own profit at the expense of our community. This is not worth my peace, and it is not worth the peace of any man or woman in this room."

He turned toward the committee members. "I propose that the town of Providence Ridge sever all ties with the Pacific Northwestern Development Consortium, effective tonight. I propose that the bridge be completed as a community-funded project, paid for through community subscription, county petition, and whatever resources we can raise ourselves." He looked at Caleb. "And I propose that Caleb Sterling be hired directly by the town of Providence Ridge as lead engineer, answerable to this committee and to no one else."

"I second it," Mrs. Hanscombe said from the kitchen doorway.

Tom looked across the room. "The motion has been made and seconded. All in favor."

The vote moved through the room like a river finding its channel. Every hand went up. Every voice carried it. Owen Gallagher raised his hand, and the act of it, the public choosing of sides that he had failed to make for months, settled something in the man's posture that Caleb could see from across the room. Emmett raised his hand. The crew members along the wall raised theirs. Ranchers who had ridden miles to attend a meeting they had only heard rumors about raised their hands because the evidence was clear and the choice was not difficult.

The vote was unanimous.

Caleb stood. The room turned toward him, and he felt the weight of what had been offered, the trust of a town that had watched him work and had decided he was worth keeping.

"I accept," he said. "I will see this bridge to completion, and I will do it without pay. This town has given me more than wages could account for, and the bridge will be my contribution to Providence Ridge's future."

The room responded with applause.

Horace Pritchard looked around the room and his composure fell away entirely, and what remained beneath it was not the smooth, persuasive man who had descended the boardinghouse stairs moments ago but something smaller and sharper, a man who had played his hand and lost the table.

"You can vote however you please," Horace said. "But I own the majority of the land north of town, and when the mining operations begin, you will all wish you had a part of it." He straightened his coat. "This is not the last you will hear from me."

"I believe it is," Tom said.

The kitchen door opened. Two men stepped through, and the room registered them instantly: the federal stars pinned to their coats, the sidearms at their belts, and the particular bearing of men who had traveled a distance to perform a specific duty. Deputy United States Marshals.

Horace's expression emptied. The confidence of the boast he had made ten seconds earlier drained from his face as he looked at the two men who had been standing in Mrs. Hanscombe's kitchen waiting for this moment.

The taller of the two deputies stepped forward. "Horace Pritchard, you are under arrest on federal charges of embezzlement and fraud against the Pacific Northwestern Development Consortium. Two additional warrants have been issued for your associates in connection with the same scheme. The United States Attorney's office in Denver has been investigating the diversion of consortium funds into private land acquisitions for several months, and the evidence gathered by Marshal Callahan in coordination with the U.S. Marshal's office for Montana Territory has been instrumental in completing that investigation."

The deputy produced iron manacles. Horace looked at them, then at Tom, and in that look Caleb saw the final collapse of a man who had believed that money purchased immunity and had discovered in the space of a single evening that it did not.

The manacles closed around Horace's wrists with a sound that carried across the quiet room, metal against metal, final, and clean. The deputies led him toward the front door, and the people standing in their path parted to let them pass. The door opened, and the evening air came in, and the door closed behind him.

Conversations broke open in every direction, the released tension of an evening that had asked people to sit still while the foundations of what they believed about a man were dismantled piece by piece. Amos stood speaking with two ranchers. Margaret had crossed to Mrs. Hanscombe, and the two women spoke in low voices near the kitchen doorway. Owen Gallagher sat with his wife's hand on his arm, his head bowed, the posture of a man who had done a difficult thing and was only beginning to understand what it had cost and what it had saved. Emmett spoke with the bridge crew, and Caleb could hear fragments of the conversation, questions about tomorrow's work, about the stone course, about whether the timber delivery would arrive, the practical language of men who had just learned their jobs were secure and whose first instinct was to plan the next day's labor.

Liam had moved from his position along the wall to stand near Marshal Tom, and the two of them spoke quietly, uncle and nephew, the younger man listening with the focused attention he brought to everything that mattered.

Winnie had crossed the room toward Mrs. Hanscombe.

Caleb turned to Belle.

She was looking at him. The room moved around them in its currents of conversation and relief, but the space between the two of them held a different quality, the stillness that belongs to two people who have passed through something together and have arrived on the other side of it and can feel the solid ground beneath them.

"It's over," she said.

"The worst of it is."

"The bridge is yours now. Truly yours."

"The bridge belongs to the town," he said. "I am just the man they trust to build it."

Belle was quiet for a moment. The noise of the room continued around them, Amo's voice carrying over the others as he discussed subscription figures with a rancher, Mrs. Hanscombe's coffee cups clinking as she began distributing them with the unshakeable conviction that people who had endured an evening like this one required something warm in their hands.

"Caleb," Belle's voice was low enough that only he could hear it. "When you told me yesterday that you were staying, you said the bridge was not the reason."

"It isn't. I meant what I said."

"I need you to know something." She looked at him, and her green eyes held the lamplight and the steadiness and the full measure of what the past weeks had built between them, tested and strained and proven sound. "I have spent years holding everything together by refusing to need anyone. I told myself that was strength. It was fear, and I am done with it." She paused. "You are the reason I am not afraid anymore. Not because you are strong enough to carry what I carry. Because you are the kind of man who would stand beside me and let me carry it, and that is something I have never had."

Caleb felt the words settle into his chest. Every prayer he had spoken since Wyoming had asked for exactly this, not relief from guilt or a second chance at a career, but the assurance that God had not finished with him, that the road from the wreckage led somewhere worth arriving at.

"Belle Callahan," he said. "I am going to build this town, its bridge. And when the last plank is laid across that span, I am going to walk across it to wherever you are standing, and I am going to ask you a question that I have been carrying in silence for days now."

She smiled. "I will be standing there at that bridge and give you the answer to that question."

Around them the room continued its business, the town of Providence Ridge doing what it had always done, gathering itself after difficulty and finding its way forward through the ordinary work of neighbors deciding together what came next. Mrs. Hanscombe distributed coffee. Amos took notes on the back of a receipt. Liam spoke with Emmett about the morning's work at the bridge site. Winnie stood near the kitchen doorway watching her sister and the man beside her with an expression that held no surprise at all, only the quiet satisfaction of a woman who had seen the truth before anyone else and had waited patiently for the rest of the world to find it.

And Caleb sat beside Belle in the boardinghouse dining room in the town that God had led him to, and he understood with a clarity that required no calculation and no proof that the bridge he had come to build was not only timber and stone across a river. It was the span between the man he had been and the man he was becoming, and the woman beside him was a gift from God.

Leave A Review

If you enjoyed this book, please consider leaving an honest review on Amazon

<u>Visit Our Website:</u>

www.vivianbelle.com

<u>Visit Our Amazon Author Page:</u> HERE

<u>Find Us On Social Media:</u>

Facebook Author Page

Instagram

Scan the QR code above to sign up for our newsletter!

About Vivian

Vivian Belle is a talented author known for her sweeping **Historical Christian Romance** novels set against the untamed beauty of the American frontier. With a deep love for history and storytelling, she brings to life **resilient heroines, steadfast heroes, and faith-filled journeys** in the vast, rugged landscapes of the past.

Nestled in the **majestic mountains of northern West Virginia,** Vivian finds endless inspiration in the rolling hills, winding rivers, and boundless sky that mirror the spirit of her stories. When she's not writing, she enjoys **kayaking on tranquil waters, hiking through breathtaking mountain trails, and, of course, getting lost in a good book.**

Vivian's novels capture the heart of **faith, love, and perseverance**—where strong women and honorable men overcome life's trials to find hope, home, and happily-ever-after. Whether she's exploring the great outdoors or crafting her next frontier romance,

Vivian's passion for adventure and storytelling shines through in every word she writes.

Visit Vivian on the web: www.vivianbelle.com

Also By Vivian Belle

<u>Stand Alone Novels</u>

Where the Heart Finds Home

Faith on the Frontier

Love in Hopewell Creek

Abigail's Promise

Beneath Montana Skies

Rocky Mountain Promise

Hearts Unbroken

Beneath the Oregon Pines

Journeys of the Heart

<u>Providence Ridge Series</u>

A Bride Worth Keeping

Stronger Than the River

9 781966 609343 5